Final Debt

INDEBTED #6

PEPPER WINTERS

Final Debt (Indebted #6)
Copyright © 2015 Pepper Winters
Published by Pepper Winters

Published: Pepper Winters 2015: **pepperwinters@gmail.com**
Cover Design: by Ari at Cover it! Designs:
http://salon.io/#coveritdesigns
Proofreading by: Jenny Sims: **http://www.editing4indies.com**
Images in Manuscript from Canstock Photos:
http://www.canstockphoto.com

OTHER WORK BY PEPPER WINTERS

Pepper Winters is a New York Times, Wall Street Journal, and USA Today International Bestseller.

Her Dark Romance books include:
Monsters in the Dark Trilogy
Tears of Tess (Monsters in the Dark #1)
Quintessentially Q (Monsters in the Dark #2)
Twisted Together (Monsters in the Dark #3)

Indebted Series
Debt Inheritance (Indebted #1)
First Debt (Indebted Series #2)
Second Debt (Indebted Series #3)
Third Debt (Indebted Series #4)
Fourth Debt (Indebted Series #5)
Final Debt (Indebted Series #6)
Indebted Epilogue (Indebted Series #7)

Her Grey Romance books include:
Destroyed
Ruin & Rule (Pure Corruption MC #1)
Sin & Suffer (Pure Corruption MC #2)

Her Upcoming Releases include:
2016: **Je Suis a Toi (Monsters in the Dark Novella)**
January 2016: **Sin & Suffer (Pure Corruption MC #2)**
2016: **Super Secret Series**
2016: **Unseen Messages (Standalone Romance)**
2016: **Indebted Beginnings (Indebted Series Prequel)**

To be the first to know of upcoming releases, please
follow her on her website
Pepper Winters

Nila

"READY TO DIE, Nila?"

Cut's voice physically hurt me as he forced me to my knees. The ballroom splendour mocked me as I bowed unwillingly at the feet of my executioner.

Velvet and hand-stitched crewel on the walls glittered like the diamonds the Hawks smuggled—a direct contrast to the roughly sawn wood and crude craftsmanship of the guillotine dais. No finesse. No pride. Just a raised podium, framework cushioning a large tarnished blade, and a rope dangling to the side.

"Don't do this, Cut…think about what you've become. You can stop this." My voice mimicked a beg but I'd vowed *not* to beg. I'd seen things, understood things, and suffered things I never thought I would be able to endure. I refused to cry or grovel. I wouldn't give him that satisfaction.

"In five minutes, this will all be over, Weaver." Cut bent to the side and collected a wicker basket.

The wicker basket.

I didn't want to think about what its contents would be.

He placed it on the other side of the wooden block.

My lungs demanded more oxygen. My brain demanded more time. And my heart…it demanded more hope, more life, more love.

7

I'm not ready.
Not like this.

"Cut—"

"No. No more talking. Not after everything you've done." Ripping a black hood from his pocket, he didn't hesitate. No fanfare. No second guesses.

I cried out as the scratchy blackness engulfed my face, tightening by a cord around my throat.

The Weaver Wailer chilled me. The diamond collar that'd seen what I'd seen and whispered with phantoms of my slain family prepared to revoke its claim and detach from around my neck.

This was it.

The Final Debt.

Cut pushed my shoulders forward.

A heavy yoke settled over the top of my spine.

I closed my eyes.

I said goodbye.

. . .

I waited to die.

One Week Earlier

"NO!"

I pushed back, gripping the handrails of the private jet, throwing my weight against Daniel's incessant pushing. "Stop!"

"Get up the fucking stairs, Weaver." Daniel jabbed his elbow into my spine.

I stumbled, bashing my knee against the high tread. "You can't do this!" How had this happened? How had mere hours turned the entire universe against me? *Again.*

I wanted to smash every clock. Tear out the cog from every watch.

Time had once again stolen my life.

Jethro!

Daniel cackled. "I think you'll find we can." He shoved me higher.

My heart hurt—as if every mile between us and Hawksridge was a blade slicing me further from Jethro's protection—a disharmony in an already discorded symphony.

One moment, I'd been love-bruised and adored, tiptoeing back into the Hall; the next, I was trapped, forced to dress in jeans and a hoodie, and obey Daniel as he lurked in my doorway, barking orders to pack a few meagre belongings.

He hadn't left me alone.

His eyes followed my every move. I couldn't grab the gun I'd hidden thanks to Jasmine. I couldn't text Jethro to tell him I'd been caught. All I could do was run around my room with my lover's release still damp on my inner thighs and submit to my nemesis.

The only saving grace was beneath Daniel's hateful stare, I'd managed to pack the clothing I'd altered a few weeks ago. The cuffs full of needles and hems armoured with tools of my seamstress trade. Those garments were my only hope. There was no loophole. No way to refuse.

I had to trust Jasmine would get word to Jethro. That he would come for me…

Before it's too late.

The desolation I'd suffered when Daniel first caught me faded to indignant anger. I'd been so close to being free. I'd been in Jethro's arms. I'd been away from his psychotic family. My heart hardened a little toward Jethro for making me go back.

Why? Why did you send me back?

I didn't know if I'd have the courage to forgive him.

You know why. And you will. Of course, you will.

I couldn't hate him because I wasn't selfish. He'd sent me back to protect *all* of us. Those precious few who'd accepted him and he'd accepted in return. Love was the worst enemy, winding its commitment, ensuring no freedom when it came to clearheaded thinking of adversity.

Jethro loved too much. Felt too much. Suffered too much. And his siblings would be our downfall. Kestrel and Jasmine relied on him—just like I did. The responsibility of settling his family's wrongs was a terrible burden to bear.

But he's not alone.

I might've been stolen. Jethro's plans to save me might be ruined. But I was still alive. Still breathing. I wasn't the naïve girl who'd first arrived at Hawksridge. I was a woman in love with a Hawk. A Weaver who would draw Hawk blood.

It's not over...

Pain exploded in my spine as Daniel stabbed me with his fist. "Get in the fucking airplane."

"No!" I threw myself backward, looking frantically at the private hangar. We weren't at Heathrow, but a small, private airfield called Turweston. "I won't!"

No strangers I could call for help.

No police or air marshals.

When Daniel had stalked me from my room and shoved me outside, Cut had been waiting. With a victorious smile, he'd stuffed me in the back of a limousine.

With a purring engine, we'd pulled away from Hawksridge, tyres crunching on gravel as we followed the long driveway off the estate.

My eyes had scoured the trees, their silhouettes growing stronger as the sun tinted the sky with pink blushes. Daniel and Cut sat opposite me, toasting each other with a chilled bottle of champagne. However, I hadn't been alone on my side of the limo—I had a guard.

Marquise, Bonnie's damn henchman, sat beside me; a mountain of muscle, unyielding and impenetrable.

"Come along." A strange voice raised my gaze.

A man in a captain's uniform smiled from the top of the aircraft steps. The private plane's fuselage glinted in graphite grey. Sparkling diamonds, inlaid in the shape of a windswept ribbon, decorated the tail.

"I don't want to leave England."

Daniel laughed behind me. "Like you have a choice."

"I always have a choice, *Buzzard*." I glowered over my shoulder. "Just like this choice of yours will not end well for you."

If I don't kill you, Jethro will.

As far as Daniel knew, his slain brother was supposedly rotting in some unmarked grave. Jethro was right. The element of surprise trumped any of Cut and Daniel's grand delusions.

He snarled, "Watch it, bitch. Everything you say to me

here will be paid in full when we're there."

"Now, now. No need for threats." The captain climbed down a rung, holding out his hand. "She'll get on board. Won't you, my dear? No need to be afraid of flying. I have an exemplary record." White hair tufted from either side of his pristine flying cap. In his mid-fifties, he looked fit and toned and impatient to take off.

"I can't leave."

I can't be so far from Jethro.

The captain smiled, waving at his vessel. "Of course, you can. Plus, I bet you've never travelled in such style."

"It's nothing against your mode of transport. It's the destination I disagree to. I'm staying *here*." I dug my heels into the metal grate, fighting against Daniel's perpetual pushing. "I don't have my passport, visa… I can't travel across borders, so you might as well let me return home."

Home.

Had Hawksridge Hall become my home?

No, don't be absurd.

But Jethro had. It didn't matter where we ended up. What we did for work. How our lives panned out. As long as I was alive with Jethro by my side…I would be home.

"Don't fuss about that." The captain waved his hand in invitation. "Travel is good for the soul."

Not my soul.

Travel meant my soul would become untethered from my body, thanks to Cut and the Final Debt.

The sun barely peeked over the horizon, hidden by soupy fog and reluctant night. The world refused to warm, unable to shed the morning frost or dislodge the claws of winter. England didn't want to say goodbye as much as I did, its reluctant dawn wanting me to stay.

"If you don't get on the motherfucking plane in two seconds, Weaver, you'll live to regret it," Daniel growled.

I glared at the youngest Hawk. "Haven't you learned by now your threats don't scare me?"

Forcing myself to stand taller, I hid the quaking in my bones, the quivering in muscles, the rampant terror scurrying in my blood. "I know where you want to take me, and I refuse."

Daniel pinched the bridge of his nose. A second later, he cuffed me on the back of the head. "Behave!"

I gritted my teeth against the wash of agony.

"Almasi Kipanga is a fucking treat for the likes of you, Weaver. Get on your knees and show some goddamn appreciation. Otherwise, I'll rip out your fucking tongue and ensure peace for the rest of the trip."

"Ah, as I said, there's no need for violence." The captain took another step, prying my hand off the railing and tugging me upward. "Come along, my dear. Let's get you inside. And don't you worry about visas and things. Leave it to me. Airport control won't be an issue."

Vertigo cast the world in monochromatic greys as I swayed toward the captain. "But—"

Cut barrelled past Daniel—reaching the end of his patience. Grabbing my arse, he shoved me upward, forcing me like unwilling livestock up the final steps. "I have your passport, Nila. Get on the plane." His breath skated over the back of my neck. "And don't think about refusing again. Got it?"

Gripping the fuselage, I looked over my shoulder. "My passport? How did you—"

He waved a black binder in my face. "Everything is in here. You have no more excuses, and I won't ask again. Get on the fucking plane or I'll knock you out and you can wake up when we get there."

Daniel laughed as one last shove sprawled me up the final step and into the captain's arms.

Shit.

"Ah, there you go." The pilot steadied me, holding my shoulders as I stumbled with another swoop of imbalance. The sickness stole my eyesight before dumping me back into hell.

Find an anchor, hold on tight. Do that and you'll be alright.

Vaughn.

His little poem for me.

My heart cried for my brother and father. Would I ever see them again?

The captain led me further inside the immaculate plane. He puffed proudly. "See how nice it is? All your concerns are over nothing. We'll take great care of you." Patting my hand, he let me go. "Take any seat you like. Don't forget your seatbelt."

My eyes widened. He spoke as if this was an innocuous vacation between father and adopted daughter. Did he not see the animosity? Not hear the pre-designed fate?

I opened my mouth to tell him. But what was the point?

He was owned by Cut. Just like diplomats, lawyers, and royals.

He didn't care.

The remnants of the flu, the vertigo attack, and the fact I hadn't slept all night caught up with me. Dropping my eyes, I padded to a black leather chair and sat. Trying to clear my thoughts, I hung my head in my hands.

How the hell do I get out of this?

Backing toward the cockpit to free up the gangway for Cut, Daniel, and Marquise, the pilot said, "Pleasure to fly you again, Mr. Hawk."

"Nice to be back." Cut nodded, choosing a seat beside the one I'd slumped into. Placing the folder on the small table bolted to the floor, he asked, "All flight plans logged?"

I glanced up, familiarizing myself with the black and chrome interior. Everywhere I looked, the Black Diamond logo embossed everything. From leather seats to plush carpet to window shutters and napkins.

The plane had three zones: two black couches faced each other at the end, a large boardroom table took up the middle section with bolted swivel seats, and eight single chairs took up the front part, looking like any first class on a normal airline.

Not that I've ever flown first class.

My heart stuttered. The last time I'd been on a plane,

Jethro had drugged me and stolen me from Milan to England on a red-eye. He'd allowed me to text Kite in the bar; all the while hiding it was him.

This far exceeded that flight in luxury, but it was just another glorified cage. And the one person I'd grown to love didn't even know I'd disappeared.

The captain nodded. "Yes, all logged and ready to go. We'll have to refuel in Chad as normal, but it should be smooth sailing down to Botswana."

I froze, gripping the soft leather armrests. "Botswana?" *Africa.*

I'd be unprotected and unprepared in the middle of a lion and hyena-infested countryside, captured by men who were worse than the wildlife.

Daniel had told me in the corridor, but I hadn't calculated the ramifications. Now I was on a plane about to take off—about to leave *England.* My motherland. My safe zone.

Oh, my God. How will Jethro get to me in time?

He wasn't fully healed. He needed to put whatever plan he'd organised into action. Even if Jasmine got word to him, he would still be too late to help.

I'm on my own.

My fingers fiddled with the pocket of the hoodie I'd slipped on before Daniel stole me from my quarters. A long knitting needle rested unseen. The needle wasn't flimsy or weak. Single pointed, metal construction, approximately thirty-five centimetres long. If my hoodie hadn't had a big front pocket, I wouldn't have been able to conceal it.

I wasn't much of a knitter—preferring to sew rather than deal with yarn and wool, but on this occasion, it'd become my most favourite implement.

Please, let it be enough.

I didn't have bullets or blades, but I did have my namesake. Hadn't I promised I would become a needle rather than thread? That I would be sharp, ruthless? Able to puncture and defeat?

The bubbling anger and capable fight returned, settling into my soul. I might be on my own, but I'd achieved a lot. I'd learned how to fight monsters and win.

So what I wouldn't be in England?

I would make Africa my personal battleground.

Cut looked at me, a vicious smile on his lips. "Not just to Botswana, Nila. To the diamond mecca. To our mine."

His words echoed Daniel's from before.

Stroking the hidden needle, I narrowed my eyes. "Why?"

Cut laughed quietly, accepting a flute of champagne from a blonde-haired stewardess. "Why do you think?"

The captain cleared his throat. "If you don't need me, sir, I'll leave you to it." With a quick salute, he disappeared into the cockpit, leaving Daniel to slink down the aisle and choose the seat behind me. Marquise kept going, not saying a word, just throbbing with sheer muscle.

The plane became a sardine can, imprisoning me with three men I despised.

"You want to tell her or shall I?" Cut glanced at Daniel.

Daniel leaned forward, fisting my newly cut hair. Every time I thought of the recently sliced strands, I froze with sadness then warmed with contentedness. Jethro had righted his brother's wrongs. Fixing his family's brutality with gentle soothing.

The new style only solidified my will to win. I would avenge. And my hair would grow back while they decomposed in their tombs.

I sat dead straight, vibrating with hatred as Daniel murmured, "I told you already, Weaver. It's time for a few catch-ups. You still owe us for the Third Debt. You still owe us for the Fourth Debt. And once your debts are paid, there's the matter of the Final Debt to call it even." He laughed, running his monstrous fingers over my scalp. "It's extremely convenient that the rest of the Fourth Debt takes place away from the estate. Not just for the change of scenery but so my fucking sister stops meddling."

Pain burned where he held my hair.

Cut stroked the back of my hand. "Yes, Jasmine proved she's strong and got her way with the new laws for the inheritance, but my dear daughter and her high and mighty morals won't be welcome where we're going."

My voice reigned with righteousness. "She'll never forgive you for what you've done."

Cut cocked his head. "What makes you think she has a choice? We're family. All sins are forgivable by those who share the same blood."

I choked on a laugh. "Seriously? You truly think that?"

"I don't *think* that. I *know* that. Families stick together. That's why our business has done so well. Why we rose above you and ensured centuries of retribution." His touch on my hand flew up to tap against my diamond collar. "Ever wondered about the story behind the Weaver Wailer? Ever stopped to think how it was created?"

I pursed my lips, not giving him the satisfaction of a reply. Of course, I'd wondered. But I wouldn't weaken myself by enquiring—not when Cut seemed to think the knowledge would hurt me.

"This collar, the one I will soon take from your corpse, was fashioned by the grandson of the woman Mr. Weaver raped every night. She sketched something so beautiful it could only be hideous in its intent and William Hawk ensured his grandmother's final wish was created once she'd died."

Confusion clogged comprehension.

I didn't understand how they were linked. "Why?"

Cut scowled. "Why?"

Breaking his hold on my collar, I turned to face him. "Why only hurt the Weaver women? Why not the men? It was Mr. Weaver who harmed the Hawks. Take your vengeance out on the men. Pick on your own sex."

"We still would have won, Nila, because like it or not, the Weavers are weak." Cut laughed, his teeth flashing with mirth. "And besides, taking their women hurts them more than physical wounds ever could."

I didn't need to ask why. I knew.

Stripping the men of their loved ones highlighted not only their failure to protect but their weakness at saving them. They would live forever haunted by those they failed—troubled and plagued by their downfalls, turning into twisted, broken men— just like my father.

I sighed, looking out the window at my final glimpse of the country I'd been born, raised, and indebted.

Cut placed his palm on my thigh, squeezing. "You'll learn everything soon enough. Every secret. Every tale. It's all yours from here on out, Nila. Ask questions. Pry and interrogate. You might as well as your time is tick, ticking away."

Closing his eyes, he settled into his chair. "I'd get some sleep if I were you. Once we land, you'll have some debts to pay."

We touched down in darkness.

How long had it taken to trade homeland for foreign soil? Ten hours? Twelve?

I'd lost track.

However, it could've been bright sunshine and it wouldn't have made a difference. With the Hawks imprisoning me, it was perpetual darkness in my world.

I twisted in my seat, catching glimpses of runway lights and buildings as the captain taxied to a private hangar. The moment the plane slipped inside, Cut yanked me from my seat and shoved me to disembark.

I didn't speak.

Cotton wool and candyfloss replaced my brain. My back ached, my energy dwindled, and my eyelids scratched like cat claws. All I wanted was rest and safety. I needed to regroup and prepare.

But I had to stay alert and ready.

The cool night replaced the stuffy heat of the cabin as Cut herded me from the plane. The chilly air tore through my hoodie and jeans. I gulped in large breaths to wake me.

Daniel grabbed my arm, escorting me to the armed vehicle waiting in the middle of the hangar. Pieces of airplane bric-a-brac littered the walls and counters lining the aviation perimeter.

Cut's logo stamped his ownership on everything—from cars to wheelable scaffolding and hydraulic tools. Everywhere I looked, I couldn't ignore whose territory I existed in and who ultimately controlled me.

The Jeep wasn't like a typical one in the U.K. This had armoured panels, large bumper guards, and tinted windows. Pockmarks of bullets and splattered mud added a story of violence.

This isn't England.

I wasn't blind or deaf. I'd watched reports on how dangerous Africa could be. How ruthless the people. How fatal the landscape. How deadly the animals.

I'd become protected by the same devils who would hurt me. Reliant on the Hawks to save my life, only so they could take it when suitable to their timeline.

"Get in." Daniel pushed me into the Jeep and climbed in after me.

Cut followed but didn't enter. His arm slung over the roof, leaning his bulk against the door. His leather jacket creaked and his crumpled shirt showed evidence of a long flight, but his eyes gleamed bright and shrewd. "Put your seatbelt on, Nila. Can never be too careful."

If I hadn't agreed with him, I would've spat in his face.

My hand shook a little from hunger as I pulled the belt over my chest and buckled in. Now, if only Daniel didn't put his on and we had a car accident—flying through the windscreen and splattering like a gnat on the road.

My stomach twisted as the images switched to Jethro. Thousands of miles now separated us. Oceans and valleys, continents and mountains. My fingers itched to text him. My hands empty of the one possession that'd allowed me communication for the past several months. My phone had become more than an outlet of transmission; it'd become a lifeline.

But I hadn't had time to grab it. The device sat abandoned in my quarters at the Hall.

I couldn't tell Jethro—couldn't advice plans or activities. *I'm on my own.*

I'm all alone.

My hidden knitting needle grew warm, humming with a war beat.

It doesn't matter.

I'm ready.

"Remember what I said, Nila. The next few days are of mutual benefit. Treat it as such." Looking at Daniel, Cut rubbed a hand over his brow. "I'll meet you there. Have a few errands to run on the way."

Daniel nodded. "Fine."

"You'll sort everything out?"

"Don't worry about us." Daniel smiled, squeezing my thigh with biting fingers. "We'll have a fantastic time on our own, won't we, Nila?"

I flinched. My mind raced with scenarios on how to stop my future from unfolding. I didn't know how long the drive would be, but the minute we arrived at our destination, I was ruined.

There was no one to tell him no.

No one to interrupt if he tried to rape me again.

And he will try again.

My left hand disappeared into my hoodie pocket, fisting around the needle.

I have to be ready to do whatever is necessary.

If that meant becoming a killer with a tool of my trade, then so be it. Cut wouldn't be there. Perhaps this was the perfect opportunity to slaughter Daniel and put one demon into his grave.

Cut leaned into the Jeep, grabbing Daniel by the scruff of his neck. The symbolism wasn't lost on me. He held his son like an animal would hold its troublesome young.

"You are not to touch her, understand? Put her to bed and guard her. Let her rest. And by rest, I mean prepare for what's in store."

Letting Daniel go, Cut wiped his hands on the front of his jeans. "You touch her, Buzzard, and you won't be in fit shape to claim the Third Debt. Got it?"

My heart galloped.

Cut was the one person I wanted to die a gruesome death, but he'd just saved me from his vile offspring. Was it jealousy at not getting first dibs? Or some sick chauvinistic protection?

Daniel scowled. "No fair. You said—"

"I said we'd make her pay the Third Debt when we arrived. However, that means we *share*." Cut's eyes glittered. "I find out you didn't share, Hawksridge gets locked in a trust and goes to Jasmine's heir."

"Fuck!" Daniel glared into the night, seething.

I'd never known a stricter, more delusional parent. Cut had shot his two sons. He willingly did whatever he had done to his own brother to inherit my mother. He had his ludicrous laws and absolutely no scruples.

Yet, he controlled Daniel so effortlessly.

Daniel puffed in retaliation then softened in respect. "Okay, Pop. You got it."

"Good." Slamming the top of the Jeep, Cut ordered, "Move out." Shutting the door, he stepped back.

The vehicle instantly became stifling. Daniel breathed hard, his temper curling around me like rancid smoke.

"Fucking arsehole. Rules. Always bloody rules with him."

"Yes, and you'd do well to remember those rules."

His eyes shot to mine. "Fuck you, Weaver."

An African man slid into the driver's seat while an accomplice took the passenger beside him. The clank of metal from his rifle struck the top of the car.

A gun?

Why the hell did he need a gun?

The guard in the passenger seat swivelled around, his black skin turning him almost invisible in the dark interior. The perfect assassin. "We'll get you there, Mr. Hawk. Not too much unrest this month. Should be safe."

My eyes flew wide.

Danger.

From all corners.

If I somehow survived the Hawks, I'd have to beg for a miracle to return to England. I was stranded in a foreign country with my archenemy clutching tightly to my passport.

Daniel inched his hand further up my thigh. "Good to hear. I want to get to camp and put my darling Weaver to bed, so she's fully rested for her busy itinerary."

In a swipe, I shoved Daniel's grip off me. "Don't touch me."

Daniel cursed under his breath.

The African man glanced in my direction, eyeing me once before turning back around. "Right you are, boss."

The driver turned on the ignition, sending silence screaming with the rumbling engine.

Daniel inched closer, deleting the negative space between us with threats. "If I want to touch you; I will fucking touch you."

I squeezed my eyes as Daniel slapped a possessive hold on my leg, sliding quickly up, up, up until he cupped my pussy. The memory of him doing something similar when Jethro first took me to Hawksridge had bile rising in my throat.

Daniel breathed hot in my ear. "You're all mine now, cunt. Away from my sister. No brothers to interfere. Just me and dear ole' dad."

His fingers pressed on the seam of my jeans, right over my clit.

I shuddered in revulsion. "Pity for you, dear ole' dad just

cut off your balls." Fire blazed in my heart. "You were told not to touch me. You're nothing more than a glorified messenger boy. Do you honestly think Cut cares about you?" My laugh echoed with ice. "Really, Daniel? He loved Jethro and Kestrel more than he loves you and he shot them in cold blood. If I were you, that would make me think twice about my worth."

His fingers dug harder. "Jet and Kes were nothing compared to me. Always weak. Always running off to play together while I watched and learned."

"Did you ever think they would've accepted you if you'd been a little nicer? Been a *brother* to them rather than a lunatic?"

Daniel snorted. "You know nothing. Jet was always a pussy, and Kes thought he could save him. We're Hawks. We're meant to be indestructible not need to be fucking fixed. Why would I want to be friends with rejects like that?"

My heart cracked as Kes and his warmth and kindness filled my mind. "Maybe if you had, you'd be redeemable and not so one-dimensional."

Daniel chuckled, his teeth white in the dark. "Who are you calling one-dimensional? I've got lots of tricks up my sleeve, bitch. Just wait till we get to the mine." Letting me go, he sniffed his fingers obnoxiously loud. "Can't wait to taste you. Can't wait to claim you. I'll obey my father, for now. But you keep pushing me and you'll see who's fucking sorry."

The Jeep lurched forward.

And for the first time in my life, I prayed.

MY PHONE RANG.

A few birds took flight, their feathers rustling in the leaves of leering trees. My empathetic illness throbbed in my blood, fanning out, searching for signs that Nila wasn't far from me. That I had time to do what I needed. That all of this would be over.

Shutting the top of the laptop, ceasing the email chain of instructions I'd been sharing with Kill, the Pure Corruption president in Florida, I swiped on my phone and pressed answer.

The number signalled the caller was at Hawksridge.

Nila?

My heart thundered. *Please, be okay.* "Jet speaking."

"Kite, it's me." Jasmine's worried voice came down the line, scattering fear in an instant.

Shit.

I loved my sister, but her call wasn't good news. Even though she wasn't close by, and our only connection was the phone, I sensed her panic and horror. My condition amplified her terror, injecting it directly into my bloodstream.

My hands curled tighter around the device. "What happened? Where's Nila?"

My heart raced as Jaz swallowed a sob. "They took her!"

What?

My legs shot me upright. "Who took her?" I winced, gripping my healing side as agony flared. *Stupid fucking question.* Not waiting for an answer, I growled, *"Where* did they take her? Where, Jasmine?"

Tears tainted her voice. "Bonnie was secretive all morning, not letting me leave my room, saying we had important things to go over. She wouldn't let me go downstairs. She wouldn't let me go to Nila's quarters."

My fingers clutched the phone like a mortal enemy. "Get to the point. Spit it out, Jaz! Where did they take her?"

Jasmine cried louder, wrapped up in her own grief. "I can't believe I did it, Kite. I grabbed a pair of her flower cutting scissors and demanded the truth." Disbelief and horror lurked in her tone. "I wheeled up to our grandmother and threatened to kill her if she didn't tell me. I've become as bad as they have. I'm the same as Cut!" Her sobs came louder. "I've become *them.*"

Shit, I don't have time for this.

Rage at her timewasting battled with my need to calm her. All her life, that'd been her ultimate fear: turning into Cut. Forgetting her humanity and being swept up in the evil romanticism of debts and death and blood.

Lowering my voice, I forced myself to remain calm. This was my sister. My blood. My fear for Nila was equal measure to my loyalty to Jasmine. "You're not the same."

Dashing into the tent, I grabbed the backpack with already packed essentials. "You did what we both should've done years ago. So what you threatened her? We should've killed her for the things she's done. She's the catalyst in all of this, Jaz. Not me, not you, not Kes. Not anyone. *Her.*"

Breathing hard, I stuffed last-minute necessities into my jean's pocket and plotted a new plan. "We're putting things right. If we have to kill to do that, we will."

Jaz hiccupped, tears still clogging the line. "I just—I've let you down. She knows I'm on your side now. The way she looked at me, Jet. All this time she let me get away with things I know you would never have been permitted to. She indulged me as I'm the only girl. But she knows now. She knows what I truly think of her. I've ruined the trust you told me to gain."

Her voice broke. "You asked me to keep Nila safe. You gave me a task. And because I'm stuck in this fucking chair, I let you down."

I slammed to a halt.

My stomach twisted; it took everything inside to keep my voice level and not wobble with guilt. "Jaz...you're in that chair because of me. It was selfish of me to put so much on you. You *did* keep her safe. You dealt with Bonnie all these years. You got Cut to change the Debt Inheritance. That's fucking huge. The rest is on me."

"No, no it's not."

Sudden wrath hijacked my hand—I pummelled a fist into a sapling. "Yes, it is. I had her in my arms a few hours ago. I thought I knew best. I stupidly thought I had time. I'm a fucking idiot. *I'm* to blame. Not you. Never you. Understand?"

Jasmine didn't reply.

My time had run out. My voice lowered to a soothing whisper. "I can't comfort you. Not yet. It fucking kills me that you're dealing with this on your own but, Jasmine, I *need* you to spit it out. Where did they take her?"

Diamond Alley?

The integration house in Devon?

Where?

Jaz sniffed loudly, shoving aside her grief. "They've taken her to *Almasi Kipanga.*"

"Fuck!"

My mind swam with images of our mine. The cavernous caves and labyrinth of chiselled pathways. Our fortune had come from there. Our name. Our titles. Everything we had came from the dirt.

Almasi Kipanga.

Swahili for Diamond Hawk.

"When? How?"

"I don't know. But they took her. They left hours ago. I checked with air traffic control. The plane left on route to Chad then to Botswana. You'll never make it in time."

Everything inside went ice, ice cold. "In time for what, Jaz? What else do you know?"

I paced in the clearing, going out of my fucking mind.

"Bonnie took great pride in telling me Cut will make her pay the Third Debt the moment they get there. And the Fourth Debt the day after...Jethro...they plan on carrying out the Final Debt by the end of the week."

Motherfucking shit.

My mind ran wild, calculating time zones and travel distance.

Even if I left now and there was a charter leaving immediately, I would still be hours behind. I would be too late to prevent the Third Debt.

My heart crumbled to ash.

How could I do this to her? After everything she'd already lived through. How had I failed her so fucking spectacularly? *Christ!*

Shrugging into the backpack, I vowed I wouldn't let Nila suffer anymore. Fuck the plan. Fuck timing.

I won't give up.

"I'll take care of it." My voice was a tombstone. Even as I swore I'd save Nila, I knew the truth. The awful, disgusting truth.

Kes had done what I couldn't and saved her from the Third Debt. He'd held her. Comforted her. Been there for her while he protected her from being raped.

All of that had been in vain.

He'd been shot because of me.

He might never wake up because of *me*.

I wanted to slaughter my father with my bare hands. I wanted to tear out my heart because no matter what I did, I would fail Nila.

She would pay the Third Debt.

And she would hate me forever.

My knees wobbled as I gasped in agony. I'd condemned her. I was the one she would blame. How would she recover from that? Why would she ever want me again after I left her alone?

She would never be mine again, but I would *never* let my father execute her.

Six days.

My father wanted to kill the love of my life in six fucking days.

My plan had just escalated.

I will stop this.

Even if it meant dying alone and unwanted because of it.

"How! How will you take care of it?" Jasmine screeched. "They're in fucking Botswana, Kite!"

My jaw locked, and I stormed toward Wings. He stood obediently, hidden in the tree line. Neither tethered nor saddled, he looked up when I got closer. His black eyes gleamed with ancient knowledge, so smart, so empathetic. He sensed my turmoil. He knew what I was about to ask him and he didn't hesitate.

Moving toward me, the giant animal placed himself sideways for me to mount. No rope or bridle, just a bond between man and beast.

"I don't care if they're at the ends of the earth. I'm going after them."

Grabbing a fistful of Wing's mane, I tucked the phone under my chin. In a practiced move I'd done countless times, I leapt upright and swung my leg over Wing's back.

My side bellowed, but I ignored my discomfort, focusing on the pain I'd caused Nila by making her return to the Hall without me.

Stupid. So fucking stupid.

Wing's silky coat offered no friction against my jeans. I'd been raised riding bareback. I'd spent many nights building a relationship with my horse. He would obey and fly wherever I needed.

The minute I was seated, he burst into a gallop. I bent low, gripping with my thighs.

Run.

Faster.

My rucksack slapped against my back as Wings flew toward the Hall. Wind stole Jasmine's voice, but I caught enough. "Jethro, what are you going to do?"

The noonday sun drenched Hawksridge, mocking my choices and who I'd become. I vowed this would be over soon. That Nila would be in my arms. That my brother would wake from his coma. That my sister might finally find peace.

So much to fix.

So much unhappiness to erase.

Wings gathered more power, shooting faster than any bullet across the paddock. My legs tightened, my heart pounded, and my fury crescendoed into a breathable entity.

Cut had made his last mistake.

I'm coming for you.

"I'm going after her, Jaz. And this time, I'm going to fucking end it."

Nila

IF DIAMOND ALLEY was the place where diamonds were sorted, raining eternal sunshine from giant spotlights, then *Almasi Kipanga* was the scar in the earth that'd created them.

The entire journey from the airport, Daniel kept his hand latched around my knee. I'd stewed in annoyance and repulsion but hadn't argued or struck up conversation.

I had so much to say.

But each word would only herald more punishment.

Besides, Daniel didn't deserve conversation. He was a lost, little boy, unable to see he was already dead. He might be a Hawk about to hurt me, but I was a viper in his nest just waiting to bite and poison him.

I had time.

I had stealth.

I'll wait.

The driver escorted us through the silent night without a syllable spoken. His passenger-guard never rested, glaring out the window, his reflexes flinching and finger soaring to the gun trigger more than once. Especially when we stopped at red lights and drove down dirt roads.

When we traded human busyness for sparseness, he unsheathed a machete, placing it reverently across his knees. Starlight bounced through the windscreen, kissing the tarnished blade.

Hoots and howls replaced sounds of suburbia, scuttling premonition down my spine.

Inside the Jeep, we were safe…but out there…out there feasted animals far more equipped at killing than we were. Out there, they hunted; their yellow eyes flashing in the headlights.

My fatigue evaporated the deeper into Africa we drove. The driver and passenger granted me copious amounts of adrenaline as I fed off their alertness. They lived here yet they didn't relax. They stayed on edge the entire journey.

What had they seen that I hadn't?

What had they lived that I never would?

I didn't want to know.

The four of us travelled together but apart—each wrapped in their own thoughts and journeys.

By the time we left barely sealed roads and clunked onto gravel trails, my muscles cramped from anxiety.

Every bump, I flinched. Every cackle from hyenas and every growl from lions, I squeezed my eyes with fear. The weapons our guides carried weren't to subdue me; they were to prevent whatever was out there from consuming us.

Civilisation was no more. We'd entered the heart of nature where survival superseded wealth and common-sense triumphed over stupidity.

As we pulled into the horrendous hell of Hawk territory, more and more animal eyes gleamed in the darkness as the high beams illuminated wilderness. My heart banged against my ribs as a flash of predator and the squeal of prey echoed in the night. Some poor creature died only metres from me.

I'm next.

If I didn't kill first.

Daniel chuckled, licking his lips at the thought of some poor animal becoming dinner.

I curled my fingers in disgust, looking out the opposite window. There, I could vaguely make out knobbly trees and sun-beaten terrain. The silver cast of moonlight forgave

Africa's sins but couldn't hide its danger.

After crossing a dried-up riverbed and navigating the death plains, we finally pulled into a permanent camp.

The driver slowed, slipping through gates that sent a shiver down my spine. For all my strength and committed confidence at killing before being killed, I couldn't swallow the lie any longer.

I finally understood that this place was more than just a mine. More than just Hawk property. More than just their ticket to wealth.

This was my grave.

"Welcome to our office." Daniel opened the door once the Jeep wrenched to a halt. His fingers pressed on my seatbelt, freeing me, then wrapped around my wrist and yanked me from the seat. I slid out the door, stumbling a little as my legs woke up after being useless from sitting so long.

"Where are we?" I stretched, working out the kinks in my spine while my eyes danced over the camp. A congregation of shipping containers had been converted into offices, wooden shacks with thatched roofs decorated the outskirts, and trodden muddy paths spoke of hardship and toil. The moon offered some illumination, competing against the watery lights strung in bushes and the brighter warmth of electricity spilling from dwellings.

If I didn't know who this place belonged to, it might've welcomed. I might've relished the thought of being in Africa for the first time. Going on a safari and witnessing the creatures I was afraid of, all from the safety of an organised tour.

Instead, all I wanted to do was run—to scale the fence barricading us and take my chances with the sharp-toothed lions prowling the boundaries.

At least I knew what they would do to me.

"Are you deaf or just fucking dumb?" Daniel wafted at the site as if it held every answer. "This is ground zero. The place where the first diamond was found. The place where your family's future became shadowed by mine." Tightening his cruel fingers around my wrist, he marched me through the encampment.

I guessed about thirty to forty shacks and canvas tents decorated the space while seven or so containers oversaw whatever work they undertook. The surrounding fence was patched like an old quilt—wood recently replaced and other wood that needed to be. Everything was sun-scorched and dust-sprinkled.

But it held a wild vibe. A homey vibe.

Somehow, the people who lived here had made the most of what they had and transformed it into more than just a mine but a sanctuary.

Out the corner of my eye, I saw something I didn't think I would ever witness.

Daniel seemed to…relax.

His shoulders smoothed out. The feral desire to be seen and noticed calmed. The insanity inside him muted by the freedom he found here. Perhaps, he wasn't just a psychopath, after all. Perhaps, I'd misjudged when I called him one-dimensional.

Just like I'd broken Jethro by using his lust for me and Kes's kindness to become my ally, I tried to do the same with Daniel. "You like it here."

His eyes snapped to mine. "Shut up, Weaver."

"No. I want to know. You've got me all to yourself, Daniel. Cut said I could ask anything I want. Alright then, my first question is about you."

His mouth hung open as if he couldn't believe I'd just willingly entered into a conversation with him.

That's right.

See me.

Hear me.

Feel me.

Then perhaps you won't try and hurt me.

It was wishful thinking, but maybe, just maybe, it might payoff.

Just like it did with your brother.

"Is this some sort of trick?"

I shook my head. "No trick." Pulling on his hold, I forced him to stop in the centre of the camp. A large fire pit charred the dirt while hacked up logs acted as seating. "You like it here. Why?"

His eyes darkened, but he answered. "Because it's away from Hawksridge."

"You don't like that place?"

"I never fucking said that." His temper smouldered.

I backtracked, trying to read between the lines. "You prefer this place over Hawksridge though...why?" Sudden understanding dawned. "Because you think of this place as yours and Hawksridge as Jethro's."

His hand lashed out, wrapping around my collar. "Wrong, bitch. Hawksridge is mine. Jethro is dead. Remember? Shot. Cold and buried."

I kept my secret while my heart warmed, rolling around in the truth.

He's alive.

Looping my fingers over his wrist, I held on while he imprisoned my throat. "It's yours now—if you behave and follow what Cut tells you, of course. But something makes me think you've always been happier here." I cocked my head. "Why is that? Because it's away from Bonnie, perhaps? It can't be because Jasmine doesn't come here. I don't see you interact, but she's harmless."

As if.

Jasmine terrified me.

He didn't answer, shoving me back and wiping his hands.

I tried again. "Jethro was hurt because of his condition. Jasmine was disabled for something I don't understand. Kes was tolerated because he kept the peace. But you...you..." I gasped. "I know. You were the mistake. The third son—the unneeded backup to an inheritance that already had two heirs."

Daniel suddenly exploded. His palm struck my cheek.

"Shut the fuck up. I'm. Not. A. Mistake."

I gasped against the pain, fighting an ocean of heat.

He could hit me. But he couldn't deny it. The way he argued throbbed with past history and conviction. How many times had he been called that? How many times had it undermined his place in the family and turned him into this evil creature?

Holding my cheek, I muttered, "I didn't say *I* thought you were a mistake. I asked if that was why you prefer it here." I rubbed my flaming skin. "You're his child. Same as all his children. It wasn't right to make you feel any less than them."

"Stop with the fucking psychoanalyzing. You don't know what the fuck you're talking about." Imprisoning my wrist again, he hauled me toward a large canvas tent.

I went with him—what choice did I have? But I did have a deeper understanding of my nemesis now. His childlike hatred. His out of control temperament. He might not have a soul to implore but once upon a time...he did. He was just a kid. An unwanted kid who did everything he could to be accepted.

The similarities with Jethro didn't escape my notice. The only difference was Jethro allowed himself to finally change, improve...see his own self-worth.

"It wasn't Cut who told you first, was it?" I couldn't stop my runaway mouth. But this might be my only chance at understanding Daniel enough to defeat him.

He didn't turn to look; his footsteps moved faster. "Shut up. Before I make you."

"It was Bonnie, wasn't it? She's the one who told you you were a mistake."

What are you doing?

Our pace increased and my eyes sought out escape paths. Climbing the few steps onto the wraparound deck, the fabric tent wasn't a temporary abode. It'd been swallowed by the ground and had become part of the landscape with outdoor chairs, a veranda, internal reception room, bedroom, and bathroom.

Breathing hard, Daniel ducked and dragged me from mud to carpet, moving forward into a large bedroom with alcoves. Immediately, my gaze dropped to the bed.

I swallowed my heart.

Daniel chuckled. "If you want to ask questions, get your fucking facts straight first. Yes, I always knew I would get shit having two brothers in front of me. Yes, I wasn't planned and Cut had great pleasure in telling me that my life is a fucking gift and to be thankful. But that isn't the reason why he's such a bastard."

Wishing I could put some distance between us, I whispered, "Why?"

Daniel stepped closer, pressing his chest against mine. "Because she didn't love him. She never loved him—no matter what he did. And that fucking screwed him up."

"Who didn't love him?"

"Rose."

"Who's Rose?"

"Peter's wife."

"Peter?" My mind raced, grasping at half-remembered recollections.

Daniel growled, "Fuck, you are stupid. Cut's brother. That's why Bonnie never liked us. We weren't supposed to exist. Get it? Cut stole Peter's wife behind his back. He got her pregnant."

My mouth hung open. "Is that why Cut killed him? To not only claim the inheritance but the heirs, too?"

Daniel shook his head. "No, he killed him because Bonnie told him to. She pretends like Cut betrayed her, but once she knew Rose was pregnant, she changed the game. She's always fucking changing the game."

My mind swam. "So—"

"No more fucking questions." Grabbing my chin, he forced me to look at the bed. His dark laugh sounded forced but evil. "Gonna put that to use very soon." He shoved me, chuckling as I bashed my knee against a coffee table with metal cups and a water jug. The jug wobbled, spilling cold liquid down the shins of my jeans and puddling on the floor.

"For fuck's sake, Weaver." Marching forward, he grabbed the back of my nape, forcing me to bend over the mess. "See what you just did?"

He treated me like a dog that'd pissed on the rug.

All conversation and questions disappeared. His actions concealed any weakness he might've shown, cleverly reminding me that everyone had issues, everyone had skeletons and secrets, but it didn't matter. What mattered was the person you became *despite* your past. And Daniel had no intention of changing.

"Clean that shit up."

Marquise entered, not caring Daniel held me so roughly. He nodded as if it were perfectly acceptable and placed my suitcase beside the bed. Without a word, he left again.

Fisting my short hair, Daniel hoisted me up and planted a foul kiss on my mouth.

What the—

I wanted to vomit.

Once he let me go, I swiped at my tongue, backing away. "Just because—"

"I've had enough. One more word, Weaver. One more fucking word." His hand shook as he pointed at the puddle on the floor. "Clean that up and have a shower. You stink. I expect you and this bedroom to be clean for our little get together when my father gets back."

I bared my teeth. "You think you're so untouchable, Daniel Hawk, but let me tell you. You aren't. I understand you a little better, but it doesn't mean I'm going to let you rape me. It might be tonight, or tomorrow, or the day after, but I will hurt you. I'll—"

He laughed loudly, cutting me off. "Such stupid promises from such a stupid Weaver. Know what I believe? Tonight, I'll be fucking you. Tomorrow, I'll be hurting you. And the day after, I'll inherit one of the wealthiest estates in the world because you'll be dead. I'm no longer the *mistake*. I'm the chosen one. So fucking shut up and get ready for me." He kissed me again, his putrid tongue trying to gain entry into my mouth.

My stomach revolted and in a flash of lunacy, I opened my lips and permitted him to lick.

Then, I bit.

Hard.

So, so hard.

Coppery blood tinged my taste buds, triumphantly splashing the first blood drawn. And it hadn't been mine.

"Fuck." He yanked me back. Pain exploded on my scalp as his fingers tore at my hair. "You do that again and you won't wake up."

"We'll see."

Grinding against me, he inhaled me like a beast. "You want me to disobey my father? You want me to fuck you right here, right now?" His nose dragged shivers over my skin. "Say one more word and you're on your fucking knees."

I gagged on horrible images but somehow found the courage to retaliate. I couldn't show fear. I wouldn't show fear ever again.

I laughed in his demonic face.

Daniel's eyes met mine, hooded and manic. "Want my cock, Weaver? I'll gladly give it to you if you piss me off again." He waited, focusing on my lips. His erection jammed against my lower belly.

Stomping on my terror, I glared. "You touch me, you die. Cut won't like you disobeying him. You'll be back to being the mistake. The unwanted. The unneeded."

Jethro.

Kestrel.

Would Cut kill Daniel, too?

From three heirs to none.

Daniel trembled with lustful rage. "You fucking—"

"Go ahead and fuck me but you'll be the third son your

father shoots."

He froze.

For the longest second, we glowered. The sound of wilderness and our shallow breathing was our serenade.

Finally, he threw me away and stormed toward the exit. "I'm not that crazy. And you're not worth a bullet. I'll wait."

I couldn't stop my muscles trembling.

Thank God.

I'd pushed too far. I'd been idiotic in taunting him. It would've been my fault if he'd raped me. But I'd gotten under his skin and unsettled his equilibrium. I'd shown him I wasn't a wallflower he could pluck the petals off and stomp beneath his shoe. I had thorns…needles…pain to deliver.

His fist grabbed the tent flap, shaking with vehemence. Turning, he smiled coldly. "You're being so patient, little Weaver. I know all those questions were to make me snap. I know how much you want my cock—you're practically begging for it." His eyes narrowed. "How do you think that would make Jet feel? Knowing his corpse is barely cold and you want to fuck his younger brother?"

Clucking his tongue, he blew me a kiss. "I'll make sure to reward you for being so patient. Expect a lot of *persuasion* to scream later."

Before I could hurl obscenities, he was gone.

I stood there forever, hugging myself. My knees shook, threatening to dump me to the floor.

What have I done?

I knew what I'd just done.

I'd made whatever my future held worse.

Why? Why did I antagonise him?

Because this was it. The end. There would be no going back from here. No second chances. They would take from me. Tear apart everything I had to give. And I hoped to God I would take from them before it was over.

With numb fingers, I stroked my knitting needle hidden in my hoodie pocket.

Stay strong. Don't stop fighting.

Daniel's silhouette graced the outside of the tent as he snapped his fingers at Marquise. His lumbering form marched closer, waiting for orders.

"Stand here. Arm your weapon. If she tries to run, shoot her."

Tears tried to crest but I shoved them down. This wasn't Hawksridge. Daniel wasn't Jethro. And this was no longer a game. The stark truth couldn't hide: I was in deep shit.

Marquise nodded. "Right-o."

Sticking his head back into the tent, Daniel grinned. "Just so you're aware, if you try to run, you'll know what Jethro and Kes felt when they died by bullet. How's that for a bedtime story?"

His boots crunched on the deck as he leapt to the dusty ground and left. Marquise popped his head inside, only to give me a cold smile before zipping up the mosquito screen across the door.

Cocking his gun, he turned his back on me.

Alone.

Finally.

I didn't waste any time.

I didn't know how long Cut would be, but it wouldn't be long enough. I needed to switch off any sentiments or remaining hints of the girl I'd been and prepare to become a ruthless killer.

Snatching my suitcase, I hauled it to the bed and unzipped it. Every garment and item were in disarray. When Daniel ordered me to pack, folding wasn't a top priority.

Tossing clothes that didn't have weapons sewn inside to the floor, I hurriedly selected the fleece jacket with a scalpel hidden in the collar and the leggings with a pair of delicate scissors smuggled in the waistband.

Daniel wanted me to have a shower?

Fine. I would shower.

I would prepare.

And I would go to war when he returned.

Jethro

ECONOMY CLASS.

Public airline.

The *worst* possible environment for a man like me.

I huddled in my seat, gritting my jaw; doing my best to remember the exercises I'd been taught.

Focus on my own thoughts.

Concentrate on inner pain. Pinch, slice, do whatever it takes to put that barrier up.

Fixate on mundane influences: reading, looking at nature.

I swallowed a groan.

None of it worked.

Glancing around the plane, my condition picked up on homesickness, regret, excitement, loss, and fear. Every person had their own thoughts and those thoughts flew kamikaze in the small space.

Squeezing my eyes, I focused on my ice. Cut had done one thing right raising me. He'd taught me how to focus on hatred and selfishness, shutting everyone out—even their pain.

The lesson hadn't been easy. If I slipped or didn't succeed, Jasmine bore the brunt. Cut understood that the pain of those I loved affected me triply hard. In a way, forcing me to listen to his emotions of discipline and control, while blocking out my sister's agony and unhappiness, gave me the strength to combat the influx of paralyzing emotions from others.

Even while she was hurt right in front of me.

I could stomach my own pain, but when it came to hers...

Just like I can't stand Nila's now I love her.

Forcing those memories away, I did my best to relapse into the capsule of snow, but even as the tendrils of ice made their way around my heart, one person centred in my thoughts.

Jasmine.

Because of me, she would never walk again. And that was another reason why I couldn't abandon her when Nila begged me to leave last night in the stables. Why I owed Kes and Jaz everything because, without them, I would've died years ago.

Maybe I *should've* died years ago.

Maybe Nila would've remained safe, and Kes wouldn't be fighting for his life.

Kes would've been next in line. If Cut followed the Debt Inheritance rules—without turning into the power hungry bastard he'd become—with the firstborn dead, the contract couldn't be fulfilled and both Kes and Nila would've been free. Nila would've married someone far away from the Hawks and would've given birth to a daughter as beautiful as her.

Only to be ruined a generation later.

The ice I tried to cultivate thawed, leaving me wretched.

It wasn't the thought of future debts, but the thought of Nila married and happy with another that flayed me alive.

She was mine. I was hers. We were meant to fall in love and finish this. Just like Owen, my doomed ancestor, and his love, Elisa, never could.

Fuck, Nila.

What had she lived through in the hours we'd been apart? What had they done to her since I'd failed her?

"Juice?"

I opened my eyes, glaring at the stewardess. Her emotions bounced between job satisfaction and claustrophobia. She loved to travel but hated to wait on passengers. If I listened harder, I would've learned most of her secrets and guessed a lot about her life.

"No." I looked out the window. "Thank you."

The darkness of the sky illuminated every few seconds with a red flash from the wing tip, keeping time with my ragged heartbeat.

I hadn't calmed since Jasmine's phone call.

After galloping to the garage, I'd left Wings to find his way back to the stables and traded him for a different kind of horsepower. My Harley snarled in the afternoon sun, hurling me down our driveway and to the airport.

I didn't think to seek out Flaw. I didn't have time to tell my sister my plan.

All I focused on was getting to the airport and a charter.

However, I should've used my brain rather than my fearful heart. There were no charters or private planes available that late in the day. No pilots on call. No one to bribe to fly.

I had no choice but to hurtle to Heathrow and board the next available flight to South Africa. Getting to the airport, buying a ticket, and arguing over the fastest service had all cost valuable time.

Time I didn't have.

No quick routes. No private planes.

My only option had been a cramped, overbooked flight with three stops before reaching my destination. Even if I'd waited for twenty-four hours and hired a private jet, the long haul commercial flight would've been faster.

So I bought a ticket.

I sent Nila a text:

Kite007: *I'm coming. Hang on. Do whatever it takes to stay alive. I love you so fucking much.*

She hadn't replied. If she had been able to take her cell phone, she wouldn't have reception in the sky. And if Cut had stolen it from her, I would have no way to warn her of my arrival.

Yet another problem in my problem-riddled future.

Flying while fearing for the life of a loved one was bad enough. But flying with an empathetic condition and a healing gunshot wound was a hundred times fucking worse.

Every takeoff and landing, every airport and taxi, I lost more of my humanity and focused on bloodlust, plotting what I would do to Cut and Daniel when I arrived.

The promise of wide open spaces and empty African plains helped me remain sane in the tinderbox of airplane madness.

I'd always avoided public spaces for long periods. Flying with Nila from Milan had been the first time I'd suffered in years. For all intents, before Nila came into my life, I was a recluse. Hawksridge my sanctuary and Diamond Alley my office. I had no need to mingle with strangers.

Another whirlpool of conflicting passenger emotions bottled up in a tiny fuselage with no outlet. I did my best to ignore them. Did my best to cultivate my hate and let the single-minded determination give me peace.

Grabbing the napkin from the cognac I'd ordered an hour ago, I shredded it as my heart worked double time. My side bellowed and a fever dotted my brow. Timelines and countdown clocks swarmed my mind as I worked out how far ahead Nila was.

At best, eight to nine hours.

At worse, ten to twelve.

Nila might've been spared pain and rape.

She might still have time.

But three-quarters of the way over the Atlantic Ocean, I knew I'd run out of minutes.

They'd arrived at *Almasi Kipanga.*

She was on her own.

45

Nila

I STOOD ON the lip of a colossal mine.

The teeth of the earth yawned wide, its tongue and tonsils butchered by spades and diggers, its innards exposed to the night sky in the hunt for diamonds and wealth.

Staring into the pit hurt something deep inside. It wasn't for the broken trees left to rot unwanted, or the ebony-skinned workers toiling in the muck. It wasn't the stagnant air of degradation and robbery. It was the sadness that something as precious and rare as diamonds—that the earth had created over millennia—had been so callously stolen with no grace or thanks.

"Impressive. Isn't it?" Cut slung his arm over my shoulders.

I flinched but didn't move away.

Not that I could.

A coarse rope bit into my wrists, wound tightly by Cut when he'd come for me.

I'd expected the Third Debt to be carried out the moment Cut returned from whatever errands he ran. I'd sat on the bed, pricking the tips of my fingers with the hidden knitting needle, never taking my eyes off the entrance to my tent.

My stomach grumbled. Energy depleted. But I'd refused

to fall asleep. I would face my nightmare while awake.

It was the only way.

The cool African night had gnawed on my skin; goosebumps prickled as the *humph humph* of lions echoed through the fabric house.

They sounded so close. So hungry.

Then, all at once, it seemed as if an orchestra conductor arranged a quartet of laughing hyenas, bays of zebras, and hoots of owls.

The animal song raised my stress levels until I'd shivered with terror.

"Are you listening to me?" Cut's voice sliced through my thoughts. I hadn't rested or slept in forever; my reactions were sluggish.

I blinked. "You were saying something about quantity and how much—"

"No!" He jerked the rope around my wrists. "I was telling you how deep *Almasi Kipanga* goes. In centuries of mining, we've found seams and seams of stones. We continue to expand and the mine is currently half a kilometre below earth. Can you comprehend that?"

I shook my head. All I could think about was how dark and claustrophobic it would be. A tomb just waiting to fall like countless dominos, smothering anyone inside it.

Daniel smiled. "That's years of digging. Millions upon millions of diamonds carved out of the dirt. If a seam dries up, a new route is planned." His teeth flashed. "One lucky worker is given the job of setting explosives to disrupt any loose landslides or cave-ins."

"What happens if the explosives set off a disaster and he gets crushed?" My eyes widened at such a dangerous occupation.

Daniel shrugged. "That's why we only send one. If he doesn't make it, then tough shit. We don't evacuate, we just seal."

I swallowed my disgust. "You kill men in so many ways."

"Thanks for the compliment."

My eyes narrowed. "It wasn't."

"I don't care." Daniel smirked. "I'm taking it as one."

I wanted to wipe that idiotic greed and insanity and entitlement right off his heinous face. "I wouldn't be so bloody cocky if I were you. You act as if killing an employee is a sport—that they're as disposable as broken tools." Tilting my chin at Cut, I snarled, "But your father doesn't just stop there. What makes you think you're safe, Daniel? When all signs point to you being the reject and least desirable?"

"Why you—" Daniel fisted my hair, jerking me from his father's grip. His free hand shot to his belt where a dirty rag was stuffed in his pocket. "Gonna shut you up once and for—"

Cut yanked me back, tucking me under his arm once again. "I don't know what happened between you two while I was gone, but stop squabbling like spoiled brats."

Squeezing me, he murmured, "Now, Nila. Behave, be silent unless spoken to, and you'll get to visit something not many people get to see."

Cut glared at his son. "Calm the fuck down and be a man, Buzzard. Nila's right. At this point, you're less than desirable. And if you keep it up, I'll be the one extracting the Third Debt without you. I don't share with ingrates."

I shuddered with loathing.

The thought of Cut touching me any more than he was now shrivelled up my insides until they turned to ash.

Daniel burned red with fury but swallowed his retorts.

Cut let me go. "Come. Let's take a closer look." He raised my bound hands, kissing my knuckles as if this was a perfectly normal night on a perfectly normal vacation. After his outburst, he looked positively carefree. Happy...

How can you be happy, you bastard?

I vowed on every fallen tree and hacked up dirt that I would wipe the smug smile off his goddamn face.

"Come along." Cut strode ahead, jerking me behind him.

My ballet flats skidded on pebbles as I struggled to match

his pace. Greyness danced on the outskirts of my vision, but I refused to give in to vertigo.

I was already in a perilous situation. I wouldn't let my body subject me to more.

My mouth dried up as we moved forward on the tiny path. The deeper we headed, the more claustrophobia clawed. The track had been carved from the mountain, steadily curving with bare earth on one side, damp and musty, and a steep drop on the other, giving no second chances if you tripped.

One wrong step…

If I could guarantee Cut's demise, I'd throw myself over the edge and take him with me.

African men and women bowed as we traded the narrow path for a wider road, exchanging foot power for an electric golf cart.

The simple cart was nothing like the armoured Jeep we'd driven in.

Once Cut had returned from his errands, he'd bundled me into another car and driven Daniel, Marquise, and me to the mine. I didn't have a watch and my phone—which I missed like a lost limb—remained in the U.K. But I guessed the trip took about twenty minutes before arriving at the wound of *Almasi Kipanga*.

I'd held my breath as a wall the size of China loomed in the distance. Gates soared high; the perimeter fortified with electricity, barbed wire, and countless notices in Swahili and English warning of mutilation and death if they were caught stealing.

"Get in, Nila." Cut's rough hand pushed me into the backseat of the mud-splattered golf cart. Daniel sat beside me, while Marquise, silent as always, took the front beside Cut.

The deeper into the chasm we drove, the more Cut's pride shone. He looked upon this place like it existed because of him. Like he was the creator, founder, and architect.

But it wasn't him. He couldn't take credit for something that'd been here since the dinosaurs roamed. Nor take pride in something the earth had created. He'd done *nothing*. If anything, he'd tainted the preciousness of diamonds and smeared them with the blood of his workers.

The battery whir of the cart could barely be heard over the squelching of mud as we descended down the serpentine road into purgatory.

Workers milled everywhere. Some with buckets on a yoke, others driving diggers and dump trucks full of earth. Armed guards stood sentry every few metres, their hands ready to shoot for any infraction. The air reeked of malnourished slavery.

Daniel caught me staring at one man as he dumped a pick-axe and bucket beside a growing tower of tools. "You'd be surprised where people will stuff a diamond, Weaver. The imagination can make a human body quite the suitcase."

I bit my tongue. I wouldn't speak. Not because Cut told me not to, but because I was done trying to figure him out. Jethro had redeemed himself, Kes never had anything to redeem, but Daniel...he was a lost cause.

The questions Cut gave me permission to ask had lost their shiny appeal. I didn't care. I truly didn't bloody care.

"Like what you see?" Cut asked as we neared the looming entrance to the belly of hell. Driving into the open-aired entrance was bad enough. The thought of entering the pitch-black crypt sucked all my courage away.

Apart from the obvious destitution of the workers, Cut's treasure trove looked like any other mine—no diamonds strewn on the ground or sparkling in large barrels in the African night. If anything, the pit was dusty, dirty...utterly underwhelming.

I faced him with an incredulous look. "Like what I see? What exactly? Your love of hurting people or the fact that you murder whenever it benefits you?"

"Careful." His golden eyes glowed with threats. "Half a kilometre below ground gives many places to dispose of a body and never be found."

I looked away, wishing I had use of my hands so I could wring his neck. *Perhaps, I'll dispose of you down there.*

My hoodie didn't offer much warmth against the cool sky, but knowing my knitting needle rested in easy reach mollified me.

If I wasn't tied up, of course.

My fingers turned numb from the tight rope around my wrists.

The lack of sleep and overall situation made my nerves disappear. "Threats. Always threats with you. There comes a time, *Bryan*, that threats no longer scare, they just make you look stupid."

Cut sucked in a breath. I didn't know if it was my use of his given name or my retaliation, but his gaze darkened with lust. "Was I threatening when I killed Jethro or Kestrel? That was decisive action—cutting out the tumour before it infected the host."

"No, I call that insanity growing more and more rampant."

His throat constricted as he swallowed. He didn't say a word as he guided the golf cart to a stop beside a sheer rock wall. The air temperature dropped even more as shadows danced around the mouth of the mine. In front of us, a large opening beckoned. There were no welcome mats or happy wreaths on the door, just rough timber frames, well-tracked mud, and the occasional light disappearing into the belly of this monstrous beast.

Cut launched from his seat and plucked me from mine. "You'll learn that I don't believe in threatening, Nila. I believe in action. And tonight, once we return to camp, you'll find that you'll *crave* action, too."

The way he stressed the word 'crave' made my heart rate spike. What did he mean by that?

"No time to waste." Stepping back, Cut stole my roped hands, guiding me toward the crudely made entrance. Daniel followed, content to listen and watch rather than interrupt.

The second we traded starlight for thick, thick dirt above

us, my urge to run accelerated. The timber framework gave way to jutting wooden poles, holding up a tin structure, keeping droplets at bay from the dripping earthen roof.

Exposed light bulbs dangled from the ceiling, casting us in stencils and shadows as we followed the corridor down, down, down then branched off to a large cave-like space.

I blinked, drinking in the array of clothes pegs and large bins labelled with what their contents entailed: dungarees, boots, hammers, chisels, and axes.

I shivered as the cold dampness ate through my clothing.

Daniel moved forward and grabbed a waterproof jacket. His cheeks dimpled cruelly as he sneered, "If only you'd been nice. I might've given you a jacket. It gets cold down here." Grabbing a torch from another barrel, he shrugged. "Oh well, guess you'll freeze and I'll have to work extra hard to warm you back up when we return."

Cut let me go, grabbing his own jacket and slinging it over his shoulders. He merely smiled and didn't override his youngest's decision not to give me extra warmth.

So be it.

I gritted my jaw, locking my muscles to hide my shivering.

Daniel patted my arse as he stalked past. "Let's go to the tally room then we'll go below."

Below?

Further…down into the ground?

I…I…

I swallowed, forcing away my panic as I focused on the other word I dreaded.

Tally.

Tally room?

Like the marks on my fingertips?

I looked down at my twined wrists. Smudges and grime covered my index but beneath it, Jethro's marks still rested.

My heart twinged, remembering Jethro bent over and carefully inscribing my skin with his initials. The ink wouldn't last forever; it'd already faded from washing my hands, but I loved having his mark there—in a way, it made him immortal. Even when I thought he was dead, his signature remained on my skin.

He'll come for me.

I knew that. But I also knew he wouldn't be in time.

I sucked in a heavy breath. If I never saw him again, at least we had the night in the stables. At least I got to see him one last time.

"Good plan." Cut took my hand, dragging me deeper into the mine. More carts and trolleys, even an old Jeep littered the underground pathway. I hadn't expected such a huge size. The mine had the air of an unseen city, complete with transportation, inhabitants, and daily commuters heading to their offices.

The lights did their best to push back the gloom, but between the strung bulbs, a cloying blackness permeated my skin and clothes. The stench of damp earth couldn't be dispelled, nor could the underlying fear that any moment the world could collapse and I'd be buried forever.

Goosebumps scattered over my arms as we entered another small cave where numerous tables had been set with scales, plastic containers, and ziplock bags. This room was brightly lit, pretending it had its own sun and not banished to the underworld.

"This is where every worker must drop his haul at the end of the shift." Cut waved at the room. "The diamonds are washed, weighed, measured, and lasered with the fair trading IPL code before being sorted into equal distribution for shipment."

My eyes widened at the willingly given information. I knew Cut had no intention of letting me spill what I'd learned to others, but I couldn't get used to how open he was.

I supposed from here on out, every secret I'd be privy to, every hidden action shown.

I frowned, remembering what he'd made me promise at the dice game at Hawksridge. He'd demanded I save him a debt in return for whatever he would share.

What did he expect me to do? And what made him so sure I'd obey, now Vaughn wasn't here to torture?

Shoving those thoughts away, I focused on the already processed ziplock bags. If he wanted to share in-depth details of his family's enterprise, who was I to stop him?

Knowledge was power.

In a few questions, I'd learned more about Daniel than I had in six months.

I could do the same with Cut.

My voice boomeranged around the cave. "How do you get the stones out of the country?"

Daniel stroked a bag gently. "Oh, we have multiple ways."

Cut prowled to a table and plucked a dull stone from a pile of dirt. "We use private planes and bribe air traffic control. We use shipping containers and smuggle contraband in the captain's quarters. Other times we use trucks and pay off officials at the borders. Sometimes, we bribe a trusted few in the Red Cross who disguise the stones in medical supplies. There is no end to transport if you start looking at avenues available. Each tactic helps us export blood diamonds to borders where ludicrous taxes and regulations don't exist."

My lips curled at the mention of Red Cross. How could he use something that was supposed to benefit those in need by turning them into mules for something that hurt to procure? "That's immoral."

Cut laughed. "You think that's bad? Silly girl, you should hear what my ancestors used to do." Coming closer, he traced my arm with his dusty fingertips. "Before your time is up in Africa, you'll learn of one such method." His eyes glowed with demons. "And then you can decide which is immoral."

I shivered, wrenching away from his touch. "You can keep your methods. I don't want to know."

Daniel gathered me close from behind, pressing his hips into my arse. "You'll get your history lesson, same as always, Weaver. Once you've repaid the Third Debt tonight, you'll be told what's in store for you tomorrow."

Tomorrow.

Tomorrow.

Jethro…

How far away are you?

A question flew into my head. I wanted to ignore it. It probably wasn't wise to ask. But I was past censoring. "Why drag this out? Why not get it over with?"

Cut grinned. "Eager for a raping, my dear?"

I balled my hands. "Stop with the torment. I get it. You're rich. You have power. I've lived with you for months. I know that already."

Cut's fingers tucked short hair behind my ear, fingering the strands he'd allowed Daniel to hack. "It's a method of torture, Nila. Just like the history lessons inform you of your demise, the delay adds weight to what will happen." Dropping his fingers from my hair, he clutched my hipbones, dragging me from Daniel's clutches into his own.

Like father, like son.

I hated that both their erections pressed against me in a matter of seconds.

My heart lurched with sickness. I'd slept with Jethro willingly. I'd made Kestrel come as a thank-you gift for being so decent, and if I didn't find a way to stop my future, I would become intimately acquainted with Daniel and Cut, too.

Four men.

Four Hawks.

One Weaver.

My stomach recoiled, threatening to evict the nothingness inside me.

"Let me go—"

"No." Cut grabbed my nape.

Before I could squirm away, his mouth landed on mine.

Stop!

He'd kissed me before. Licked me. Touched me. But this was the first time he let down his guard and fully gave me a part of himself. His tongue fluttered over my tightly pressed lips. His goatee bristled my tender chin. His rough skin hinted at his age. And his impatience at getting me to respond unravelled his decorum.

His nostrils blew scalding air on my cheeks as he forced me to kiss him back.

I stood there unmoving. I didn't open. I didn't budge. He might be able to drag out my persecution, but he didn't have the power to make me fear it.

His kiss suddenly switched from savage to sweet, peppering soft kisses on my lips.

For one tiny second, he wasn't a monster. He projected a fantasy that he truly cared for me. That somewhere, deep inside his rotting chest, beat a heart that wasn't pure evil.

But that was a lie. A terrible, *terrible* lie.

The worst one yet.

Yanking my mouth away from his, I spat at his feet. "Don't *ever* do that again."

He chuckled. "Oh, I'll do more than that, Nila." Slinking his arm around my waist, he smiled. "You taste just like your mother."

"You're a pig."

"That's your misconception. I'll have great pleasure showing you otherwise." His whisper tangled in my hair. "Tonight, you'll want me just as much as she did. I give you my word on that."

"No way in hell will I ever want you, you bastard."

Chuckling again, he let me go. "We'll see." Snapping his fingers, he stalked to the exit. "Come, I want you to see what your mother saw on the eve of her final task. I want you to know how insignificant a human life, especially a Weaver life, is compared to all that we have."

Daniel grabbed my elbow, guiding me from the tally room. "I suggest you enjoy your tour, Nila, because once it's over, there's a certain protocol that has to be followed here. Certain superstitions to be entertained, local spirits to appease."

I ducked beneath a mildew covered beam. "What do you mean?"

Cut said, "He means that you're more than just our bed companion tonight. You're our sacrifice."

I gasped.

What?

Tucking my hand into the crook of his arm, Daniel guided me toward the gaping black hole and the unknown world beyond. "Now, let's go explore, shall we? Time to see below the earth…time to see where diamonds are born."

Drumbeats.

Heartbeats.

Wingbeats.

It all melted into one as Cut guided me from the Jeep and back to the camp. My bones ached from the dampness of the mine. My clothes hung with icy humidity. And my mind couldn't shed the tunnel of blackness where expensive stones were found.

How long had we been underground? Two hours? Three?

Either way, I'd seen enough of the birthplace of diamonds and never wanted to return. I couldn't stop shivering, even as I thawed beneath the open skies. Fresh air fed my lungs, doing its best to eradicate the earthen soup found below the ground.

Cut had taken great pleasure in showing me catacombs where the first seam was found then scars where workers had pinched diamonds from the soil. He'd taken me in a wire-cage elevator to the furthest point in the mine. He'd shown me underground rivers, white-washed crosses on walls where cave-ins had claimed lives, and even skeletons of rats and vermin that'd stupidly decided to dig beside the workers.

The entire experience had ensured I loved my vocation even more. Material couldn't kill me. Velour and calico couldn't suffocate me.

I never wanted to go near a mine again.

However, I couldn't stop fingering my collar, counting how many stones had been torn from their home. I'd expected the weight of the diamonds to grow heavier the longer I was in *Almasi Kipanga*. If anything, the necklace grew lighter. Almost as if the diamonds were of mixed decision. Half of them wanting to return to their beds of dust, and others happy to be in sunlight rather than perpetual darkness—regardless of the bloodshed they'd witnessed.

Cut smiled. "Time for the next part of the tour."

The cacophony of drumbeats tore me from my thoughts. Cut shoved me through the camp, barred behind fences, ensconced in a human habitat rather than diamond tomb.

Drumming and singing guided us toward the central fire pit.

"What the—" My mouth fell open as we rounded the path, entering a different dimension. I felt as if I'd time travelled—shot backward a few decades where African tribes still owned the land, and their life was about music rather than gemstones.

The pounding of fists on animal-hide drums echoed through my body, drowning out my nerves of what was to come. The air shimmered with guttural tunes and barbaric voices.

I'd never seen such a cultural fiesta. Never been enticed to travel to somewhere so ruthless and dangerous. But witnessing the liveliness and magic of the group of ebony-skinned dancers made tears spring to my eyes.

There was so much I hadn't seen. So much I hadn't done or experienced or indulged.

I was too young to die. Too fresh to leave a world that offered so much diversity.

This.

I want more of this.

Living…

"Your mother liked this, too," Cut murmured, his face

dancing with flame-ghosts from the bonfire. Topless women weaved around the crackling orange, their skirts of threaded flax and feathers creating stencils on the tents and buildings. Men wore loin clothes, pounding an intoxicating beat on animal drums of zebra and impala.

"This is what you meant when you said superstitions being appeased?"

Cut nodded. "Every time we return to *Almasi Kipanga*, our workers welcome us home."

"Why? They must hate working for monsters like you. You treat them like the rats living in the mine."

Cut grinned, softened by the tribal spectacle. "To them, we are their masters. Their gods. We feed them, clothe them, keep them safe from wildlife and elements. Their families have grown up with my family. As much as you hate me, Nila, without our industry, these people would be homeless."

I didn't believe that. People found a way. They would've found a better life rather than slaving for a man who didn't deserve it.

Daniel patted his father on the back. "Gonna get something to drink. Make the rest of the night extra special." Winking at me, he faded into the mingling workers and guards.

I ought to be relieved he'd left. I only had to focus on Cut. But somehow, Cut's promises of *craving* action and enjoying what he would do to me layered my lungs with terror.

Cut pressed on my lower spine. "Come along. Time for your part in tonight's festivities."

My heels dug into soil. "My part?"

"I told you." His gaze glowed. "You're the sacrifice."

"No. I'm nothing of the sort."

I'd been my father's sacrifice. Tex had given me up to Jethro that night in Milan with no fuss. I was done being forfeited for the greater good.

"You don't have a choice, Nila." Cut dragged me closer to the fire, despite my unwillingness.

Nervousness exploded in time to the tribal drum as he led

me through the dancing throng and pushed me onto a grass mat at the head of the bonfire. My wrists burned in their twine, sore and achy.

The entire time we'd been in the mine, he hadn't released me. What did he think I'd do? Grab a pick-axe and hack away at his head? Run and dig myself to safety?

The texture of the woven mat beneath my toes told me this tribe were weavers, too. It took great skill to create items from plant life and not cloth or silk.

Cut sat beside me on a raised platform decorated with ostrich feather and lion skin. He didn't look at me, just wrapped the rope tethering me in his fist and smiled as the women danced harder, faster, wilder.

I didn't want to be distracted. I didn't want to fall under the spell of magical music and sensual swaying, but the longer we sat there, the more enthralled I became. I'd only seen this culture on documentaries and television. I'd travelled to Asia with V and Tex to gather diamantes and fabrics, but I'd never been on this continent.

My horizons were so small compared to what the world had to offer.

Sitting there at the feet of my murderer, watching his employees dance and welcome, highlighted just how much my life lacked. I'd let work dictate and rob me of living.

If only Jethro was here.

His handsome face popped into my mind. I wanted to run my fingers over his five o' clock shadow. I wanted to kiss his thick, black eyelashes. I wanted to kiss him, forgive him; pretend the world was a better place.

The more the music trickled into me, the more my body reacted. Sensual need replaced the damp panic of the mine, making my nipples ache at the thought of Jethro touching me.

My body grew twisty and excited, cursing the distance between us and the circumstances I was in.

My eyes smarted as smoke from the fire cast us in sooty clouds. The rhythmical footsteps and infectious freedom of the melody slowly replaced my blood.

There was something erotic about the dance. Something slinked nonverbally, speaking of connection and lust and love and forever togetherness. Bodily communication superseded that of spoken languages.

My heart throbbed with lovesickness. I missed him. I wanted him. I needed to see him one last time and tell him how much he meant to me.

I love you, Jethro…Kite.

Cut hadn't lied when he said superstitions had to be acknowledged. Over the course of three songs, the local tribe welcomed their boss with handmade gifts of beads and pottery, delivered food of roasted meat and fruits, and danced numerous numbers.

At one point in the ceremony, a woman with bare breasts and white paint smeared on her throat and chest reverently placed a flower headband on Cut's head.

He nodded with airs and graces, smiling indulgently as the woman merged back with her tribesman.

My skin prickled, a sixth sense saying I was watched.

Squinting past the brightness and sting of the fire, I searched for the owner's gaze.

Buzzard.

Daniel lurked on the outskirts of the fire, his eyes not on the half-naked women but on me. His lips parted, gaze undressing me, raping me from afar. In his hand rested a crudely made cup, no doubt holding liquor.

One song turned into a mecca of soulful salvation. A young girl broke away from the dancing women, moving forward with a small bowl and a blade.

I sucked in a breath as she looked at Cut and pointed at me with the knife.

A knife?

Why the hell does she have a knife?

Cut nodded, tugging my leash. I tried to fight it, but it was no use. Effortlessly, he forced me to present my tied hands.

My lungs seized as the girl bowed at my feet, placing the bowl on the dirt. Unfurling my palms, she kissed each finger, murmuring a chant that sent spiders scurrying down my spine.

I tried to tug away, but Cut held me firm.

"Wait—"

The girl flashed her blade.

I gritted my teeth. "No—"

Before I could stop her, she sliced the flesh of my palm and held the bleeding cut over the bowl.

Ow!

Pain instantly lashed over the wound, stinging and raw. Blood welled, dripping thickly into the girl's collection.

"Why did you do that?" My voice bordered on rage and curiosity. My hand begged to curl over the wound and protect it.

The girl didn't reply; she merely waited until a small crimson puddle rested in the bowl before letting me go.

The music turned to a fever, the men pounding their drums, the women kicking their heels. The little girl returned with her bloody prize, dancing and howling at the moon as voices rose in an ancient euphony.

My entire body was on fire.

My blood flowing fast.

My skin flushing bright.

My fear twisted into intoxication.

I wanted to join them. To become *wild*.

My wound was forgotten. My predicament and future peril ignored.

The moment the girl took my blood, I'd become more than just an outcast in this foreign land, I'd become *one* of them.

Cut sucked in a breath, something odd and not entirely unwelcome throbbing between us. He tore his gaze from mine as the girl finished her pirouette and with a squeal the bowl landed in the fire, shattering against hot coals, hissing with burning blood. A potent smell laced the air as the dance turned crazed, choreographed by gravity-defying shamans.

To be somewhere where life wasn't about TV or work-stress or mundane normalness—to see people having fun and partying—intoxicated me better than any experience.

The night came alive with singing and stomping feet and the unravelling power inside billowed faster. I wanted to get up. I wanted to dance. I wanted to forget who I was and let go.

This was an experience of a lifetime and my lifetime was almost over. My mother was here. My grandmother was here. Every ancestor had somehow come to life and existed in the flames of the enchanted fire.

We all lived the same path…and failed. I was supposed to be the last Weaver taken but time no longer held sway on my plans. It charged forward, dragging me with hardship, hurtling me toward a conclusion I didn't know how to stop.

A woman appeared in front of me. Coconut beads and crocodile teeth decorated her neck, draping between naked breasts. "You. Drink." Shoving a crudely made bowl beneath my chin, she tipped the milky substance toward my lips.

I reared back, shaking my head. "No, thank you."

Cut tugged on the rope, his face alive with power. "Drink."

I pursed my lips.

"You must." The woman tried again.

I turned my face away. The liquid smelled rank and rotten.

"You will drink, Nila." Lashing out, Cut fisted my hair, keeping my head in place as the woman once again held the bowl to my mouth.

I scrunched my face, protesting. The silty liquid splashed against my lips.

I didn't know what it was, but it was powerful—the otherworldly smell warned me I wouldn't be the same if I ingested it. I wouldn't like the results if I gave in.

Stop! Please, stop.

The woman tried again, bruising my mouth with the rim of the bowl. Crushed up leaves and smashed up roots lingered on the bottom, splashing with her attempts. The woman cursed in Swahili, looking at Cut for help. "She won't."

"She will." Still holding my hair, he reached with his free hand and captured my bleeding palm. "Open." With ferocity, he dug his fingernail into the fresh wound. I did my best to prevent drinking, but his hold was agonising.

The heat and pain wrenched my mouth open, and a gulp of disgusting liquid shot down my throat.

My eyes watered.

My stomach retched.

I spluttered.

The woman nodded with satisfaction. "Good." She stood, slipping back to her fellow dancers.

Alone, Cut hugged me, kissing my cheek. "Good girl." His tongue slipped out, licking a droplet off my lower lip like a lover would his bride. "Let it transform you. Let it own you."

I shuddered, fighting his embrace. "Let go of me."

Cut chuckled, kissing the corner of my mouth. "Don't fight it. You *can't* fight it."

"I'll fight whatever you do to me." Our eyes clashed. My heart roared with hatred.

But then...

Something mellowed.

Something simmered.

Tiptoeing through my blood, stealing rationality and sanity and coherence.

"What...what did yo—you give m—me?" My ability to speak in correct dialect fumbled as the drink merged faster with my thoughts.

Cut beamed wide; his face rollicked as my vision washed in and out. "Give it another moment. You'll see how useless fighting is." His lips caressed mine again. Softly, teasingly, coaxing me to react.

And this time...I couldn't hate it.

My loathing turned to liking. My hatred to harrowing welcome.

My heartbeat left the epicentre of my chest, cannonballing into every extremity. My toes felt it. My ears felt it. Even the strands of my hair *thump-thumped* in time.

I'm hot.

I'm cold.

I was sick.

I was cured.

What's happening?

A gust, a gale, a monsoon ripped through my body. Whatever the woman had given me tore up my denials and aversion, switching them into the sudden overwhelming desire to kiss him back.

God, a kiss. Such a delicacy. A tongue, such a gift.

Kiss him.

I tore myself away, spitting on the flax mat. "No!"

Cut turned into a rippling watermark, decorated with flames and starlight. "I don't believe you." His fingers traced my skin, drawing hungry blood to the surface. My mouth said no but my body said *yes.*

No...this can't...

I moaned, struggling against the ropes as I fell deeper and deeper into whatever spell he'd fed me.

I didn't know what lacquered my mouth.

I didn't know what made its fiery way into my belly.

But I did know it was aggressive and possessive and persuasive.

Vicious.

Far, far stronger than anything I'd ever had before.

I can't fight it.

My tongue went numb, followed by my throat and skin. My pussy throbbed for release. My mind howled for connection. I'd never been so disappointed in myself nor so annoyed at preventing such delicious need from billowing.

I split in two.

I became something I wasn't.

I became a creature with no morals or humanity, just an

animal wanting to fuck.

Shivers hijacked me as I fought against the overwhelming sensation to let go. To give in to the magic. To be swept away by the river of sin.

"Do it, Nila. Let it take you." Cut's fingers were tiny birds upon my spine, feathering into my hair.

I moaned, trembling and wanting.

"Let it win and tonight won't be rape. Tonight will be the best fucking sex of your life."

No.

Yes.

No!

Oh, my God.

His words were invitations to my destruction, beckoning closer with every word.

My heartbeat thundered harder, feeding the drug into every part of me.

"That's it. Let go. Forget about the past and future. Think about how good my cock would feel. How delicious it would be for me to fuck you right here."

Fuck.

Sex.

Mate.

God…

I squeezed my eyes, swirling down a rabbit hole of fanaticism.

His fingers licked through my hair, blazing with lust and horror. "You want me, Nila. Admit it."

My soul turned wild, snarling at the power of the drug.

The fire burned brighter.

The stars twinkled faster.

The dancers twirled harder.

The world twisted and turned, rushing quickly then slowing down as the hallucinogenic played havoc with my senses.

I lost track of time.

I lost track of myself.

My mind swam with images of the dark dripping walls of the mine. My hands locked and squeezed, smearing my blood over Jethro's initials, wanting nothing more than to touch myself and orgasm.

I need to come.

I need to fuck and love and consummate.

I was a black and white painting, an enigma, a shivering contradiction.

I was numb.

I was alive.

I was dead.

I was reborn.

What's happening to me?

I shook my head, fighting the intensity, refusing to become hypnotised by sex and want and music.

But then hands were grabbing mine, tugging me to my feet.

Cut's laughter laced around me. Commands to dance consumed me.

I tried to dart away, but the ground rolled like a funhouse. Vertigo latched me in its horrendous arms.

I fell forward. I was caught.

I swayed to the side. I was propped up.

Daniel's eyes. Cut's eyes. Laughter. Dangerous promises. Lust and greed and pain.

I couldn't.

I couldn't fight it anymore.

My vertigo balanced. My veins sang with drunkenness and I lost everything.

In a circle of sweaty ebony women, I shed my worries, my fears, my hopes. I ceased to be Nila. I stopped being a victim.

The diamonds on my throat increased in weight and warmth, squeezing me tight and drenching me in rainbows from the fire.

I stopped pining for Jethro.

I stopped fearing my future.
I stepped into the magic and danced.

Jethro

AFRICA.

The witching hour stole the continent as I ran through customs and exploded through the arrival gates. Sir Seretse Khama Airport welcomed me back before spewing me out into the chilly night of Gaborone. I hadn't been in Botswana for two years, yet it felt as if I'd never left.

I avoided coming here. I couldn't handle the emotional currents from our workers. I hated feeling their toil and trouble. I hated seeing secrets and shimmers of how unhappy they were.

The last time I'd come, I'd talked to Kes about doing something about it.

He became our official mediator. Behind Cut's back, he travelled often and built a rapport with the men who'd been in our employment for centuries. In his quintessential style of helping and generosity, he improved the living conditions, gave them higher salaries, safer workplace, and secret bonuses for their plight.

He ensured Cut's slaves turned into willing employees with health benefits and satisfaction.

Cut didn't know.

There was so much he didn't know.

But then again, what Cut didn't know didn't hurt him. And it meant our enterprise ran smoother because no ill will and destitution could undermine it.

"Goddammit, where are the fucking drivers?" I jogged toward the vehicle stand, searching for any sign of hailing a lift.

Taxis were few and lingering opportunists rare at this time of night.

I hadn't slept in days. My wound had ruptured and my fever grew steadily worse. But I didn't have time to care. My senses were shredded from the flight and it was all I could do to remain standing.

But Nila was with my father.

Nila was running out of time.

I'm coming.

A single shadow appeared up ahead. Turning my jog into a sprint, I clenched my jaw and approached the scruffy African man. His long hair was braided and his jeans torn in places.

I pointed at his muddy car. "Is that your four-wheel drive?"

The guy glowered, crossing his arms. His black eyes looked me up and down, his muscles priming for a fight.

In Africa, you didn't approach strangers unless you had a weapon and were prepared to battle. Humanity wasn't as civilized here, mainly because so much strife kept the country salivating for war.

"What's it to you, white boy?" His Afrikaans accent heralded memories of playing in the dirt at our mine as a child. Of digging beside workers and chipping unwilling diamonds from ancient rock.

"I'll pay you two thousand pounds if you'll drive me where I need to go."

His territorial anger faded a little, slipping into suspicious hope. "What about I just steal the money and leave you dead on the side of the road?"

I stood to my full height, even though it hurt my side. "You won't do that."

The man uncrossed his arms, his fists curling. "Oh, no? Why not?"

"Because in order to be paid you have to take me. I don't have the money on me."

"This a scam?"

"No scam."

The guy leaned forward, his eyes narrowing for battle. "Tell me who you are."

I smiled.

My name carried weight in England, just like it carried weight here.

However, here I was more than an heir to a billion dollar company. I was more than a lord, and master polo player, and vice president to Black Diamonds.

Here, I was life.

I was death.

I was blood and power and royalty.

"I'm a Hawk."

And that was all it took.

The man lost his indignation, slipping into utmost respect. He turned and opened the door of his dinged-up 4WD, bowing in welcome. "It would be an honour to drive you, boss. I know where you need to go."

Of course, he did.

Everyone here knew of our mine. They knew it was untouchable. They knew not to raid or pillage. That sort of respect went a long way in this country.

I clasped his hand in thanks. "You'll be repaid. But I expect you to drive fast."

"No problem." He smiled broadly. "I know how Hawks fly."

I curled my hands, unable to ignore the ticking time bomb in my chest.

Nila.

Glaring at my driver, I ordered, "Do whatever it takes, but I want to be at *Almasi Kipanga* before sunrise."

"LET HER GO."

Daniel dropped his hold.

I spun to face them. I didn't know why; I knew what was about to happen and should hide. Hide deep, *deep* inside. Hide from everything they would do to me.

However, I preferred to stare at the devil than go into this blind. I would rather pay attention, so I knew that I fought. That I'd won against whatever Cut had made me drink. That he hadn't taken my refusal away from me.

I won't let myself submit.

I vibrated and throbbed. I still begged for a release.

The drugs from the bonfire ran rampant in my veins. Cut had let me dance. He'd cut the rope from around my wrists and sat beside the fire and watched. At times, I caught him pressing a fist between his legs; others, I thought I witnessed affection on his face.

Every step, I succumbed more and more to the drugs. Every drumbeat, my pussy clenched. If Jethro had touched me, I would've dropped to all fours and begged him to fuck me.

I wouldn't have cared about people or fires or watchful gazes. I would've given myself completely in to the fantasy and thrown myself into every debauched act imaginable.

But he wasn't there.

And buried beneath lust and shameful wetness, I remembered enough to be disgusted at my urges. Below the tremors of salaciousness, I hung on with fingernails so I didn't double cross every moral I had left.

The more I danced, the more the fire chased away the chill of the night sky, coating my skin with dew.

The sweating and heat helped.

Perspiration helped shed a little of the drug's claws, bringing me back from untamed animal to a woman I vaguely recognised.

I'd won.

Against the hardest battle of my life.

But now, all that existed was desire and the knowledge there was nowhere for me to run.

Not this time.

No Kestrel to fake it. No Jethro to save me.

Just Daniel, Cut, and me in this flimsy fabric tent.

Drumbeats pounded outside, the occasional whoop and incantation fading into the starlit sky. I'd never battled myself so hard. Never tried to cling to right and wrong when faced with impending doom and wanting so fucking much to give in.

Sex.

They wanted sex.

And whatever they'd given me made me want it bad, too. Terribly bad. Stupidly, fearfully *bad*.

But I couldn't.

I couldn't forget. I *wouldn't* forget.

And so my body split further into two, quaking and twitching, demanding I give in.

Cut came closer, cupping my cheeks with his rough hands. My skin sparked beneath his touch and I hated, hated, *hated* myself for the way I swayed closer, focusing on his mouth and heat and charred smell from the fire.

He chuckled softly, running his thumb over my bottom lip.

It took everything, absolutely everything, inside not to

open for him and suck his finger.

"You're still fighting, little Weaver. I suggest you give in."

Never!

I moaned as he kissed me, encouraging me to just let go. Cut no longer played by whatever ancient rules that'd bound him. He played a different game. He seemed younger, softer…and the occasional similarity between him and his eldest son shot confusion into my brain like the worst vertigo attack.

He's not Jethro.

He's not!

I might've given in to the music and danced. I might've become one of the clan as I cavorted around the burning blaze. But now I would control myself, even if it meant shackling everything my body wanted and ensuring I was taken against my will.

Rape would destroy me.

But willingly participating…I would rather die a thousand times on the threatened guillotine.

"Do you need me to go into details, Nila?" Cut ran his nose along my jaw. "You know what happened to our ancestor. He was buggered from one a.m. to one p.m. He was shared. There were no rules on what could be done to his body. He was given as a debt."

I swallowed hard.

The terrible tragedy of what'd befallen his relative helped fortify my resolve.

I leaned away from his touch. "No, you don't have to. I remember."

Jethro…

God, I wished he was here.

Kestrel…

He'd saved me last time. He'd remained true and honest and so damn selfless—I'd wanted him in that moment.

I wanted him now.

The drugs made me want anyone as long as I earned

pleasure and an end to the incessant drive for a release.

I balled my hands. "Whatever you gave me—I won't give in to it."

My eyes glazed as Cut grabbed his cock. "You sure about that?"

Animalistic primal urges overrode my humanity. I was sick. Sick, sick, *sick* to want this murderer. The man who'd slaughtered my mother. The man who killed my lover and his brother—his very sons.

No!

A wash of clarity helped me stand firm. "Get out! Get *out*. I won't enjoy this. I won't. No matter what you do, I won't welcome this. You want me to give myself willingly? You want me to love you like I love your son? But I won't. I never will. You're a twisted bastard who deserves nothing more than death!"

Silence smothered us as my outburst hung loudly in the tent.

Daniel ran his hand over his face, chuckling. "Oh, fuck, Weaver. Now, you've done it."

Cut didn't say a word, but the loose enjoyment on his face tightened with rage. Lashing out, he grabbed my hair, jerking my head back. "Love my son? I think you meant to say *loved*, my dear. He's dead."

Shit!

I forced desolation into my gaze, burying the truth deep inside.

Cut's gaze probed mine, searching for my lies. "You're strong, I'll give you that. Stronger than your mother. Do you want to know how she begged me to fuck her? Want to know how wild she was? How she confessed she loved me and would die happily after the night we had together?"

Lies. All lies.

My heart formed a callus, a scar, thickening against his taunts. "I don't believe you." The diamonds on my throat pressed heavily on my larynx as Cut yanked me harder.

"You think you'll fight us, but you won't. The minute I lay a finger on that wet pussy of yours, you'll be screaming for more." Letting me go, I stumbled backward.

Cut prowled to a small table where a decanter of cognac had been delivered. His white shirt clung to his lanky body, almost translucent with sweat from the ceremony. His skin glimmered with dampness and his eyes glowed with sickness as he turned with a poured shot in his hand.

If only he *was* sick. If only he caught a disease and died.

He raised the goblet in a toast. "To the Third Debt, Nila." Throwing back a large mouthful and tossing away the glass, he came forward. Reaching into his pocket, Cut pulled out a one pound coin. "Heads or tails, Dan."

My heart ran wild.

My breasts tingled.

Arousal battered at my hatred, urging me to bow to the false euphoria. I wouldn't be subdued or seduced by trickery. I would stand and *fight*.

I will kill you, Cut Hawk. I will kill you!

Daniel rubbed his nape. "Ah, shit. Um…heads. Gimme the queen."

Cut flicked the coin into the air. Catching it on its downward sweep, he slapped it on the back of his hand and revealed it. His lips pulled back. *"Fuck."*

Daniel punched the sky. "Fuck, yes." Darting forward, he lassoed an arm around my waist. "I guess that means you and I get the first round, Nila." Possession leaked through his pores.

No!

A bone-deep sob tried to claw free.

Pointing at the tent flap, Daniel growled, "Come back when the screaming stops, Pop. I'll make sure to leave her alive for you."

Everything inside me withered like a flower in autumn, dying, dying, dead.

Cut ran a hand over his face. "Motherfucker." His golden eyes turned dark, but he snarled reluctantly. "Fine." Storming toward the door, he looked back one last time. "See you in a little while, Nila. Remember what I said—the minute I touch you, you'll be on your knees begging me to fuck you. Don't let Daniel steal everything. Save some of your strength for me."

And then, he was gone.

Leaving me alone with an insane Hawk who deserved to be torn apart and devoured by wolves.

Stay strong. You can do this.

My lungs ceased to work. I wanted the earth to open up and consume me.

"Ready for some fun, Weaver Whore?"

I gritted my teeth, refusing to look at him.

Daniel came closer, capturing my chin, raising my eyes to his. I hated that his touch felt good. That my body craved more. That whatever drugs in my system chipped away my strength, my panic…just waiting for weakness to consume me.

"Don't touch me." I tried to remove my face from his grip, but he only pinched me harder.

"Ah, don't be shy. Now isn't the time to be shy. Not when I finally get to see what made my brother such a fucking idiot over you." Trailing his hand down my cleavage, he muttered, "Don't like your small tits. Perhaps it was your pussy that drugged him, huh?" Pushing me backward, he laughed. "Let's find out. Shall we?"

I screeched as he shoved me toward the bed.

No torments or games. No history lessons or delays.

He wanted me. He would have me. And then his father would. And I'd be mentally, physically, spiritually broken.

Tears sloshed inside me like a storm upon a sea, smashing against my ribcage.

Don't give in.

Time sped up as unsteadiness latched onto my brain, throwing me to the side. My skin crawled. My blood boiled with misplaced disgusting lust.

Being in this place, this awful foreign place, imprisoned me worse than Hawksridge.

I'm all alone.

Even my body was a traitor as it hummed and melted, ignoring my demands to remain frigid and fighting.

"Get on the bed, whore." Tossing me onto the mattress, Daniel cackled. The alcohol he'd consumed glazed his eyes, turning his touch sloppy and cruel.

I bounced on the soft bedspread, shaking my head to rid the imbalance. The tent parried and pirouetted, refusing to remain in one place.

Daniel threw himself on top of me. The air erupted from my body with his heaviness.

Instantly, fire exploded through my system. "Get *off* me!"

"Oh, yes. Scream all you want. No one will care." His hands fumbled with the waistband of my jeans, tearing at the zipper.

"No!" My voice broke as the scream tore my throat.

"Fuck, that makes me hard." Daniel licked my cheek, spreading disgusting saliva. "I'll make sure you prefer me to my father, you can count on it." His hand soared over my ribcage, latching onto my breast.

I squirmed and kicked and screamed and *thrashed.*

"Goddammit, you're wild."

I kept fighting. My petrified fear buried beneath lawyers of rapidly failing courage. "Stop. *Stop!*"

Daniel only laughed. "Tire yourself out. There's a good fucking bitch." He shoved my shoulders against the mattress, pinning me down. His legs spread over mine. "Been waiting for this day for months, little Weaver."

His fingers tweaked my nipple and heinous pleasure shot through my system.

Lust.

Desire.

Pleasure.

No.

I could handle fighting. I could handle battling for my life. But I couldn't handle wrestling with my body. That was supposed to be on *my* side. Mine. Not his.

Mine.

A surge of power swatted the drug's effects away; I soared into life. My knee shot upright, colliding with soft balls and hard cock.

Daniel crumpled in slow motion, a guttural groan tearing from his mouth. His skin shot white as pain-perspiration decorated his forehead. Gasping for breath, he fell to the side, releasing me to hold his precious equipment.

Writhing away, I flew to my knees and rolled off the bed. "I hate you! *Hate you!*"

Somehow, Daniel fought through the agony, hurling himself after me to grapple around my legs.

We tumbled to the tent floor, pricked by twigs and debris beneath the canvas lining.

Daniel turned red. "You fucking bitch!"

His fists pummelled my side, stealing the oxygen from my lungs. I squirmed and kicked, but the liquor in his blood muted whatever I managed to land on him.

Stumbling to his feet, Daniel kicked me in the belly. "That's for hurting my dick, bitch."

Agony radiated out as fast as lightning. I groaned, sickness dousing every inch. I curled up, holding my stomach, cursing him in every religion. Somehow, I compartmentalized the pain and lashed out with my foot. My toes hooked around his heel, sending him toppling to his knees.

He grunted, but it didn't stop him from punching me again in the thigh. "Plenty more pain where that came from. Like it? Do you like it when I kick you like the bitch you are?"

I moaned in torture as he rolled me onto my back. "You're not going anywhere, whore. Not this time."

The tent turned fuzzy as the drugs made everything so hot. My muscles were weak from lack of food. I wouldn't be able to win the fight.

You can win.

I growled, aiming for his nose.

He deflected my hand as if it were nothing more than pollen.

I can't.

I tried again, slapping his cheek, connecting with his hot flesh.

I can!

Daniel snarled, his fingers fumbling with his belt. "That's the last time you'll hit me." His head came forward, cracking his forehead on mine.

The mutual pain crested through my skull, rendering me numb and lost. Swimming through it, I did my best to scramble backward, kicking him. "Leave me alone!" Somehow, I got free of his putrid embrace, crying in fleeting triumph.

"Fuck!" He grabbed my ankle.

"No!" My skin tingled, awoken by the drugs from the fire. I moaned as another flush of heat and hatred became bedfellows in my heart. Every inch of me was swollen and wet with desire. I'd never wanted sex so much but fought so hard to avoid it.

The awful contradiction stole every last dreg of energy.

He yanked me back, a morbid chuckle on his lips. "Getting tired yet?"

"Never."

Yes, so much yes.

Tears torrented down my cheeks even though I didn't permit myself to cry. My body bypassed synapses, defending, slipping into preservation. "I'll kill you. You're nothing. *Nothing.*"

"I'm nothing? I'll show you fucking nothing." Rearing upright, Daniel cocked his fist and ploughed it straight into my cheek.

Stars.

Galaxies.

Lions and tigers and bears.

I lost consciousness.

How long, I didn't know. I floated in an ocean of

affliction, vaguely aware as cold air licked around my hipbones, then arse, then thighs, then toes.

Lucidity slammed back as the rotten feel of his fingers on my pussy jerked me awake.

I came to with my jeans ripped away and my knickers wrenched to my knees.

The room spun as my cheekbone shrieked in pain. "No..."

"Yes." Daniel grinned. "I'm going to show you punishment. I'm going to teach you a lesson you'll never forget."

The sound of belt buckles and zippers rapidly gathered my wits.

Fight, Nila.

Time had run out.

Daniel would rape me on the floor of a tent in the middle of their diamond empire. I was alone. If I didn't win, Cut would take me next, and I would crave the day I paid the Final Debt as I wouldn't be able to live with myself.

Please...

Sobs wanted to take over rather than fight. I'd burned through everything I had.

How can I win when I have nothing left?

Daniel shifted, jerking down his trousers, freeing his red-angry cock. "We're in fucking Africa." Daniel breathed hard, his breath reeking of liquor. "Know what happens in Africa?"

I didn't respond. I never liked his answers. I *hated* his answers. Instead, I wriggled, trying to get free.

I'm done.

It was over.

It's not over!

Memories of altered garments and sewn weapons flooded my mind. How could I forget?

My vision narrowed, searching, flying around the tent.

My jeans.

They rested an arm's stretch away. In the leg, I'd hidden a

scalpel.

The scalpel!

My heart catapulted in my chest with joy. The hidden blade would be my guardian. My saviour. Grunting, I stretched my arm out, fingers fumbling with the denim.

Daniel didn't care about my attempt to grab discarded clothes. His fingers latched around my collar, shaking me with frustration. "You know, this would be a lot more fun if you played along. Answer me. What happens in Africa, Weaver?"

Spit welled in my mouth—partly from grey sickness and partly from vile disgust. My fingers stretched harder.

I can't reach.

"Fuck, answer me!"

"I'll answer you." Turning my head, I spat in his demonic face. "Shut up! There? That make you happy, arsehole?"

His features contorted, but he didn't move away. "That's the last fucking straw. You pushed too far. Gonna do what I've wanted for months." His breathing turned sporadic. "I'm going to break my promise."

My heart stopped.

What?

I was torn between straining to reach my jeans and paying attention.

Get them. Before it's too late.

"I promised Cut I'd leave you alive for him. But after that—" He chuckled coldly, his eyes darkening into golden blackness. "After that blatant disregard, I'm going to fuck you dead, you hear me? I'm going to make you scream and cry and beg and pray for motherfucking *death*."

He smiled, showing perfect teeth that only childhood braces could deliver. "Get on your knees, bitch."

Before I could respond, he hooked his fingers tighter in my collar. The thick filigree and impenetrable diamonds were the perfect lasso to jerk me up and flip me over.

No!

My jeans were no longer in reaching distance.

The moment I was on my knees, Daniel spread my legs and grabbed my hips. "Shit, yes."

I screamed as he dug fingernails into my skin so hard he drew blood.

I gave up trying to reach for help. I gave up trying to remain human. The drugs buzzed in my blood, twisting me with horror and desire. But the desire was no longer for sex or pleasure. Oh, no. This desire was for *murder*. To rip out his entrails and stuff them in his bleeding mouth. To slice off his cock and present it to Cut as my trophy. This desire was my ignition.

This desire was my *annihilation*.

Clearheadedness settled into every cell, even as Daniel yanked me back and fisted his cock to thrust inside. Purity and precision slowed my breathing. Certainty and courage stopped my shaking hands. And proficient power guided my fingers to the hem of my hoodie.

I forgot.

But now I remember.

The knitting needle.

The one implement I'd stroked and caressed since leaving Hawksridge. I didn't need a scalpel. I had something better.

A thirty-five centimetre, single-pointed metal spear.

Closing my eyes, I conjured everything I loved, everyone, every reason why I would survive and Daniel wouldn't.

Jethro.

Vaughn.

My father.

I would survive for them.

No matter what it takes.

I gave myself over to bloodlust.

I did the one thing I was born to do.

I carried out my promise to my ancestors.

My fingernails were blades as I sliced through the loose stitching and pulled free my weapon of choice. My life might be over. I might be alone. But I wouldn't die without taking a

Hawk with me.

Daniel grunted, lining himself up to rape me.

My skin went cold. My heart went calm. And I fisted my knitting needle.

"You ready for this, Weaver? Ready to be fucked?"

I didn't reply as his knees touched the back of mine.

I didn't move as his thighs pressed against mine.

I didn't flinch as the tip of his cock entered me.

I waited.

I hunted.

I swallowed my tears and fears.

Another inch inside me.

His awareness faded, focusing entirely on sex.

Weaker…weaker…

And still I waited.

Another centimetre of my enemy's cock inside me.

I paused for the perfect moment.

Now.

I attacked.

Rage stole everything.

I wasn't afraid of repercussions or consequences.

I wasn't afraid of getting hurt or dying.

All I cared about was ending this monstrosity before he took my soul.

"Fuck you!" Throwing myself to the side, his cock slipped out and Daniel's hold fumbled. The ground kissed my shoulder, rattling my teeth as I flipped onto my back beneath him.

For a moment, I drank in the final image I would have of Daniel. He stood poised on his knees, his cock swollen and hungry, his face rageful and surprised. A simple man turned into a despicable creature. He was no longer human. Just the mistake. The unwanted.

I did the world a favour.

I did the only thing I could do.

"Goodbye, Daniel."

Sitting upright, I hugged his shoulders, lining my trajectory for perfect aim. I wrapped my fingers around the needle; I pressed my face into his throat. Energy exploded. Righteousness detonated. I bared my teeth and bit his neck as my arm soared up, faster and faster, guided by the divine, flying with ghosts of my family, winging with the precision of fate, and pierced my mortal enemy.

The sharpness of the knitting needle slipped as easily and as cleanly as a knife slipped through expensive steak. Up and up, puncturing through his ribcage, slicing through his lung, and finally, finally, *finally* perforating his heart.

Time stopped.

The world ceased to spin.

Daniel turned from rutting animal to shocked puppet.

His eyes popped wide as the softest cry tumbled from his lips. His gaze met mine. His hand flew to where the knitting needle lanced his side. He was no longer my adversary but merely thread, welcoming my needle, ready to be transformed into a seamstress's masterpiece.

And then, he toppled.

Falling, falling, *falling* to his side.

Vertigo teased as death swooped across *Almasi Kipanga* and whipped into the tent. My wrist twisted as I fell with him, never letting go of the needle. I rolled, straddling him, forcing the weapon further into his heart. I almost lost my grip as he bucked and lurched, but I didn't let go. Using two hands, I pushed down. Harder. Harder.

Die, Daniel. Die.

I'd researched how to take a life while existing at Hawksridge. I'd read articles, watched examples, planned the perfect murder. To puncture a heart didn't guarantee death. A 'stiletto' type perforation could be survived.

I had no intention of letting Daniel survive.

Locking my knees either side of his chest, I ripped the needle free.

An agonising groan came from his chest as blood oozed

from the hole.

Daniel's stupor fell away. His hands reached for my throat, his fingers shaking and weak as his blood pressure dropped from the orifice gushing in his chest. His brain starved for oxygen the longer his heart bled. He only had seconds before the machine of his body shut down.

His arms flailed. His palm struck my cheek, desperate to hurt.

Tears spurted and pain smarted, but I didn't move. I wouldn't have the power to fight him if his body hadn't turned traitor, poisoning him from the inside out. But right now, I had all the power in the world.

"You fucking cu—" He coughed, his fingers slipping in their attempt to curl around my neck, grasping my collar instead. The impenetrable diamonds kept me safe from being throttled as I arched my arm and prepared to complete my final strike.

"Die." The needle glistened with dripping crimson as it hurtled through the air and kissed his skin again. The wickedly sharp point crunched its way through flesh and fat, returning to lodge in his most important organ.

Daniel howled, his torso thrashing, face straining. He hit me, struck me, tried to knock me over. But I had an anchor— the needle. I held on, pushing down with all my might driving the end home.

"You can't stop me."

He bellowed as the needle tip slid deeper, deeper, past gristle and bone, impaling my victim inch by inch. He twitched and bucked, his fingers unable to snare as his nervous system shut down.

The wet squelch of my needle ripping another hole in his heart brought rushing nausea, but I didn't falter. All masterful killers knew to make the result permanent, dedication and desire had to be invoked.

I was dedicated.

I desired freedom.

I would finish this.

Holding the base of the needle, I twisted it like a corkscrew.

"Ah!" Daniel jerked. His arms fell to his side, scrabbling at the needle, but it was too late. Adrenaline would keep him animated for another few seconds, but it was already done.

I took his life, not with horror or regret, but with no mercy and complete acceptance.

A life for a life.

He owed me that.

Watching him succumb iced my blood, turning me into a ruthless executioner. His golden eyes met mine, gasping for hope and help. His motions turned languid and dull, a broken pawn, never to live again.

"How does it feel, Daniel? To know you've lost?" I gasped, but my nerves remained calm. "How does it feel to know a Weaver took your soul?"

He never had the chance to answer. His face froze of vitality. His breath wheezed, his heart stopped, and in those final seconds before his soul leapt free, he snarled with sinister hate.

Then…emptiness.

There were no longer two people in my tent, only one. Just me.

Just me.

I killed him.

As if the universe rejoiced in one less monster breathing its air, a lion bayed on the dawn's horizon. Daniel's blood slowly seeped in an odd little trickle around my needle. Weeping wetly and warmly, staining his chest like spilled wine.

He twitched.

I rejoiced.

I'd killed my first Hawk.

Daniel…

…

was dead.

THE LUMINESCENT glow of imminent dawn welcomed me to *Imasi Kipanga.*

I knew the compound well and ordered the driver to wait a kilometre from the perimeter. He obeyed because he trusted my family's name. And I trusted him because I hadn't paid him yet. I had no intention until I found Nila and had her safe in my arms.

He was my ticket to freedom, and I would reward him handsomely for it.

Jogging through the long grass of the plain surrounding the encampment, I hoped the dried blood from my side wouldn't attract unwelcome predators. I'd stepped into a world where teeth and fang were much more dangerous than bullet and gun.

The camp sat like a giant growth in the centre of nothing. Armed guards patrolled the fence line but I knew another way in that would go unnoticed. I'd used it when I was young, when hanging out with too many people overwhelmed me. Kes had found it——the unfortified entrance——kindly giving me an escape route to find silence and sanctuary.

Keeping low, I avoided the main entry and dashed to the service area and staff quarters. Keeping my footsteps light and breathing shallow, I pulled on the loose wooden panel and slipped into the latrines. Either the guards had never found the perimeter's weakness or they had no intention of doing repairs while breathing in the stench of excrement.

Animals avoided the scent of human waste, and men who wanted to rob us didn't think to follow the malodour for a way in.

Smoke from a dying bonfire crackled in the centre of the camp. Fast asleep tribesmen and their families slept in lean-tos while some preferred to dream in the elements beneath the stars. My lips curled, remembering the ceremony that'd almost incapacitated me emotionally.

I'd been fifteen.

I'd been an unwilling participant.

But that hadn't stopped them from forcing me to ingest the drug-liquor, consuming me in their drumbeats and chanting.

It'd fucked me up worse than normal. I'd never felt so unhinged and aroused, turned on by the tiniest touch, overwhelmed by the simplest emotion. The entire camp had become an orgy, and I'd run far and fast.

I'd barricaded myself for twenty-four hours, remaining alone and far away from rutting sex-crazed humans. But it hadn't stopped me from pleasuring myself or spilling orgasm after orgasm on the dusty African plains.

Holding my breath, I wrapped my arm around my painful side. Every heartbeat activated the wound, highlighting my lack of rest and fever. I wouldn't have the strength to fight many men if they woke up.

Tiptoeing through the scattered sleeping forms, I calculated where Nila would be. The faster I could get in and out, the higher our chance of survival.

But at least we would be together again—regardless of what happened.

One particular woman moaned and rolled over in her sleep, hugging a black-skinned man beside her. The one blessing of the drug was insane lethargy. After the passion and demands of animalistic behaviours, they'd be out cold until the heat from the African sun forced them to move indoors or incinerate.

My heart remained in my mouth as I weaved around tents and shipping containers. Cut's sleeping quarters were across the compound, upwind and in a prime location. Daniel's rested four tents away which left the guest one beside it.

My gaze shot to the fabric A-frame in question.

Lights.

The only one with lights illuminating the inside like a trapped firefly in a jar.

It took a few minutes to skirt around the edge, stepping through shadows, avoiding open spaces. I listened for noises. I hoped to God Nila hadn't been harmed. And I wished for a gun to protect her.

A noise sounded inside the tent. A gentle thud followed by a female moan.

Nila!

I couldn't wait any longer.

Surprise would be on my side, but I hoped righteousness and fate would be, too.

Ducking beneath the entrance canopy, I charged inside.

My heart stopped.

My mouth fell open.

It couldn't be.

"Nila..."

Her head shot up. She looked as wild as the animals of this country. She crouched beside my brother, her hands covered in blood, her hoodie hanging off one shoulder, and her legs bare and exposed. Bruises marred her porcelain skin, scratches and blemishes hinting at a fight I was too late to stop.

She jerked to the side, wielding a long red weapon. "Don't—" Her eyes focused, then love poured from her. "Jethro? It can't...it can't be true."

I staggered toward her, glancing between my half-naked woman and my dead brother. His cock was still hard on his belly. My skin crawled even as my heart stopped beating. "How…how did this happen?"

Her skin was white as milk, her frame shaking with adrenaline. My eyes drifted to her naked pussy and rage unfurled inside me.

"Did he rape you?" My hands curled as I stood over my brother's corpse. "Did that motherfucker touch you?"

She shook her head, throwing down her weapon and wiping bloody hands on her hoodie. Her eyes flashed, hiding the truth she didn't want me to see. "No." Standing, she huddled into me.

My arms automatically wrapped around her, protecting her, even though I begged her to be honest with me.

He'd touched her.

That motherfucking animal touched what wasn't his.

My embrace became shackles as I dropped my head in despair. Inhaling the softness of her scent and sharpness of spilled blood, I trembled with rage.

Nila let me hold her, her arms returning the furious hug.

I'm sorry.

So fucking sorry.

Her emotions collided with pride and purgatory. She'd killed him and hadn't processed what his death would mean.

I hugged her harder.

I'm here.

Her voice whispered into my shirt. "He didn't rape me, Jethro. I swear. I'm sorry…sorry…so sorry."

Liar.

I understood why she'd lied. Even now, even with death on her hands and fear in her heart, she still tried to save me.

I was the one who'd let her down.

I was the one who made her return to the Hall.

This was *my* fault. "I did this."

Her quaking arms wrapped tighter, hurting my unhealed side. "No. Don't blame—"

"If I don't blame myself, who can I?" I pressed my face

into her throat, the short ends of her hair tickling my cheeks. "I sent you back. I fucking sent you back to be raped and—"

She struggled in my arms. "He didn't—"

I pulled back, anger cresting. "Don't lie to me! You can't lie to me, remember?"

Her lips pursed; she battled between looking at the floor for privacy and fighting me like she'd fought my brother. "Don't. Don't get mad. I'm only trying to save—"

I bared my teeth. "Save me? That's my fucking job, Nila. Not yours. Don't you get it? I should've been the one to protect you. Not the other way around."

She didn't reply, her eyes burning black holes into my soul. There was no judgement in her gaze, only forgiveness for making her leave when she'd begged me to reconsider.

"Fuck." My back rolled, and I grabbed her close again. "I'm sorry. Shit, I'm so sorry."

Her arms twined around me, her love giving me somewhere to hide from my own fucked-up emotions. "I know. It's okay."

It wasn't okay. None of this was okay. But I wouldn't press it further. Not here. Not now.

Whatever had happened before my arrival spilled out of her, lapping around our feet.

Her fingers dug into my spine, reliving what she'd done. "I wanted to kill him. But now...now, maybe...I didn't. God, I killed him, Kite. I—I took a life." She hugged me impossibly harder as she lost herself to tangled thoughts. An odd overtone layered her emotions the longer I held her. The sensation of need and desire so strong it superseded her misery at killing.

I winced at her strength but didn't care about the pain. All I cared about was her. About taking her far away from here and protecting her like I should've done from the start.

I crushed her in my embrace, holding her so fucking close. "It's over now. Whatever happened, it's over." I kissed the top of her head, her brow, her eyes. "Are you okay? Don't lie to me. I need to know you aren't hurting." My eyes trailed over her injuries. Daniel had done more than touch her, he'd hit her, possibly kicked her.

Her hair stuck up in places, and her cheek flamed red from a slap. She'd been to hell and back, but she'd left my brother in damnation.

I'm so fucking proud of her.

She nodded, breathless and broken. Tears washed down her face. I'd never seen her so primitive, focused only on survival and death. "I'm okay. I'm okay. I am. Truly. I'll be okay." The same shadow of lust tainted her voice. I could understand sudden joy at winning over an enemy, but lust?

Taking a few steps back, I pulled her away from Daniel. He lay on his back, blood clotting on his side, a blue tinge already creeping over his lips.

I didn't want her to look. I'd been around death before. I'd been the instigator of taking another's life. It wasn't easy to stare into the eyes of your victim once it was over. Especially when self defence forced your actions.

"Don't look. Forget what happened. I'm here now, and I'm never leaving again." I kissed her hair, so, so thankful I had her back in my arms.

Nila squirmed, disobeying me and looking at Daniel's corpse. Her muscles locked; a haunting hollowness entered her eyes. "He deserved it. So why do I feel like such a monster?"

I clamped my hands on her shoulders. "He *did* deserve it. Don't second-guess. You did what you had to do."

"Did I? Was there no other choice?"

I shook my head firmly. "None. It was the only way."

Nila bit her lip, her eyes overflowing with liquid. "But...he was the youngest. He couldn't help that Bonnie and Cut called him a mistake. He couldn't stop being ridiculed or believing in what he'd been told."

What?

What did she know about our upbringing and who Daniel had become because of his childhood? I'd caught him hurting for fun, killing animals for a rush. I'd told him off for being so egotistical and crude. Kes dealt with Daniel's fuck-ups more than I did because being around him was too hard. I'd slowly feed off the nastiness inside him. But because of my condition, I could wholeheartedly say he deserved what he got. Nila hadn't killed him. Karma had.

"Putting tragic tales to villains is a sure way to destroy yourself when they force you to do something cruel in order to survive, Nila."

Nila clenched her jaw, ready to argue. To judge herself into torment. Yet again another ripple of need, completely out of context to the situation, polluted the air.

Forcing her to twist and look at me, rather than Daniel, I cupped her cheeks. "Nila, listen to me. Don't look for redemption in those who don't deserve it. If you hadn't fought back, he would've raped you and possibly killed you. You don't know him—not like I do. And I can safely say, he deserved it."

She sniffed, dropping her eyes. "I'm so sorry, Jethro."

"Sorry?" My heart thundered. "What for?" Letting her go, I marched toward the bed and whipped the sheet free. Wrapping her bottom nakedness, I guided her further away from the body. "Why the hell are you apologising?"

I'm the one who should.

I'm the one who left you on your own.

Her body quaked as she looked over her shoulder, unable to stop staring at Daniel. "Because...because I just killed your flesh and blood."

I grabbed her waist, holding her tight. "I'm *grateful.* Not mad. Did you think I would care? Nila, I love you. Ever since you replied to my first text, my heart has put you above everyone in my family. *I love you.* And you're killing me by hating yourself for doing what was needed."

Softening my voice, I tucked her short black hair behind her ears, rubbing away her tears with a thumb. "Nila...he deserved to die. You need to trust me on that. You can't hold his death inside you. You can't feel responsible. I'm glad you ended him because if you hadn't, I would've made his demise a lot fucking worse. You did the right thing—that's all you need to know. Promise me that's all you'll remember?"

She sucked in a breath, leaning into my touch. "But—"

"No buts."

My heart cracked at what she was going through. I wished I'd arrived sooner. Been the one to stab him and wear his life on my soul, pinned there for eternity. Anything to prevent her from feeling the pain of aftermath. However, I hadn't been. And knowing Daniel had hurt her—taken something that didn't belong to him—that was my punishment to bear.

I shook as my own hurt surfaced. I had no right to ask. Not now when she struggled. But I couldn't stop the question falling from my lips. "Please...tell me one thing...and be truthful."

Her eyes met mine. "Anything."

I swallowed hard.

I swallowed again.

I lost courage but spoke anyway. "I know he touched you, Nila, you can't hide that from me. But how badly did he rape you? How much do you hate me for letting that happen?"

I hated my question. *How badly did he rape you?* Were there gradients of rape? Every form, no matter how long or brutal, were equally as terrible.

Christ!

I wanted to kill myself for being so useless.

But I had another question. One I didn't want to ask. Why did I feed off her overwhelming desire for sex? Why did she have such powerful thoughts when the current predicament was so inappropriate?

A slight pause, another lie formed. She shook her head. "I could never hate you. And I already told you. I stopped him—before..."

My shoulders sagged.

She rushed. "Jethro, don't torture yourself. Let me keep some secrets. Let me choose which ones to tell you and which ones to let die." Her voice cracked. "*Please*...you don't need to know. Just…leave it. I'm sorry…"

I died a little as my condition flared into full reception. Her emotions told me everything I needed to know. He'd been inside her. And she'd defended herself the only way she could.

Fuck.

How could I ever forgive myself for this?

Would she want me now? Would she trust I could protect her?

My arms latched around her, crashing her face to my chest. "Goddammit, Nila. You put me to shame. For the rest of my life, I'll make it up to you. I'll keep you safe. I'll stop all of this because I'm never letting you out of my sight again."

She kissed my shirt, moaning in gratefulness as she finally allowed me to take some of the responsibility. Her fingers fluttered over my hips, questing more than just a hug…more violent affection.

Her thoughts begged me to give in. To grant her some relief from the intensity in her mind. But I couldn't. Now was not the time.

"It's over now. It's done. You're safe."

For a moment, she let me soothe her. Her lustful taint gave way to sobs, and she crumpled deeper into my embrace. Together, we fell to the floor—me to my knees and Nila in my lap. I rocked her. I kissed her. I promised so many, many things.

Time ticked onward, putting seconds then minutes between her and taking Daniel's life. Nothing else would be able to fix her—only time and distance.

Finally, the shock of killing left and her eyes opened to focus resolutely on Daniel. Any hint of desire disappeared with clear-headed determination. "Cut will be back for his turn soon." Her voice shook. "What do I do, Kite? What do I do with the body?"

"You?" I laughed harshly. "You aren't doing anything. You've done too much already." I ran a hand through my hair. "I should've been there for you and I wasn't. I'll deal with this."

Her skin turned frigid beneath my fingertips. "No, you have to go. If Cut sees you—"

"I don't fucking care if he sees me." Pushing Nila off my lap, I stood. Marching across the tent, I tore through her open suitcase and threw fresh knickers and leggings her way. "Put these on. And shoes. I'm going to get rid of Daniel and you're coming with me."

"But—"

I cut my hand through the air. "But nothing, Nila. I'm not letting you out of my sight. Got it?"

"But Jasmine and Kes. You have to think of them. Cut can't know you're still alive, he'll—"

Kill me. Yes, I know.

But my life was worthless compared to hers. I would willingly trade it if it meant she walked away from this with no more bruises or battered memories. She'd already endured so much. She wore the marks of war, and I refused to let her endure more. I'd tried to save too many people. Kes would understand, and Jaz would expect me to do what was right.

This was right.

Nila was my only choice.

"Don't worry about them. I know what I'm doing." I glanced at my dead sibling, feeling nothing but relief. His cock taunted me with what he'd done to my woman. If he wasn't already dead...he would die with severe mutilation to purge myself of the wrath in my blood.

"So...how will we dispose of the body?" Nila whispered.

My mind ran with scenarios. "We could cover him in liquor and make it seem like he drank himself into the grave."

Nila swallowed. "Is that believable?" She looked at the floor where the long bloody weapon stuck to the tent covering. "I stabbed him in the heart with my knitting needle. The two wounds are small, but there. They'd know it wasn't self-inflicted."

She killed him with a needle?

An awed smile lit my face. "You're so fucking strong."

She glanced away, despair still prominent.

I rubbed my face, willing tiredness and pain to fade so I could come up with a solution.

Think.

Where could I put him that Cut wouldn't find him?

The diamond mine!

The idea sprang from schematics to doable. "We can make it look like an accident. I can bury him in the mine. Make it look like he fell."

Nila paused, tasting my plan, nibbling at it for flaws.

"Shit, that won't work." I shook my head. "I couldn't get him there without someone hearing the Jeep." My eyes narrowed, rushing forward with a new idea.

Then, it came to me.

Africa would take care of it for me.

I snapped my fingers with decision. "I know what to do."

Nila opened her mouth to argue, but I stormed across the room and grabbed her face. I couldn't help myself. She was so fucking courageous. Her emotions so clear. Her love so deep. Her passion so pure. Not one inch of terror or hate that I hadn't been there for her. Not one smidgen of hostility or judgement.

She's so damn selfless.

I kissed her.

The instant my lips touched hers, it was if a nuclear explosion mushroomed inside her. The lust I'd gleaned in her mind erupted into full force, drowning everything. Her tongue snaked into my mouth, decaying my resolve not to touch her.

Dropping the clothes I'd given her, she groaned long and low, her mouth tempting mine to give more. The sheet fluttered from her hips as her naked leg twined around my hip, grinding against me.

"Fuck..." I stumbled forward as she turned crazed with desire. I'd never felt such passion pouring from her. "Nila...wait..."

Her tongue shot swifter, sexier into my mouth. Kissing.

Licking. *Demanding* I respond.

"Nila…"

"No, Jethro. Give me this. I *need* this." Her lips recaptured mine, pulling me under.

"Shit." It all suddenly made sense. The clouded residue on her thoughts. The flowing undercurrent of something stronger than death and pain. She wanted sex. She *needed* sex.

They'd drugged her.

They'd given her the same thing they'd given me when I was fifteen. Something so potent and heady no one could say no to the aphrodisiac power.

Goddammit.

My gut twisted into a knot as her tongue licked and flicked. I forced myself not to listen to her tainting thoughts—I didn't want the urgent need to fuck to consume me. But my cock thickened, drawn to her even as I tried to battle the rapidly building need. "How—how did you fight it for so long? How did you stop?"

Her hands flew up my t-shirt, skirting over my wound, dancing over my skin like compelling butterflies. "Stop talking. Please…give me what I want. I need to feel alive. I need to take back what Daniel tried to steal. *Please*, Jethro. Please, fuck me."

The memory of our first kiss in her room—the way she'd chopped my resolve to pieces with her demands to kiss her, fired into lustful flames.

Kiss me.

Fuck me.

She'd fought him; she'd killed him, even while under the influence. If she were anyone else, she would've willingly submitted. She would've enjoyed whatever Daniel did because her body would've given her no other choice. The drugs were beyond powerful, but somehow she'd been able to fight them along with fighting my brother's advances.

I don't deserve this woman.

This Weaver. This answer to my wrongness. This salvation to my condemnation.

"Jethro...please." Her kiss deepened.

"Goddammit." In a vicious yank, I plucked her into my arms and stalked to the bed. Her hands flew into my hair, tugging as her mouth danced over mine.

Our breathing grew laboured. Our skin slick and sensitive. My entire body stiffened. The tent crackled with lust so painful it crippled us.

How much time do we have?

We were tempting fate. Beyond stupid to give in.

There's a dead body...

It was macabre.

It was wrong.

But I'd failed her in so many ways.

We didn't know what awaited us.

We didn't have the luxury of time.

She wanted this. It was the least I could do to obey.

Throwing her onto the bed, I stood over her. Her jaw-length hair fanned out on the white bedding, her legs spread, and her hand dipped to her pussy. Her fingers weren't shy as she rubbed her clit.

My lungs refused to operate. "Shit, Needle."

"Take me, Kite. I need you to take me." Her finger smeared wetness around her entrance, her stomach tensing with pleasure. "I fought him. I managed to stay true to myself and not let the lust take control. But I'm tired. I'm empty. I can't—I can't fight it anymore." Tears glittered on her eyelashes. "I need it. I need a release. I need to forget, for just a little while. I need to live, to remember, to be happy, to be free. *Please.*" Her fingers swirled faster, her skin flushing with need. "Oh, please...*please.*"

I couldn't speak.

I was hypnotised by her.

My hands shook as I wrenched open my belt. The idiocy of fucking her when Cut could return at any moment had no power over us. Common-sense died on the pyre of desire and all I could think about was filling this stunning creature and claiming her over and over and fucking over again.

Her eyes met mine, and everything that'd happened the past few months fractured. *This* was all that mattered.

Making love. Connecting. Merging into one.

She was my all and only.

My world.

Her tongue licked her bottom lip, her teeth biting as her finger dipped inside. "Jethro...please!"

"Shush. You have me. I'm here." My heartbeat drummed in my erection as I shoved down my jeans and boxer-briefs.

Nila's eyes hooded as I fisted my cock, stroking hard and fast. "Tell me." My voice was guttural.

"Tell you what?" The diamonds around her neck refracted light.

"My cock...how do you want it?"

A seductive smile lit her face. She moaned low and full of invitation. "Hard and fast. God, so hard. So fast." Her hands skated to her nipples through her hoodie, twisting cruelly. "I've never felt like this before. This unhinged. This horny. God, please don't make me wait any longer." Her spine arched off the bed. *"Fuck me."*

Fucking hell.

I lashed out. My hands captured her hips, yanking her toward the edge of the bed. "You want me? You can fucking have me."

She cried out as I forced her thighs wide, presenting her pussy to me—glistening and perfect. I bowed and bit her knee, running my hand up her thigh and pressing a finger deep inside her.

She screamed.

I slapped a hand over her mouth. "Quiet!"

She was my punishment and penance all in one.

Her eyes rolled backward as I forced another finger inside her. Her hips rocked dangerous and demanding. She was liquid and heat. She didn't want foreplay. She wanted to be fucked, used, abused, *claimed.*

My mind shattered; I couldn't stop.

Her breathing turned ragged as I strummed her clit. My cock wept at how fucking beautiful she was. How needy and fierce.

"I'm going to take you." I thrust my fingers hard. "I'm going to claim you. I'm going to give you everything because you deserve fucking everything. You deserve to be worshipped and praised. You deserve to be loved every damn day of your life."

She gasped, her skin sticky with sweat.

Withdrawing my fingers, my heart filled to bursting.

Nila panted, whimpering beneath my hand.

She looked so fragile and delicate, but I knew that was a lie. She was stronger than anyone. And I wanted to bow at her feet for the rest of eternity.

Keeping one hand over her mouth, I rubbed my fingertips together, slick from her desire, and grabbed my cock to position at her entrance.

I sucked in a gasp as her body heat cremated me.

I slammed inside her.

Stretching.

Fisting.

Tight.

Tight.

Tight.

"Goddammit, Nila." My blood boiled with feral hunger.

My mouth watered to bite her throat.

Her hands latched around my wrist as I held her silent, her lips parting wide beneath my palm. I sank deep, so fucking deep. She spread her legs, her body yielded, and I sheathed into my soul-mate.

For a second, we paused. Heartbeat to heartbeat. Desire to desire. Sex turned to saturated connection, and I couldn't stop the words spilling from my lips.

"I love you, Needle." My hand fell from her mouth as I slammed my palms on either side of her head on the mattress, rocking into her. My toes curled in my shoes, my jeans tightened around my thighs as I stood over this goddess and fucked her like she begged.

"I…love…you…" Her pants destroyed her voice, but I didn't need the words to know. Her emotions screamed it louder than anything. My condition swam in her contentment and affection, and I knew there would be no going back from this.

This was the moment she became totally mine.

And whatever happened afterward, we would be together forever.

I couldn't live another moment without her bound to me. Without knowing this creature belonged to me for every day after, every year, every decade.

I *needed* her.

"Marry me."

Nila gasped, her body flinching with shock. "What?"

I grabbed her legs, wrapping them around my hips. Her shoulders remained on the bed, arching into my hold. Her pussy fisted my cock, giving me an answer to my question.

The most important significant world-changing question.

"Marry me. Become mine."

I groaned as I rocked harder, fucking her with everything I had. My knees bashed the bed, my balls smashed against her arse. Emotions and feelings and sensations grew out of control. "I need you so much."

Her breasts bounced as my pace turned crazed.

"I need you forever."

My hips bruised against her inner thighs as I rode her so hard.

"I need you as my wife."

A release snarled into being, hungry, savage in intensity.

My heart twisted as Nila licked her lips. "I…I—"

Everything else faded.

I drove into her over and over again. Our eyes locked and we fucked into promises. "Say yes…. Fuck, please say yes."

I lost myself to the rhythm, sinking my fingers into her thighs.

Her pussy clenched; her head thrown back as her body prepared to release. Her eyes glazed as the pain of riding her and the pleasure of her building orgasm turned our connection into an almost unbearable fight.

I couldn't think straight. I was lost, owned, *consumed*.

I couldn't get enough oxygen. My arms trembled as Nila finally gave me the greatest gift I'd ever earned.

"Yes…Yes, I'll marry you."

"Christ." My heart shattered into fractals.

I gave up.

Our rhythm turned frenzied, fucking, rutting, taking everything we could.

"God, yes. I'm coming…I'm *coming*." She cried and laughed and cursed as she drowned under the crest of her release. Her gaze locked with mine and midnight irises consumed me as fireworks turned into catastrophic detonations.

"Yes," I hissed. "Yes. Shit, yes." Electricity charged through my toes, my quads, my balls, my dick. Spilling deep as I pounded inside her, delivering every last drop of bliss. Pleasure I'd never experienced stampeded with a thousand heartbeats.

She was mine as much as I was hers.

Now and for always.

Alive or dead.

We were one.

Nila

"THIS WON'T WORK."

Jethro shushed me, inching through the wonky panel hidden in the toilet block. The wretched air almost made me gag.

The moment Jethro had come, he'd made me dress, and hoisted Daniel's carcass over his shoulder.

His eyes blackened with nerves and resolution as he ignored me. "It will." Under his breath, he added, "It has to."

Another shiver darted down my spine. The millionth shiver since I'd arrived in Africa.

It felt like an eternity had passed since I'd claimed a life, pierced my needle and taken someone's last breath, last gasp, last thought. It felt like eons since I'd finally succumbed to the raging lust in my bloodstream and forced Jethro to take me.

But in reality, only forty minutes had ticked past.

How long would Cut give Daniel to rape me? An hour? Two? Or would he wait until Daniel tired and went to tag him for his turn? Either way, time was finally on our side—for now.

Every step, I couldn't stop the remembrance of Daniel's heart giving way to my needle point. Every breath, I couldn't stop reliving the final moments of victory, followed by a canyon of regret.

I'd killed someone.

I've murdered.

I no longer had the right to heaven or angels or eternal paradise. In order to win against the devils, I'd had to become one. Before, I was willing to make that sacrifice, but now...now I knew what a weight it was to value my life above another's. And I wasn't so sure. Did I have the right? Did anyone— regardless of circumstance?

I kept seeing the trickle of blood, oozing and pooling on the floor—unwilling to leave its host, copper and crimson...slowly turning to unwanted rust.

Dirt to dirt.

Ashes to ashes.

Daniel had been raised with diamond spoons and diamond toys. Would his body eventually fuse with the earth, transforming from bone and becoming the sparkling gemstones his family coveted?

Reborn.

Into the one thing his family treasured the most.

Was that karma?

Or serendipitous endings?

Stop it.

You heard what Daniel said. He would've raped me until death.

If I had died, he wouldn't be moping about mourning my loss or regretting his decision.

Straightening my shoulders, I stopped thinking about the murder and dealt with the aftermath.

Jethro moved silently and stealthily. I refused to look at Daniel's sheet-wrapped body. A bloom of blood was the only sign that beneath the burden existed something sinister.

"Jethro..." I whispered, cursing the remnants of the drug-liquor still hammering my heartbeat. My orgasm had been blistering and explosive, but it hadn't nullified the urge entirely.

He looked up, stepping through the fence opening, leaving the encampment for the free world. "What?"

"I—I—" I didn't know what I wanted to say. I'd apologised for killing his brother. I'd let him console me when really I should console him for losing yet another member of his family.

He hasn't lost Kes...not yet.

I felt responsible. I should be the one to destroy the evidence, not him.

"I want you to go. If Cut—"

His teeth bared. "*Don't* bring that up again. I'm. Not. Leaving. I don't fucking care if he sees me. I'm here for good. I'm with you *for good.* Got it?"

His gaze entrapped me; I sucked in a breath. The magical question he'd asked filled my mind.

Marry me.

Marry me.

Marry him?

I'd said yes, but nerves tap-danced on my ribcage. I wanted him as mine more than anything, but there was so much we had to defeat before we were free.

Looking over my shoulder, fear tiptoed through my shadow, terrified Cut would find us.

Repositioning Daniel on his shoulder, Jethro held the panel wider. "Come on." Perspiration and strain etched his forehead. "We have to hurry."

I didn't hesitate again.

Ducking through the fence, I stayed by his side, crunching through long grass, keeping my eyes wide and wary. We were no longer in the den of Hawks but entered a much larger one of lions and hyenas. I'd never been to a place where humans weren't on the top of the food chain. It made me very aware of how vulnerable and edible we were.

A few hours ago, the plains had been shrouded in darkness so thick, my eyes were completely blinded. Now, the black turned pinky-grey, slowly yawning as daybreak appeared.

We had to hurry.

Hurry.

Jethro had to hide.

We have to run.

Trailing in his wake, I didn't ask about his plan. I trusted him. However, being so exposed out here—visible to both man and beast—I didn't like it.

I had to pinch myself to believe he was truly here. When he'd run into the tent, I thought I'd finally snapped. That whatever drugs Cut had given me had consumed me whole.

But then he'd touched me and the repellent desire in my blood became an incinerating demand. His arrival was a miracle. And I'd appreciated that miracle by making him fuck me.

He'd helped me forget for just a tiny moment.

The further we travelled, the more numb I became.

Shock was a weird thing.

It had the power to anesthetize even the most horrifying situation. It could dull the most excruciating pain and make it liveable. But it could also abolish instinct and make a bad idea seem good.

Was this a good idea? Or terrible?

Jethro stumbled beneath his dead brother's weight.

Dashing forward, I reached out unthinkingly. My hand touched cooling flesh. I swallowed the urge to retch. "Let me help."

Jethro shook his head, pain scrunching his face. "I can manage. Just stay close." Blood trickled down his side where his gunshot wound had torn. The heat in his eyes wasn't just from rage but fever. As much as he would deny it, he wasn't fully healed and should be resting.

Instead, he's out here…saving me.

We were both in pain. The kick from Daniel throbbed and the hits and scratches didn't appreciate being ignored. Even the slice on my palm from the ceremony still stung. We both needed to be held together with stitches and bandages.

"Jethro, please, you're not well. Let me help. We're in this together. Don't carry this burden on your own." By burden, I didn't just mean Daniel's death, but the entire situation.

He smiled softly. "Nila, I can feel your urge to help. I feel your love, your fear, your uncertainty." He sighed. "I even feel your confliction about saying yes to marrying me."

I sucked in a gasp. His condition gave me no room to hide. No secrets.

"I'm sorry. I can't—"

He moved forward again, his knees kissing the long grass. "I know you can't help it. But don't ask me to lean on you when there is so much I made you survive on your own." His jaw clenched. "I *need* to do this. And I would appreciate it if you didn't interfere."

"Interfere?"

"You know what I mean."

"Jethro—"

"No!" He slammed to a halt. "Nila. Stop. Just stop. Be quiet in both voice and thoughts and let's get rid of him."

I looked down, rubbing my fingers together, hating the sticky residue of Daniel's blood. I hadn't even washed my hands after stealing a life. A life he didn't deserve but still a life.

The terrible crime would shade me forever.

Who am I? Who have I become?

"Please, Needle," Jethro murmured when I didn't respond. "Be quiet. Just…focus on happier things. It will help me immensely."

Forcing a door closed on my thoughts, I nodded. "Okay." If blocking my feelings was the only way I could help him, I would do it.

"Thank you." Jethro's back bunched as he slowly moved ahead with his slain sibling.

A rustling sound shot my head up. Every thought dispersed like the wind while fear squatted heavily on my spine. "Jethro…"

"Shit." He froze.

"Shit?" I couldn't breathe. "What—what is it?" My ears strained for more noise while my eyes frantically searched the thigh-high yellow grass.

Jethro took a determined step forward. "Don't look. Just

keep moving. We need to get a little further."

I disobeyed, locked into a statue.

A chilly morning breeze rustled the grass, making it dance and weave. But there was something else…something other than plant life…something very much alive.

Stalking us.

Hunting us.

"It's watching us…" My voice barely escaped.

"Do as I say. Don't run. Don't panic. Just stay calm."

Something glided, hunting closer and closer.

Jethro slowly turned to face me, his eyes narrowing on a spot to the side. Daniel's arm escaped the sheet, hanging loosely over his shoulder, his frame morbidly sprawled.

Jethro tensed. "Fuck."

My heart rate exploded. Instincts ordered me to run. But I couldn't unlock my knees.

Never tearing his eyes from the speck in the grass, Jethro very gently, very methodically slid Daniel off his shoulder. His legs, hips, torso, arms, until finally Daniel lay on the ground. The moment he was down, obscured partly by foliage, Jethro tore off the sheet, threw it away, and paced toward me.

Stupidity made me speak. "People will find him. It's too close to the camp."

Jethro shook his head. "Believe me when I say, they won't." He backed up, splaying his hands as if showing no threat to whatever hunted us.

I knew why.

Don't ask why.

"Why?"

Ignoring me, his voice dropped to a whisper as his face skittered between fear and fight. "Nila…back away. Return to the camp. I need you to run, understand?"

My mouth fell open. I gulped terrified breaths.

Jethro came close enough to touch me, swivelling my shoulders until I faced the fence. His voice burned my ear as he growled, "Run. *Now!*" He shoved me hard. "Run!"

His command was a gun and I became a blur of motion. My knees shot high, bouncing over the tall grass; my hair flying in all directions.

Movement immediately exploded beside us, disrupting the peace of the plain.

Shit!

Run.

Run.

Run, run, run.

I wanted it to be explainable—grass stroked by the breeze. But it wasn't. There was no wind anymore.

Prickles on the back of my neck had nothing to do with the cold morning. Basic instinct knew what this was—why I ran for my life.

I was prey in the middle of a hunt.

My legs sprinted harder.

My lungs burst as we covered the distance back to the base in seconds compared to minutes.

We collided with the fence, Jethro grunted as he wrenched open the panel. "Get inside. Quick." Shoving me through, he was rough and aggressive, before tearing inside behind me and slamming it shut.

I buckled over, planting my hands on my knees as I inhaled air and life. The whiff of ammonia and excrement hung thick in the space, but I didn't care.

I'm alive.

I'm alive.

We made it.

Jethro didn't move. He pressed his face against the crudely made fence and stared.

That was when I heard it.

Not a howl or grunt or purr. But a loud *crunch*.

"Oh, my God." I sidled up beside him, staring through the slats to the plains beyond. Daniel had disappeared in the grass, the sheet caught on the stems, fluttering in the breeze. But he wasn't alone.

Two lionesses had found him. Their tails flicking in greed, tan coats camouflaging them perfectly, and muzzles covered in Hawk blood.

"Oh…" My stomach roiled as the larger feline ducked and grabbed Daniel's throat, hauling his carcass into view. I slapped a hand over my mouth as she tore through his jugular, ensuring I'd done the job correctly and he was dead.

The other lioness swatted her companion, taking a bite of Daniel's shoulder.

Jethro vibrated beside me, silent but merciless.

We didn't say a word as the cats gnawed a snack from the man I'd lived with, a brother Jethro grew up with. They ate a few large mouthfuls before grunting with triumph at the dawn sky.

With tan fur rippling, the head huntress snarled over Daniel's gashing throat and with powerful muscles, carted her trophy away. The black tuft on her tail bounced back and forth as the evidence of my murder slowly disappeared.

His death to give life.

His evilness to feed purity.

We watched until there was nothing to see. No lions. No Daniel. Nothing.

Finally, Jethro pushed away, swiping a hand across his face. His shoulders rolled as he battled and segmented whatever emotions had risen. His voice was gruff as he said, "That's why."

I blinked, ignoring the stench of toilets and smarting realness of what had just happened. "What?"

He smiled sadly. "Out there, you asked me why he wouldn't be found."

A shudder stole my nervous system. "They'll eat him?"

He nodded. "I doubt there'll be any remains. And if there is…it's the perfect alibi. Daniel got drunk after raping you and stupidly went for a walk to clear his head." He grabbed my shoulders, holding me tight. "Promise me you'll only remember that part, Nila. You didn't kill him. He didn't touch you. He didn't rape you. And you didn't have to defend yourself. Wipe it from your mind. It will help you live easier. He had it coming—even nature agreed with you."

I cupped his cheek. "Is that what you're worried about?"

His face tensed. "It's what I feel from you."

"Really?"

Dammit.

He was too in-tune, too perceptive.

He sighed, nudging my forehead with his. "I sense what you're not saying. I know he went further than you want to tell me. I know you're in pain—most likely from the slap to your face and kick to your stomach—and I know the drugs in your system from the ceremony made fighting that much worse."

How—? He'd picked up on not just emotional but physical woes, too.

"I'll never get used to you doing that."

His arms wrapped around me. "Well, you agreed to marry me—unless you're having second thoughts—so I guess you're going to have to get used to it."

My body suddenly burst into a blistering sunrise. "I did, didn't I?"

"Did what?"

"Agree to marry you."

Jethro shuddered. "Fuck, I love hearing that."

"That I'll marry you?"

He smiled. "No, that you'll be my wife."

I did my best to squash the pessimism that we might never be granted something so precious. That the Final Debt might still come to pass, no matter he wouldn't leave me again.

I used to be such an optimist…now…it was hard after the past six months. I smiled and kissed his lips. "You'll be my husband. How did I ever get so lucky?" I did my best to project confidence and joy. However, I couldn't hide anything from him.

Pulling back, he ran a hand through my hair. "We'll win in the end, Nila. You'll see."

I sighed. "I know."

I hope.

"We will. I promise." Taking my wrist, he pulled me toward the panel. "Come on. Let's go. I've got a driver waiting a kilometre away. We can leave."

My heart galloped. "Wait. Through *there?* No. No way." I tugged on his hold. "That fence is the only thing stopping us from being breakfast to the pride that's already taken Daniel."

Jethro frowned. "They have food. I doubt they'll come after us."

Food being his brother.

Knowing Jethro could see into the souls of others made a smidgen of relief settle. He didn't care Daniel was gone. In fact, he seemed more than okay with it.

That said something.

I looped my fingers through his. "I'm not willing to take that chance. We're together now. No lion or Hawk will take you from me."

Pacing away, he looked like a wild animal trapped against this will. "I could run ahead. Get the driver and come back for you."

Slamming my hands on my hips, I shook my head. "There is no way you're leaving without me again. No way. You promised. Will you renege on that so soon?"

He exhaled heavily. "Agreed. I was wrong to leave you at Hawksridge. If I'd listened to you, none of this would've happened."

I softened. "If you'd listened to me, then your sister and Kes might have been hurt." I snuggled into him. "You did the only thing you could."

He groaned, gathering me close and kissing the top of my head. "I don't deserve you. Not after what Daniel—"

I kissed him. "Shut up. I won't let you think that way."

I would never verbally tell him I let Daniel enter me—just a little—to ensure my trap was sprung before killing him. He didn't need to carry such knowledge. It was a price I willingly paid. Jethro didn't need to know how repulsive those few inches had been, or how much I loathed myself for letting it happen. I couldn't stop him from sensing what I refused to say. But they were my thoughts and I wanted them to remain unspoken.

His lips grazed over mine. "You're right. Let's get out of this hell hole."

"That's a good idea."

"Stay quiet and follow me." He twisted to leave, a painful hiss escaping his lips.

I yanked him to a stop, inspecting his side. "Are you okay? You need a doctor." Pressing the back of my hand on his forehead, I whispered, "You're burning up, Kite. You need medicine."

He scowled. "I'm fine. Don't worry about me. Just focus on getting out of here. Then we can both heal and relax once we've won."

I didn't ask how we would do that. But I did ask, "Are we going to the driver a kilometre away?"

"No. You're right. It's too dangerous." His eyebrows furrowed, thinking of a new plan. "The Jeeps that the workers take to the mine aren't far away. I know where the keys are stored. If we stay hidden, we can get there in time to leave when the employees do."

"What about Cut?"

"What about him?"

"Will he have come looking for me by now?"

A harsh look filled his gaze. "Cut will leave you to Daniel. Call it training. Like a lion leaves its cub to maul its dinner before stepping in and killing it. He wants Daniel to use you. He won't interfere with that."

I wasn't so sure. The way Cut had looked at me spoke of rage that his youngest son got me first. He'd hated Daniel had won the coin toss.

Stepping away from the smelly latrines and into fresh, morning air, I squeezed Jethro's hand. "I trust you."

His golden eyes glowed with their own daybreak. "I'll make sure to finally deserve your trust, Nila."

Tugging me forward, he smiled. "Now, let's go home."

Jethro

I HID MY fear as I held Nila's hand and guided her through the camp.

She didn't need to know I had no fucking clue how to keep my promise. She didn't need to hear my worries or concerns about this new plan. What she did need was for me to be strong and get her out of this mess.

And I would do it.

Gritting my teeth, I pulled her faster. I'd told her Cut would wait until Daniel had had his fill, but that was wrong. Cut had a fascination of claiming everyone for himself. His tolerance for time would've ended by now.

I had no doubt he would be on his way, if not already pissed at waiting so long.

Bird-song and awakening animals heralded in the new day. The calls and chirps sent chills down my back. Daniel had deserved to be devoured. Nature had taken care of it. But it didn't mean it was easy to watch.

Flashbacks of him growing up, of him chasing Kes and me, of the rare times we got along all unspooled in my head as pieces of him were sliced and disappeared down lionesses' throats.

Guilt for not trying to understand or help him festered

and I wished for a moment that I'd been a better brother to all my siblings.

But I couldn't change the past. I barely had power over my future.

I had to pay attention to the present so I could save the woman I'd chosen above my family.

"Stay low." I jerked Nila behind a shipping container, sticking to the darkness and shadows. The workers and guards who'd been sprawled unconscious after a night of debauchery had disappeared. The dusty footprints signalling the camp might still be quiet, but people were awake, in their homes, cooking breakfast, readying for work in a few short minutes.

We need to move faster.

Nila trotted beside me, her breathing shallow. She mimicked me without noticing, ducking when I ducked, scurrying when I scurried.

She wasn't stupid. She knew what was at stake. And for some goddamn reason, she trusted me to lead her to safety.

I almost got her killed by the lions.

For the tenth time, I berated myself for taking her onto the plain with a body oozing blood. I knew the predators would come. That was my plan—for them to cart Daniel off and turn his body into animal shit—but I hadn't planned on them coming so soon.

"Stay hidden." My voice barely registered as I guided Nila down a small alley, bypassing the open paths and doing my best to remain unseen.

However, I knew it wouldn't be enough.

Eventually, we would be spotted…it was just a matter of time.

We need to be closer to the Jeeps before that happens.

Nila tugged on my hand, pointing to the side where the fire had burned itself out and the strewn men and women had disappeared.

"I know." I narrowed my eyes. "Stay quiet."

She nodded.

My side panged with agony as I twisted around to continue our perilous journey. My fever gradually made me weaker, draining my system of reserves. Nila was right about needing a doctor. We both did.

I couldn't stomach looking at her bruises without wanting to repay like for like. My short-term goals included getting her on a plane where I could assess how badly hurt she was and how much she'd hidden from me. My next plan was to secret her away where she couldn't be touched while I went back to Hawksridge and finished what I should've finished years ago.

I refused to leave Jasmine in Bonnie's clutches any longer. Especially now Bonnie knew the depth of Jasmine's deception. And I needed to see Kestrel. To touch him and encourage him to wake from his coma and come back to life.

The Hawk children were down from four to three.

I didn't want any more of us to die.

Nila stumbled, hissing through her teeth. I pulled her upright, matching her hiss with one of my own. I chuckled morbidly. We were both running on fumes.

Our footsteps made no noise as we moved forward. For all intents, the camp wasn't large—housing upward of thirty to forty people. But this morning, it seemed as if we crossed the Serengeti with hyenas on our heels.

We ducked and froze, scampering across an open distance to the cover of another container.

We're close.

Squeezing Nila's fingers, I motioned with my chin that we were almost there. The parking lot was just around the corner.

Pointing at the ground for her to stay put, to stay safe, I untangled my fingers from hers and prowled forward to the edge of the fence line. I didn't look back, but I sensed her annoyance with me leaving her.

It's only for a moment.

No one.

Nothing.

Only vacant property between me and the first Jeep.

Could it be that easy? Had fate finally decided to let us win?

My eyes danced from guard box to guard box. Last night's ceremony was a special occasion where the rules on security were loosened. However, there should be at least one guard.

No one.

It wasn't uncommon, but it didn't ease me. It only made my condition fan out, seeking any emotional sway to signal humans were there just unnoticed.

My attention fell on the single cabinet bolted to the ground in the middle of the parking lot. The lock box housed the keys to the twenty or so Jeeps waiting to take the freshly slept workers to replace the night shift.

The cabinet didn't require a key but a pin code.

And I knew the pin code.

My mother's birthday.

Waving at Nila to follow, I dashed across the dirt and quickly fumbled with the tumbler.

Please, don't let it be changed.

That would just be my fucking luck.

It took three long seconds before the padlock sprang open.

Thank God.

My hands shook as I grabbed the set labelled with the closest Jeep's license plate.

So close.

Please, let us get out of here.

My thoughts became prayers, paving the way to hopeful freedom.

Waving for Nila to dash from her hiding spot, I shoved her toward the car. "Go."

She didn't hesitate.

Together, we bolted around the vehicle and I unlocked the doors. Throwing myself into the driver's side, I swallowed the gasp of pain from my side. Nila leapt in the passenger side and I shoved the key into the ignition.

Nothing happened.

I stomped on the gas, twisting the key.

Again, nothing.

"What the fuck?" My eyes flew between the dead dashboard to the rapidly cresting sunshine.

We're running out of time.

I tried again, shoving the pedal to the floor.

Start. Please, fucking start.

The engine suddenly sputtered into life, coughing.

Then the worst sound imaginable.

It backfired.

The loud crack ricocheted through the quiet morning, ripping through silence, announcing to the world where we were.

"Fuck!" I pounded the dash with my fist. My heart stopped beating.

Nila huddled in her seat, panic glistening in her eyes. "What do we do?"

I wanted to tell her this wasn't the end. That we still had a chance. But I didn't have the breath.

I tore my gaze to the entrance gates.

Shit.

A guard appeared, bleary eyed and not doing his duty. He jogged to his post, raising his weapon, searching for the threat.

I didn't wait for a bullet or an invitation to leave.

This was the only chance we had.

"Hold on!" Wrenching the gear stick, I forced the old Jeep into gear and shot forward.

Nila squealed as we fishtailed and pebbles pinged below us. The tyres chewed up dirt, snarling faster and faster.

The guard aimed.

"Go!" Nila screamed, gripping the dirty fabric of her chair. "Go. Go. Go!"

I forced the car faster. It lurched forward, squealing in a cloud of dust.

The guard dropped his arm, ducking out of the way as we

careened over the half-way point, swerving around parked cars.

Closer.

Closer.

Come on. Come on.

He fisted a walkie talkie on his vest, his face bouncing between shock and surprise.

Yanking the steering wheel, we hurtled straight for him. I wouldn't let him gather forces. Not now. Not when we were so close.

The gate and final freedom rose before us, promising happiness the moment we barrelled through it.

"We'll make it. We'll make it," Nila chanted, holding the dash with white fingers.

I stomped harder on the gas, preparing to ram the entry. "We will. Almost there."

My heart chugged and hope unfurled with joyous frissions at the thought of finally, *finally*, saving Nila and living up to my promises.

Only…

Fate wasn't on our side, after all.

The gates swung wide and a barrier of men appeared from either side, marching in perfect combat, weapons drawn and armed.

"No!" Nila yelled, her voice mixing with the screaming engine.

What the hell—?

And then a man in a white shirt, goatee, and glistening colourless hair stepped pride of place in the line-up. He stood with his legs spread in the middle of his henchmen and pointed a finger right into my soul.

Motherfucker.

I was right. Cut hadn't waited.

He probably gave up waiting the same time we left with Daniel.

While we gave the lions breakfast, Cut had amassed a counter-attack.

"Fuck, fuck, *fuck!*"

"No!" Nila cried as I stood harder on the gas. "Don't stop. Please, Kite. Do. Not. Stop. I don't care. I don't care if they shoot. Just…don't stop!"

Feral ferocity exploded in my veins. "I won't."

They were in my way. I had a car. They didn't.

"Put your belt on. Now!" I downshifted, granting more power and more screams to the angry engine. Our trajectory turned from hurtling to flying.

I would kill every last guard barricading my way. And I would do it gladly.

Nila's eyes bugged, but she did as she was told. Trembling hands grabbed her seat belt, securing herself tightly. I did the same, juggling between belting myself in and steering the old Jeep.

I gritted my teeth against the influx of emotion pouring from the men before me. Their bodies might form a wall, but their emotions did, too. Fear, obligation, unwillingness to get hurt regardless of what threats Cut had delivered.

My heart skipped a beat as the youngest of the men—just a boy—stepped from the line and raised his gun.

He aimed.

I drove faster.

He fired.

The explosion hurt my ears as the kid recoiled, his arm soaring upward from the kickback. Nila screamed as the bullet pinged off the bonnet.

"Get down!" Grabbing her neck, I forced her to bend over her knees.

"What about you?!" She looked sideways, frantic terror in her eyes.

"Don't worry about me."

Worry about them.

I swerved, placing my side of the car more prominent than hers. If anyone was going to get shot, it was me. I'd already survived one bullet. I could do it again.

"Jethro!" Nila disobeyed my orders and looked up. "Watch out!"

We stared down the barrels of guns. Machine guns. Shotguns. All types of guns. Armed and cocked and ready to—

They fired.

We didn't stand a chance.

The wheels blew, the metal carcass became pockmarks and mangled debris.

The car kept flying, but not on the ground. The front end crunched as the axis buckled, sending us tumbling through the sky.

Slow motion.

Loud noises.

Utter carnage.

The last thing I remembered was skidding, smashing into a boulder, and flipping end over end over end.

Then...

Nothing.

Nila

I LIVED IT all.

Jethro fighting with the wheel.

The rain of gunfire.

The buck and kick of the Jeep as its nose ploughed into earth and sprang upward into the air. I witnessed Jethro's head snap sideways, his temple crunch against the windshield, and the bone-shattering landing when air turned to ground and the Jeep morphed from car to flattened sandwich.

Vertigo had affected me all my life. But this...the flipping, ricocheting, swerving nightmare was ten times worse. The hurl, the roll, the loop de loop forced our bodies to forsake our bones and turn into cartwheels of flesh.

Down was up. Up was down. And fate had well and truly abandoned us as we came to a teeth-chattering stop upside down.

I hurt.

I throbbed.

The engine wouldn't stop whining. The shattered glass rained like fractured crystals. Blood stung my eyes, but I refused to tear my vision from Jethro.

Jethro...

Tears clogged every artery. Panic lodged in every vein.

We'd been so close…

He hung unnaturally still. Blood dripped from his temple, splashing against the roof of the car with morbid artwork. His side bled a rich scarlet while the gash on his forehead oozed almost black-red. His arms dangled, wrists bent and lifeless on the roof.

No…no. Please, no…

He couldn't be dead.

He couldn't.

Life wouldn't be that cruel.

It wouldn't bait hope before us and then yank it away as we reached for it.

It can't be that cruel!

Jethro…

I wanted to reach out and touch him. I wanted to speak and assure him. I wanted to pull him free and drag him far, far away.

But my brain had no power to send the message to bruised limbs.

So I hung there—a broken marionette held up by strings.

My lungs suddenly demanded breath. I gasped and spluttered. My seatbelt hugged me too tight, cutting my ribcage, keeping me pinned upside down. My hair hung around me, droplets of my blood tracing their way over my forehead, like incorrectly flowing red tears joining Jethro's on the roof below.

"Ki—Kite…" I groaned as the word ripped me in two. I begged my arm to move to him, to see if he was alive.

But I couldn't move.

Jethro didn't move.

Nothing moved apart from the spinning tyres and settling dust, cocooning us in a cloud of yellow ash.

Blinking away blood, I sucked in another breath, willing the oxygen to knit me back together and revive me.

Come on.

We weren't safe. I couldn't remember why. But we weren't safe.

Lions?

Hyenas?

Footsteps crunched closer. The click and snap of weapons being disarmed echoed in my skull. Instructions given in a language I couldn't understand.

I suddenly remembered.

Hawks.

Someone tried to open my door, but it wouldn't budge. I didn't look at them. Keeping my eyes trained on Jethro, I wordlessly told him everything he deserved to hear.

I love you.

I trust you.

Thank you for coming for me.

I'll follow you.

I'll chase you.

This is not the end.

Horror that he might've gone forever consumed me. I'd watched him die twice. *Twice.*

I knew what it was like to survive without him. If he'd died, I wanted to go, too.

Tears streamed from my eyes, joining the blood dripping from my forehead.

More footsteps.

More crunching and conversation.

"Jethro…" I battled against the pain and misfiring synapses and managed to force my arm to move. Inch by inch, cripple by cripple, I reached for him.

When my fingertip touched his elbow, I burst into ugly tears. "Please…wake up."

He didn't twitch.

I poked him.

He didn't flinch.

I pinched him.

He only hung there like a butchered corpse.

The windshield suddenly shattered. I screamed as a rain of safety glass pebbled in a waterfall.

My arm wrenched back of its own accord, sheltering my head instinctually. The butt of the gun came too close to my face.

Then a human replaced the gun. A dark-skinned masculine human. His gaze met mine. "Alive, boss."

I squeezed my eyes. Outside, the view mocked me. We'd managed to soar free of the compound before succumbing to bullet fire. We'd been free. We'd made it past the fence.

But now...I would be dragged back and Jethro...I doubted reincarnation would happen a second time.

I drifted in and out of consciousness; half pictures and stuttering images showed me a story of African workers, slowly making sense of the wreck. Someone reached inside and undid my seat belt.

Instantly, gravity yanked me into its embrace and folded me in two on the roof.

A moan tore past my lips, aching with pain.

The moment I was undone, someone grabbed my ankles, yanking me through the jagged hole where the windshield used to be and into the bright morning sunshine. Sharp shards of metal cut me as they pulled me free. Sand burned my bleeding skin as they dragged me across the dirt.

"No!" My fingers latched onto the bullet-riddled car. "Not without him. No!"

No one listened.

Instead, arms plucked me effortlessly and carried me away from the Jeep. They put me down, spreading me onto my back. My spine creaked and stretched, my brain rapidly cataloguing pain, agony, and excruciating discomfort.

My body had been through so much in such a short amount of time.

I hurt, but it didn't matter anymore.

Pain was only temporary as I focused on more important things.

While part of my brain catalogued my injuries, I looked at the destroyed Jeep. Everything bellowed, but I could move in small increments. I didn't think anything was broken.

The man who'd dragged me from Jethro left me alone. However, his sunburned silhouette was replaced with the man I hated the most.

His shoes crunched as he stood over me like a devilish avenger. "You were leaving before the best part, Ms. Weaver." Cut spread his legs, placing his hands on his hips. "I can't permit my guest to leave before the festivities are over."

I had no more to give. No more to fight with.

Ignoring him, I twisted my head to stare at the 4WD. My heart leapt as Jethro was dragged from the wreckage.

I didn't look away as the man who'd carried me placed Jethro's inert form beside mine on the ground. His head lolled to the side. Dirt and grease smeared his handsome face, braiding with the blood on his skin.

Cut nudged me with his toe. "So...you were telling the truth when you said you 'love' not 'loved' my son." Squatting, he poked Jethro in his broken side—the side where he'd shot him.

My arm flailed with uncoordinated projection. "Don't— don't touch him."

Cut smiled, placing his hand on his son's throat. His forehead knitted together, searching for a pulse.

I bit my lip, begging him to find one while at the same time hoping he wouldn't, so Jethro would be free of more torture.

Slowly, Cut's lips spread into a grin. "Well, well. He's still alive."

Thank God.

Thank you, thank you, thank you.

Softer tears fell, enjoying the moment even knowing the future would be anything but happy.

Cut's fingers landed on my cheek. I swallowed back rage, pushing unsuccessfully off the ground to get away.

"I'm so glad to see you're in one piece." His fingers latched angrily around my chin. "However, you have a lot of explaining to do before I let you stay that way."

"Let's start with a few easy questions, shall we?" His other hand smeared blood from Jethro's forehead. "How is he here? How is he alive? Where the fuck is Daniel?"

Gritting my teeth, I used every avenue of energy and shoved Cut's hand away from my lover.

You can touch me, you bastard. But not him. Never him.

"I'll tell you everything if you let him go."

"Let him go?" Cut chuckled. "Why on earth would I do that? It's not every day a ghost comes back from the grave."

I tried to crawl closer to Jethro, to place myself between him and his father. He was alive but unconscious. Cut could kill him so easily, and he would never know until his soul untethered and became homeless over the African plains.

"Stop it. Leave him alone."

Cut dropped his hand, his smile deepening. "You're telling me what to do now, Weaver?"

"Yes."

His eyes glowed. "And what do I get in return?"

My heart clanged and the pits of Hades opened up beneath me.

Marry me.

Yes.

Husband.

Wife.

None of that would come true now.

But I had the power to keep Jethro alive. I would do whatever it took.

"Me, you get me. Just…let him go."

Cut stood upright. "No. I have a better idea." Snapping his fingers, he ordered a guard closer. "Bind his hands."

The guard nodded. Dropping to his knee, he rolled Jethro roughly onto his stomach, not caring his bloody face squashed into the dirt. Efficiently, the guard wrapped the same coarse rope that'd bound me in the mines around his wrists.

It physically hurt watching them maul him while he

couldn't defend himself. Then again, it was better this way. This way, he couldn't antagonise his father or somehow manage to get shot a second time.

Please, wake up.

Please, don't leave me.

Selfishness rose. It would be better if he left in peace. If he slipped quietly away. But I couldn't stomach his loss.

Whatever Cut had planned would make both of us wish we'd died. The belief that we'd get out of this intact and alive was left in the disfigured Jeep, crushing our dreams into African soil.

Cut wiped his hands on his jeans, glaring at the workmen. "Has anyone seen Daniel?"

Men scuffed their boots, fiddling with their guns. None of them made eye contact.

Finally, someone found a backbone. "No, boss. Not since last night at the ceremony."

Cut scowled, running a hand across his face. "Well, find him. He can't have run off too far." His glare landed on me. "Unless you have something you want to share with me, Nila?"

I glared right back, silent.

"Fine." Pacing, Cut growled, "Search the compound, head to the mine to see if he was stupid enough to go there, and check the plains around the camp. I want him to be a part of the afternoon plans, and he doesn't get to skive off just because he has a fucking hangover."

My lips twitched. I'd won in some small measure against Cut.

Daniel was suffering the worst hangover of his life.

In *pieces*.

The workers nodded, fanning out in levels of importance to carry out Cut's orders.

When only a few men remained, Cut said quietly, "That damn son of mine has to learn a thing or two." Pointing at the man who'd rescued me, he ordered, "Take them to cave 333."

"Yes, boss." The man ducked to collect me.

Cut grinned, stepping closer, blotting out the sunshine with this evilness. "I think it's time you learned a few secrets, Nila, and for my eldest to learn that nothing he does can stop me."

I wanted to scream. I wanted to kill. But I bit my tongue and stewed. I'd had my chance to leave. We both did. We'd done what we could, but it wasn't good enough.

Now, we would pay yet another price.

Another debt.

Another toll.

My entire body howled as the worker hoisted me to my feet. My imbalance threw me sideways, turning the world into a broken jigsaw. I groaned as I gave up trying to find an anchor and swam in vertigo.

"Carry her, for fuck's sake," Cut snarled. "She won't make it otherwise."

"Yes, boss." The worker's arms scooped me up, holding me firm. I squirmed, looking drunkenly over his shoulder as he carted me away.

Bye, Jethro…

I didn't relax.

I didn't cry.

But I did die inside as another worker hauled Jethro into his arms and together we were thrown into a Jeep and taken to perpetual hell.

The stickiness of Daniel's blood stained my hands as his father paced before me. Luckily, it threaded with the blood from my sliced cheek and grated legs from the car accident, hiding my sins.

We were no longer above ground but below it.

Cave 333.

Deeper than the caves Cut showed me. Bigger than the sorting or paraphernalia storage caves by the surface.

My bruised body craved sunlight. To beg the sunshine to grant me its healing power so I could run.

But in here…with dampness and rankness and darkness— I was already dead and buried.

There would be no exhuming into daylight. No one to disembalm us when Cut had finished his morbid chores.

Cut dragged his hands through his hair, never stopping his pacing. His white shirt stained and jeans dust-smeared. "Answers, Ms. Weaver. I expect them. This very fucking second."

I bit my tongue, glancing at the earthen walls, wrapping around us with a cold, moist welcome, swallowing us whole like a greedy giant.

This wasn't a cave. It was the giant's stomach. Its entrails.

"You have exactly three seconds to tell me what I want to know. Otherwise, I'll stop treating you as my guest and hurt you as my prisoner instead."

I snorted. "The past six months was you treating me as your guest? Last night with the coin toss? This morning with the gunfire? That's typical behaviour for your *guests*?" Flames smouldered in my belly, suppressing my injuries and allowing me to focus on staying alive.

Cut spun to face me, stalking quickly to slam his hands on the armrests of the wooden chair he'd tied me to. "Six months in my house and haven't I kept you fed and content and given you free rein to explore? Last night, didn't I give you something to make the Third Debt more bearable? I let you dance, smile. You had *fun*, Nila. You can't deny that." His voice lowered to a hiss. "You had fucking fun and you cannot say otherwise."

I trembled. "You want to continue thinking of yourself as a gentleman? A maverick making sacrifices for a good cause? Go ahead. Fulfil that fantasy by letting Jethro and me go. Then I'll answer any question you want. Give me your word we're free to go and I'll tell you everything."

Not everything.

Because the moment he knew about Daniel, there would

be no guillotine or Final Debt. He would wring my neck within seconds. He would avenge his youngest because he hadn't been the one to decree it should be over.

Pushing off from the armrests, he resumed his pacing. "Let's begin with the elephant in the room, shall we?" He pointed at Jethro. "How the fuck is he alive and here?"

My heart cracked, taking in Jethro's beaten form. He slouched unconscious in an identical chair. However, the ropes holding him in place were triple mine. Twine snakes licked around his thighs and torso, gluing him to the chair. His wrists hung lifeless, trapped behind him while his ankles were locked against the chair legs with yet more rope.

There would be no escape. Not even if he was a magician with every spell in the world.

My mind raced with ideas on how to get free, but so far...I had nothing. Blank. Zero. Zilch.

"I shot him. He died on the rug at my feet. He's meant to be dead." Cut's face turned red.

I flinched but held his gaze. "Just let us go. No one else has to get hurt."

His eyes narrowed. "No one else? You say it like someone just got hurt, Nila. Was it Daniel?" He soared forward, his fingers biting into my cheeks. "Where is he?"

Survival kicked in. I'd never been a good liar.

"No idea." Keeping my chin high, I aimed to be honest but obtuse. Forthcoming but mysterious. "Why would I know where your despicable son is?"

"It seemed you knew where my oldest was, even while living under my roof." His face etched with fury. "You ate my food, slept in my rooms, and lied to my fucking face."

"No, I didn't."

Cut laughed coldly. "Don't be a bitch. You knew. All along, you knew."

"I didn't!" I swallowed back my shout. "I thought he was dead. Same as you." Granting him a smidgen of truth, I added, "I only found out a few hours before you put me on the plane."

Cut glared. "How? How did you find out?"

What could it hurt? Jethro was here. Whatever plans he had, they wouldn't come to fruition. "He told me himself. He came to get me."

Cut's mouth fell open, a surprised cough falling free. "You're telling me he *willingly* came back to Hawksridge, had you to himself for however long, and then left you again?" His eyes glowed. "Wait, *that's* where you were when Daniel found you outside your quarters."

I didn't respond. He already guessed with conviction. "What a fucking idiot." He shook his head. More shadows darkened his soul.

Shoving aside the new knowledge, he said, "Speaking of Daniel. Let's get back to what's important. Jethro is alive. I'll need more information on that. But for now, Daniel is more pressing." His eyebrows knitted together. "You were the last one with him. What did you do?"

"Me?" I scoffed. "How could I win against Daniel? I wouldn't stand a chance."

"Did he rape you?"

Blood flowing over my needle.

Oxygen leaving a corpse.

Lions chewing on flesh.

"Yes."

He tried.

"You're lying."

"No."

He paced around me, standing behind my chair so I couldn't study his face. "I find that very hard to believe."

I sat taller in my imprisoning seat. "Why?"

Cut's voice licked over my nape, stroking my dust-blanketed hair. "You're bruised and bleeding, but I don't know if that's from the car crash or my son. You're hurting but not broken. Not exactly encouraging if Daniel had his fill of you." He sneered, "I think you're lying because you're still alive." His fingertips glided down my throat to my breasts. "You can walk. Talk. Answer back. I know my son, Ms. Weaver, and if he'd taken you the way he planned, you wouldn't be sitting there with rebellion in your eyes." His hands fisted my hair, jerking painfully. "You'd be in fucking pieces."

Shit.

Tears pricked as he moved to stand in front of me again. His hands on his hips, he towered like judge, jury, and executioner. "You're lying to me."

"No." I fought my shivers. "I'm not."

Cut bowed, his face to my face. "Tell me the truth. *Now.*"

"I *am* telling you the truth."

His eyes blackened. "One last time. One more chance and then you'll get a painful reward for each lie."

My heart flung itself against ribs. "I'm telling you the truth. Daniel took what he wanted."

"Implausible." His hand curled. "There is no proof and my son is suddenly missing."

Lie better.

Fight smarter.

Taking a deep breath, I snapped, "I didn't say he took what he originally wanted."

Cut froze. "What do you mean?"

Please, let him believe my lies.

"After you left, he—he changed his mind."

Cut raised his fist. "I don't believe you—"

"Wait!" I tucked my chin, tensing against his strike. "The drug-liquor you gave me. He'd had it, too. He said he thought he wanted me to fight and struggle, but then he decided he'd rather I participated."

Cut paused, never dropping his fists. "Go on."

Words tumbled in a rush, tangling with bullshit and storybooks. "I kissed him and said I would willingly submit. That I wanted him because of what you'd given me. That I found him so sexy and I wanted him so, so much."

Filth.

Trash.

Scum.

"He didn't need to hurt me. I participated. I happily gave him pleasure because I earned pleasure in return."

Soap.

I desperately wanted soap to wash my mouth.

Silence fell, cloying and sticking to the cave walls. I hoped my lie wasn't so farfetched to believe. The past few months at Hawksridge gave no hint to who Daniel truly was. He was awful, but I did understand what it would be like to be rejected from birth, told you were unwanted, stripped from human connection. *Love*. He'd never had unconditional love.

Was it too hard to imagine that with his guard down and happiness in his veins, he wouldn't want togetherness rather than rape? Jethro and Kes were kind-hearted and loving— beneath the bullshit layered on them by Cut. But at least they'd had some semblance of family. Their mother had cared for them. They'd been raised in a marriage not a regime.

Daniel hadn't been so lucky. Was that why he'd never evolved past a spoiled brat? Did he lack everything that made him human because he'd never been given tenderness and mothering? Had I gone too far by hinting in my arms he'd found sanity for a change?

"I gave him more than he asked for. I gave him affection." My eyes narrowed with anger. "I gave him what you were never able to give."

Cut froze. His entire body locked down as if I'd stripped back his shell and revealed a grotesque truth inside him.

Oh, my God.

Was that Cut's issue, too?

Lacking love from his own mother?

Bonnie…how much had she warped her son?

His lips pulled back, revealing glistening teeth. "Where is he then? If you gave him a night of fucking wonder, why wasn't he in your bed? Why were you fleeing with Jet? Why does every word spewing from your motherfucking mouth reek of horseshit?"

I stiffened, curling into myself for protection. "I've always said I would run if I got the chance. Jethro gave me that chance. As for Daniel, he left after he finished. I assumed he went to fetch you."

My mind grabbed a new idea.

"Perhaps, he found another woman to spend the remainder of the night with. Perhaps, he got too drunk and is sleeping it off in the shade." I kept my voice level, even though it begged to wobble with uncertainty and plead Cut not to hurt me. "I don't know where your son is. And no matter how many times you ask me, my answer won't change."

Cut swiped a tired hand over his face. A tiny part of me wanted to shout so loud my admission would echo in every cave within the mine.

It was me.

Me.

I slaughtered your offspring.

I was the one who took his life before he could take mine.

And I'll take yours before we're through.

But I swallowed it back, letting my rage rejuvenate me.

Cut snarled, "You're lying. Stop fucking lying and tell me the truth."

"I'm *not* lying."

He grabbed my hair in a feral fist. "You had something to do with his disappearance. I know it. You can't spin it away, Nila. I'll tell you what I think happened." Cocking his chin at Jethro, he growled, "Kite arrived and together you killed him. You plotted this and—"

"No!"

He yanked my head back. The diamonds around my neck bruised my larynx. "Tell me the truth then. Where. Is. My. Son?"

I gasped. "I didn't do anything."

"Liar!"

"No!" My eyes flew to Jethro. "Besides, it doesn't matter

now. Your firstborn is back from the dead. He's your original heir. He can be again." My injuries all flared in time with my raging heartbeat. Fighting against his hold, I did my best to cajole. "You know in your heart Daniel wasn't fit to rule your empire. But Jethro is. You groomed him. He's—"

"Shut up!" Cut's palm smashed against my cheek.

Stars.

I groaned in pain; my head hanging heavily as he let me go.

Cut breathed hard, pacing away.

Trying to tilt my chin and blink through grey and black, I willed Jethro to wake. I didn't want to be alone anymore. I didn't want to face whatever would happen by myself.

I'm selfish.

Wake up. Please…

Jethro didn't move, slumping in his matching chair, barely breathing.

Cut continued pacing, his boots kicking up diamond dust and soil. "I don't care if Jethro is back from the dead. You're forgetting I wanted him hurt. He betrayed me—with you, no less. I shot him on purpose."

"No." I shook my head. "That's not true."

Cut paused, his eyebrows shooting upward.

I rushed, "You shot Jasmine, but Jethro protected her." My heart raced, doing my best to touch some sort of humanity before it was too late. "I don't think you wanted to shoot Jethro. You've never understood his condition, but you're proud of how strong he is—how loyal he is to your family. How much he endured to be everything you ever asked him—"

"Shut the fuck up." Cut reared backward, wiping his hands on his trouser leg. "You have it all wrong."

"Enlighten me then. Tell me your secrets. You said you would. You told me I was entitled to know everything." I couldn't suck in a proper breath with fear. "I want to know. I have questions. So many, many questions. Tell me the truth of what happened when you claimed my mother. Did you love her? Did you ever feel anything for her to stop from killing her?"

A cold smile spread his lips. "Out of everything, *that's* what you want to know? Unpractical, stupidly romantic things?"

I nodded. "Yes. Because those stupidly romantic things will show me if you ever had a soul."

He chuckled. "Oh, I have a soul, Nila Weaver."

"Show me."

"What do you want to know?"

"Everything."

Keep him talking. Keep stalling.

"Tell me your story, Cut. Before you end this, make me understand."

Cut didn't reply. Instead, he strolled over to an empty table lining the wall and stroked a finger in the thick dust. "I can see through your ploys. I know what you're doing, but it so happens your request falls in line with my intentions."

A chill sent fearful frost down my spine.

Throwing me a smile, Cut changed his path and headed toward the crudely made wooden door. The only entrance and exit. "Seeing as extracting truth from you is proving tiresome, let's move onto more exciting things, shall we?"

I couldn't speak as terror cloaked me.

I'd tried to stall and now Cut had twisted my agenda with his. I had a feeling I would've preferred a fist to the jaw every time I lied rather than what he planned now.

Grabbing the door handle, Cut wrenched the entrance wide. Immediately, two men marched in. Men I hadn't seen before. The whites of their eyes glowed in the darkness of their skin; yellow dirt stained their skin with war paint while their clothes of jeans and dirty t-shirts marked them as workers inside the mine.

"Put it on the table." Cut sidestepped, moving out of the way as the men pushed a cart across the cave to the mentioned table.

I couldn't look away as they placed random but terrifying things in place. A rubber mallet. A bucket full to the brim with water. A square shallow container. A ziplock bag with black pouches which I assumed were diamonds. A packet of something with medical jargon on the front, scissors, gauze, and lastly a small stick.

What does all of that mean?

None of it made sense, but my stomach twisted with percolating horror.

Once the workers had emptied their cart, Cut motioned for them to leave. "That will be all for now." He followed them to the door and locked it behind them.

I hated how similar his gait was to Jethro's. Powerful, no-nonsense, a masculine stride. As much as I loved the son, I would never care for the father.

Tearing my gaze from Cut, I looked at the cave ceiling. If I died down here, would my soul find its way from the mine and into the heavenly sky? Or would I sink further into the ground toward hell for murdering Daniel?

A droplet splashed into my eyes, leaving its entourage of teardrops above, balancing precariously until finally giving into gravity's beckons. The occasional splash on the top of my head and the tiny ding as droplets hit plasticware and containers added another dimension to the cave-crypt.

Cut smiled, coming back toward me. "Before we begin, I think my son has slept long enough. Don't you?"

My heart hurled itself into my mouth as he stalked toward a large barrel in the corner full of silty water and grabbed a small pail. With liquid sloshing over the sides, he beelined for Jethro. With a savage smile, he tossed it over him.

Jethro burst into life.

His mistreated body lurched as he gasped and choked, shaking in his shackles. His face drenched and dripping, his tinsel hair plastering against his head.

Tears shot to my eyes as his head flopped backward, gulping air as if he'd been drowning forever. His lips parted wide, his eyes squeezed closed as he rallied.

Watching him come back to life was a miraculous thing. To be so close to death, so inert and broken, and be able to wake up astounded me.

The cave echoed with sounds of his crippled gasps. His head lolled to the side, fighting the weight to take in his surroundings. His eyes glowed wild and worried, drinking everything in at once.

I didn't need to suffer his condition to understand his thoughts. He saw the cave, his father, and then me.

Me bound to a chair with the saddest smile on my lips.

He shattered internally and I heard every smash.

His shoulders flopped further, his soul slipping deeper into a grave. He couldn't move thanks to the rope, but even if he was free, his weakness at hurting kept him tethered.

"It's okay…" I murmured, fighting tears. "It's alright."

Nothing is alright.

Nothing went to plan.

We never got free.

His own eyes glassed with longing and fury. Apologies and unconditional love blared toward me before slipping into hateful rage at his father. The longer he was conscious, the stronger he became. His back straightened, forcing energy to keep him tall rather than slouched.

He coughed again, convulsing with heavy chokes.

My body begged to go to him, to help him breathe. At the very least, to brush aside his dripping hair and dry his face.

Cut didn't do a thing, letting his son fight through the pressure of pain.

Jethro's chin landed on his sternum as he did his best to calm his wheezing and gather a nourishing breath. Finally, he swallowed and glared at Cut beneath his brow. His eyes sparkled with tears from suffocating, but his temper snarled with peril. "Le—let her g—go."

Cut clasped his hands in front of him, letting the pail fall to his feet. "Suddenly, you're in the position to give me orders?"

Jethro groaned and spat on the floor, clearing his mouth from filth and water. "I'll do what—whatever you...want." His voice resembled sandpaper on a skill saw. "Just le—leave her out...of this."

The irony. I'd said exactly the same thing.

Wasn't that true love? The conviction of self-sacrifice in the face of your loved one's agony? It was the greatest selfless act anyone could do.

"I have a better idea." Cut snatched my face, imprisoning it in nasty fingers. Looking at Jethro, he squeezed me until I flinched with pain. "Instead of letting her go, I'm going to have some fun."

Jethro groaned, still breathless and gasping. "Please...do whatever you want t—to me but forget the de—debts. Forget whatever it is you th—think she's done. Just let her go...Father." His voice slowly smoothed, pronouncing words more clearly.

Cut paused at the term of endearment. "Do you hear that, Nila? He wants me to be a better man and hurt him instead of you. What do you think?"

I swallowed, wincing in his hold. "I think you should let him go. He's suffered enough. Let him leave and I'll stay in his place."

Jethro spasmed in his ropes. "No!"

Cut let me go. "You're both as stupid as the other. Seeing as you refuse to save your own skin and prefer to be fucking martyrs, the only course of action is for me to oblige you."

Stalking around my chair, he sawed through the rope holding me against the wooden seat and hoisted me to my feet. I swayed with wobbliness but blinked it back. The incurable illness had been my gaolers, my prison guards for too long. I refused to be weak while Cut destroyed me piece by piece.

"Let her leave." Jethro's gaze bounced between Cut and me. He smothered a cough, his face blazing. "Nila, run."

My wrists remained bound but being free from the hard

wood granted a false sense of freedom.

Cut clucked his tongue. "She's not running anywhere. Are you, Nila?" Capturing my elbow, he dragged me to the centre of the cave. "Stand there."

"For fuck's sake—" Jethro's words tore short in a vicious cough. "Le—let her go!" He fought the rope around him. The chair legs wobbled, creaking with pressure. "Stop. Nila…don't be an idiot."

It hurt so much watching him struggle to protect me when he hurt himself so much.

"Leave, Nila. He doesn't care about you and the debts. Not now I'm here to take his anger out on." His eyes glowed golden and sad. "Please, you ha—have to let me save you."

Tears tracked silently down my cheeks. I wanted to give him what he wanted. I wished I was able to turn my back on him and value my life above his.

But I'd done that with my hated enemy, and I'd almost buckled under the right and wrong of taking his life.

I wouldn't survive if I sentenced Jethro to death when I had a small chance of preventing it.

"I'm sorry, Kite." I dropped my eyes, unable to look at him. "While you're here, so am I. I'm not leaving you."

Cut slung his arm over my hunched shoulders. "It's too depressing in here. It's time for some fun."

I shuddered.

"Let. Her. Go!" Jethro's voice vibrated against the cave walls, threatening an avalanche of dirt. A cascade of soil kissed the top of our heads, a verbal earthquake.

Cut growled, letting me go to prowl behind Jethro's chair. "She's been a part of this since the day she was born, Jet. The sooner you understand that she *will* pay the Final Debt and there's nothing you can do about it, the easier your life will be."

Jethro stiffened, his nostrils flaring with the urge to fight. "What do you mean, my life? I thought I was dead."

Cut bowed over his son, wrapping his arms around his shoulders in a sinister hug. "I mean, I've reevaluated my decision to kill you. Haven't you found it strange you're alive and not currently being gnawed on by hyenas?"

I bit my lip.

His hypothesis was eerily close to what'd happened to his third-born son.

Three boys.

Three heirs.

All gone in different ways.

Only one actually killed.

It was the perfect murder.

And I got away with it.

Jethro shivered with disgust. "Stop with your games. Spit it out."

"Fine." Cut pulled out a dirty rag and duct tape from his pocket. "I mean I'm not going to kill you."

I sucked in a gasp. Thank God! Had he decided to reinstate Jethro as his heir, after all? Had I got through to him in some small way?

You don't believe that.

The tiny voice undermined my hope, tainting everything with sloth-like anticipation.

With measured motions, Cut held Jethro's cheeks and unceremoniously stuffed the rag into his mouth. Jethro thrashed, shouting around the material. His nostrils flared, fighting once more for hard to earn oxygen.

Cut didn't stop. His fingers manhandled his son until he'd forced the gag into Jethro's mouth. Once done, he roughly stuck duct tape over his lips sealing his mouth and gluing to five o' clock stubbled cheeks.

Jethro twisted and squirmed, searching for a way free. But it didn't stop the inevitable. He was silenced, bound...stuck.

"I mean I'm going to grant you a long life, son. After what happens today, after watching what I do to the girl you've fallen in love with, your fate will be worse than death."

Patting Jethro's cheek, he moved toward me. "Much, much worse."

"Don't come near me." I backed away, eyeing up the door to run. Even if I did manage to flee, I couldn't open the door with my wrists tied. And I couldn't fight countless workers scurrying around the mine like mice.

"I'm going to do more than that, Nila." Cut caught me, dragging me close. "Remember the dice throw back at Hawksridge?"

I gulped.

Heretic's fork.

Vaughn.

Kissing Daniel.

I knew, but I played stupid. "I have no idea—"

"Yes, you do." He stroked my arms with threatening fingers. "You rolled the dice and I claimed the roll was to be paid once we got to *Almasi Kipanga.*" His voice dropped to a deep baritone. "Well, we're at *Almasi Kipanga.* And if you refuse, your brother, Vaughn, will be hurt. It doesn't matter that we aren't in the same country. All it takes is one little phone call."

I *hated* him.

I threw myself sideways in his hold, trying to get free. "No!"

Cut didn't let me go, giving me enough leeway to tire myself out but not run. His voice lowered with mirth. "Not only will your brother pay for your refusal but Jethro will, too."

He paused, letting the warning sink into my blood.

Jethro growled, gagged and furious. His bleeding body twisted and jerked in his ropes.

I tore my eyes away. I couldn't look at him. "What—what do you want?"

"I'm going to give you a history lesson, then take what you owe me from the dice game. The Third Debt might once again be elusive, but I have a better idea." Cut's eyes flashed. "Once I've taken my fill, you'll pay the remainder of the Fourth Debt...the Fifth Debt as it were."

Moving me so I stood directly in front of Jethro, Cut murmured, "And my son will watch it all. He'll remain alive, but his soul will die knowing he couldn't help you. And then, once I've taken what I'm going to take and done to you what needs to be done, he's going to continue living with that agony eating him away day after day. I'm going to leave him here, alive, knowing he can't stop me from carrying out the Final Debt. That I'll fulfil the prophecy because he was too much of a chickenshit to do it. And he'll live with your death forever."

Kissing my cheek, he sighed. "That is what I want from you, Ms. Weaver."

It wasn't a happy sigh or even satisfied he'd won—more like a weary, ancient sigh speaking of a man who showed nothing but violence. "My son loves you, Nila, and not a day will go by he won't remember this cave or your death. That is your legacy to him."

Wrapping his arms around me, he whispered, "Don't worry, I'll give you time to say goodbye."

Pulling back, he smiled at Jethro. "Now we all know what to expect, let's begin."

Jethro

I'D LOVED HER for months.
Yet it seemed like my entire life.
I'd fallen for her as an adult.
Yet she'd intrigued me as a child.
She'd been born for me.
I'd been born for her.
We were linked. Joined by fate and history and destiny.
Star-crossed, doomed from the start, absolutely forbidden lovers.

Bound and gagged and utterly fucking helpless, I faced the truth head-on. I'd entertained fantasies of living a normal life. Creating my own family, putting an end to grief and wretched revenge.

But I think I'd always known that no matter what we did, no matter how hard we fought, no matter what we sacrificed, there would be no other ending than the one signed in blood by my ancestors.

I'd said I'd loved her.
I'd proved I'd loved her.
I'd vowed to love her forever.
But the Debt Inheritance was too strong.

It wanted what it'd been given time and time again. Fate marched us faster and faster, stealing everything we'd promised.

Not many people had lived in hell. Not just visited for a while, but actually slept and ate and breathed there. As I watched my father manhandle my woman, the girl I wanted to marry, I set up home in hell. I breathed its sulphur air. I ate its brimstone hate. And I gave my soul over to the devil because what good was righteousness when only evil prevailed?

I was a demon's son.

The demon's son.

Wrought in fire and moulded by sins. My blood forged with terror; my body formed from mistakes and wrong turns. Debts. Contracts. Vengeance.

And no matter how I raged to be free, to end my predetermined inevitability, I couldn't find a way to triumph.

Nila had fixed me.

She'd helped me escape my purgatory.

She'd been the nebula of perfection. The freedom of flying with no wings. Granting wind to a kite with untethered strings.

I'd soared. I'd rejoiced.

And now, I'd fallen.

Whatever Cut would do, whatever he would make me witness and Nila endure, I wouldn't walk away intact.

I would breathe, but I would die.

I would blink, but I would be soulless.

I would vanish inside.

My heart would split open, veins slashing bloody substance all over a life I no longer wanted.

I knew what hell was.

As I fought the rope and begged for salvation.

As I blinked back tears and resigned myself to living the worst day of my life.

I knew what hell was.

I knew…

Because I was there.

Nila

"THE BEST WAY to tell the full story is to start at the very beginning."

Cut left me standing in the middle of the cave, pacing around me pompously. His nose elevated with smugness, arms crossed with self-confidence. Each footstep, he slipped into the history lesson that Jethro ought to deliver. I preferred Jethro's eloquence. His raspy, delicious voice. His melodic accent. His love pouring through every syllable.

But Jethro was gagged, and I had no choice but to hover where I'd been placed and listen.

"You've read the Debt Inheritance," Cut said, "You understand Frank Hawk was whipped for stealing, which you repaid in the First Debt. You know his daughter was killed for witchcraft, which you repaid in the Second Debt. You know Bennett Hawk was sodomized, which I still don't believe you paid with Daniel for the Third Debt, and you understand the mother did anything necessary to keep her family alive. That particular sacrifice was touched on at Hawksridge but will be fully repaid while you're here."

I balled my hands, trying to stop my mind racing with scenarios of what he would make me do.

Cut spun around, pointing a finger like a professor teaching a vital lesson. "Here's where it gets complicated, Nila, so pay attention. Bennett Hawk despised what the Weavers did to his family. He ached constantly from the rape and time moved forward where daily atrocities were delivered. As much as he hated it, his family continued to work for the Weavers. Indebted to them with unpayable taxes and outstanding warrants. They could never leave the Weaver's employ, thanks to a bribed police officer.

"More years passed where no hope of being saved seemed possible. Until Mabel Hawk, the mother who saved, not only her family but her bloodline, did what she had to do to repair their future."

Cut smiled broadly. "She thought outside the box. She used whatever assets she had and fought against society and social standing." He shook his head, almost in awe of his ancestor. "She took out a loan, Nila. Not just a loan, but a carefully plotted move and effortlessly executed design. Once her husband, Frank, died of sickness, instead of giving up, she blossomed. She approached a wealthy earl and bedded him. She'd learned the art of seduction thanks to Percy Weaver raping her every night and put that training to good use. Through sheer determination, she earned the good graces of the earl, who agreed to grant her money for revenge.

"His heart grew fond of her. After her tale of what the Weavers had done, along with evidence of her nightly terrors, husband's death, and her son's troubles, he agreed to take the Hawks in and helped them with legal counsel and the drawing up of the Debt Inheritance.

"Bennett Hawk was mentally unstable from his tragedy when it came to signing the Debt Inheritance. However, it didn't stop the document being lodged with the crown thanks to the earl who'd become mesmerised by Mabel Hawk. On the day of the signing, Bennett didn't have an heir but Mabel circumnavigated that problem by writing an unborn son called William Hawk into the binding contract. She thought of everything, never resting as she prepared to overthrow the Weavers. It didn't matter to her there would be an age gap. She had bigger plans than taking Sonya's life.

"In a few short years, she'd earned the affection of a powerful gentleman, all for her own ends, protected her family, and ensured retribution to those that'd hurt her."

Cut stopped pacing. "But it wasn't enough."

He ran a hand through his hair. "She was on her own with no husband or help. If she failed, the Weavers would ensure she'd be arrested and rot in jail for ever daring to leave their employ. The Debt Inheritance was flimsy at best. She had no wealth to back up her claim. No court on her side. No crown to defend her. She'd done all she could with the earl's help, but she needed more. More money, more power, more protection.

"As it was, living in the earl's house, she and Bennett were untouchable for a short time. She worked tirelessly, never failing in her quest to bring the Weavers down, but despite the earl helping her, his small amount of power wasn't enough to ensure the Debt Inheritance would be enforced.

"A few years passed and the threat of the Debt Inheritance kept the Weavers from coming after her. However, Sonya grew older and Bennett still had no heir. The ages to be claimed would become void, and Mabel wasn't getting any younger. So she put the next part of her plan in place.

"Despite her hoodwinking the earl in the bedroom, he wouldn't do anything more. He wouldn't publicly announce his involvement with her—relationships outside classes were forbidden—and she grew tired of being yet another secret and burden.

"Instead, she set her sights higher. Her family had their freedom—for now—and were the proud owners of a document stating Bennett Hawk's heir could claim Sonya Weaver to extract the debts his family had endured. However, Bennett refused. His fight was gone and he slipped into sickness and depression.

"Mabel noticed her son fading and did what any mother would do to immortalise her family's lineage. She hired a girl off the street—a whore she knew in passing, a girl who'd fallen for the malicious sins of the upper class. She interviewed this girl, got close to her, and ensured she was good stock to breed the perfect offspring. Only once she was sure she was strong and untouched by disease did she get her son drunk enough to make love to her night after night until she was pregnant with a new heir."

Cut pursed his lips. "What was the name of that heir, Nila?"

Despite the sudden switch from storytelling to questioning, I remembered easily. "William Hawk." A firstborn son. Fate smiling kindly on a family who'd endured so much. How different would history have been if he'd had a girl instead?

He nodded, satisfied. "Yes, exactly."

Breaking eye contact, Cut continued to roam the room, unable to stay still. Jethro followed him with his gaze, like me. While Cut talked, we were safe. However, the moment the lesson was over...we wouldn't be.

I didn't want to listen. I wanted to plot an escape. But Cut's voice dragged me back under his tortuous spell.

"Bennett sprang to life when the whore gave birth to his son, but it wasn't enough to completely drag him from his demons. He lived a little longer, enough to see his son grow up from toddler to young boy, before succumbing to the sweating-sickness that plagued London with no warning.

"Instead of mourning her son's death, Mabel Hawk kept it a secret and summoned a meeting with Sonya Weaver. She had already hit maturity and was old enough to understand her place in society. She was of claiming age, but William was still too young. However, that was never Mabel's intention, and it didn't stop her from setting things into motion. Things she'd planned for years now she had an heir to fulfil her prized future.

"Waiting until Sonya was away from her family with a new lady's maid in the park, she approached her with the contract. The girl tried to deny it, but she was old enough to know what went on in the household. Smart enough to know Mabel had been hurt by her father and crimes such as those had to be answered for.

"No doubt Percy Weaver had told her about the preposterous contract, laughing with his wife at such a thing. But Sonya, in her wise young way, saw the Debt Inheritance as something strict and serious rather than a joke.

"She didn't scoff or run when Mabel uttered, 'The time is nigh to pay your debts,' and passed her a sealed and signed copy of the agreed contract.

"Sonya didn't believe she had to answer for her father's sins and tried to refuse—as anyone would—but she'd witnessed what her family had done. She'd heard Mabel's screams while lying in her bed. She'd been too young to stop it but not young enough to stop the guilt festering inside for not trying to help."

"Even as a young woman, she was a good person," I interrupted. "Not all my ancestors were cruel. You can't hate my entire bloodline for two rotten people."

Cut tutted. "No but the same cruelty that ran in your ancestor's veins runs in yours. No matter how small. We merely keep it at bay by making you pay for what you did." Marching away, Cut slid back into his tale. "Mabel knew she ran a risky game by approaching Sonya. For weeks, she sat on edge, waiting for Percy Weaver to storm into her sanctuary and drag her from safety. She didn't venture outside; she didn't let William leave to play with his friends. He was all she had, now her son was dead, and waited with worry. However, nothing happened. Sonya hadn't told. She'd proven a worthy martyr and there was no need to enlist the help of her quiet benefactor the earl."

I rolled my wrists, spinning in place as Cut patrolled the cave. Jethro's eyes glazed with pain and vexation, the gag and duct tape stretching his cheeks. He looked half in this world and half in the other, fading before my eyes.

No matter his story dragged out Jethro's discomfort, Cut

continued, "In that fateful meeting with Mabel and the first indebted girl, a new deal had been struck. Unbeknownst to Percy Weaver, the new bargain was in favour of everyone involved."

"What?" I bit back the question, hating I'd become involved in Cut's story.

He smiled. "Sonya would be spared the long and agonising death by debts if she did two things." He paused for me to ask him what those two things were, but I refused. He'd tell me without me playing his twisted game.

Cut sniffed. "Those two things bound the women together as another year ticked past. Mabel endured living with the earl even though his affection came with more and more bruising fists, and William grew up, faster every month.

"Mabel was prepared to wait however long it took for Sonya to fulfil her promises. However, she didn't have to wait as long as she feared." Cut grinned. "Item number one for Sonya to achieve, to ensure she would be spared, came true without much trouble."

Cut spun, running his hand over his chin. "The silly girl fell in love, and in a night of passion, ruined the life Mabel agreed to save."

I shivered. "What do you mean?"

"I mean, the first condition was fulfilled. Mabel wanted Sonya to get pregnant, to give birth to many offspring for William to inherit. He would never be of age to inherit his original indebted. But there would be others. Amendments to be made. New rules to be scratched into parchment. Sonya wasn't married, but had stupidly gotten with child from her secret lover. Mabel immediately ensured the earl took care of the dowry and married the pair.

"Percy Weaver stood by in shock as his daughter accepted the terms because her name would be disgraced if news got out she'd slept around. He hated that his ex-housekeeper and sex-slave had left his employ and was now protected by a man he couldn't touch. Mabel wasn't stupid; she didn't antagonise the

Weavers without putting solid foundations down first. And with the one good deed of marrying Sonya to her lover, she held her life in her hands.

"That very life she offered to give back to her on one condition." Cut paused for dramatics.

The rhyme of his words wrenched to a stop, leaving the silence in the cave eerily cold. My eyes landed on Jethro. We shared a silent conversation.

I love you.

I love you more.

Whatever happens, I'll find you.

Whatever happens, we'll be together.

"What was that one condition, Nila?" Cut asked, coming close enough to run his fingers through my hair.

I shook my head, dislodging his hold. "From what I'm beginning to learn of Mabel, the one condition would be their deaths."

Hurry up.

I'd listened long enough. I didn't want to become consumed with past rights and wrongs. I always ended up feeling hatred toward my own flesh and blood and unwillingly on the Hawk's side.

Despite that, I needed to know. I would never have guessed the story was so tangled or full of deceit and double-cross. I ached to think of Bennett Hawk living such a sad existence only to die unhappy and tormented by his past.

Cut smiled, his goatee bristling. "You're a fast study. Good girl." He continued his journey around the cave. "Exactly. Sonya would live a full life with a husband and children…if she agreed to kill her parents."

My heart raced. *A hard bargain but, dare I agree, a justified end?*

"Sonya sullenly agreed, and Mabel found a woman in the ghetto selling potions and poisons. The same witchcraft that her daughter was killed for thanks to the Weaver Wife. With money from her earl, she purchased two vials of deadly poison and gave them to Sonya."

Cut's voice sped up, reaching the end and rushing toward other things. "Two weeks later, Sonya met Mabel in their agreed meeting place. There was a new wedding band on her finger, a growing baby in her stomach, and the news that both her parents—the very same ones who'd raped, mutilated, and killed the Hawks—were dead from fatal poisoning."

"Did the police not investigate?"

Cut laughed. "No. The authorities didn't get involved. Weary from the paperwork and previous nightmares caused by the Weavers, they stayed out of it. The Weavers' standing within the community was tarnished and nobody really cared about a suspicious death when it solved so much propaganda and ill will."

Cut clapped his hands. "So there you have it. Mabel Hawk single-handedly ensured the continuation of the Weavers by Sonya's pregnancy, made it so her mentally broken son impregnated a whore, and the two people who'd been the crux of her pain were dead.

"Unfortunately, Bennett had died before her triumph. Her revenge came years after his brutal rape, but it didn't dampen the pleasure in knowing she'd won the first battle."

My voice replaced Cut's deep one. "That doesn't explain how she became so wealthy or how the Hawks crushed the Weavers. A scandal like that would fade in time. My ancestors had a skill. They worked for the crown. Even if Mabel married the earl, her title wouldn't be enough to be highly influential in court—not to mention she was a commoner, regardless of marriage."

Cut smiled, savouring the rest of his secrets. "Don't rush the story, Nila. I never said she married the earl. In fact, quite the opposite. After a time, she faded from his affection, and he tossed her out on the street. He finally saw she'd used him and wanted nothing more to do with her. Over the years, he'd become a drunkard and a wife-beater, ripping apart what they could've shared.

"Mabel went from living in a nice abode to begging for

scraps on the street. The only possession she took with her was her grandson, William. The boy had just turned twelve and was a troublesome child."

Moving closer, Cut whispered in my ear, "And that leads to the next part of the tale. The part where the true rise to diamond power began.

"The part that destroyed your family, once and for all."

Mabel

TOO MANY YEARS had passed since my family fell apart thanks to Percy Weaver and his hellish family. So many years since he'd raped me for the final time. Excruciating years since I secured our lineage and ensured my son's heritage was passed to another.

My daughter was dead, drowned for lies of witchcraft. My son was dead, raped and mentally broken. And my husband was dead, leaving me to defend our legacy on my own.

The hate toward the family who'd taken my everything never ceased—bubbling, billowing, wanting so much to deliver revenge.

And now, I had a way to extract that revenge.

In the days before we worked for the Weavers, I'd been a hopeful girl looking for love. I'd met Frank young and fell pregnant within months. For years, I thought our troubles of living on the streets, of begging and stealing, would be the lowest point in our lives.

However, we hadn't met the Weavers yet. We hadn't entered into their employment. We didn't know how bad things could get.

I wanted to rest. I *needed* to rest. But I couldn't.

For a time, things had been good with the Earl of Wavinghurst, but then I ran out of energy to perform and beguile. He had an issue with his fists, and although I willingly paid for my freedom from the Weavers with a little pain, I'd reached my threshold.

It was mutual—the day he asked me to leave.

I had nothing of my own, only my precious grandson, and traded the staff quarters of his manor for the slums of the London poor.

The Weavers were dead.

Sonya gave birth to a boy followed by twins—a boy and a girl—a year and a half later. The firstborn girl had been delivered, and in order to claim the Debt Inheritance and finally balance the karma scales, I had to find more power and immeasurable wealth so William was in a position to claim his birthright.

In the meantime, I had to find a way to put food in my grandson's belly. I didn't want to, but I had no choice—I returned to what I'd become with the earl. I sold my body; willingly giving the only asset I had left to stay alive.

William's mother—the whore I'd interviewed, given to my son, and bought her child—helped me gain employment with her current madam. And I was grateful. William was growing well. He wasn't sickly and grew strong. He would make a fine Hawk someday. All I had to do was provide for him at his youngest, so in turn, he would provide for me at my oldest.

We moved around a lot that first year, living up to the last name Hawk given to us by the court. Hawks were scavengers, predators, always ready to swoop and steal. I'd never liked the name, until now. Now, I embraced it and nurtured my grandson. All his life, I'd told him bedtime stories of what the Weavers did. I took him to the neighbourhood park where Sonya would walk her children and show him the daughter who would soon belong to him.

He watched that little girl with untold interest, begging me to introduce them, to play with her. It took a lot to ignore his requests. I didn't know what would be better. For them to meet as children or as adults. What would be easier to carry out the terms?

More years passed and I picked up work in sculleries and

markets. Along with the occasional trick in a dark alley, we had enough to get by. We made do. William continued to grow, his interest in our history and what the Weavers had done increasing as the years rolled on.

However, he took matters into his own hands when it came to meeting Sonya's daughter. On his fourteenth birthday, I gave him a few coins and told him to head to the local market to pick up whatever he wanted for his birthday treat.

Only, he came back with the money and a story of meeting a Weaver girl who asked to be called Cotton, even though her name was Marion.

Time had sped up and soon both firstborn children would be of age to begin the Inheritance. However, I often caught William doing strange things. He was strong, oh yes. He was well-spoken, kind-hearted, and hard-working, but there was an oddity about him I couldn't explain.

I would lay in bed at night pondering why he was so different. Why he was so aware of others' plights, why he would often give our hard-earned money to those deserving, or soothe random acquaintances in the street.

As he grew older, he couldn't handle crowds as well as other young men. He'd shake and sweat, striking fear into my heart that he would fall ill with the sweating-sickness like his father.

I did everything I could to shelter him. I saved every penny and prepared for a better life.

And finally, that better life arrived.

Our new existence began one evening at the local brothel, where a share of my nightly profits provided a mouldy bed. After work, I headed back to the temporary home I'd found thanks to a local baker's kindness.

William looked up, covered in flour—as usual—working all hours of the day for the baker and his customers. He preferred this job—away from people, hidden in a kitchen with only his thoughts for company. He'd bloomed into a delightful, handsome man.

I couldn't believe he would turn twenty-one next month.

I was proud of him. Proud of myself for never quitting, even when life became so hard.

Dropping my shawl on a flour-dusted chair, I said, "I heard something, Will. Something that will get us far away from here and somewhere better."

My grandson, my darling grandson, looked up. His golden eyes, courtesy of his father glowed in his icing-smeared face. His hands kneaded the fresh dough, and his smile warmed my soul.

Every time I looked at him, my heart broke remembering my daughter and son. Despair and fury never left me alone—they fed me better than any other substance, and until I got back at those who'd wronged me, I would remain alive and deliver vengeance.

William wiped his hands on a tea towel, sitting on the roughly-sawn stool by the oven. Moving to the bucket of water, I rinsed my arms and neck wishing I could cleanse my body from the foul stench of men who'd used it.

I might have a grandson, but I maintained myself. I looked better than most of the whores downtown.

"What did you hear, Grandmamma?"

I smiled. "The street criers said the man from Genoa—the explorer, Christophorus Columbus—has set out on his second journey. They say not since the Vikings has anyone been so brave to risk the dangerous seas and commit a voyage to new worlds." My voice rose with eagerness. "His successful first journey has inspired many ship merchants to follow in his stead. Exploration is the new wealth, William. Those who risk will come back with untold treasure and knowledge."

My heart raced as I recounted what I'd heard on the streets this morning. News from Europe travelled fast, spreading like a disease to infect those who listened. "He took three ships last time. Seventeen this time. Can you imagine, William? Seventeen brave boats to find out what's yonder over the horizon. He left this morning." I wished I could've seen the departure of such a fleet. To have travelled to Spain and waved a white handkerchief in good luck.

William smiled indulgently, his cheekbones slicing through his short beard. "Grandmamma, you need to give up these fantasies of leaving. We live here." He stood, using the tea towel to pull out handmade bread from the crackling fireplace. "I know you don't like it here. I know you and your family didn't find happiness. But it's all I know."

William took after his father. And just like Bennett, he was a quiet soul. He preferred to be gentle and kind, rather than battle and wage war on what was rightfully his.

"We might live here, but I refuse to die here." I crossed my arms. "I'm leaving this country one way or another, and you're coming with me."

He shook his head, smiling softly. He was used to my rambling of finding a better life, a better world. I would give anything to move. To seek what we were owed after such tragedy.

"It's a nice idea. But this is our life." He winced as he sat back down—his body already overused even at such a tender age. I didn't want him labouring to an early grave when I had the gumption to find a way to deliver a splendid upper-class life.

Standing, I fumbled in my skirts for my one saving grace. I'd worked for decades to acquire such a sum. I never went anywhere without it and hid it within my petticoats.

Money.

Enough for two passages on the next boat leaving port.

Moving around the table, I handed him the meagre purse that offered so much. "We're leaving this place, William. There won't be any arguments. We're going to make our fortune and only then will we ever come back."

Eight weeks and counting.

Almost half of those passengers who'd boarded and paid for a hammock in the rat-infested bowels of the ship, *Courtesan Queen*, had died. My gums bled. My stomach wouldn't hold food. And my eyes only saw blurs and shadows rather than vibrant pictures.

But England was far, far away from us.

The ship had no final destination. No advice on where they would deposit us. But I hadn't cared. I believed in fate, and would rather die chasing my dreams than sitting at home never brave enough to try.

True to my word, I'd bought us passage on the next departing boat. The seafarers had seen Christophorus Columbus' triumphs and raced to chase him. When I offered money and my body in exchange for a safe journey, the captain had agreed.

We'd left the very next day. No belongings. Nothing but hope in our hearts.

I'd either condemned us to die at sea, forever lost beneath the waves, or set us free for a better future.

I just wished seasickness hadn't made my new life such a misery.

Groaning, I grabbed the pail again, retching as another swell rocked the creaking vessel.

Twelve weeks.

Even more of us had died. Storms had come and battered the crew and ship. But still we bobbed and travelled.

Sunshine broke through the clouds, granting nutrition in the form of its heated rays. William lost weight. He looked like a walking skeleton, but I was no better. My ribs had become so sharp, my skin bruised where they stretched my sides. I'd lost teeth due to rotting gums and my vision sputtered with useless blurs.

But hope still blazed.

We were owed happiness. I had no doubt we would be

paid.

Fourteen weeks after leaving mother England, my hope was justified.

Land.

Sweet, life-giving land.

The next few days gave new energy to the ship and its remaining inhabitants. Celebration ran rife and excitement levels gave us the final push to reach salvation.

The first steps on terra firma lifted my heart like nothing else could. I'd made it. I'd left hell and found heaven. Here, my grandson would find a better life. I owed him that.

Only, I didn't know how hard this new world would be.

For three long years, we lived in squalor and hardship. Our newfound existence turned out to be no better than England. Instead of buildings, we lived in huts. Instead of food, we had to hunt and kill. And instead of streets, there were dirt tracks and violence.

However, every day William thrived. He shed the shy baker from England and transformed into a warrior matching the courage of the black-skinned neighbours of our new home. They taught him how to track and trap. They taught him their language, and eventually, adopted us into their tribe.

Once accepted, we made the choice to return with them to their home. We had nothing holding us in the port town and agreed to make the pilgrimage to their village. It took weeks of travelling by foot. My old age slowly caught up with me and eating had become a chore with very few teeth from bad nutrition on the boat over. My body was failing, but I hadn't achieved what I'd promised.

Not yet.

I had to provide for William. He had to go back and claim the Debt Inheritance before he was too old. My to-do list was still too long to succumb to elderly fatigue.

William was a godsend, helping me every step. He held my hand. He carried me when I collapsed. He helped the shamans break my fever when I was sick. He never stopped believing with me that one of these days we would find what we were owed.

And then one day, five years and four months after leaving England, we finally found it.

My eyesight had deteriorated further but every night at twilight, William would take me for a walk around our adopted village. He'd guide me to the riverbed and guard me from local predators while I washed and relaxed.

However, that night was different. A hyena appeared, laughing and hungry, and William chased it off with his spear. I stood in the middle of the water, not daring to leave but unable to see my brave grandson.

He wouldn't respond to my calls. No sound gave a hint that he'd won. Tears started to fall at the thought of losing him. If he'd died, I couldn't keep going anymore. Why should I? My stupid hope and blind belief that something good would happen would no longer be enough to sustain me.

However, my worry was for nothing because he returned. Blood smeared his bare chest as he dragged a hyena carcass behind him. He looked as wild and savage as our ebony-skinned saviours. He dropped the carcass and waded into the water directly to me. My animal hide skirt danced on the surface, lapping around my thighs as he held out something large and glossy and black. Black like a nightmare but an ultimate dream come true.

"What is it?" I whispered, my heart rate climbing. I didn't know what I held, but it felt right. It felt true. It felt like redemption.

"I don't know, but the stories they tell us around the fires might be based on truth. Remember they sing of a magical black rock? I think this might be it." He kissed my cheek, hefting the weight of the suddenly warm stone. "I think this is worth something, Grandmamma. I think this might be the start of something good."

I'd like to say I lived to see the good arrive, but I'd done all I could for my grandson. A few months later, I fell sick and remained bed-ridden as he found more black stones, digging with spears and hipbones of lions, slowly sifting through soil and rock. Black stones gave way to white stones, clear stones, glittering beautiful stones.

Our tribe gathered and hoarded, filling bushels and burying them safely so other clans didn't rob us. William gathered a hunting party to return to the bustling port and trade his magical stones.

I remained behind, clinging to life as hard as I could.

My body had done its task, but I didn't want to leave…not yet.

We'd heard tales of a gold trader who made a fortune in saffron and bullion. That same trader took William aside and whispered in his ear that he might've found a rare diamond.

Diamond.

I'd never seen one up close. I'd heard of them on the king's finery but never been lucky enough to witness.

The night William returned from port, he told me he'd traded enough clear stones for passage back to England. And that was when I knew the tides had finally turned. The Weavers had ruled for long enough.

It was our turn.

By candle-light, we negotiated his plan upon returning to the United Kingdom. I gave him my elderly wisdom and what I'd learned the hard way. In order to become untouchable, he had to buy those who would protect him. He had to give the king everything to purchase his trust. He had to spend money to make his fortune last longer than fleeting.

I hoped he'd heed my advice.

Unfortunately, I never knew.

I died two weeks before William named a handful of trusted warriors the Black Diamonds and booked passage on the first boat back to England.

I never got to see him strip and destroy those who'd ruined us.

I never got to see the fruition of my sacrifice.

But it didn't matter.

I loved him with all my heart.

I'd given him everything.

I'd finally set him free.

Nila

"COULD YOU FEEL her loyalty, Nila? Her unfailing spirit toward her beloved family?"

Cut's voice tore me from the hypnosis of learning about Mabel Hawk. She was the only reason the Hawks had become the superpower they were today. Without her, without her determination and willingness to do whatever it took, the Hawks would've remained poor and unknown.

I rolled my shoulders, forcing myself to snap out of the trance he'd put me in. I couldn't forget I stood in a dank mine——the very mine William Hawk started so many centuries ago. Cut wasn't telling me history for the fun of it——he gave me a prelude to the debt I would soon have to pay.

Listening to Mabel's tale, I couldn't figure out what the payment would be. Mabel had given up everything for her grandson. What a strong, commendable woman she was. Even if she was the reason for my pain.

"Yes." I nodded. "She did so much." My eyes met Jethro's. His nostrils flared wide, sucking in damp air, unable to talk with the gag lodged in his mouth. My heart overflowed with love and affection. I fully understood Mabel's drive to save someone she loved.

She saved them.

I smiled sadly to think two things in both our families had been passed down from generations. One, my family had always had the tendency to breed in multiples. Twins were common and triplets a regular event. And Jethro…his empathy had come from William. Mabel wouldn't have understood his plight, but listening to the characteristics of her grandson, I had no doubt he suffered what Jethro did.

"Can you see how everything we are is owed to that woman? That she is, without a doubt, the bravest Hawk." Cut paced in front of me.

Yes, I can see.

I asked a question of my own. "Why don't you have her portrait up in Hawksridge? You have so many men hanging in the dining room, where is Mabel—considering she is the founder of your family's fortune?"

Cut paused. "There is a portrait, or as close to her likeness as William could make it. When he returned and created a new life for himself in England, he did his best to describe his grandmother to a local artist. The poor couldn't afford painters, Nila. And she died before she had the means for such frivolous items."

"Where do you keep her painting?"

Cut's lips twisted into a smile. "It's interesting you should ask that."

"Why?"

"Because you'll see, soon enough. You'll see her portrait, along with many other Hawk women before the Final Debt is paid."

Jethro growled, struggling in his binds.

Cut chuckled. "Don't like me mentioning your girlfriend is on borrowed time? I'm glad I gagged you. It's nice being able to have a conversation and not have you interrupting us."

Jethro's eyes glowed with rage.

Turning his back on him, Cut gave me his full attention. "Now you know how we found the diamonds. Let's continue with William's story when he returned to England."

I didn't approve or deny as Cut moved around me, his voice taking on a story-time timbre. "William grieved his grandmother's death, but he knew she would want him to reach the heights she'd dreamed. So he left on the boat with his Black Diamond warriors and returned to England without his grandmother.

"When he reached English soil, he went directly to the king. He didn't try and find someone to value the stone or seek backhanded deals. He knew that was a sure way to get himself killed.

"Instead, he announced he'd been on a voyage and had returned with a gift for the king. It took him four months of hanging outside court, following dukes and duchesses, and slipping through the king's guard before the king finally agreed to an audience.

"In a meeting attended by courtiers and advisors, William presented the black diamond. The stone was the largest ever found at the time and the king immediately gave him authority to return with a fleet of ships to collect more on his behalf.

"William remembered what Mabel told him. He was willing to give up the wealth he'd found, pay exorbitant taxes, and lavish gifts upon the crown in order to have the most powerful monarchy behind him."

Cut ran a hand through his hair. "Imagine that. Giving up every stone you'd found, returning home richer than the king, and leaving penniless once again."

I kept my chin high. I had to admit it would be a hard decision to swallow but smart at the same time. No king wanted a richer subject than he. This way, the crown became insanely wealthy and the Hawks cemented a lifelong partnership, ensuring better things than money.

Friends.

Allies.

Kings in their feather-lined pockets.

Was that how the crown became so rich? Were the jewels on their garments and diamonds on their scepters all thanks to the Hawks?

I gasped, my mind running away with the new angle of thoughts.

Every war. Every triumph and takeover of other countries—had they been possible and financed entirely by the Hawks?

Cut interrupted my epiphany. "William returned to Africa and found yet more diamonds. His Black Diamond warriors increased in number, his mine and village became the most protected piece of dirt in Botswana, and he returned to England with far more than before.

"The king once again welcomed him with open arms. He granted William a title, land, property—anything he wanted. He agreed to the terms that all Weavers—related to Sonya or not—were no longer favoured in court and banished them to Spain. He also approved the Debt Inheritance to be binding for future years.

"By his third trip, the young Hawk boy had become an untouchable aristocrat. He'd grown in wealth and power and wore his self-worth like the expensive tailoring he commissioned. The fleet of ships given to him by the king grew until the crown jewels filled to bursting with diamonds of all shapes and sizes."

"What about the Debt Inheritance?" I tried to do quick arithmetic. "He would be nearing his thirtieth birthday—if not older. What about claiming Marion?"

Cut's forehead furrowed. "Don't rush me, Ms. Weaver. I'm getting to that." Jamming his hands in his pockets, he continued with his tale. "It was almost a decade before William found another black diamond that trumped even the one he'd given to the king, the one he'd named his entire brethren and brotherhood in honour of. This new one...this black monster found beneath the soil of the African plains, made the one the king owned pale in comparison. To this day, it sits carefully guarded in our safe at Diamond Alley."

Diamond Alley?

My eyes flew to Jethro's.

Oh, my God. He'd shown me. He'd allowed me to hold the menacing stone that'd become the most treasured item in his family history.

Jethro scowled, shaking his head slightly. *Don't mention it.*

I bit my lip. *I won't.*

"For years, the arrangement with the king prospered but then an aspiring courtier tried to kill William and take his trade routes and diamond mine for himself. The man ambushed the boats journeying home. His entourage robbed the crates of gems when they arrived at port. And they killed members of William's Black Diamond brothers in order to weaken the wealthy Hawk importer.

"William obviously didn't put up with such behaviour and fought his enemies by becoming a smuggler."

I rolled my wrists, encouraging blood to flow into my fingertips. "How?"

"The mines at *Almasi Kipanga* gave many ranges of diamonds. Some of low grade. Some of high. The lower grade, William mixed with quartz and other invaluable gemstones, pretending the shipment contained millions worth of invaluable cargo. He'd allow the hijacking and sacrifice the haul without losing anything of value.

"The king was aware of the ruse and allowed him to create tales and fiction of robberies and bankruptcy. But what the thieves didn't know was, William had found better ways to transport. He lost his reputation of respectful decorum and embraced a notoriety of strict and fearful.

"His trusted warriors ensured his mystery increased, killing those who opposed him, creating a formidable empire no one could take down. Not even the king."

Cut stopped before me. "That wealth started our dynasty and the power that ensured we were above the Weavers, even though they'd been the court seamstresses and royal designers for decades. It was the same power that made the Weavers run like vermin, hiding in their new Spanish home, believing they were safe from any other claimant on the contract."

I frowned. "So William never made Marion pay the Debt Inheritance? He let her live?"

Cut smiled. "There's something you didn't know about William. Something Jethro shares with his great-great—too many great ancestor."

I smiled, happy I'd seen within the lines of his story. "I think I know what that is."

Cut narrowed his eyes. "I suppose, after being so close to my son, that would make sense. For the purpose of full disclosure. What is it?"

My arms ached to hold Jethro. My heart throbbed to be with him, away from this place. I held my lover's eyes as I muttered, "He was an Empath, too."

"Exactly." Cut nodded. "An unfortunate trait that runs in the family. It wasn't diagnosed or even recognised as a condition. But records and voyage logs give hints into William's emotional perception. His disease prevented him from hurting the one girl he was owed."

Cut moved toward me, his body heat defiling mine. My feet moved for every one of his, moving in a slow waltz around the room.

"Because William was so weak emotionally, he felt the brunt of inflicted pain. He'd endured discomfort in his merchant world. He'd seen things, done things, and lived through things he couldn't shake when having to deliver agony firsthand. Unfortunately, the thought of carrying out the same punishment, of whipping her for his grandfather and ducking her for his aunt, and raping her for his father—he knew he couldn't do it."

Cut's story achieved two things. One, it showed that although my ancestors had been conceited and cruel, Sonya had been compassionate and kind. And even though the Hawks were insane today; back then, they sounded upstanding and courageous.

Cut's voice cut through my musing. "Instead of taking her

for his own, William let Marion marry and breed. He married himself and accepted the gift of land from the crown to build our home, Hawksridge Hall."

Cut stopped moving; I stopped backing away.

His white hair flickered with the electric lamps around the room. His voice turned raspy from delivering such a long tale. "Unfortunately for William, his firstborn, Jack Hawk, was nothing like his father. Jack willingly accepted the Debt Inheritance when he came of age."

I finally understood why, through so many generations, only a select few inheritances had been claimed. There would've been more Hawks like Jethro—especially if it was a common trait. And my family didn't take the threat seriously because the claiming wasn't strictly enforced.

Cut didn't speak again for a minute, letting history fade around us, allowing ghosts to settle back into their coffins.

Taking a deep breath, he finished, "So you see, Nila. We had our own hardships. We knew what it was like to rise from the gutter. And the Weavers couldn't stop us."

I squirmed in my ropes, hating he'd come to an end—knowing it meant only one thing. I'd enjoyed the lesson, but I wanted to run from whatever debt he would make me repay. "But you have so much. Why bother hurting others when you no longer need to?"

Cut scowled. "Why do politicians lie? Why do the richest families in the world create war? Why do those who have the power to fix global poverty choose to exploit and murder instead?" His fingers kissed my cheek. "Nila, the world is black beneath the skirts of society. We aren't any different from others."

"That's not true. I don't believe that."

"Don't believe what?"

"That other men do this. Hurt others."

Cut laughed loudly. "Don't you pay attention to the news? Do you not see between the lines of what a corrupted, blackmailed globe we live in?"

I looked away.

Jethro continued to wriggle. Nervous sweat beaded on his forehead while wildness glowed in his eyes.

We both understood time had run out. Cut was ready for the next part of this sick and twisted game.

"I do agree some families control every earthly asset." I stood tall and defiant. "I agree death to them is as simple as a signature or a whispered word. What I don't agree with is *why*. *Why* do you have to do this?"

Cut marched quickly and gathered me close in his arms. "Because I can, Nila. That's all." Letting me go, he prowled to the table where items I didn't want to look at rested. "Now, enough history. I've rambled on long enough, and it's starting to get boring. Let's get to the exciting part, shall we?

"Let's pay the rest of the Fourth Debt."

GET YOUR FUCKING hands off her.
Don't touch her.
Let her go.
Leave her alone, goddammit!

Every thought hurricaned around my head, blistering with outrage but not able to spill thanks to the rancid gag inside my mouth.

I wanted to kill him. Motherfucking slice his godforsaken head off his shoulders.

Every inch of me cried with agony—from the gunshot wound to the fever to the pounding headache and potentially cracked ribs from the car crash.

Yet nothing hurt more than listening to Cut deliver the story of Mabel and William——the same tale I'd heard over and over again——and counted down the minutes of when it would be over.

Nila paid attention, rapt beyond her will, absorbing my family's history. To hear it for the first time would've answered so many of her questions but I had my own about William Hawk. Along with Owen, I felt most connected with him. I had documents of when William was inducted into the House of Lords while building Hawksridge. I had countless notes of his rise to wealth and the ledgers from his ships.

He was the keystone to my family, just like Mabel. He'd managed to deliver our rightful happiness without spilling any more Weaver blood. I liked him. But I hated what'd happened after his time had passed.

Nila struggled in Cut's control. "I paid the Fourth Debt at the Hall."

Cut laughed. "You paid one element of it, that's all. This is the main part and must be completed for the contract to be appeased."

Snatching her tied wrists, he stroked her tattooed fingertips. "You've only earned two tallies. You need two more marks before the Final Debt can be paid."

Nila snarled, "If you think you can etch your name into my skin, I won't let you. Jethro's initials are what I bear. Only he can tally me. Only he can claim me as per the Inheritance rules."

Cut let her go, tutting under his breath. "As you no doubt have figured out, Ms. Weaver, I'm not exactly playing by those rules any longer."

Another wash of crippling pain from my headache dulled their voices. My shoulders ached from flipping in the car and my sockets bellowed from being wrenched behind my back.

They continued to argue as I grappled for coherency.

I willed them to continue talking. Every extra stolen minute could help.

Gritting my jaw, I struggled with renewed force. For the past half hour, I'd done everything I could to get free.

My fingernails sawed at the rope; my tongue pushed on the gag. But Cut hadn't tied me with half-measures. He'd tied and triple tied.

All I achieved was more pain and tiredness. Despite my bitterness and hatred, I'd become helpless. All I could do was sit there like a fucking arsehole while my father tortured Nila with anticipation.

The Fourth Debt.

Originally, the debt ensured ultimate pain and a quick

delivery to the Final Debt. Not many would've survived for long—especially a few centuries ago when anaesthetic and disinfectant weren't used. The Fourth Debt was the last to be claimed and the most barbaric.

Missing body parts.

I shuddered, breathing hard through my nose. My innards crawled with what would happen, what Nila would endure, what I would witness.

I have to find a way to stop it.

Thankfully, Nila wouldn't be subjected to Cut's surgery skills. Not in this day and age. The debt had evolved a little since then. But it would still be painful. It would still be brutal and cruel.

I twisted in the ropes, wishing for just a small loosening that I could use. But the twine only gathered tighter, rocking the chair legs against the floor as I writhed.

Cut glanced at me, his eyes narrowing. "I'd save your strength, Jethro. You have a new task, remember?"

I threw every inch of hate into my gaze. If only looks could kill. I would've ripped his motherfucking head off with one glance.

"Your fate is no longer death." Cut came toward me, calm and collected. He acted as if this was a business meeting discussing new terms of the estate. "Your destiny is to stay alive, missing her when she's gone. Forever alone with memories of her death."

Nila swallowed a cry, her eyes darting to the exit. "That doesn't have to be the case. He's your son. I'm in love with him. Let us go and be a father rather than tormentor." She could run, but her hands remained tied—without her fingers to open doors and arms to defend, she was as trapped as I was.

Cut ducked to my eye level. He hid so much of himself but throughout my childhood, I'd seen parts of him in direct contradiction to the man before me now. Was there any goodness left inside, or was he nothing but a black shadow, a grim reaper of Weaver souls?

Don't hurt her!
Don't do this.

He didn't need words to understand what I begged. If the ropes didn't lash me to the chair, I'd fall to my knees and plead. I'd give him anything—my life, my future—*anything* to save Nila from what he would do.

With a smile, he patted me on the head. "Keep your eyes open. Nila agreed to do a certain something for me back at Hawksridge. It's time to see if she'll obey." Leaning closer, he whispered so Nila wouldn't hear. "If she does it, it will rip out your fucking heart but she'll remain intact. If she doesn't, she'll be loyal to you but will pay the price with pain."

Taking a step back, he grinned. "Let's see what she chooses, shall we?"

I looked directly at Nila. How could I tell her to behave and do whatever Cut asked? How could I tell her to choose between two horrendous things?

Her eyes widened, confusion settling on her face from my scattered questions.

Trying to calm down, I did my best to silently share a message. *Do what he asks.*

She flinched. *Never.*

Please.

Don't ask me to do that.

Her emotions waked around the space, tainting the walls and air. I couldn't turn my condition off, and I wouldn't survive feeling Nila's agony.

My muscles bunched as I struggled harder. I choked on saliva, sucking on the disgusting gag.

Cut placed himself in front of Nila with his back facing me.

I couldn't see.

I can't see.

I strained to the side, seeking a better vantage, but I couldn't see around Cut's large frame.

"Now, you've heard the history, so let's focus on the

present." Cut's voice echoed in the cave. "But first, you owe me from the dice throw in Hawksridge. I won't tell you what you'll avoid if you obey, but I will tell you if you don't, worse pain than you've endured so far will be delivered."

His hand landed on her cheek, brushing aside glossy black hair. I *hated* his hands on her. I *hated* I couldn't see Nila's reaction or read her face. I hated, hated, *hated* he'd already stolen so much from her—her long hair, her happiness…her smile.

She looked nothing like the young seamstress from the runway show nor any hint of the sexy, shy nun in her first text messages.

Together, my father and I had stripped her of everything she'd been and created this new creature. A creature being led to the slaughter.

No!

I growled.

Cut looked over his shoulder, rolling his eyes. "A growl? That's all you have to say?" His gaze landed on the duct tape over my mouth. "Like I said, Jet. Save your energy. All you need to do is watch."

I'll fucking watch.

I'll watch wolves tear apart your carcass.

I'll watch demons suck your soul into hell.

My breathing crescendoed until my ribs creaked and my head swam.

Nila trembled in place. Her emotions stuttered, fading a little as she locked down internally. I'd felt it happen to many people. When stress overloaded the system, a human's natural response was to go quiet. To focus. To numb. To delete every distraction.

I'm here with you, Nila.

I'm with you every step.

Nila's voice was a blade as she replied, "If I refuse, will you hurt Jethro?"

"No, my son isn't going to participate in this next part."

She sniffed. "In that case, you can't inflict worse pain than I've already endured. The day you shot him and I believed he was dead is the worst you can ever do." Her tone strengthened until it shone with steel. "So do your worst, Cut Hawk, because I can survive you."

Cut didn't reply, but his hand lashed out to wrap around her waist. "We'll see about that." Jerking her elbow, he spun her around to face away from him. "If that's how you want to play this." Letting her go, he pulled out a switchblade from his back pocket.

My heart splattered into my toes.

Stop!

I growled and struggled, but it was no use.

Shit!

Maybe I was wrong. Maybe the Fourth Debt would still include slicing off a limb or appendage. I had to stop him!

Don't!

Don't fucking touch her!

With a flick of his wrist, Cut sliced through the rope around Nila's wrists and spun her around to face him again.

The relief at no blood being drawn layered my shoulders with heavy relief. I slouched, breathing hard, fighting through the *thump-thump* of my headache.

Thank fuck.

Tucking the knife back into his pocket, he smiled. "Now you've had time to think about your lies, Nila, let's try again. Where is Daniel?"

Black hair flicked as she shook her head. "I've already told you. I don't know."

"You do know."

"I don't."

Cut gathered her close, wedging her body against his. "When I find out the truth, you'll understand I can deliver pain outside of the original debts to be claimed." He ran a hand over her chin. "If I find out you've hurt or somehow killed my youngest, you'll wish to God you died in the car crash today."

Pacing away, he gathered his temper. His boots scuffed the earthen floor.

My eyes immediately latched with Nila's. Now Cut's body didn't block hers, I shot as much love and pride that I could.

I'm so fucking in love with you.

She smiled sadly. *I know.*

We'll get through this.

Her body folded with depression. Her eyes didn't return a response.

Cut moved behind Nila, folding his arms around her in a rotting embrace. Locking eyes with me, he whispered in Nila's ear.

I couldn't hear, but the change in Nila faded her heartbeat by heartbeat.

Christ, I wanted to stop this. Hadn't he done enough?

My tongue pulsed against the gag, doing my best to curse and yell.

Her spine rolled, her cheeks whitened, her hands opened and closed by her sides. When Cut finished whispering, she bit her lip and shook her head.

He murmured again, his breath disturbing her short hair.

Once again, she shook her head, gritting her jaw against the sudden sickness rolling from her. Not sick from a malady but sick to the stomach with hate and disgust.

What did he say to her?

What happened at Hawksridge with the dice?

Cut whispered harder, his voice hissing like a snake. Again words were non-existent but his tone was insistent. He pointed a finger at me, his lips forming rapid threats.

Don't listen to him.

Whatever he does to me, I'll take it.

If it means you're safe, I'll do anything.

Nila looked up, her dusky skin as white as the clouds far, far above us. She studied me. Decisions fluttered then shredded. Conclusions formed then discarded with revulsion.

I sensed her battle but wanted to howl when she finally

nodded.

Don't…don't…

Whatever it is…don't.

"Fine."

Cut smiled. "Good girl."

My eyes bugged as Nila willingly spun in Cut's embrace, facing him in the cage of his embrace. Her back blocked what her hands did, but the muscles in her spine rippled beneath her clothing.

My stomach knotted as she sucked in a breath; her hands moved to Cut's belt.

No. Fuck, no.

I tripled my efforts, my head roaring, my ribs screaming.

I growled and grunted and groaned. I sounded like a wild beast fighting for its life.

No!

Her elbows moved as her fingers flew over his belt and fly, undoing both effortlessly. I hated her skills with zippers and buttons. I hated her gorgeous hands and strong fingers and how they disappeared into Cut's trousers.

My voice garbled around the gag, swearing in every dialect as Nila swallowed a moan and touched my father where she should never have to touch.

Cut's eyes darkened as her hand wrapped around him.

My gut clenched, appalled and outraged he'd forced her to do something so wrong.

"Good girl," he murmured as her hand worked up and down. I didn't need to see what happened to have foul images splash across my mind. She touched him. She fucking stroked my father's cock.

The chair creaked and splintered as I shook—fighting, *fighting* against the ropes.

Nila stiffened as Cut whispered loud enough for me to hear. "That's it. Make me hard. The drugs from last night might've left your system, but I'll make you scream while you pay my part of the Third Debt."

Fuck, he was going to rape her in front of me?

He was going to emasculate me and kill me all over again by stripping Nila of her rights as a woman.

I won't.

She can't.

Throwing myself to the side, the chair legs buckled. Gravity latched on, slamming me sideways to the floor. Pain radiated through my shoulder, but I didn't care. My feet kicked, trying to unravel the rope from around my ankles. I stretched, slowly inching the twine down the chair legs.

I gave everything I had.

I ignored the splitting headache. I forced bruised muscles to gather power beyond normal limits. I turned rogue as Nila continued to stroke Cut.

Stop!

Don't touch him.

Cut smiled, wrapping one arm around Nila as she did what he commanded. But his eyes never left mine. They gleamed with triumph. Knowing this would break me worse than any bullet, better than any guillotine.

Soil smeared against my cheek as I rolled on the floor, doing my best to get free.

You won't get away with this, you bastard!

Flashbacks of Emma, Nila's mother, being in Cut's embrace merged with the present. She'd tolerated my father. She'd played him better than he knew. But I'd known all along her true thoughts. I'd felt her repellent dislike for him, even while she smiled affectionately and let Cut believe she was in love with him.

She'd done what Nila had attempted to do; only Nila fell in love with me. Emma never fell in love with Cut. And that'd only layered to his fundamental issue.

No one loved him. No one cared.

People respected and feared him, but it wasn't the same as being completely devoted through affection. And he knew that.

Nila cried silently as her hand worked harder. What had he

threatened? Why had she agreed to touch him?

I knew Nila. It wouldn't have been anything toward her. Her own pain she faced far too easily. No, he would've threatened me—even though he'd said I wouldn't be used in this debt. Bastard. Utter fucking *bastard*.

Nila!

The shout warped unintelligently around the gag as Cut dropped his face into the crook of her neck and inhaled.

Her shoulders quaked; tears making her tremble and shake.

I would've killed countless innocent people if only I had the power to stand and shove a dagger into Cut's heart.

Tears stung my eyes at being so fucking helpless.

Cut brushed aside Nila's hair, kissing the diamond collar. "God, that feels good. I hope you're wet for me, Weaver. Because I can't take much more of your teasing."

Everything changed.

Nila's hand ceased stroking. Her shoulders stopped quaking. And the room turned stagnant with possibility.

"I—I can't—" Ripping her hand from his trousers, she shoved him hard. "I won't!"

Cut wobbled from her push, his legs spread and jeans undone. The shadow of his erection tightened the fabric. His voice was blackness personified. "Think wisely, my dear. Are you sure?"

Nila nodded, frantically wiping her right hand on her leggings. "I won't. I won't grant you pleasure. No matter what you say. I won't!"

Storm clouds covered Cut's face. He lowered his jaw, glaring at her beneath his brow. "Have it your way." Marching toward her, he grabbed her wrist. "This way, please."

Nila looked over her shoulder. Her eyes widened, taking in my change of sitting upright to lying on the floor. Her features contorted with sorrow and guilt. *I'm sorry.*

I shook my head, dispelling ancient dust. *Never. There's nothing to be—*

Cut forced her to turn, stealing our private moment.

Her feet stumbled as he threw her against the table at the perimeter of the room. Yanking out a chair, he shoved her into it. "Sit."

She breathed hard, red spots of fear and fury on her cheeks. "Cut...please, whatever you're about to do—don't. *Please.*"

"You're getting repetitive, Ms. Weaver." With an angry swipe, Cut shoved the paraphernalia the mine workers had brought in and cleared a spot on the dirty table.

His hands shook as he rearranged his cock and zipped his jeans. His belt buckle clanked as he fumbled to do it up. "You could've paid the Third Debt without pain. I wouldn't have hurt you. I would've even granted you pleasure."

Nila spat on the floor. "Pleasure? Rape would never be pleasure. Your touch is grotesque."

I sucked in useless air through my nose. Her strength astounded me but also pissed me off. Answering back would only deliver worse things. As much as it would've butchered me to witness the love of my life submit to my father, watching this...whatever this was...would be worse.

At least Nila would be intact.

You don't believe that.

Her strength came from answering back and standing up for herself. If she let Cut willingly strip her of sexual rights and permit him to take her...I doubt her mind would remain so rebellious and untouchable.

Christ, I'm so sorry, Nila.

I wriggled on the floor, trying to get closer, doing my best to get free. Every inch of my body worked against me, slowly draining with every sordid breath.

Cut panted hard as he brushed back his hair, centring himself. "Give me your arm."

Nila froze. "What? No? I won't touch you again."

"I didn't ask for your *hand*, Nila. I asked for your arm."

She slowly shook her head, crossing her arms defiantly.

"You ask and I deny. No, you may not have my arm."

"You're wrong. I didn't ask to begin with. I said *give*."
Cut's anger rose to the surface. I was surprised he'd let Nila's outbursts last as long as he had. No matter how he would deny it, Cut had feelings for Nila. Feelings he still nursed for her mother. He wanted her. He wanted to keep her. But it fucking killed him that the daughter fell in love with his son when the mother cursed him to hell the day he took her life.

He'd given her a choice...

My mind skipped back to the private conversation I hadn't meant to overhear. A week before the Final Debt with Emma, Cut had admitted to his Weaver prisoner he loved her too much to kill her. He wanted more from her. More time. More togetherness. He was willing to hold off the Final Debt indefinitely if she agreed to be his completely.

Marry him.

Submit to him whenever he desired.

His one condition for her life—she was forbidden from seeing Tex or her children ever again.

It was a testament of Emma's love for her family and husband that she turned him down and chose death instead.

"For fuck's sake, give me your bloody arm." Cut lashed out; snatching Nila's arms and breaking the hold she'd formed. She struggled but was no match for Cut's strength.

Slamming her forearm on the table, he growled, "Did you listen to the part of the story about smuggling diamonds?"

Nila wriggled in Cut's possession, doing her best to take her imprisoned arm back. "Yes. I listened."

"In that case, you'll understand what the rest of the Fourth Debt entails."

She stopped breathing. "No...I don't..."

He chuckled, fighting her tugging, keeping her arm against the table. "Yes, you do." Holding her down with one hand, he reached to the side with the other. Plucking a narrow stick from its resting place, he pressed it against her mouth. "Open wide."

Her face arched away from the offer. "What? No."

Cut pinched her arm. The shock stole her attention, parting her lips. Taking advantage, he slipped the stick inside her mouth so the ends stuck out either side of her cheeks. She looked as if she'd been bridled.

Turning her head to spit it out, Cut held the stick in place. "Ah, ah, ah. I wouldn't do that if I were you."

Her eyes glared daggers.

"Bite down." Cut slowly removed his hand, daring her to dispel it.

Nila paused, the stick remaining lodged in her teeth. Her eyebrow rose with questions as Cut slowly picked up a black rubber mallet. A type of mallet used for hitting unwilling pieces of timber or coaxing nails into holes. A hammer that would bring untold pain.

She sucked in air around the stick, her struggles renewing. "No!" Her voice wavered around the obstruction.

"I told you, bite down." His fingers latched tighter around the mallet. "This will hurt."

No!

My heart lurched as I twisted and bucked. "Stwrop!" I despised not being able to move, to talk, to shout, to help. "Nwoooo!"

Nila.

Fuck, I'm so sorry.

"What—what's—" Nila couldn't tear her eyes away from the mallet. Her entire body went on lockdown. "Cut...don't." The stick remained in her teeth, her tongue forming words with care.

His eyes glinted. "When William's reputation of priceless diamonds made its way around the city, more and more people tried to rob him. Opportunists and pirates all wanted a piece of his good fortune even when he'd paid so much for it. Thieves. Cheapskates. They all deserved to hang."

Nila whimpered, fighting his hold as Cut braced his legs, preparing to deliver the Fourth Debt.

My heart bucked, smashing against bruised ribs, leaping

into the throbs inside my head. From my angle on the floor, the world tilted sideways, my mind straining to stay with her, to find a way free.

"William constantly had to come up with new ways to smuggle his cargo into the country. He started with the obvious: the orifices of his men. The switch and ruse. The fake packaging ploy. But after time, each one would fail as word got out of the latest scam.

"Even in the last few decades, we suffered our own setbacks. Our smuggling mules would swallow the diamonds or wrap small quantities around their stomach and legs, and fly in sweating guilt and terror—guaranteed to have the shipment ceased upon arrival. Or they'd shove them in arseholes and pussies but that's become too widely used by drug traffickers and with tighter border security, not practical. So…we came up with a new plan."

His voice thickened. "Know how we solved this problem?"

Nila shook her head, black hair sticking to sweaty cheeks, tears cascading in streams.

"Sewing into flesh."

She sucked in a horrified breath, the air whistling around her stick.

Cut frowned. "The sewing was rather barbaric and didn't have such satisfactory results. A doctor would cut a mule in the least invasive place, insert a few packets of diamonds, and sew them back up. Once the traveller arrived at their destination, the wound was reopened, diamonds removed, and their sum paid. However, the risk of infection and hospitalisation was too high.

"So…we came up with a better idea."

He twisted his wrist, dragging Nila's attention back to the black mallet in his fist. "We don't cut anymore, we break. We offer legitimate disabilities while using the fracture as the perfect alibi." He grinned. "Understand what I'm saying, Nila?"

Shit.

I gave everything I had left. My wrists soaked with blood as I fought the rope. My back splintered with every wriggle. I couldn't watch. I couldn't prevent what Cut would do. I couldn't do a thing as he broke her and dressed her in diamonds.

I yelled profanity, choking on the gag. I wanted to talk to her. Comfort her. I didn't want to fail her all over again.

Shock electrocuted her system. She spat out the stick even though she'd need it to ride the upcoming pain. "You can't be serious."

"I'm deadly serious." Cut's smile twisted his face into horror. "You had the choice to make me hard and deliver pleasure with your right hand. You had my cock in your fingers, your future in your grasp, yet you threw it in my fucking face. Well, your right arm will pay, Nila. It now has a different task."

Nila fought harder, scratching at Cut's hold with her free hand. "No, let me go. Let me—"

"You really should've bit down like I told you. Too late now." Cut didn't soften, raising the mallet above his head. "Do you repent? Do you take ownership of your family's sins and agree to pay the debt?"

"No! Hell no!"

"Wrong answer." Cut prepared to strike.

"No. Wait!"

His jaw clenched.

"Stop, please!"

"With or without your ownership, I won't stop."

His gaze glowed.

His arm sailed down.

The mallet became a black boulder of agony.

"This is going to hurt."

Nila

THE MALLET SOARED downward.
No!
The whistle of wind heralded imminent agony.
Please!
The small cry was my soul escaping.
Don't!
The silent scream from Jethro was my undoing.

* * *

The crack of impact.
Pain.
The loud splinter of skeleton giving way.
Torture.
The wave of sickness as mallet defeated bone.
Torment.
The cloud of unconsciousness that numbed everything.

* * *

The room spun and tilted.
I'm crippled.
The agony swelled and crested.
I'm mutilated.
The mallet left my burning broken bone, resting innocuously beside my wrist like a fallen executioner.

I'm in pieces.
I'm in splinters.
I'm broken.
I threw up.

* * *

There were two worlds.

The one where I'd existed only moments ago—intact, whole, afraid but complete.

And now, this new one. The one where I shook with excruciating pain…was in pieces…destroyed.

A delayed scream fell from my lips as I cradled my shattered forearm.

I screamed

and screamed

and *screamed.*

It hurt.

God, how it hurt.

I'd broken pieces of myself in the past. How could I not living a life with vertigo? But I'd never felt it coming. Never seen the pain unfolding. Never heard the agony delivered.

I moaned, battling wave after wave of deep throbbing pain.

Please…make it stop!

Gentle arms cradled me, embracing me, fingers wiping tears from my cheeks. "Told you it would hurt," Cut murmured.

I couldn't look at him. I couldn't breathe around him. I couldn't stay alive in a world where he existed.

No!

Shying away from his touch, I bit my lip hard enough to bleed. My intact fingers wrapped around my broken arm, soothing the burn, wanting to erase the damage. The flesh turned red and swollen, bloating with pain. It wasn't disfigured or deformed but the hot swell hinted he'd done the damage he'd intended.

He broke it.

He hurt me.
He did this!

Noises clanked beside me.

I didn't look. I let my hair curtain the outside terrors. I didn't glance at Jethro. I didn't blink. I didn't care.

All I cared about was nursing my battered body and surfing the tsunami of suffering.

Time ticked onward, dragging me further into this new world where I hugged a broken limb. He broke me. He struck me. And all for what? So he could use the wound as a suitcase for his disgusting diamonds.

"Give it to me, please."

Cut's voice cut through my horror.

I curled tighter around my injury. "Fuck you." Tears shot to my eyes. Not again. *Please, not again.* I couldn't handle that pain twice.

I should've agreed to the hand job. I should've got on my knees and performed the blow-job he'd commanded. I should've let him fuck me—even if it meant Jethro would forever remember my willingness to be raped.

That was what Cut whispered, what he'd promised. He'd vowed I would enjoy it. That if I gladly made him hard, if I obediently removed my clothing and spread my legs, he would make me come, moan, beg for more.

I didn't believe him. How could I ever do that? How could I ever betray myself in such a way? But I couldn't trust he wouldn't play my body better than I could control it. I couldn't know if the drug-liquor had left my system entirely, and I wouldn't give in. My options had been submit and let Jethro leave Africa unhurt and alive. Or not agree and watch Cut rip him apart once he'd raped me anyway.

What good were options when they only offered one conclusion?

I'm sorry, Jethro.

He'd come to my rescue only to find Daniel had touched me and I'd touched his father. What a fucked-up situation to be in.

Cut leaned against the table, his fingers tucking my hair behind my ear. "It's a simple fracture, Nila. You should be thankful I didn't slice you open and insert my diamonds directly into your bloodstream." His touch dropped, tracing an outline on my wrist. "You've kept all limbs. You've retained your precious body. This is merely a means to the final end."

I looked up, shaking with anger. The pain plaited with rage as I stared him down. "One day, someone will do to you what you've done to others. Someday, your crimes will come back to visit you, and I hope I'm there to tell you to be *thankful*."

Cut scowled. "If that day ever comes, Ms. Weaver, I can safely say you will not be in attendance." Holding out his hand, he snapped, "Now, don't make me ask again. Give me your arm."

I twisted my body away, hugging my broken limb. "No."

"I'm not going to hurt you."

"You already did."

"What does that tell you?"

I didn't reply.

He growled, "It tells you I'll rectify the pain I've caused. I have no doubt after each debt Jethro would've tended to you. Am I right? He would've fixed his wrongs and ensured you were healthy to continue."

My mouth fell open. "You're sick."

I couldn't stop my eyes flying to Jethro. In my haze of pain, I hadn't given him attention. I hadn't seen him thrashing on the floor, desperately trying to get free. I hadn't witnessed him covering himself in mine dust, furious tears tracking mud down his cheeks.

Oh, Kite.

My heart hurt almost as much as my arm.

Cut pointed to the equipment on the table. "Open your eyes, Nila. What do you think this stuff is?"

Despite myself, I looked closer. Before, the items made no sense...now, they began to.

Gauze, water, padding, and medical packets with jargon stating their contents as plaster strips.

A cast.

He's going to make you a cast.

I sniffed, fighting back another wash of agony. "If you're honestly going to set my arm, I want painkillers first."

I expected a scoff and refusal. But Cut merely nodded and opened a small plastic case. Popping out two tablets from a blister foil, he handed them to me with a bottle of water. "They're codeine. You're not allergic, are you?"

I bared my teeth. "Why? You going to care if I have a reaction?"

He frowned. "Despite what I've just done, I want you to remain well. We have a long journey ahead of us, and your pain needs to be managed accordingly—minus any allergies."

I swallowed my fear. "Long journey?"

Cut nodded as I threw the tablets into my mouth and drank. The water slipped down my parched throat like liquid life. I hadn't eaten or drunk in so long. *Too long.* The water splashed in my stomach, reminding me how empty it was.

"I didn't break your arm for fun, Nila." Cut shoved away the plastic container, ripping open a packet of plaster strips a moment later. "I told you. We smuggle diamonds. We're going home, and I want to take a few high-quality stones with me. They're larger than normal and rare. I want to keep them with me at all times."

"With *you* at all times? Me, you mean?" Another wave of pain made me hiss.

Cut dumped the plaster into the fresh bucket of water. Steam gently rose from the surface.

"Yes, you." He busied himself with opening packets and preparing to set my broken bone. I didn't know what to think. He'd pre-empted this. He'd sat down logically, cool-headedly, and planned to break my arm then gathered enough supplies to fix it in the same location.

Who does that?

The answer dripped with sarcasm. *A Hawk.*

Once his supplies were in order and the plaster reaction had ceased, Cut held up a plastic splint. Three sides, smooth and well formed, with little compartments hidden where my arm would rest.

"Now you know I'm not going to hurt you, will you give me your arm?"

I hugged my wrist, looking at Jethro rejected in the dirt. "Let him go."

Cut looked over his shoulder before glancing back. "No. Now, give me your arm."

Shakes stole my body, shock trying to erase everything that'd happened. "Please, at least untie him."

Jethro looked in pain, squashed on his side. I dreaded to think how he coped with my internal and external screams when Cut broke my arm.

Had he felt it?

Had he lived through it like Vaughn used to whenever I fell and hurt myself?

Shit, Vaughn.

He always knew when I'd broken something. Twin intuition. Would he ache in his right arm in sympathy? Would he terrorize England trying to find me, or worse, stampede Hawksridge Hall trying to save me?

Cut laughed. "Why? So he can stupidly attack me and get himself re-killed in the process?" He rolled his eyes.

It was such a juvenile, simple thing to do that it sent chills scattering down my spine.

His temper thickened. "I won't ask again, Nila. Arm. Now."

The painkillers already siphoned into my blood thanks to no food delaying the absorption. I had no other choice but to let Cut fix me.

Not that there was any fixing me. Not after the past six months.

Gingerly, breathing hard through my nose and hissing

through my teeth, I gently laid my arm in the three-sided cast.

Cut tutted. "No, not in there. Not yet." Slipping it free, he opened the opaque ziplock bag and pulled out multiple black velvet pouches. Holding one up, he smiled. "In each of these parcels rests over one million pounds worth of stones—total of five million." His eyes landed on my diamond collar. "Almost as priceless as the gems around your neck."

Meticulously, he slipped the parcels into the sections cut out of the plastic splint. "They'll be hidden. They're not metallic, so they won't set off the alarm, and they won't be inside you, so they won't show up on the body scanners."

Alarms?

Body scanners?

He's going to fly me home and force me to lie to airport security.

A terrified lump lodged in my throat. "They'll catch me."

Cut shook his head. "I have full belief you'll be fine. The nervous sweats will be blamed on the new break. The waxy pallor of your cheeks on overwhelming pain. They might ask you questions, but they won't find anything untoward with the cast. You'll see."

Tears prickled my eyes at the trials I still faced. My lips twisted with hate. "You could've just put me in a fake cast. No one would know the difference."

Cut cupped my face, holding me firm. "Wrong. People can tell. Liars are spotted easily in airports. And besides, we'll have an extra arsenal that will prove our tale isn't false."

I ripped out of his hold, gasping at more pain. "What's that?"

Cut inspected inside the bucket, lifting out the plaster strips to rest in a plastic tray. "We'll have x-rays stating your accident, evidence of the fracture, and time and date."

My eyes widened. "How?" I scoffed at the dirty cave. "You're telling me you have a state of the art x-ray machine down here, too?" A half-crazed, half-diabolical laugh escaped me. "Not only a diamond smuggler but doctor, biker president, and doting father as well. Is there anything you can't do?"

Cut narrowed his eyes. "Careful, Nila. Just because you're in pain, it doesn't mean I can't discipline you. I demand respect at all times. You'd do well to remember that while we travel home together. When you go through security, I'll be with you. When you board and land, I'll be beside you. You won't be free and you'd be wise to hold your tongue." He pointed a finger at Jethro. "Otherwise, he doesn't live like I promised. Obey me, and he survives. Pull something stupid and he dies." He shrugged. "Stupidly simple."

Stupidly simple?

How about I kill you on the plane?

That would be stupid as I'd end up in jail for the rest of my life. But so simple because Cut would no longer be breathing.

I laughed sarcastically. "Sounds as if you've thought of everything."

His forehead furrowed, but he didn't respond. Instead, he ignored me in favour of inserting the diamond packets and layering soft padding over the compartments. Even if airport security shone a light or poked a stick in my cast, they wouldn't find the stones.

Cut held up the tampered cast. "*Now* you can place your arm inside."

My heart raced, but I did as I was told, breathing a sigh of relief as the gentle cushioning helped soothe some of the pain.

Cut grinned. "See, I told you I'd make it right."

My voice transformed into scissors, cutting him into pieces. "Just because you're tending to me now doesn't mean I forgive you for before."

Jethro groaned, dragging my attention to him. His beautiful golden eyes were dull and anger-filled. Love linked us together, forged stronger despite such adversity.

He'd proposed to me.

I'd say yes to him.

Yet, horribly, time was running out.

Once Cut had immobilized my injury, I had no doubt we

wouldn't be in Africa much longer. He would want to get home. He would want to finish whatever else he'd planned.

Will he carry out the Final Debt before he partakes in the Third?

I shuddered. How wrong was it that I hoped he would kill me instead of rape me? I should value my life over anything my body was subjected to. But having Cut inside me wouldn't just be physical; it would be mental and spiritual, too. It would mess me up completely knowing he'd been with my mother and killed her. Then done the same with me.

I'll kill him before that happens.

The memory of stabbing Daniel in the heart granted me a much-needed boost. I'd been terrified of him. Yet, I'd won. I could do the same with Cut.

Cut pressed down on my arm, making me cry out with pain. I flinched, trying to pull away. "Stop!"

His strong fingers ceased tormenting me. "Just making sure you're wedged comfortably."

"Bastard." The curse fell beneath my breath.

If Cut heard me, he didn't retaliate.

Letting me go, he layered another lot of padding on top of my arm, followed by the gauze. He wrapped it around and around, binding my arm into its new prison. Once it was secure, he placed surgical gloves on his fingers, and pulled out a strip of plaster from the drying tray.

"Don't move."

I didn't respond as he industriously wrapped warm, wet plaster around my broken limb. The chemical reaction offered hot comfort to the throbbing ache, and I relaxed a little as the painkillers worked their magic.

It didn't take long. In the past, the doctors would wrap three or four layers of plaster around my cast, ensuring no way could I break or damage myself further. However, Cut only wrapped two layers, finishing off the top with a gauze sleeve, smoothing the plaster with wet fingers.

"There. Don't twist or move your arm for sixty minutes while it hardens."

I wanted to laugh. He knew how to apply basic medical help. But his bedside manner was atrocious. No doctor had ever caused his patient's injury in the first place.

Sitting upright after leaning forward for Cut to work on my cast, I held it away from me to dry but wanted to hug it close. For some reason, a hug—even from me—helped the pain fade.

My eyes soared to Jethro. His face was red and furious; his eyes glassy with sorrow.

I'm fine.

You're not.

I'll live.

You better.

I smiled at the last silent message. I would live because I deserved to. Jethro, too. We would find each other again—even with imminent separation about to tear us apart.

Washing his hands in a fresh bucket of water, Cut smiled at his handiwork. "All done." His eyes glinted. "How does it feel to be a millionaire with so many diamonds against your skin?"

I tapped the collar condescendingly. "Like I've felt ever since Jethro put the Weaver Wailer on me."

I looked at Jethro shooting an apology. *I didn't mean that in a bad way.*

He squeezed his eyes, flinching against the memories of our fucked-up beginning.

Cut nodded. "That's a fair comment. You've worn more diamonds than most Hawks in their lifetimes." He cocked his head at Jethro. "Did you notice Kite's lapel pin? That two carat diamond was handed down for generations. I gave it to him on his sixteenth birthday when he assured me he had his condition under tight control. I wanted nothing more than to believe him." His voice softened. "I know you can't comprehend it, but I do love my son, Nila. More than you'll know."

I snorted. "Did you love Kes when you shot him? Or Daniel when you let him grow up believing he was an unwanted mistake?"

Cut froze. "What do you know about that?"

Unwittingly, I handed weight to my previous lie. "I told you. We shared the night together. He shared a little of his past. He opened up to me because I gave him what he needed."

Jethro didn't move on the floor.

For the first time, Cut paused. His eyes narrowed as his brain mulled over my answer. He looked unsure...contemplating it might be the truth, after all.

I doubted he would ever find Daniel's remains. I might get away with his murder, all thanks to a hunting party of lionesses.

I never knew nature can be such a competent alias.

"Regardless, when Daniel is found, I'll learn the truth and shall decide on your punishment." Cut dried his hands and ran both through his white hair. "Now the Fourth Debt has been paid, it's time for us to depart."

Striding across the cave, he squatted by Jethro and swatted his son's dirty cheek. "Make yourself at home. I'll give the staff instructions to release you once we've been at Hawksridge for a few days and there's no way for you to interfere." Standing, he smiled at me. "All you have to do, Nila, is get through security with my diamonds still in your possession and your lover will remain alive. That's not too much to ask, is it?"

I slid off the chair, wobbling a little with vertigo and residual pain.

Moving toward Jethro, I ached to hug him, kiss him, tell him I loved him and always would. But Cut stopped me half way, planting a stern hand on my breastbone. "No. Say your goodbyes from a distance."

I shook my head. "Why can't I touch him? What harm can it do?"

Cut clenched his jaw. "More harm than I'd like."

"You know I have no weapons to give him." My temper surged. "You know I have a broken arm and am suffering a serious case of shock. Let me say a proper goodbye. You *owe* me that."

Cut breathed hard, preventing my path. But slowly, he nodded. "Fine."

The minute he'd cleared my trajectory, I rushed forward and landed on my knees. My good hand tugged at the awful duct tape around Jethro's mouth. "Breathe." That was all the warning I gave him.

With a quick rip, I tore the stickiness away from his five o' clock shadow and yanked out the disgusting gag.

He hacked and spluttered, sucking in a noisy breath.

Cut stomped forward, towering over me. "Nila fucking Weaver—"

I glared at him, balling the sodden gag and throwing it at his face. My left arm never had strong coordination, and the toss ended up soaring past his cheek. "He can barely breathe. Shut up! Letting him talk won't change things, you monster."

"Needle—" Jethro coughed, spittle landing on his chin.

Needle.

The name I'd asked him to call me so many months ago when I didn't know he was Kite007. Tears sprang to my eyes. "I'm here."

I wished I could sit him upright, but he'd broken the chair and without cutting the ropes, I couldn't help him.

God, I hate this. All of this.

Jethro smiled, grimacing with pain. "Fuck, Nila, I'm—"

I placed a shaking finger over his dried lips. "Don't. I know."

We shared an endless look, weighted with past and present. The unsaid words sank into my soul like a heavy anchor, lodging itself in my heart forever.

Bending over him, I brushed my lips against his temple. His bloody temple from the car crash. How badly was he injured? His forehead still burned from his fever and the gunshot wound on his side hadn't scabbed.

He needs help. And fast.

Glancing at Cut, I begged, "Please, bring him with us. He needs a doctor."

Cut crossed his arms. "He'll stay here until I say."

"But—"

"No fucking buts." Holding out his hand, Cut snapped, "You've said goodbye. Time to go."

"No!"

Cut towered higher. "The longer you deny what will happen—regardless of your willingness—the longer Jethro has to go without medical help." He cocked his head. "Does that encourage you now? Knowing you have the power to get him much-needed attention by behaving?"

I hated I had the power to save the man I loved by obeying the man I hated.

Gritting my teeth, I looked down at Jethro one last time. "I have to go."

He shook his head, his lungs rattling and wet. "No."

"I love you, Kite."

His eyes glossed with fear. "Nila...don't. This isn't the end. I don't care what he says. I'm coming after you. I'll stop the Final Debt. I promise." He shook hard in his binds. "I fucking promise, I'll stop it. You're mine. I won't let the Debt Inheritance have you. I won't!"

His pouring unhappiness and despair cracked my heart. I couldn't let him drain himself of whatever reserves he had left. Cupping his cheek with my good hand, I guided his face to mine.

I never closed my eyes and neither did he as I kissed him.

His lips parted, his tongue threaded with mine, and we agreed he would fight for me. He would chase me. And who knew, maybe he would save me one last time.

Cut shattered our moment, yanking me away from Jethro and dragging me toward the exit. My arm bellowed, but it was nothing compared to the internal shattering at leaving Jethro behind.

At the door, Cut pulled me closer and I staggered in grey imbalance, imprinting Jethro on my soul forever.

His chin cocked, keeping me in his sights for as long as he

could. "Don't give up, Nila. It's not over."

Silent tears dripped from my eyelashes as Cut shoved me out the door and separated me from my soul-mate.

The door closed behind me.

Tears fell faster.

Pain billowed thicker.

And all I could do was whisper, *"Goodbye."*

Jethro

"FUCK!"

The door closed. Nila was gone. I remained crumpled on the floor like a discarded fucking prisoner.

I'd been in worse binds.

Have I?

I liked to think I had and overcome them. That I would overcome *this*. But how?

My stomach hadn't unknotted since Cut started his creepy history lesson and worked up to the most horrendous thing I'd ever witnessed.

The slam of the mallet on the love of my life's arm. The scream as her bone broke.

I shuddered.

It won't remain the worst thing you've ever witnessed if you don't get your arse off the floor.

The Final Debt.

Jasmine had said Cut planned to carry it out before the week was finished.

The moment he returned to Hawksridge, Nila would be dead.

Ferocity spread through my veins, and for the millionth time, I wriggled and struggled, trying so fucking hard to get free.

The ropes around my ankles had slid off the chair legs, but my wrists and torso remained tight.

Think. There must be something you can do.

Forcing my breathing to calm, I glanced around the cave. The table with remnants of cast-making equipment was too far away. I might be able to shuffle with the chair attached to my body, but it would waste valuable time and energy. Besides, Cut hadn't used any sharp implements and the knife he'd utilised to slice Nila free had disappeared with him in his back pocket.

Kes.

It was times like this—when I'd fucked up and couldn't see a way free—that he'd come to my rescue. He always came. Always answered his phone if I'd had a relapse, or shared a beer with me when I needed his welcome support.

Kes was the only one I knew who could regulate and calm his emotions to the point of soothing rather than a battering ram. I didn't know how he did it but being around him was the opposite of being around others.

I miss you, brother.

The door opened.

My eyes shot to it, my heart leaping with hope.

Nila…

Only, it wasn't Nila.

Marquise stomped inside. His burly size and Black Diamond leather jacket blocked the exit as he turned and relocked the door. He didn't say a word, merely raised an eyebrow in my direction and sat in the chair Nila had when Cut broke her arm.

He. Broke. Her. Arm.

Motherfucking *bastard*.

I'd felt her pain, bewilderment, and terror as the mallet crushed her. I'd felt her fear that she wouldn't make it through airport security with the bushel of diamonds in her cast.

I wanted to tell her to scream when she boarded the plane. Let the pilots know she had contraband and ought to be detained. If she was caught, they'd hold her, possibly convict her, and she'd remain alive in prison until I could figure out a way to free her.

If she was locked up, Cut couldn't kill her, and I could hire the best attorneys to dismiss her case. I could show the entire world what my family had been up to. I could rip open the truth and finally, *finally* show what money could do.

What loyalties it could buy.

What sins it could cover up.

How happy middle-class families were duped by the few who held the wealth of the globe.

If it meant I'd go to jail, so be it.

At least my conscience would finally be clear and Nila would be alive.

And Cut would rot right beside me in an eight by eight cell, never seeing his precious Hawksridge or diamonds again.

The daydream shattered as I twisted to glare at Marquise. I couldn't get free on my own. But he could help me.

"Free me and I'll pay you two million pounds." I tugged on the ropes around my wrists, inhaling hard against the bruising binds across my chest. The car accident battered me and my vision hadn't stopped spluttering with the massive headache. I hadn't kept my promise to pay the driver who'd brought me here, and I hadn't done what I'd vowed by rescuing Nila.

This entire trip had been one big fuck up. However, I would trade ever feeling whole again, every good thing I'd ever done, if I could rewind time and stop Cut from breaking Nila's arm.

Marquise grinned. "Your grandmother has paid me far more for my loyalty." Crossing his arms, he glared. "Stop talking. I won't let you go for any amount."

"What about a title? An estate of your own? Shares in our companies?" I spat the lingering taste from my tongue thanks to the awful gag. "Everyone has a price. Name it."

Marquise inspected his ragged fingernails as if he was a

fucking king on his throne. "I'll get all of that if I remain true to Bonnie." He sniffed. "So shut the fuck up."

I exhaled heavily. For now, he wouldn't budge, but he would. I just had to find his weakness. Everyone could be bought. We'd learned that prime example through years of bribery and control.

My mind returned to Nila and Cut, keeping count of time and distance slowly separating us.

I have to get free.

A shrill tune ripped around the cave.

Marquise slouched and pulled out his phone. He stabbed the screen, holding it to his ear. "Yes?"

Silence as he listed to instructions.

"Still on the floor and tied up. Yes, will do. Got it."

He hung up, a sinister smile spreading his lips. "Looks like you should get comfortable, Hawk. Got orders not to let you up until the Prez is on a plane. And then...he wants me to give you an extra special surprise."

Of course...

I didn't expect Cut to let me survive—not after trying to kill me. He might have a sick fascination with making me survive in a world where Nila didn't exist, but he understood the moment I was free, the moment I had a chance, he would be dead.

It was only a matter of time if he let me live.

He won't let me live...

I clenched my jaw. "What's the surprise?"

I already know.

Pain and then death.

Cut wasn't overly original.

Marquise clenched his fists, showing scabbed knuckles and ropy forearms. "You'll see."

CUT GRIPPED MY unbroken arm tighter, hauling me faster through the airport.

He'd manhandled me and corralled me ever since we'd left Jethro in the mine and flew by Jeep to a small doctor's surgery on the outskirts of Gaborone.

While the African doctor nodded and smiled and arranged my arm for x-rays, Cut had washed his face and changed his clothes, discarding the dirt-smudged jeans and white shirt in favour of black slacks and shirt.

The doctor didn't remove my cast, and he didn't show me the x-rays once the decrepit machine had whirred and snapped grainy pictures of what Cut had done to me.

Once the large black and white images were tucked safely into his briefcase, Cut allowed me five minutes to wash as best I could in the surgery's small bathroom. The blood from Daniel and the car accident siphoned down the plug hole, revealing scratches and bruises in their colourful glory.

I had no makeup to cover the marks and no choice but to change into whatever clothing Cut had grabbed from my suitcase on the way out from *Almasi Kipanga.*

Unfortunately, he hadn't selected any of the clothing I'd artistically amended, leaving me without scalpels or knitting needles, leaving me vulnerable.

The one good thing about the doctor's surgery was the sweet-eyed man gave me a homemade honey muesli bar— either noticing the way I ogled his sandwich sitting on his desk as he x-rayed me or the wobbles of weakness as Cut dragged me outside.

I didn't think much of his practice, considering he didn't check if my arm was set correctly, or there was nothing majorly damaged inside, but I inhaled the food offering before Cut could snatch it away.

With Cut's timeline, he envisioned my head in a basket within a few days. Who cared if my arm was set wrong? It wouldn't be needed much longer.

That's what you fear.

But it isn't what will happen.

I curled my fingers, testing the pain level of the break. My grip was weak, and it burned to move, but I still had mobility. My fingers still worked, which I was thankful for. I couldn't stomach the thought of never being able to sew again or hold intricate needles and lace.

Cut had stolen so much—he couldn't steal my entire livelihood and skill, too.

"Hurry up." Cut pulled harder.

I staggered beside him, breathing hard as every footstep jarred my aching arm. The pain resonated beneath muscle and skin, a hot discomfort stripping me of energy.

The moment we'd arrived at the airport, Cut had abandoned the Jeep in a long-term car park and only bothered to carry his briefcase. At the time, I wondered if we'd be questioned for suspicious behaviour travelling long-haul with no luggage. But I'd rolled my eyes and hid my snort.

This was Cut Hawk.

This part of Africa *belonged* to him—no doubt the airport security would belong to him, too.

"For God's sake, Weaver." Cut slowed, forcing my half-trotting, half-lagging footsteps to fall in line with his. "We'll miss the plane."

Fresh throbs brought scratchy tears to my eyes.

"I want to miss the plane. I want to go back for Jethro."

The entire travel I couldn't stop thinking of Kite. Of him bleeding and feverish tied to a chair. Of him having no choice but to watch as I was taken.

The muesli bar I'd eaten roiled in my stomach. "You'll keep him alive…won't you? You'll keep your promise not to hurt him."

Cut smiled coyly. "I wouldn't worry your pretty head about it. Soon, trivial things like that won't matter to you."

The veiled hint at my death should terrify me. I should fight and scream and act like a terrorist to prevent boarding the plane. But the fear of interrogation and imprisonment kept me silent.

Cut was insane, but there was only one of him. One beating heart to stab. One life to extinguish. If the police took me, I wouldn't know who or how to fight. I'd be alone.

Yes, but you might stay alive.

Perhaps in England I would cause a fuss. But not here. I didn't trust the Hawk's power in Africa. Cut might have the means to murder me even in the custody of the law. Buy a cop—arrange a convenient suicide in my cell.

No, I'll wait.

I would return to England, to my home, to a land I knew and could gamble my life with better odds.

Checking us in, Cut never let me go as the agent handed over our passports and boarding passes. Dark-skinned security and airport personnel didn't look our way as Cut guided me roughly through customs and immigration to the baggage x-ray.

The closer we got to the metal detector, the more my heart galloped.

Don't think about the diamonds.

Cut whispered in my ear, his fingers digging into my bicep. "If you bring unwanted attention or do anything stupid, I've given Marquise strict orders to make Jethro pay."

I shivered, joining the queue to pass through the detector.

My heart permanently relocated into my mouth as my turn fast approached and I held my broken arm protectively. I didn't know if I hugged it for the pain or the illegal diamonds. Either way, the flush and wax of my skin played right into Cut's masquerade that I was under the weather from agony rather than smuggling.

The woman officer smiled, waving me forward. "Come through, ma'am."

I shuffled through the arch, cringing as it beeped.

"Stand there." The woman came closer, waving her wand over my front and back.

I squeezed my eyes, expecting her to detain me. Terrified she'd find the millions of pounds worth of diamonds and sentence me to death by hanging.

What would be better? Hanging or guillotine?

What kind of morbid thought is that?

Cut stepped through without setting off the alarm and gave me a smirk as he collected his briefcase off the x-ray belt. He stood close by, not interfering as the woman did one more pass and the wand failed to beep.

She dropped her arm, waving for me to go. "Have a nice flight."

"Uh—uh, thanks." I scurried forward, sweat dripping down my spine with nerves. An itch developed on my forearm beneath the cast, slowly driving me mad as Cut placed his hand on the small of my back and guided me into the departure lounge.

"See, wasn't so bad, was it?" He spoke quietly, not making eye contact as we dodged travel-weary passengers.

My uninjured hand ached from holding the cast. I wished I could keep it close to me but not have to hold it. Wait...

That was what was missing.

I stopped in the centre of the duty-free shop we'd cut through. "A sling. I need a sling."

Cut frowned. "What?"

I held up my arm. "It hurts. I need to keep it close so it doesn't bump or dangle, but my other shoulder is sore from the car accident. I need a sling."

When his lips curled with dismissal, I rushed, "Besides, a sling will only add evidence to the break. It doesn't have to be much. Just something to give me some relief."

Cut scowled, his throat working as he swallowed. "Fine." Storming toward a bookshop, he quickly bought me a canvas tote bag and asked the sales clerk to cut it straight down the centre.

Guiding me from the store, he quickly cradled my arm with the sliced tote and knotted the handles around my side and shoulder, creating an imperfect but practical sling. The ease and quickness in which he'd done such a tender thing made me freeze.

If I was honest, I hadn't expected him to listen, let alone *help* me.

"You—you—" I looked away, hating him but grateful. "Thank you."

Cut stiffened, his golden eyes meeting mine. "I wouldn't thank me, Ms. Weaver. You know I didn't do it out of concern for your well-being."

Now that my other hand was free, I pushed hair out of my eyes and relaxed a little. "No, but you can't hide there's more to you than just a crazy man hell-bent on ruling everyone."

He smirked, the skin by his eyes crinkling. "You might have figured out Daniel, but you'll never figure me out, so don't bother." Stepping closer, we formed a little island as flowing passengers darted around us. The fear for Jethro and the nervousness in my gut layered my aching muscles, but I didn't move back. I didn't show a weakness that Cut's proximity irked and irritated.

His gaze fell to my lips. "You're strong, Nila. I'll give you that. You remind me so much of Emma that it's sometimes hard to remember you aren't mine. That you aren't *her*. You might think it would be a good thing for me to think of you kindly, but it wouldn't, believe me." He lowered his voice. "Your mother ripped out my heart before I cut off her head. And nothing will give me more pleasure than doing the same to Jethro and you."

My lungs stuck together, unable to gather oxygen.

Cut cocked his head, smiling at my dumbfoundedness. "Why does that continue to shock you? Why do you, even now, still look for the good in others?" Patting my hand, he looped his fingers through mine and pulled me back into motion. "You should know by now no one is what they say they are, and everyone deserves to pay for something. People have been covering up or blaming their mistakes on others for centuries. I take control of mine. I do the best I can to better myself and I refuse to let you or anyone else stand in my way."

I didn't speak—what could I say to that?

We moved through the large departure gate, heading toward the plane.

Cut smiled as he pulled out our documentation for the gate staff. His gaze met mine. "This is the easy part." Handing over the boarding passes, Cut guided me down the air bridge, keeping me close to him, controlling me at all times. "It's the stress of landing that's the hard part."

Landing.

English security.

Maximum penalties for lies and incorrect declarations.

Marching onto the plane, we moved down the aisle, through first class, through business, right into the dregs of economy.

Cut pushed me into a row with a window and aisle seat. "Sit."

I sat.

Stretching, he placed his briefcase in the overhead lockers before sitting smoothly and unhurriedly beside me.

The moment he settled, I asked, "Why a commercial airline? Why not the private jet we flew in on?"

"Why do you think? Because the private plane would be

far too easy. This way is much harder."

My eyes widened. "Harder?"

"Harder on you." His voice lowered into a threat. "This way you have to sit with hundreds of strangers, wondering if they suspect you. You'll have to hide your fear when we land and lie through your teeth when they question you. The stress of being watched, of being surrounded by countless people, of having to lie—it's to show you how hard it is to transport a secret. You'll value the cost so much more."

Reclining, his long legs spread out in front of him. "You'll learn what it's like to protect something so precious by any means necessary."

I swallowed. "You forget I don't care about your diamonds. I don't care if they find them."

His eyes narrowed. "It's not the diamonds I'm talking about, Nila. It's my firstborn rotting in *Almasi Kipanga* watched over by Marquise. You fail, and he dies in the most horrifying ways. You win, he lives even when you die. It's a fair trade—don't you think?"

I bit my lip against the torrent of hate and helplessness.

I couldn't reply. It would be an explosion of retorts and profanity.

Reaching between our wedged hips, he yanked out one end of my seatbelt. "Now, buckle up, Nila. You can never be too safe."

"I'll never be safe as long as you're alive."

I will kill you.

I'll find a way.

His eyes darkened. "Careful."

"Why are you doing this?"

Cut smiled, looking the perfect distinguished gentleman travelling on business. "Because William Hawk smuggled his wealth numerous times. He completed his grandmother's legacy, but despite his hard work and terrible history, the king wasn't satisfied with taking half of his profits, he wanted it all."

Cut gathered tension around him, suffocating me. "So

William went one step further. He gave the king his dues, he paid taxes, indulged in bribery, and ensconced himself in the good graces of the court, but he managed to keep the exact location of our family's mine a secret.

"And the stones, well, he used extra ships he purchased to smuggle quantities the king could never contemplate. He sacrificed millions in order to cement his place, but he also saved untold wealth by being smarter than the pompous arse on the throne."

Another flush of agony washed over me from my arm. I hugged the cast, slipping it free from the sling to rub the gauze, wishing I could rub the pounding break beneath. "I don't care what you think. I don't care how much money or power you have. One day, karma will catch up and make you pay."

Cut ran his hands through his hair, smoothing the white strands into snow perfection. "You can make empty threats all you want, Ms. Weaver, but the truth will forever stand."

"What truth?"

"The truth you can't make someone pay when they're completely untouchable."

I tore my eyes from his, glaring out the window.

Oh, but that's where you're wrong.

Your son was a prince to your empire, untouchable, unkillable——a Hawk.

Yet, I touched him.

I killed him.

I murdered him.

And I'll murder you, too.

One hour into the flight.

I groaned in agony as the pressure of the cabin swelled my broken arm.

* * *

Two hours into the flight.

Food was served. Some overly microwaved rubbery concoction with salad and a slimy strawberry cheesecake. I devoured the entire tray, even the hard-as-a-brick bread roll. Food helped replace a small piece of the emptiness inside me.

* * *

Three hours.

I squirmed beside Cut dying for pain-killers. He barricaded me in, sitting in his aisle seat like my jailer. My bladder protested and my thoughts swam with Jethro.

* * *

Four hours.

I lost my promise not to cause issues and pressed the button for an air-hostess. Cut glowered when the woman with coiffed red hair appeared. Ignoring him, I begged for some Panadol, some Advil, anything to lessen my pain.

She looked at Cut.

He shook his head.

I never did get my painkillers.

* * *

Five hours.

I stared out the window, counting stars, following wisps of clouds and pleading with the universe to keep Jethro safe.

"Stop fidgeting." Cut narrowed his eyes at my tapping fingers and dancing legs.

"Let me walk the cabin. I need to stretch."

And use the bathroom.

His jaw twitched. "Five minutes, Nila. If you're any longer, or I suspect you're disobeying me, I'll give you a taste of Diamond Dust."

"Diamond Dust?"

His lips curled. "You remember…the drug Jethro gave you from Milan? The magical substance that turns you mute and obedient while you can scream all you want in the inside?"

I gulped.

I completed my stretches and a bathroom break in four minutes.

* * *

Six.
Seven.
Eight.
Nine.
Ten hours.

Clammy sweat broke out over my skin. Adrenaline drenched my system the closer we flew to England. The cast itched with hot imprisonment, eerily heavy with its tormenting cargo. Lack of sleep clouded my mind and I swore the facets and sharp edges of diamonds burrowed their way into my flesh, gnawing me like a worm gnawed an apple.

* * *

Eleven hours.

The captain announced our upcoming arrival. Breakfast was served and cleared away in record time. Cut smiled and patted my hand. "Almost there, my dear. Almost home."

I cringed, looking out the window.

I just want this to be over.

* * *

Eleven hours and forty minutes.

The plane left clouds for earth, flying me toward my greatest challenge and worst debt yet. It wasn't my pain on the line. It wasn't Vaughn's like the night with the dice. It was Jethro's.

The man I'd willingly given my heart to. The man I said I would marry. The man who needed me as much as I needed him.

If I failed, he would die.

And not just die but be tortured until he begged for death.

My ears popped and my arm distended as the airplane

tyres skimmed the horizon before skidding onto tarmac.

I didn't speak as we taxied to the gate. Cut filled in arrival cards, running his fingers possessively over my passport.

My stomach performed circus tricks and trapeze stunts as the air-bridge attached and the flight attendants announced we could disembark. Passengers exploded into action, grabbing cases, children, and blocking the aisle in their rush to leave.

None of them were aware of what a monumental task sat before me.

Stay calm.

Don't think about what's in your cast.

Cut grinned, standing upright and holding out his hand. "Ready, Nila?"

I longed to scream and tell the truth. I wished I could tell everyone what I smuggled. If they knew, perhaps they could take away the worry that I wouldn't make it.

Jethro.

Think of Jethro.

You'll do this because of Jethro.

Standing, I took Cut's hand for balance and followed the other passengers onto English soil.

"Miss?"

Shit. Shit. *Shit.*

I turned slowly, doing my best to swallow my nerves. "Yes?"

"You don't have any hand luggage to put on the x-ray belt?"

I blinked, holding up the line waiting to go through the body scanner. The new equipment did a better job than the metal detector in Africa. Upgraded facilities, shrewd airport staff, and suspecting officers kept my heart permanently lodged in my throat.

"Oh, no. No bag."

The middle-aged security guard wrinkled his forehead. "No luggage on a long-haul trip?"

My stomach hurled itself against internal organs, knotting with kidney and spleen. "Well, I—"

"She's with me." Cut slung his black briefcase onto the conveyor belt, raising his eyebrow as if daring him to deny it.

I froze.

Why had he come to my rescue? Wasn't it his intention to make me sweat? To give him reasons to hurt Jethro? *Not that he needs a reason.*

The man eyed Cut, taking in his expensive clothes and white hair demanding respect. "Okay…" He glanced back at me, beckoning me to step into the round chamber with its curved glass and two footsteps painted on the floor. "Hold your arms above your head and wait until I tell you to move."

Tears sprang to my eyes. Tears of fear. Tears of pain.

I pointed to my tote bag sling. "I—I just broke my arm. I can't—"

The man behind me snapped my forearm with a mallet.
He's going to kill me when we return to his home.
Help me…

No sympathy glowed in his eyes. "Do the best you can."

Jethro.

I still had his fate in my hands. I couldn't falter.

Swallowing my racing heart, I slipped the cast free and raised my arms as best I could. Blood pressure throbbed in my fingertips and shooting pain bolted down my forearm. A terrible image of diamonds spilling out the end of the cast had me swallow a gasp-cough.

Closing my eyes, I waited as a two large sensors swung around me with the whirring noise of rotor blades.

"Thank you. Come out, please."

I obeyed, forcing my legs to remain firm and not buckle. Standing beside the man as the screen lit up with an image of a nondescript person, he frowned as black splotches appeared on the screen where my cast, my bra, and diamond collar were.

The officer cleared his throat. "Miss, you'll have to undergo a pat down." Looking behind him, he said, "Jean, can you help this lady?" He sidestepped, giving room for the female staff member to move into my personal space with her rubber gloves and judgemental stare.

"Do you wish to go into a private room?" Her voice screeched across my nerves.

A private room.

I could tell her what Cut did. I could inform her of what I carried. I could destroy not just my life, but Jethro's, too.

Cut met my eyes through the scanner. He hadn't gone through yet. He didn't say a word, crossing his arms, waiting for my decision.

I bit my lip. "No, here is fine."

"Alright." Clasping her hands, she ordered, "I need you to spread your legs and hold your arms out to the side."

Other passengers milled around, slyly watching as they grabbed their bags and slipped into shoes and jackets.

I did my best to comply, but my arm burned. God, how it burned.

Without asking for permission, she swept swift hands from my wrists to my shoulders and down the front of my chest. My white jumper with a unicorn in the same grey colours of Moth gave way beneath her touch. Her fingers pried at the underwire of my bra, ensuring there was nothing hidden. Skimming my leggings, she returned to my chest and slipped her fingers beneath my diamond collar.

I held my breath, forcing myself not to choke as she tugged a little, running her touch right around my neck.

She pursed her lips. "You'll have to take the sling off. I want to x-ray it."

I awkwardly shrugged out of it, passing it to her one-handedly.

She placed it onto a tray and gave it to another guard to run it through the x-ray machine.

"I'll also need to see inside your cast." Pulling free a torch from the arsenal on her belt, she said, "Stand to the side and hold out your arm."

Air suddenly turned to soup.

Tears pricked as I handed over my broken limb, throbbing with the crime of diamonds.

Cut was wrong.

A cast didn't offer sympathy these days. Perhaps in the past it had. Once upon a time, the sign of weakness and pain might've allowed a trafficker free range to import whatever they wanted by tucking a parcel of contraband in a fake cast. But not anymore. People had no empathy these days. High on their careers and pompous on their commitment to protect the borders—any shred of compassion had disappeared beneath strict training and no-nonsense.

I stiffened as the woman bent closer, her torch illuminating the inside of my cast. Could she see? Did the sparkle of diamonds glitter through the plaster?

Cut came through the body scanner, cleared by the male officer. He never took his eyes off me as he collected his briefcase and my sling from the conveyer belt. Coming closer, he pulled free the envelope the African doctor had given him before we boarded. "I have the x-ray if you need it. She's my daughter-in-law." Yanking out the images of my abused arm, he shoved it at the woman currently peering down my cast.

She pulled back, frowning. "I didn't ask for evidence. The signs of pain are obvious."

Cut smiled smugly. I knew his thoughts—they glowed in his eyes. *I told you people could see a faker from the truth.*

Dropping her torch, she inspected the x-ray quickly. The light of the airport showed what Cut had done to my arm with clear precision.

Stupidly, I'd hoped Cut had been wrong. That the mallet had only severely bruised me. That the snapping sound I heard wasn't an internal structure giving way, merely a movement of the table.

However, the image clearly showed a clean break on one

of the two bones in my forearm. The two pieces hadn't separated, but the large shadow was enough to make me faint. Cut obviously had practice. The fracture would knit together, eventually.

Won't it?

He'd broken me, and I hadn't had proper doctor care.

Would it need to be reset? How long did something like that take to heal?

I squeezed my eyes. *Will I die with this fracture?*

"How did you hurt your arm, Miss?" The officer pursed her red-painted lips.

My heart fluttered as fear ran amok. "I don't—I'm not—"

Jethro.

Lie better.

Cut crossed his arms, crunching the x-ray in his grip.

"I—I fell." Standing taller, I sucked in a breath. "My father-in-law and I were on a safari. One of those open top, no door Jeeps. I didn't listen to the guide and we went over a gully and bounced quite hard." I dropped my eyes. "I fell out of the car and broke my arm."

Cut laughed. "Kids. Can't teach them survival skills these days."

Annoyance painted her face. "Sir, I'm going to have to ask you to step back." The woman pointed toward baggage claim. "Your daughter-in-law will catch up with you when she's finished here."

I narrowed my eyes.

Morbidly, I didn't want him to go. I didn't want to give him any reason to hurt Jethro. He'd bolstered my tale, given x-rays with evidence. I wasn't delusional to think it was to keep me from breaking my promise to Kite.

All he cared about were the diamonds stuffed in my cast—smuggling his own wealth to avoid taxes and government thresholds.

My stomach twisted.

He would cut off my head before Jethro managed to find

a way to chase me back to England. And Jethro would have to live every day knowing that he failed.

That fate was worse than death.

My shoulders slouched as a rogue tear escaped my control. The airport officer softened. "It's okay."

Cut moved a few steps away, always watching, always controlling.

"Is there anything you want to tell me, Miss?" The woman widened her eyes. I guessed she tried to come across as sympathetic and helpful, but it only made her more duplicitous.

I shook my head. "No, I'm just in pain, that's all."

Holding up the sling Cut had passed back to me, I asked, "Can I put this back on?"

She paused for a long moment, eyeing up my cast while chewing on the inside of her cheek.

She's going to arrest me.

She's going to lock me up and Cut will hurt him.

Finally, she nodded. "I hope you get better soon." Turning off her torch, she waved me through. "Go on. Get home and sleep. You look positively drawn out."

"I will."

Unfortunately, I had no idea how many hours I had to breathe. I wouldn't sleep…I wouldn't waste a minute. After all, I wouldn't wake from death—the longest sleep imaginable.

I gave her a watery smile, trudging in Cut's footsteps toward the exit.

I've won but at what cost?

Cut's diamonds had entered England undetected, and I'd just condemned Jethro to a life of hell when I paid the Final Debt.

Jethro

NO MATTER WHAT I offered Marquise, he didn't bite.

He flat-out fucking ignored me, tapping on his phone, sitting like a troll in the corner. I hated he had reception down here. It used to be that being metres beneath the ground there would be no signal, but that was before technology and routers and modems.

My shoulder screamed for mercy like it had for the past few hours. My neck ached from lolling on the floor and my headache flickered with hazy tiredness.

I wanted to sleep but couldn't.

If I were concussed—which I feared I was from the car accident—I couldn't afford not to wake up. I had to keep going. Keep trying.

Blood slicked my wrists from trying to get free. I'd hoped, once I broke the skin, that the crimson lubrication would help me. If anything, it'd just clogged the twine and wrapped it tighter.

Nila.

Was she on a plane now?

Had Cut helped her through security?

"What time do I get my surprise?" My voice tore through the stagnant silence. We hadn't talked since Marquise informed me of Cut's final plan.

I had no doubt my time was running out. I would remember the pain I was currently in with fondness once Marquise started delivering.

Marquise looked up from the glowing screen in his hands. "Eager to begin?"

"Eager to leave." I cleared my throat, desperate for some water. Not that I'd ask him for some. He'd only taunt and torture. "Come on. Name your price."

He chuckled. "You don't have a clue, do you? You think you're in charge. You're not. I know the way your family's wealth moves. Bonnie is the one with full jurisdiction and she's the one I work for. You have no money—it's controlled by your tiny grandmother, and I bet that pisses you the fuck off."

I clenched my jaw. "She's old. How much longer do you think she'll last?"

Marquise shrugged. "Alive or dead, it doesn't matter. I'm written into her Will. Loyalty is what she bought and loyalty is what she'll get." His eyes dropped to his phone. "Now shut the fuck up and prepare yourself for all the fun we'll have."

I fell silent. Not because he told me to, but because my energy levels were dangerously low. I had to be smart. I had to find a way out of this godforsaken crypt before it was too late.

Something shuddered above us. A sprinkling of dirt shivered from the ceiling, merging with the dirt below. I twisted, looking up, squinting as another dusting landed on my face.

What the—

Then a boom sounded. Low and echoing and terrifying.

Shit!

An explosion or cave-in.

When I was young, Cut had brought Kes and me to visit for the first time. I'd rather liked the oppressive tunnels. The thickness of earth and loneliness so far beneath sunlight appealed to my chaotic, oversensitive brain. But I'd explored too far. I'd got lost.

I'd tried to find my way out, only to crawl and get trapped in an unused part of the mine. A section of wall had caved in, partially blocking my exit. Luckily, a worker had come to reinforce pretty quickly and found me.

I'd laughed off the experience and Kes had used my tale as a fascinating story of diamond warfare, but I never forgot the instantaneous terror at being buried alive.

Another reverberation travelled through the walls and floor, shivering like a beast waking up.

Marquise shot upright, his phone clutched in his hand. "What the fuck was that?"

That isn't normal.

The mine was sturdy, despite its ancient age. The rarity of a continual yield in diamonds after so long was another reason why the shafts and cylindrical passageways were well maintained. No one wanted to destroy a never-ending wealth creator, especially after centuries of collecting.

I flinched as another curtain of soil landed over my tied-up form.

Marquise charged toward the door. We humans were alike in that respect. We craved oxygen and sunlight. Put us underwater and claustrophobia could kill you better than any shark. Put us underground and fear could drive you insane.

My heart charged out of control as another smaller cannonade sounded.

Fuck.

If Marquise didn't kill me on Cut's behalf, it looked like *Almasi Kipanga* would.

The mine shouldn't behave in such a way. The tunnels dived deeper and deeper as the years went on, but the workers knew how to reinforce. Their lives were on the line. They didn't cut corners.

Yet another boom. Louder. Stronger. Closer.

The cave walls trembled, scattering earth over the table and medical supplies Cut had used.

I raised my eyes, fearing cracks and sudden crashing of

rock and earth.

"Fuck this shit." Marquise grabbed the handle and wrenched open the door.

Armageddon broke out.

Gunfire.

It ricocheted into the room with a sudden spray of bullets. Flashbacks of Jeep metal crumpling and crash landings swarmed my mind. I pressed my face into the ground, curling up the best I could while tied to the chair.

What the hell—

Whizzing bullets and the dull thud of their pockmarked landing ratcheted my heart rate until I inhaled dirt from the floor. Terror lacerated my blood, setting up residence in my pounding head.

My system had a healthy dose of fear when it came to lead projectiles. When Cut shot me, I'd reacted instinctually. I wasn't thinking about pain or death but saving my sister's life. I didn't know how it would feel. But now I knew what happened to a body in the path of a mortally wounding weapon.

It fucking hurts.

I didn't want a repeat.

Fighting the ropes to protect myself, I couldn't stop my mind doing a mental cleanse, saying goodbye to everyone and everything I ever loved.

Nila.

Jasmine.

Kestrel.

Even Wings.

My life story flickered pitifully lacking and empty of experience.

And then…it was over.

As suddenly as the gunfire began, it ceased.

The silence was almost as deafening as the shots.

A howl replaced the bullets, growing in decibels as the seconds ticked on.

I looked up.

Marquise.

He lay on his back, his hands glued to his chest where multiple red spots bloomed on his t-shirt. I couldn't unravel what'd happened. It was just us in the room. No one entered. No more firing.

I looked at the open door. The wooden frame had dings and splinters from a spray of firepower, but the exit remained empty. Within the depth of the mine, feet pounded, guns erupted, and the sounds of a battle exploded out of nowhere.

What the fuck is going on?

Marquise's howls slowly turned into moans. The soil beneath him accepted his blood like a tree accepts fresh rain, sucking it deep into the ground.

I put up a blockade between him and me. I didn't like the guy, but couldn't help sharing his pain as he died in front of me. Death was private, and I had no intention of participating in his final moments.

Somewhere in the mine, a war had broken out. I didn't know who was on what side. I didn't know if it would work in my favour. But I did know I'd been granted a second chance; I wouldn't waste it.

Kicking, I somehow managed to rock sideways, propping myself awkwardly on a fulcrum of brittle chair leg. My shoulders sagged in relief, but the way I repositioned put immense pressure on my chest and ribs from the ropes.

I couldn't suck in a deep breath as I jerked and twisted. The chair cracked and groaned, fighting against my encouragement to break.

Footsteps suddenly sounded closer, scuffing pebbles and belying numbers.

I froze.

Sweat dripped off the end of my nose as I squirmed harder. If they were new enemies, I couldn't be there still fucking tied up when they—

They entered the cave.

Five men poured inside, blocking the exit. Their dark skin

sucked the meagre light from the lamps, the whites of their eyes hell-bent and focused. The rifles in their hands were old but still capable of murder.

I glowered, drinking in their warrior thoughts and violence. One of the men moved forward, scuffing the blood-soaked dirt where Marquise lay.

Marquise erupted to life, pulling a pistol from his pocket and firing. His aim struck one of the men in the heart.

No!

Everything happened at warp speed. More workers poured through the door, launching themselves at the mountain of muscle, swatting his pistol, slamming his hands onto the floor.

He hollered like a beast attacked by insects, but in sheer numbers, he was overwhelmed.

Another man entered, this one wearing the patch of manager on his dirty t-shirt. He was older, more Cut's age, and full of authority as he stood over Marquise. Without flinching, he hacked at his neck with a machete.

One moment, Marquise was alive, keeping me from Nila. The next, he was gone to the underworld. Gruesome to witness but humane to put him out of his misery. He was a dead man already...this way...the pain had gone—even if he didn't deserve such compassion.

Bonnie will need to buy someone else's loyalty.

If she survived what I would do to her when I returned home, of course.

If *I return home.*

A man moved toward me. My muscles stiffened as he cocked his head. Up close, he appeared younger. His skin unblemished and pupils as dark as his skin. Without a word, he went behind me.

I swallowed hard, waiting for a knife to slice my throat or a bullet to lodge in my brain.

The swish of a blade being drawn from a scabbard set my heart racing but then the pressure around my chest suddenly vanished.

I toppled sideways, freed from the chair, ropes trailing after me. The sawn ends landed on the floor like decapitated snakes. The moment the chair no longer held me captive, the young man grabbed my wrists and sawed through the remaining twine.

I couldn't understand…why?

Why had they done this?

The man helped push me into a sitting position. My head thundered with pain, but I blinked and stretched my spine. It felt amazing to sit up and roll my back without stiff wood holding me in place. My ribs complained and the wooziness of my vision didn't help, but I could move, I could breathe, I could survive.

Pearly white teeth, almost as bright as diamonds, appeared in the gloom. He smiled, speaking rapidly in Afrikaans.

My memory of their language was rusty, but I let my condition and the few remaining words I recalled give me a hint of what he said: *We save for you save.*

It made no sense.

The worker who'd cut me free gave me a hand. Without hesitating, I clasped fists, staggering to my feet. I stumbled sideways, finding yet more injuries now I stood upright. My right kneecap ached and a large bump on my thigh swelled with a new bruise.

The weakness from lack of rest and nutrition caught up with me as the room spun.

Holding my elbow, the worker didn't say a word as I blinked and forced myself to be stronger.

Pushing the help away, I brushed off damp mud from my clothing with shaking hands. The movement helped remind my body how to react, fresh energy filtered, and the pain faded a little. Looking up, I glanced at the men all watching me. "I don't understand."

The manager came forward. His once white shirt was now stained a rusty ore from digging all his life. His skin glistened while his eyes shone with vengeance. His hand shook around the machete—still glistening with Marquise's blood—as he raised it to my heart. In English, he repeated, "We saved you so *you* could save *us*." His blade wobbled as he breathed hard. "We've taken care of the guards. We're in control of the mine now. We thank Kestrel Hawk for his help, but the guards obey the bossman's orders and our conditions are no better."

Temper strained his voice. "We have had enough of being treated like slaves. Tonight we rise. So answer me honestly, diamond son, or share their fate." His weapon shook as he pointed at Marquise and back to me. "Are you like them? Or are we right in thinking you are not like your family?"

I rubbed my face, forcing myself to focus on conversation not bodily pain. All Kes's work here had been for nothing? Had none of his generosity and deals behind Cut's back been delivered?

Injustice for our men and my brother's cause pissed me off. "You're asking if I'm not a Hawk?"

He shook his head. "No, we're asking if you're like them."

I didn't move. "Why? Why ask this now?"

The young man who'd freed me said, "We saw you."

My eyes landed on Marquise's corpse, unable to look away from the gash in his neck from the sword. "Saw what?"

"Saw you drag your brother's body and the lions take it. You killed your own flesh and blood."

Fuck.

I froze.

I didn't think now was the time to mention Nila had killed him. I'd just helped tidy up.

The manager moved closer, his fingers tightening around his blade. "You killed him because you don't agree with his practices, yes?"

I frowned, trying to keep up. How long had they hated my family? How long had they waited to overthrow us? My heart thundered with their combined hurt and hope. They'd killed in order for me to help them.

We were on the same path.

Bracing myself, I banished myself from my family, vanquishing any relation. I let myself be true with the men who'd saved my life. "No, I don't agree with his practices. If I'm honest, I never did."

"We can tell." The manager smiled. "We watched you while you were younger. You are not like them."

He didn't know he'd just given me a compliment I would always remember. All my life, I hated the fact I wasn't like my family, that I was an outcast, a disappointment. But now...now, I couldn't be more fucking thankful.

It just saved my life.

I pressed a fist over my heart. "I'm forever in your debt."

Debt.

Indebted.

It seemed Nila wasn't indebted any more, but I was. A Hawk owing a debt. I rather liked the responsibility of paying them back after something so unforgettable.

The manager lowered his machete. "You'll help us?"

I nodded. "I give you my word."

He grunted under his breath. "Good."

"I promise I'll change everything you are not happy with. But first...I really need to go after my father. I need to save—"

"The woman. Yes. I know." The manager sidestepped, waving at the exit. "A Jeep is waiting at the top of the mine. The driver will take you to the airport."

I couldn't stop the swell of gratitude. Moving toward the ziplock bag Cut had left behind after loading up Nila's cast with as many diamonds as he could fit, I scooped out a handful, stuffed them into my dirty jeans, and handed him the remains.

Inside rested countless jewels to be included in the next shipment. Hundreds of thousands of pounds worth of stones. "Please, call me Kite. Spread this out amongst your men. I'll be back as soon as I've controlled the situation at home."

He grinned, taking the diamonds. "Thank you, boss."

I shook my head. "No, thank *you*."

Moving a few paces, my legs argued and my gunshot

wound protested, but I had bigger things to worry about.

I had to get home.

I had to fly.

Looking one last time at the manager and workers who had changed my future, I stalked from the room as smoothly as I could. I ignored my headache. I dismissed the pains and discomfort in my muscles. I charged through the earthen labyrinth and exploded outside.

Fresh air.

New beginning.

Blinding hope.

This is it.

This was my true inheritance.

I'd earned the loyalty of men by remaining true to who I was.

Now, I would make the world a better place and end those who didn't deserve to survive.

A worker beamed, revving a Jeep with the Hawk crest on the side as he waited for me to climb inside.

The moment my door slammed shut, we tore off toward the airport.

Nila

"AH, SON, I'M so glad you're home."

My eyes wrenched upward as Cut threw me inside Hawksridge Hall.

Bonnie.

She stood with prideful smugness as I stumbled over the threshold.

A Black Diamond member had collected us from the airport. Cut hadn't said a word to me on the drive back, preferring to type furiously on his phone the entire journey home.

Home?

Hawksridge was never home.

Not without Jethro.

He was my home.

I hugged my cast harder, trying to push away the fears of Jethro's safety. I had double terror now I was back in the one place that would steal my life.

How many breaths did I have left?

How many heartbeats and moments?

Bonnie inched forward, leaning heavier than normal on her walking stick. When I first arrived, she'd refused to use her stick, moving around without any aid. Now, she seemed to have aged decades in the months I'd been her prisoner.

I smiled slightly. The trouble I'd caused had withered her—trading her youth for my longevity.

If I died, at least she wouldn't be far behind me.

My fingers curled with defiance, activating the break in my arm. It'd taken almost an hour for the adrenaline to leave my system after dealing with airport security. I'd burned off what food I'd eaten on the plane and felt shaky and sick.

However, there was one silver lining to being back in the rat's nest.

We'd returned to Hawksridge minus a Hawk.

Daniel.

His body was now lion shit turning to dust on an African plain.

Was that what Cut was emailing about? Trying to find his wayward son?

I'd been surprised Cut left without waiting for news of him. Leaving his offspring behind seemed callous, but I supposed he'd done worse. What was a departure without a note in the scheme of what he'd committed?

Bonnie seemed to sense my thoughts. Her hazel eyes narrowed on me. "Where is my grandson?"

Cut stormed forward, pecking his mother on her cheek. She stood in the grand foyer of the Hall, where Jethro and I had guided the *Vanity Fair* interviewers for our photo session in the grove.

Her skirts hung regally, her chin tilted just so, offering a royal welcome.

"I'd like to know that, too." Cut gave her another peck. "Hello, mother." Turning to face me, he growled, "Nila knows something. She's not talking currently, but she will. Have no doubt about that."

I gulped as Bonnie turned frigid. "I see." Shuffling forward, her eyes landed on my cast. "Despite that blip of bad news, I understand the Fourth Debt went okay."

Cut nodded. "Yes. No one suspected." Marching toward

me, he grabbed my good wrist and yanked me toward Bonnie. "I'll leave you to remove the cast and retrieve the merchandise. I have to attend to something." His eyes glittered, filling with secrets. "Ask me what I have to attend to, Nila."

I clamped my lips together. I didn't need to ask. He'd threatened me for too long.

The Final Debt.

There would be no more dallying or delays.

No more reprieves or hope things could end differently.

I'm not going down without a war.

Fisting my hair, he kissed my cheek. "I have an old friend to dust off and prepare for its latest victim. You have a date in the ballroom tomorrow, my dear."

"Tomorrow?"

My heart splintered. Was this how prisoners felt on death row? Having a date for their execution? Wishing for more time all while begging it to slow?

"Tomorrow." His mouth pressed against mine.

I squirmed, but he held me firm. "Daniel might've made you pay the Third Debt but don't for a second think I've forgotten that I didn't. You chickened out at *Almasi Kipanga*, but you won't have a choice tonight."

I refused to let him see my fear. "I fought you then. I'll fight you now."

Cut chuckled. "We'll see."

"I'll die fighting. I'll fight every second for Jethro."

"Jethro?" Bonnie snapped, full attention brimming. "What about that traitor?"

Cut smiled at his mother. "Long story. I'll tell you later." Turning his gaze back to me, he whispered, "Jethro will know you'll fight. His imagination will run rampant of images of me doing all sort of things to you now we're home." He kissed my cheek again. "The eyes paint an awful picture, Nila, but the mind is far worse."

Letting me go, he strode off, saying over his shoulder. "When you're dead and Jethro's been taught a lesson, he'll no doubt try to find a way to kill me. What he doesn't realise is, I'm one step ahead of him. I'll hurt him. I'll ruin him. And I'll tell him word for word what I did to you and watch it break him apart."

Rounding the corner, Cut's voice sailed back with promise. "He won't kill me because he'll be ruined before he ever gets the chance."

Jethro

FINALLY.

Finally, fate decided to throw me a fucking break.

The captain hesitantly accepted my pocket full of uncut diamonds, swiping a hand through a bushy moustache. I'd never met him, but he'd heard of me—like everyone in Botswana. "You want to leave *now*, now? Like right now?"

I nodded, anxiety pinging in my blood. "Yes. Like this very fucking minute."

Nila...

He frowned. "Just you?"

I nodded.

"To Turweston Airport, England?"

I nodded again.

We'd been over this, but I felt his confliction. He wanted the diamonds. He wanted to fly me. He just needed a moment to let the magnitude of logging a new flight plan and departing the moment he landed from a previous contract compute.

Lowering my voice, I encouraged, "I know you've just arrived with another client. But I need to go this very moment. If that's not a possibility, then I'll have to look elsewhere."

I held out my palm, requesting the return of the glittering stones.

The captain clutched his fist where the diamonds lay. He bit his lip, slowly working out what tiredness was worth compared to an instant fortune. Amazing how such simple stones could corrupt even the most innocent.

"I didn't say I couldn't take you."

I crossed my arms, wincing a little at the aches in my body. "Decide. We need to leave."

His eyes darted to the private jet sitting serenely by the hangar. After arriving at the airport, courtesy of the worker who should've been a racecar driver rather than a diamond digger, I'd found there were no commercial flights for thirty-six hours.

That was too long.

It wouldn't work.

I fucking refused to go through the nightmare of flying economy while fearing for Nila's life. Last time, I'd arrived late. Daniel had touched her and Nila had to defend herself by taking a life.

I won't let that happen again.

But the gods of fate had finally smiled at me as the captain I now propositioned had walked through the terminal with his flight bag and weary eyes ready for a nightcap and bed. He paused, eavesdropping on my conversation with another pilot offering all number of things if he'd charter a plane and get me to England tonight.

He'd interrupted and guided me outside where no other ears would hear.

The moment it was just us, I'd pulled free the pocketed diamonds and given him my terms. There were a few missing—I'd paid the worker a big bonus for driving me so quickly before sending him back to the mine to find the guy who'd driven me last night. I'd promised my previous ride two thousand pounds. Who knew if he still waited by the gates, but he deserved to be compensated for his loyalty.

I would never take people's willingness to help another ungratefully again.

The pilot rolled a clear stone in his fingers, a decision solidifying on his face. Finally, he nodded. "Fine. Let's go."

"Good choice." I wanted to fucking kiss him. Instead, I prowled toward the aircraft and prepared to face my father one last time.

I checked the clock above the cockpit for the millionth time.

Almost there.

By my calculations, I was only a couple of hours behind Nila and Cut. Their international service had been delayed—I'd seen the departure board at the terminal—and their airliner travelled at a slower speed.

Also, once in England, clearing customs would've taken a while depending on Nila's acting skills.

Even though I was so close, chasing Nila through the skies—it wasn't quick enough.

Come on. Fly faster.

The air-hostess, who hadn't looked happy when the pilot asked her to pull a double shift, came forward. The co-pilot had also grumbled, but nothing a few bribes and promises couldn't fix. Both the flight attendant and the crew had assumed they'd finished for the day. But they'd agreed. Everyone agreed for money. Even if tiredness and common-sense told them otherwise.

We were all running on fumes, lethargy and stress slowly polluting the interior of the plane. Mile after mile we travelled and I drank coffee after coffee, refuelling on pre-packaged sandwiches and fruits stocked in the plane's galley.

My stomach was no longer empty and with edible vitamins came healing. My body knitted together enough to get me through the day. My vision stabilised and my headache receded. My fever remained, however, staining my hope with an unwanted film.

"Another drink, Mr. Hawk?" The air-hostess with her plaited dark hair was pretty enough but held nothing compared to Nila.

God, Nila.

I'd never been so attracted to someone both physically and emotionally. The shared text messages had made me proud of her, pissed at her, lusting for her. She'd become a friend...then lover. But mostly, she'd become everything I ever needed.

Clenching my hand, I rubbed at the sudden ache in my heart.

I fucking miss you, Needle.

I shook my head. "A phone. Do you have an in-flight phone I can use?"

She nodded. "I'll get it for you." Disappearing down the back of the aircraft, she returned with a satellite phone.

The moment I turned it on, I forgot all about her and focused on rallying every plan I'd put into place before Jasmine called to say Nila had been taken to Africa.

How long ago was that?

A decade? Two?

Shit, it felt like an eternity.

The first call was to Tex.

He answered on the first ring, almost as if he sensed the magnitude of the situation and the peril his daughter was in.

"Arch speaking."

"It's Jethro."

His voice turned sharp. "You said you'd call me hours ago, Hawk. What the hell happened?"

"Change of plan." I swiped a hand over my face. "Look, they took her before I could put everything into place. It's happening right now. You need to gather whoever you've been working with and get to Hawksridge this very fucking second." My heart charged with gunpowder. "Can you do that?"

"What the fuck happened? Is my daughter okay? Tell me what the hell you did!"

"She is for now, but she won't be if we don't move fast.

Get ready. I'll meet you outside the gates to the estate in—" I checked the clock. Landing was in two hours. The local airport I'd ordered us to land in was closer to Buckinghamshire than Heathrow. Every extra minute I gained on my father counted. On a commercial service, Cut would've had no choice but to land at Heathrow.

Local time would place my arrival at late morning.

I'm closing in.

Working out the time differences, I said, "Meet me at eleven thirty a.m. Bring everything you have. I'll tell you what we need to do when I'm there."

"Jethro—"

"No, I don't have the time to console or repeat myself—just be there." I hung up and dialled the next man on my list.

Kill answered on the third ring.

"Speak."

"Kill, it's Hawk."

"About time you fucking called. Been sitting in this damn bed and breakfast waiting for the green light to move."

"You're in Buckinghamshire?"

"Where the fuck else would I be? I said I'd come. I came. Brought three of my best men with me, too."

I slouched in my seat with gratitude.

Thank God for friends in random places.

I took a deep breath. "I need you to get to Hawksridge as soon as you can. Sneak onto the grounds. Hide. If you see anything threatening Nila Weaver's life, you have full permission to do whatever's necessary." My voice faded. "Just keep her safe for me. I'm almost there."

"The woman I met at your diamond warehouse?"

I pinched the bridge of my nose. "That's the one. My father will have her, or possibly my grandmother. I want to deal with them on my own so keep them alive if possible. But above all, do whatever you need to keep Nila unharmed—even if it means slaughtering them."

Kill's voice grew cold and calculated. "You have my word.

We'll leave now. See you soon, Hawk."

Hanging up, my fingers shook as I dialled the final number.

"Flaw speaking."

"Flaw…it's Kite."

It didn't escape my notice I'd made three phone calls and used three names. Was that who I'd become? Three facets of myself? How would I choose which was the better side of me and settle into one person after so much strife?

"Shit, man. Cut just arrived ten minutes ago. Bonnie has Nila up in her quarters. Where the fuck are you?"

Shit!

"I'm on my way. I've sent reinforcements, but I need you to do something for me."

"Name it."

"I'm making you vice president of the Black Diamonds. I need you to gather those you trust to take down the members loyal to Cut. Fracture and Cushion should swear allegiance to you. Colour might, too—he was friends with Kes and not a bad guy. But the rest, I'm unsure of. You'll have to work out who to trust and who to peg for a rebellion. You think you can do that?"

Silence before he gulped. "You want me to start anarchy?"

"I'm asking you to get the brothers out of the way. The war is happening right now. It's going to end tonight. I can't have the club getting in the way."

"I know which members will stick by you and which won't. Leave it with me. I'll make sure to keep them out of the way and deal with those who won't behave."

I smiled with thanks. "Appreciate it. I'll be there soon. Help will arrive with me. I have reinforcements. Just stay low and get ready."

"Been born ready, my man. This is yours. Don't fucking care it's not your thirtieth or you haven't inherited the estate yet. This became personal when that motherfucker shot Kes in cold blood."

Leaning against the window, I sighed. "It's personal. And it's almost over."

Flaw growled, "Let's finish this for him."

The ache returned to my heart—this time for my brother. *I fucking miss you, Kestrel.*

"For Kes." Hanging up, my eyes fell on the clouds and world far below us.

Up here, I was closer to my brother. Closer to his untethered soul.

If you can hear me, brother. Don't leave. Not yet. Things will be better after tonight. You'll be safe. Jaz will be safe. We can have the life you always dreamed.

Turbulence hit the plane, bouncing us like a skittle.

I liked to think it was him…telling me he'd heard and wouldn't give up.

Stay alive. Give me a little more time.

And then wake up and come home.

Nila

"COME HERE, CHILD."

All I wanted to do was escape, to be alone so I could drop the mask of defiance and indifference. It took every effort to come across contrite and fearful but not guilty and sinful.

Daniel's death glowed inside me, giving me power. But I couldn't deny I was tired. I needed to rest...in case I said something stupid and escalated my death from tomorrow to today.

Jethro...keep breathing.

Every time I thought of him, the image of dank mines and oppressive walls came back. I hated him trapped down there, alone, hurting.

I knew so much now. I knew about Mabel and William. I knew a secret both Bonnie and Cut didn't know.

The secret burned a hole in my soul because what good was a secret if I died with it—especially when it would grant pain to hear it.

If I tell her, I could kill her before she tells anyone else...

My heart skipped.

Yes, I like that plan.

Bracing my shoulders, I moved toward Bonnie. She'd escorted me into her quarters, ferrying me into the lift I assumed Jasmine used to move around. I'd never been in the silver box and hated travelling even a small distance with Bonnie in such a tight space.

Jasmine.

Does she know I'm back?

Could she sense her brother's predicament? Was she like Vaughn and in-tune with her sibling's well-being?

Vaughn.

Could he tell I'd been hurt? Where was he? The entire drive from the airport, I'd feared he would be at Hawksridge, firing cannons and charging with some fictional cavalry to rescue me.

But he wasn't.

I was both glad and heartbroken.

Jethro couldn't save me this time. I would do my best—I wouldn't die without a fight—but what if it wasn't enough? I was more alone here than I was at the mine. At least there I was surrounded by strangers. Here, I was surrounded by enemies.

Stop that.

It took every last reserve, but I shoved my fears deep, deep inside and embraced antagonising pompousness.

Bonnie expected me to be as broken as my arm.

She was very much mistaken.

Cocking my chin, I pranced toward her. "Did you miss me?" I eyed up her quarters. "Last time I was in here, I seem to remember I taught you seamstresses are better than flower arrangers."

Bonnie's rouge-painted cheeks whitened. "And I seem to recall I showed you what happened to Owen and Elisa and proved Jethro played into the hands of fate. He's dead because of you. Congratulations."

Goosebumps darted over my skin. I probably shouldn't but Cut would tell her. I wanted to be the one to deliver the news. "He's not dead. He's alive and coming for you."

Wishes were free. Threats were cheap. I could taunt her

even knowing Jethro remained bound to a chair and lorded over by Marquise.

She fisted the top of her cane. She didn't break decorum, merely looking a little ruffled and a lot annoyed. "I highly doubt that. How is he still alive? What exactly is the meaning of this nasty business?"

I glided forward. "You don't deserve to know." The pictures of Owen and Elisa still graced the walls. The overwhelming perfume of her flower arrangements poisoned the air.

My skin crawled with how much I despised her.

Die, witch. Die.

Bonnie came closer, her cane sinking into the carpet, her red lipstick once again smeared on pencil thin lips. "You look at me as if I'm the devil. You're such a stupid child. Go on, you have my permission. What do you see when you look at me?"

My mouth parted, sensing a trap.

She waved her stick. "Go on. I want to know."

I balled my hands, rising to her challenge. "Fine. I see a twisted, old woman who's controlled her son and grandsons with no mercy. I see a soulless creature who doesn't know the meaning of love. I see a scorned hate-filled Hawk who never understood the true value of family." My voice lowered to a hiss. "I see a walking dead woman."

She chuckled. "You have more perception than I gave you credit for." Sniffing, she looked down her nose. "You're right on some accounts. I *have* controlled my son and grandsons because, without me, they wouldn't have the discipline required to maintain the Debt Inheritance and future responsibilities of this family."

"When you're dead, your legacy will die with you."

"Yes, perhaps." She smiled. "But you'll be dead long before me, Ms. Weaver. Perhaps you should remember that so you don't forget your place." Stabbing her cane into the carpet, she sneered. "Now, enough, what do you have to say for yourself?"

My hands fisted. I stared at the flower arrangement on the trestle by the door. I'd had to stand there and listen to her high-class airs and demands, seething while she speared lilies and roses into oasis foam.

I hated the perfection of lilies. I *despised* the bright red of roses.

My temper swirled out of control. "I'll tell you what I have to say, old witch."

Bonnie froze. "*What* did you just say?"

If I did this, there would be no turning back.

I would die tomorrow.

But I could live today.

I could achieve more in one act of cruelty than I ever could in a coffin.

No one knew when death was coming.

I supposed I was lucky in a way—knowing the grim reaper waited for me gave me a certain kind of freedom. The knowledge gave me power to face my nightmares rather than run.

Plucking the vase with my good hand, I held the bushel of flowers as a weapon. Petals fell by my feet, dripping slowly in the heat of her boudoir. "You make me sick."

Her eyes flared. "Put that down this instant."

Tucking the arrangement haphazardly into my sling, I stalked closer. Wrenching the head off a red rose, I threw the petals in her direction. "You set a bad example for all grandmothers around the world."

She stood taller but stepped backward. Not wanting to give up ground but wary at the same time.

I threw another destroyed rose in her direction. "You've polluted this earth for long enough."

She lost to my invasion.

Her cane tapped for traction as she scuttled backward.

The door soared open and a Black Diamond brother came in.

Shit!

I breathed hard, fistful of petals and a standoff with Bonnie Hawk.

Instantly, Bonnie's face transformed into feral confidence. "Ah, Clarity. Good timing." She pointed her stick at me. "Kindly remove the vase from Ms. Weaver's control."

"Right away, ma'am." I had no hope of holding onto it one-handedly as he snatched it from my sling. He was smaller than Marquise but had the same evil glint and malicious satisfaction. His bald head shone with the sconces around the room.

He didn't look at me again as he placed the flowers back on the trestle. "You summoned me?"

Bonnie nodded, smoothing fly-away hairs from her chignon. "Go and fetch the Dremel and a bucket of water and vinegar."

He cocked his head in my direction. "You okay alone?"

"I'll be fine. Go."

Clarity nodded. "On it." He left, closing the door behind him.

I *hated* she trusted she could be in the same room with me—even after my outburst. I hated I came across so weak that she didn't feel she needed protection.

Make her regret that.

"Trust me alone with you now?" I tilted my head. "Rather a stupid thing to do, don't you think?"

My hands curled as thoughts of killing her ran wild. I had nothing to lose anymore. Jethro was in Africa. I didn't know where Jasmine was. V was hopefully back with Tex. And Kes was in the custody of doctors and nurses. We were scattered to four corners, no longer touching but still linked.

I could kill Bonnie before Cut killed me.

Bonnie smirked. "Child, you have a broken arm, most likely a fever, and death looming on your horizon. I have no need to fear a guttersnipe like you. You just used whatever energy you had. You can't deny it. You're positively dripping with exertion and fatigue." Turning her back on me—showing just how little she viewed me as a threat—she snapped, "Now, after that highly inappropriate incident, return to the subject. What about Jethro?"

"What about him?"

She cleared her throat angrily. "Am I correct in assuming he's still alive?"

Rage spread like wildfire through my system. I might not have knitting needles or scalpels, but I couldn't stomach this old bitch any longer. "Yes, as a matter of fact. He *is* alive, and I was telling the truth. He's on his way to kill you all."

She flinched, unable to hide her sudden suspicions. "I don't believe you."

I shrugged. "You don't have to believe me for it to be true."

For a second, silence was a third entity in the room before Bonnie laughed. "Cut would've mentioned such a thing. You're lying. Didn't your mother ever tell you liars go to hell?"

"Was she supposed to tell me that before or after you killed her?"

Bonnie tensed. "You're getting mighty bold for a Weaver about to die."

I drifted forward. "Bold enough to kill you before I go?"

Say no so I can prove you wrong.

One Hawk soul tallied my own. I wanted two. No, I wanted three before I was through.

The door sailed open, shattering the tension between us. The Black Diamond brother strolled in and placed a bucket of water, sour smelling vinegar, and a power tool on the flower-arranging bench.

Glancing at Bonnie, he wiped his hands on his jeans. His bald head caught the rays of late-morning sunshine.

My body clock was so screwed up; I didn't know if it was meant to be night or day, sleep or awake.

"Need anything else, ma'am?"

Bonnie pursed her lips, glancing at me with a mixture of wariness and disdain. "Yes, stand by the door. Don't leave."

I laughed softly. "Afraid of a Weaver, after all."

Bonnie snapped her fingers. "Shut that trap and come here. I have work to do."

Damn.

Now I had an audience; my plans shifted slightly.

Be patient.

She'd grow cocky again and send the brother away. And when she did…

Playing along, for now, I moved toward the table. "What are you going to do?"

She didn't reply as she shuffled toward a chair, dragged it closer to the bench, and perched on the padded seat. "What do you think, you stupid girl? You're carrying our money. I want those diamonds. Your arm is currently worth more than your entire family history."

"I don't believe that. My family earned its wealth through skill and hard work. Weaving and sewing for dukes and duchesses. We didn't lower ourselves to smuggling stones and calling it hard work."

She spluttered. "Soon that tongue of yours will no longer be attached."

"Why? You plan on cutting that off along with my head?"

She smiled coldly. "Such a temper."

I smirked back. "I've learned from the best."

I would never bow to her again. *Never.*

Bonnie huffed, busying herself with an attachment for the small power tool. "Stand here."

Looking over my shoulder, I calculated how much time I would have before the brother managed to stop me. If I slashed her throat with a pair of scissors, would I have enough seconds or not?

Mulling the problem of murder, I moved to where she pointed.

"Don't move."

I didn't move; too consumed with my own ideas to care about hers.

Bonnie grabbed the Dremel in shaking, arthritic hands and switched on the battery-operated machine. A loud buzzing filled the room as she ordered me to remove my sling and place the cast on the table.

The ache in the broken bone had faded a little, or maybe my body had become fed up with letting me know it was hurt. Either way, I did as she asked. Obeying for now—purely biding my time.

How should I do it?

Cutting shears to her jugular?

A fire poker to her heart?

My fingers around her throat, strangling, *strangling?*

I flinched as the sharp teeth of the Dremel chewed through the cast, removing the heat and itch. It didn't take long for Bonnie to slice from wrist to elbow. Her hands shook, trying to pincer it open—her age not granting enough power to break the mould.

"Open it," she commanded, growing weary. A sheen of sweat covered her brow, a grey tinge painting her skin.

My heart skipped to see her struggling. Her heartbeats were numbered. My mind started a countdown.

One beat.

Two beats.

Three beats.

Four.

My hand was steady as I cracked open the cast, almost as if contemplating murder worked wonders for my peace of mind. I winced as the cast fell away, destroying whatever support I'd had.

Once the pieces hit the table, Bonnie immediately scooped them into the bucket. They sank into the water and vinegar mixture.

Air bubbles popped on the surface, faster and faster.

She caught me looking. "Allow me to teach you a few things before your final hour. The vinegar dissolves the plaster. Once it's reduced to nothing but sludge, the water will be sifted, any wayward diamonds scooped from the bottom, and washed in preparation to go to Diamond Alley for processing."

She snapped her fingers. "Give me the rest of the cast. I know the pouches are hidden in the padding."

Fifteen beats.

Sixteen beats.

Seventeen beats.

Eighteen.

Pain amplified as I slipped out of the cushion and handed over the plastic tray. My arm held marks and indents from the padding, red from the cast's itch. However, the swelling hadn't gone down. An angry bruise already marred my skin, black and purple and blue.

Immediately, she scooped the diamonds out and placed them beside the bucket. "Once they go to Diamond Alley, then where do you think they go?"

Nursing my arm, I tested my fingers. They worked but with no power or grip. If I had any chance at killing her, I'd have to work through the agony and force my limb to obey. Otherwise, I wouldn't stand a chance.

"Well, Ms. Weaver?" Bonnie slapped the table. "I asked you a question. Answer it."

"Oh, I'm sorry. You mistook my disinterest for attention." I rolled my eyes. "I don't care."

"You should." Prodding my vulnerable break, she hissed. "Hurts, doesn't it?"

Flinching away, I fought the pain as I grabbed the edge of the table. A horribly frustrating and terribly timed vertigo wave attacked me. I hung my head, anchoring my feet to the floor, riding out the vicious swell.

She chuckled as the greyness subsided, leaving behind the serendipitous knowledge that Bonnie's flower shears rested only a finger breadth away.

Scissors.

Blood.

Death.

255

She didn't notice my sudden hope and fascination with the weapon within reach.

Wrapped up in her own importance like a fluffing peacock, she looked at the brother by the door.

She pointed at the bucket and pouches. "Take those downstairs and make sure each diamond is accounted for." Her eyes narrowed. "I'll know if any go missing and you'll be subjected to a cavity search once the diamonds are bagged and labelled."

The man came forward, cringing a little at the thankless task and the reward he had to look forward to once completed. "Yes, ma'am."

I held my breath.

The brother grabbed the items and departed through the door.

She made him leave.

We're alone.

Thirty.

Thirty-one beats.

Thirty-two.

Thirty-three heartbeats.

Stupid, stupid Hawk.

Slowly, I fisted the shears with my unbroken arm, wrapping tight fingers around the handles.

Bonnie didn't notice, so consumed with her own self-importance as she stood and brushed plaster dust from her blood-red skirt.

Blood-red.

The same colour she wore at the dice game a few days ago.

My fury fired and I held up the twin blades. "You asked me before if my arm hurt. I'll now ask you a similar question. Do you think this will kill you if I lodge it in your heartless chest?"

She scooted off her seat, shuffling backward. "Drop it, Ms. Weaver."

I advanced, brandishing my weapon. "No."

Her mouth opened to scream.

Fifty-two.

Fifty-three heartbeats.

I'd lost my opportunity last time.

I'd been too slow. Too weak.

I had no intention of screwing this one up.

I charged, stopping her before she could make a sound.

I slammed my palm over her mouth, tackling her. My break bellowed and my good fingers weakened around the pilfered scissors, but I didn't let her go. She tripped, but I managed to right us. Bolts of agony and shards of pain drenched my nervous system from my uncasted arm.

"Ah, ah, ah. I think silence is better in this newly developed situation, don't you?" My vocabulary mimicked hers, thriving off the power of manhandling the wicked Hawk witch.

Bonnie's papery breath fluttered over my hand as her nostrils flared.

She struggled. But her brittle bones were no match for my rage. Her eyes tried to hurt me with unspoken curses, but I wouldn't put up with it anymore.

In a burst of power, she ripped out of my hold, swatting my broken arm.

I groaned in agony as she sucked in a breath for help.

I had two choices. Let her scream, give into the overwhelming pain, and let this end without victory, or fight through everything and win.

I fought.

Tackling her again, I didn't care about my arm as I wrapped the broken one around her tiny waist and slapped my other hand over her lips.

Seventy-four.

Seventy-five.

Seventy-six heartbeats.

She folded as delicately as her beloved flower petals, crashing to the floor. I didn't try to protect myself. I didn't relish the impact or brutal pain.

I fell with her.

Agony I'd never felt before ripped through my bones.

I bounced on her decrepit body, squashing her into the carpet. I gasped, willing myself to keep going. "Not this time, Bonnie. You don't get to win this time. This time…it's *my* turn. It ends here. Just us."

I was better than this. Better than her and all Hawks combined.

I would take this grandmother's life, and I would *enjoy* it.

She was frail, ancient—the matriarch of a power-crazed house. Yet she was just human—same as me, same as Jethro, same as every person on this planet.

She wasn't immortal or scary.

She's already dead.

She batted at my hold with wrinkled hands, her strength rapidly dwindling.

"You deserve to die, Bonnie." I pushed her further into the carpet. "You asked me when I came into this room what I saw when I looked at you. It's my turn to ask you." I held her wriggling form, breathing hard. "What do you see when you look at me?"

Your killer?

Your demise?

Not letting her answer, I snarled, "I'll tell you what you should see. You should see a girl who's reached the end of her limit. A girl who won't hesitate to kill. A girl who fully intends to survive this massacre and burn your legacy to the ground."

Her eyes shadowed with fear.

She fought me—surprisingly strong, but she couldn't defeat the cold animosity siphoning through my veins. My rage turned into something not entirely sane as I stared into Bonnie's terrified gaze. "Want to know a secret?"

Her nose whistled as she sucked in ragged breaths around my silencing palm.

"I know something you don't know." I had meant to kill her quickly, but taunting was too much fun. I wanted to do to her what she'd done to my family and me.

A dose of her own medicine.

And my secret about Daniel had to be shared. Who better than his grandmother who would soon be joining him in the afterlife?

Her hazel eyes glared into mine. I understood her silent message. *You'll die because of this.*

I giggled, hovering over her. "I'm dead already, so what does it matter if I take you with me?"

The fight left her. An eerie calm replaced it instead. Her face filled with conversation, dragging curiosity through my blood.

Dammit.

Despite my need to end her, I had an intolerable desire to hear her final words.

"Don't scream and I'll let you speak."

She nodded.

Was it stupidity or possibly insanity making me trust her? Whatever one it was, I removed my hand.

Her face turned to the side, sucking in oxygen, her white chignon falling apart thanks to the carpet.

I squeezed her tiny body with my knees. I was her death shroud. A crow hovering for murder.

One-hundred and four.

One-hundred and five.

One-hundred and six heartbeats.

"You're not stupid, child. You know you'll pay for this the moment Clarity returns. There are worse things than death. Haven't you learned that yet?"

"I know."

"Then get off me and I'll make sure they don't maim you too much." Her smile was evil personified. "However, wait another moment longer, and I'll personally tear you limb from fucking limb."

The curse fell from her red painted lips.

I smiled, cocking my head. "Not yet. I want answers first."

"I've given you plenty of answers."

"No, that was convoluted history seen through your twisted eyes."

She snorted.

"I want to know why you are the way you are. Why you're ludicrously set on an ancient vendetta. Are you just mad and passed that defective gene onto your son or did you grow into this despicable creature?"

"You stupid, *stupid* girl. I've helped keep this family together. There is nothing wrong with loving blood over others."

"Even murder?"

She grinned, showing yellowing death and bad breath. "*Especially* murder." She raised her head off the ground, bringing our eyes closer together. "Especially your bloodline's murder. You *owe* us."

"What did we ever do to you to deserve such barbaric treatment?"

"You know what!"

"No, I don't. I will never understand because there is nothing rational to understand. It's just a sickness inside you that needs to end."

She coughed, her ancient lungs rattling. "You don't know a thing about me."

"Tell me. I'm giving you the opportunity, right now." I glared. "I want to know. This is your last chance." A contorted smile spread my lips. "Call it your last confession. Purge your sins, Bonnie, because I'm sending you to your grave—secrets told or not."

No fear shone on her face, only black rebellion. "I have nothing to confess."

"Bullshit."

I don't have time for this.

I wanted to know Bonnie's tale. I wanted to try and understand why someone would go to such lengths. But I wouldn't sacrifice my only opportunity to kill her.

"You don't want to talk? Fine. I changed my mind." Gritting my teeth against another influx of pain, I grabbed her scarf—the pretty silk decoration to match her despicable outfit—and tugged it tighter around her neck. "Want to know what I promised myself when I first came to your home and was told what would become of me?"

She pushed at my hands, sending a shard of agony down my break as I slowly tightened the scarf. Her eyes bugged wider and wider.

"I made an oath to be the last Weaver stolen. At times, I didn't know how I would honour that vow. But now...I do."

She begged for air, her lips gasping. I wasn't throttling her...yet, but the fear of strangulation sent droplets of panic across her overly powdered face.

The stench of rose water and summery perfume gave me a headache, but nothing would stop me doing this.

I lessened my hold a little. "Now, before I go too far. Do you want to know what I know or would you rather die clueless?"

Are you sure this is wise?

My arm throbbed as I doubted my actions.

Daniel's death wasn't only my secret. Jethro would be implicated, too. I couldn't risk his life if Bonnie told—

Told!

I laughed out loud. *Who is she going to tell? She'll be dead within moments...*

Something corrupted inside me. Something I didn't want to acknowledge. Straddling Bonnie, I was cold-hearted and focused—more Hawk than Weaver and ready to bloody my hands for revenge.

"No, you have nothing of value to tell me. Get off me, you heathen." Bonnie tried to buck me off, but her ninety-plus years meant it was like pinning down a fluttering leaf.

I bent further. "I know where Daniel is."

She went deathly still.

"Do you understand?" I bared my teeth. "Do you get what

I'm telling you?"

Her gaze narrowed, disbelief shadowing them. "You're saying you killed my grandbaby?"

"I'm saying he hurt me and paid the price."

Bonnie shifted, trying to kick beneath me. The grey tinge staining her face slowly spread over her cheeks and throat. "You're lying."

"I'm not." I laughed softly. "What if I explained a bit more? What if I told you a bed-time—? No, a *kill-time* story. And prove I'm telling the truth?"

No reply.

Digging my knees, imprisoning her skirt tighter, I wrapped her scarf around my fist. "He won the coin toss against Cut. He got first right to rape me. *Rape.* A word so abhorrent, a family should disown any offspring who would ever do such a thing. And yet, you encourage them. You like your sons and grandsons to take what isn't theirs to take.

"Well, Daniel would've made you proud that night. He hurt me. Kicked me. Knocked me out for a few moments. But he didn't understand how powerful the will to live is, or the single-minded determination sheer hate can deliver.

"He did take me—just a little—and I let him. Does that shock you? That I didn't fight the final part when he invaded my body just enough to taint my soul?"

Bonnie swallowed, her breathing erratic, her chest lurching beneath my hold.

"I let him think he'd won, but really, I guided him to his death. I'd come prepared and I had my weapon of choice within my grasp. While he focused on rape and pleasure, I turned cold and ruthless."

I tugged the scarf. "I hugged him, you'll be glad to know that. I hugged your grandson as I jammed my metal knitting needle through his heart."

Bonnie sucked in a noisy breath. "No…"

"Oh, yes. I took great satisfaction driving that needle through Daniel's soulless chest. He didn't see it coming. He was too arrogant to notice until it was too late." My mind skipped back to the tent, recalling the last breath, the final topple of his corpse. "It was over so fast."

Bonnie spluttered, "But, they—they haven't found his body. You're lying. He's alive. I don't believe you."

"You don't have to believe me. It's the truth." I smiled brutally. "Only you know what really happened. Cut suspects me, but he has no proof."

"But how…" The muscles in her neck stood out, straining against translucent skin. "How did you hide his body?"

Even on her back, with death hovering over her, Bonnie remained frosty and aloof. If I didn't hate her, I might've respected her. She was the same formidable force Mabel Hawk had been. The same invincible dowager.

I stroked her papery cheek. "I didn't."

She glowered. "Then it can't be—"

"A Hawk did." I twisted her scarf a little more.

More sweat dotted her forehead. Her fingers scrabbled at the obstruction.

"The Hawk who's in love with me and is fully on my side."

Her eyes popped wide, then glared with the hate of a thousand hells. *"Jethro."*

"Yes, Jethro…Kite. The man I agreed to marry."

Sharing my secrets even to a gnarly old cow lightened my heart. In two breaths, I'd admitted to murder and marriage. Not exactly two subjects that went hand in hand.

But they do in this case.

Without murder, Jethro and I would never be allowed to get married. We'd never be allowed to live.

The deadline of my own demise tried to shred my confidence. I might be the killer currently, but soon, I would be back to being the prey.

Spittle flew from Bonnie's lips. "Impossible. Jethro is loyal. He knows his responsibilities—"

"Responsibilities?" I laughed in her face. "Your son *shot*

him. That loyalty died the moment you had him killed in cold blood. We're together. Against all of you."

Bonnie shuddered. "Never. A Hawk would never work with a Weaver."

"Lies. I know more of your history now. I know that Hawks gave Weavers leniencies throughout the years. I also know there was more than one generation who tried to stop this ludicrous debt."

"You know nothing, you insolent child."

My heart raced as I shook my head. Short black hair curtained my cheeks, giving the illusion we were already in a coffin, blocked off from the world.

"I know Jethro walked in and saw his brother dead. I know he helped me clean up. I know he—"

"How that boy is still alive is beyond me." Bonnie interrupted me as if she couldn't stand to hear more. Perhaps she did care, after all. "It's an abomination of nature."

My fingers tightened. "No, I'll tell you what's the abomination. That's you. *You're* the abomination. You twisted your family into criminals."

I waved at the room, the majestic Hall, the entire Hawksridge estate. "This is more than most people will have in their entire lives. You have everything, yet you seek to destroy everyone."

I rushed my parting words. "Once Jethro arrived, he helped me dispose of Daniel. We took him outside the fence of *Almasi Kipanga*. We left him on the plains…"

Understanding etched Bonnie's grey-washed face.

"You know, don't you? You know what happened from there."

Her pallor turned sickly, her lips tinting blue. "They ate him."

I nodded. "They ate him. Piece by piece. Chunk by chunk. Daniel no longer exists. Just like you will no longer exist."

My arm pushed harder, pressing her against the carpet. "I've killed your grandson, but I haven't finished."

Bonnie tried to yell.

I clamped a hand over her lips. "Ah, no bringing attention to us. I haven't told you the best part yet."

She shook her head, trying to free her mouth.

"I'm going to kill your son. I'm going to ensure your mad family tree dies. Only sane Hawks will continue. I'm going to kill Cut. I don't know how, but I will. The only one who will pay the Debt Inheritance is *him*."

Her struggles became frantic.

I held her down, riding her like she was a bucking bronco. I waited for her to tire herself out so I could look her in the eye as I strangled her. Only…she never tired.

Her body moved inhumanely, twitching like the undead, knocking me off her with super strength. Her gaze locked with mine; she stiffened and bowed. Her right arm flailed outward and the ire in her gaze changed to terror.

My stomach tangled as her entire body scrunched up in agony.

Shit.

Four-hundred and five.

Four-hundred and six.

Four-hundred…and seven…heartbeats.

She's having a heart attack.

Seconds whizzed past as the knowledge sank deep.

No!

Fate stole her death away from me.

I wanted to take it.

Her heart.

Her life.

She *owed* me.

But the very thing I'd stabbed in Daniel was now failing in Bonnie.

Thump—thump. *Thump…*

"Damn you, Bonnie." I climbed to my feet, standing over her with the flower shears. I'd wanted to capture her soul as it escaped her body but destiny hadn't judged me worthy.

Perhaps claiming Daniel's soul was all I was allowed. Bonnie's belonged to more powerful entities.

The ghosts of my ancestor's filled her chest cavity, slipping into heart chambers, blocking veins and arteries.

Her back arched as if an exorcism was performed. She reached for me. The greyness of her face slipped straight into starch white. "He—hel—help…"

"No…"

I backed away.

I wasn't worthy enough to take her life, but I would watch every moment. I would stand vigil as she passed away at my feet and would cherish the moment when she existed no more.

But then the door swung in.

The fucking door swung and Cut entered.

He stormed into the room. Summoned by deep family bond, his posture switched from confident and assured to frozen in shock. His eyes bounced between me standing over his mother with sharp scissors and Bonnie convulsing on the floor. His eyes glittered, his face arranging into symptoms of disbelief, shock, and outrage.

How long did it take someone to die of cardiac arrest?

Die, Bonnie. Die.

The mantra repeated from when I'd killed Daniel.

Die, Hawk. Die.

"Fuck!" Cut launched into action, sprinting across the boudoir and slamming to his knees beside his mother.

She rattled and chortled, breathless and wheezing. Her eyes begged for help while her heart suffocated.

"Hold on. Hold on." Raising his voice, he screamed, "Someone call a fucking ambulance!"

No one replied. No Diamond Brother's spilled into the room. No one to take orders.

I just stood there.

A morbid spectator as Bonnie faded from this world.

"Call a fucking helicopter!" Cut didn't seem to notice his orders fell on deaf ears. I'd never seen him so normal. So afraid and lost.

I paced back and forth, hugging my smarting arm, hoping no one heard his commands. An ambulance would be too slow...but a helicopter? That might be too fast.

Die faster, Bonnie. Faster.

And fate listened.

Life chose its victor.

Me.

Thump...thump-thump—*thump*.

Heartbeats failing.

Heartbeats ceasing.

Cut cradled his mother as she quickly lost the elderly crone persona and tumbled into an emaciated corpse.

My secrets dying with her.

My sins silencing with her.

However, Bonnie didn't go quietly. She gave a parting gift, granting her final breath to me, sending me straight to damnation.

"She—" Bonnie gasped. "Dan—Dan—Daniel. She—"

Cut wiped her forehead, pushing away soaked strands of white hair. "Shush, save your strength. The doctors are coming."

Bonnie spread her lips, lipstick staining her teeth. She knew as well as I did she wouldn't be living another day. Gathering every last remaining strength, she raised her quaking arm, pointed her finger, and hissed, "She kil—killed hi—him."

And that was it.

Last heartbeat.

Last breath.

Her eyes latched smugly onto mine, then closed forever.

I'd killed my second Hawk.

But she'd delivered me into terrible torture.

Her arm tumbled to her side, bouncing off her dead flesh, coming to rest awkwardly by her side.

For a moment, the room mourned its owner. Flower petals drooped and curtains twitched with a non-existent breeze.

Then Cut raised his head, eyes glittering with unshed tears, face swelling with unadulterated hatred. *"You..."*

I raised my scissors, backing away.

He didn't move, hugging his dead mother, my second victim—stolen, not at my hand, but by the poltergeists of my ancestors.

"*You* killed Daniel."

Two choices.

One future.

I was so sick of running. So sick of hiding. So sick of being *weak*.

I didn't run.

I didn't deny it.

Instead, I held my chin high and claimed all that I'd achieved.

I'd won; they'd lost. So be it if my life was now over.

"Yes. Yes, I killed him. I took his life, I disposed of his body, and I enjoyed every damn second of it."

Cut gasped.

I smiled.

We didn't move as the next battle was drawn.

Bonnie

NO ONE WANTED to listen to the story of the sinner. The bad guy. The villain.

No one truly cared about my agendas or goals.

No one could comprehend that my actions stemmed from a place of love, family, and commitment to those I cherished.

Did that make me a terrible person?

Could I not put those I cared about before a total stranger?

People did it all the time.

They murdered to protect themselves and loved ones. They willingly forgot the commandments in favour of how they viewed what was acceptable and what was not.

I was no different.

Those who knew me understood my passion and drive. And those who didn't. Well, I didn't give a rat's arse what they thought.

There were rarely two sides to every story. In my long life experience, I'd come to see the truth. There were multiple sides. Pages and pages of sides. A never-ending battle where humans picked what they believed, causing friction and intolerance. Sometimes the choices were for understandable reasons—not justified or rash or right—just...understandable.

And when I understood that magic, I learned how to create the same spell within my own empire.

There was no right and wrong.

There was no black and white.

Those two simple lessons guided me through my life forever.

My reasons for doing what I did made sense to me. They were my dreams, and I was lucky enough to have the power and authority to press those dreams on others.

Was I right? Depended on who you asked.

Was I wrong? Not in my eyes.

And really, that was all that mattered.

I believed in what I did. I loved my family. I adored the power and wretchedness my loved ones could deliver. I gave my entire being to ensuring they thrived.

It all started on the day Alfred 'Eagle' Hawk asked me to marry him. The day he went from courting to bent knee, I knew my trials at living within my place in society were over. I hated the airs and graces of stuck-up princesses at the seasonal parties. I hated dealing with egotistical jerks who thought one manor and a career slaving for others meant they could take care of me.

Idiots.

That was just a prison sentence, and I had no intention of sharing a cell with middle-class achievers.

I came from wealthy stock myself. The Warrens owned most of South Hampton and a fleet of transportation that travelled all over the world with merchandise. Mainly, other people's merchandise—a fact I didn't like. I didn't like that we helped others improve their footing in this world.

Finite resources meant me and mine had to *share*.

I believed those I loved and shared blood with should prosper and those who didn't shouldn't. A simple decision that came with so many different sides.

As I grew used to my newfound authority, I decided to forgo my first name of Melanie and rechristen myself as Bonnie.

Bonnie Hawk rose from the ashes of Melanie Warren.

And I became a true wife and supporter.

When I fell pregnant with Peter, my first child, I swore he would be the reason I worked beside Alfred and gathered more power. Hard work and dedication didn't scare me. Failure and destitution did. So I did everything in my power to make my husband great—beyond great—unsurpassable.

One night, Alfred told me of the Debt Inheritance. It took me years to get him to fully explain what it meant. Wives of Hawk men were not supposed to get involved with the so-called Indebted business, but Alfred was mine, and if it was in my power to bring him greater glory, I would do it.

I was then graced with another son, Bryan. Life smiled on us, doting on my perfect children, ensuring they would become great masters and lords of a universe I would help maintain and create for them.

However, one stormy night and a few too many cognacs, Alfred told me how he claimed a Weaver before he met me. He carried out a few debts but couldn't carry out the final one. He didn't attach the Weaver Wailer, and he lied about killing her to a save face with the history books.

He let her go. Told her to run. To hide. He buried an empty coffin, pretended he'd completed the debts, and covered up the truth on the moor.

Stupid bastard.

That kind of weakness was not tolerated. I lost all respect for him. I saw him for what he was—a wimp. So I moved out of his bedroom to new quarters. I could no longer stomach his unwillingness to deliver a perfect future for our sons. Years later when he died of lung cancer, I didn't mourn his loss. I celebrated it.

Now was my time to triumph or meddle—again, it depended on whose opinion.

Peter took after his father. A hard worker, loyal and kind. I truly hoped he would be a good replacement and heir but time slowly changed my opinion.

Bryan took after me. He had my soul, my discipline, my drive for the impossible. Peter preferred to study and donate our wealth to charities. Bryan preferred to take that wealth and turn it into even more wealth for us—not others.

We were blood, but battle lines had been drawn and as age separated my two sons, I taught the one who listened. Bryan had been my student since he was little, and he remained my student all his life.

I'd wanted more children. I wouldn't deny it. Lots and lots of children to ensure a greater probability of world domination. We traded in the most priceless of wealth. We owned countless empires in countries around the globe. I was finally in a position to ensure we were unstoppable, but I only had one son on my side. However, he was a son who was happy to oblige.

While I was busy teaching Bryan how to run the Black Diamonds with better efficiency, digging through Hawk history books and immersing myself in my new family more than I ever did as a Warren, Peter fell in love.

A woman he met at an animal shelter. He brought her home to introduce us a few months into their relationship. Behind my back, he'd asked her to marry him and she'd agreed without my consent.

Rose Tessel was everything I wasn't. Softly spoken, obsessed with dogs and cats and horses. She didn't care about Hawksridge. She didn't care about diamonds or money. All she cared about was making Peter happy and spending time at the stables with my firstborn.

That bitch completely clouded Peter's mind. As my eldest son, he had a duty to perform. His father hadn't followed the rules of the Debt Inheritance, but my son sure would. However, he left it too late. He didn't collect Emma Weaver and pretended it didn't exist—burying himself in storybook romance and stupidity.

Bryan tried to make him see sense, but Peter and Rose fought a good battle. They were so wrapped up in their own plans; they forgot we were family and family sticks together through *everything*.

It was Bryan who came up with the idea.

He was such a good son, so attentive and switched on. He made a promise that if I put him in charge of Hawksridge, he would grow the empire to ever-new heights. He would always look after me and would grace me with many grandchildren to rule.

However, he had one condition.

He wanted to claim the Debt Inheritance. He'd spied on Emma Weaver. He'd coveted what should've been Peter's and a dislike for his older brother festered deep within his heart.

I pondered my decision, not because I doubted his capabilities, but because it would do him good to stare defeat in the face before granting his dreams. Unfortunately, while he waited for my deliberation, his jealousy of Peter overflowed one drunken night.

Peter was at a business meeting in London, delayed overnight. Rose had agreed to wait for him at the estate in his quarters instead of returning to her place in Buckinghamshire. I hated having that hussy under my roof—unmarried, no less. But Bryan did something unforgivable.

He raped Rose.

He took what should've been Peter's.

But what he took, he gave back. He impregnated her with my first grandbaby.

I cursed him for that. I was disappointed in him. Disgusted in his weakness for flesh.

But after he'd taken what he wanted, he regretted the choice immeasurably. He came to me with the weeping woman and together we put her back together again. I held a meeting that very evening and said Rose could remain in my household, but she would have to marry Bryan. If she didn't, Peter would pay the price.

She refused but wisely reconsidered when I threatened Peter's life.

The next few months were fraught with drama I didn't care for. I realised too late that my eldest would never accept his love was betrothed to his brother. Peter reminded me too much of his father, and I'd had enough of his indecision and weakness to have the strength to deal with it again. So I told Bryan he could have everything he ever wanted. A family. Children. An empire. And the Debt Inheritance.

All he had to do was put an end to his brother.

And he did.

He strangled Peter while I was at a council meeting. I pretended to grieve and act disgruntled with his actions. I made it known that the incident was on his head alone. But in secrecy, I was awed he'd had the gumption to do it.

Peter's death was reported as a horse riding accident. Rose was married to Bryan. And life moved on. Jethro was born followed by Jasmine and Angus. Bryan became known as Cut as he stepped into the role I always knew he was capable of and took the Hawk name to even greater heights.

He strengthened our relationship with authorities. He befriended new royals and smoothed out age-old alliances. And then one night, he announced Rose would have another child.

Daniel.

Cut hadn't planned on more, but he'd said he'd been to watch Emma and couldn't wait any longer to claim the Inheritance. He'd used his wife to dispel some of his lust that night—even though they'd barely talked for years.

After Jasmine's birth, Rose had moved out of Bryan's rooms, living a sham of a marriage, only glued to us by her children. My dislike for her grew year by year.

Unfortunately, Daniel's birth unravelled the perfect family I'd gathered.

Rose insisted on a hospital birth—regardless that her other deliveries had been at Hawksridge with a midwife and no complications. Bryan felt guilty for his treatment of her and softened. He gave her her wish.

Stupid man.

A few days after the birth, Bryan returned to the hospital to bring his son and wife home. Only, his wife had vanished. She'd abandoned her family—the greatest sin of all. She left behind four children and a husband who would've protected her for life.

Only, she didn't get far.

For a few months, she managed to escape our notice, but then Bryan—my ever resourceful, capable son—found her awaiting an international flight. She'd willingly traded her children for freedom—an unpayable crime.

He brought her back to the Hall. He kept her by his side while the children grew a few more years. But then the incident occurred.

I didn't approve of what happened that night, nor will I ever forgive him for the slip of Jethro and Jasmine seeing what he did to their mother. But what was done was done and there was nothing more to be said.

She was finally gone.

Good riddance.

However, her death taught me one final vital lesson: even family could disappoint. In fact, family could do more than disappoint—they could destroy everything with one ungrateful action.

I wouldn't put up with any more nonsense. Jethro turned out to have the same condition plagued by previous generations of Hawk bloodline. I ordered Cut to beat it out of him until he learned that as firstborn he had responsibilities, destinies, obligations to fulfil.

Angus pleased me but only because he had a gift not many others had. He could read people and only show them what would be appropriate to the situation. He was a chameleon within my ranks, but he was family and did what he was told. So he was left to his own devices.

Jasmine listened and obeyed, but she was rebellious in her heart like her older brother. Yet she was my only girl and despite myself, I doted on her. I wanted a mini-me. It would take time, but eventually, she would see the light and mimic all that I did.

However, recent events made me see what a foolish wish

that was. I didn't show how much she hurt me when she picked sides against me. She needed to be disciplined. I knew that. But…for some reason, my ruthless laws faded when it came to Jasmine. I couldn't hurt her—not when she'd already been hurt so much.

I shouldn't have been so weak toward her. It would remain my greatest regret.

And Daniel.

Well, not having a committed mother screwed him up from the start. He was a needy, attention-seeking, reckless child. Strictness didn't work with him. Time-out. Smacks. Nothing. At least he idolized his father and ensured he wouldn't turn out like Peter or Alfred. That was his only saving grace—that and the fact he was blood and obeyed me.

And now, my beautiful family—the son I'd groomed who'd pleased me so much; the grandson who'd disappointed and destroyed everything—would now have to fend without me.

My legacy was long. I was proud of what I'd achieved.

The Hawk name was who I was.

I was born to become a Hawk even if it was only through marriage.

I'd strengthened our lineage. I'd played my part precisely.

And death could never take that away from me.

Nila

"*YOU!*"

Cut stumbled to his feet. His fists clenched and every muscle in his body spasmed with hatred.

I forced myself not to run as he shot across the room, weaving and wobbling. I tensed for the pain of him tackling me, hitting me, delivering his sadness and rage into my flesh.

Fear of his inevitable revenge and repercussions of my actions wouldn't let my knees unlock to flee. I wouldn't look weak by running.

Not anymore.

I'd achieved two out of the three lives I promised I'd steal. Those were good odds. I might not achieve every goal before my life was done, but I wouldn't turn my back on two victories.

Cut was broken. *I* did that. I broke him. His reign over the House of Hawks still stood strong and powerful, but I was the mole beneath him. Digging through foundations, chewing on support beams, gnawing at everything he held dear.

So no.

I wouldn't run because there was nowhere to run to, and I'd earned the right to stare at my defeated before he defeated me.

Those thoughts sucked to a violent stop as Cut charged

toward me.

Whatever conclusion spilled into my head must've filled his. Perhaps in the same order—the knowledge he looked upon a worthy competitor and not just a Weaver—or the newly forming plan to strip me of everything now I'd stripped him.

Either way, he slammed to a halt, breathing hard—almost as if he didn't trust himself if he touched me. Giving time to gather his scattered self and focus on so many new developments.

"You killed her."

I balled my hands. "I wanted to, but I didn't."

His breathing billowed like dragon smoke from his nose. "You did. You fucking did!"

"It was a heart attack. Her own body killed her."

"Lies. Just like you lied about Daniel. It was *you*."

My spine straightened even as I winced at what my truth would bring. "I did."

His fists shook. "You fucking bitch." He wanted to strike me—it lived in every cell—but at the same time, there was something else...relief? Traitorous gratitude instead of mournful grief?

Did he hate his mother as much as the rest of us?

Pain from my arm gave me false bravado. "Can I help that I learned from you? You killed two of your sons. I only killed one."

Cut lowered his chin, glowering beneath his brow. "They were *my* sons. Mine to do what I like. They were only alive because of me. *I* created them."

"You might've created life, but they created themselves into the men they are."

He went deadly still. *"They?"*

I swallowed.

Shit.

"Kestrel is fucking alive, too?" His eyes bugged, ignoring the death of his mother so easily. "You're telling me I didn't murder either of my children, yet you killed my youngest, the one I'd promised to make my heir?" His voice gruffed. The air tinged with…regret?

Relief and regret—two very contradictory emotions I never expected Cut to feel.

What does that mean?

Backing away, I held up the scissors. "I said nothing of the sort."

Cut prowled toward me, slower this time, as if he couldn't comprehend such blasphemous facts. "They. You said *they*. Who's *they*?" His gaze flew around the room, to the open door, to his dead mother. "What do you mean by that? Where is he? Where the fuck is Kestrel if he didn't die with the bullet in his godforsaken heart?"

Kes was anything but godforsaken. God chosen perhaps. Protected and watched over and given friends who ensured his healing and safety.

"Answer me!" Cut's hand shot to his back waistband, pulling free a pistol.

I froze, staring down the black muzzle, expecting any moment a flash of gunpowder and a cold kiss of lead. Cut bounced between so many emotions, I couldn't keep track.

Was it the pistol he'd shot Jethro and Kes with? He didn't have it with him when we cleared customs at the airport. What outstanding matters had he attended to once we returned to Hawksridge?

Despite facing a grave, I kept the truth hidden. Jethro was trapped in Africa subjected to survival only if I obeyed Cut and gave up my life. I couldn't help him. But I could help Kes by staying silent. Kestrel was safe. I wouldn't tattle on his whereabouts, and I definitely wouldn't tell Cut that both lives had been saved thanks to Flaw and Jasmine.

Flaw!

He's on my side.

The tentative friendship we'd sparked when Kes let me into his chambers at the start. The jokes and conversation around late afternoon snacks when Jethro avoided me after the

First Debt was paid. Flaw had come through for me, for Kes.

Could he help me now?

Where is he?

My heart thundered with despair. Even if Flaw was close by, it wouldn't be a simple matter of screeching for help. Hawksridge Hall swallowed men whole, disappearing for days in its cavernous corridors.

He'd never hear me.

Cut suddenly stopped, leaving a few metres between us. His eyes narrowed as sorrow, anguish, and loathing crossed his face. The hand holding his gun lowered until the nose threatened the carpet and not my life. "I underestimated you, Nila."

My lungs siphoned oxygen faster. My spine wanted to roll, to give in to the sudden ceasefire, but I knew the armistice wouldn't last long.

His mother had just died in his arms. His mourning and rage fought to take ownership of what his next move would be. He was as unpredictable as a penny in the air.

"That's the first compliment you've given me."

He looked over his shoulder at the cooling, decaying body of Bonnie. "Emma was right."

I flinched. "Don't talk about my mother. You have no right to mention her name."

His eyes landed on mine with ferocity. "*I* have no right? I have every fucking right. Did you think I didn't see her playing me? Pretending to love me while all along I knew her love was for her wretched family left behind. Even when she was nice to me, she warned me what would happen if Jethro claimed you."

Chills darted over my skin. "What did she say?" As much as I hated discussing my mother with Cut, I wouldn't stop him sharing more of his weaknesses. Because Emma was definitely his biggest weakness.

His shoulders sagged as he swiped a hand over his face. For a short second, he looked defeated. As if without Bonnie, the drive to be the worst, the most despicable overlord had vanished. "She said you'd finish us."

An icy smile lit my face. "I guess you should've listened to her."

His lips spread in a snarl. "Want to know what else she was right about?"

The atmosphere switched. Cut shed his melancholy, gathering the storm of venom he so often carried. "She said you would steal the heart of my oldest and the Debt Inheritance would end with your generation."

I gasped. How had she known how the future would unfold? How much time had she spent with Jethro to understand that my soul and his would find peace with one another?

Cut chuckled. The sound sliced through the envelope of death, fast-forwarding through his grief. "I'd wipe that smug smile off your face, Nila. Because that wasn't all she told me."

Throwing the gun to the floor, his hands fisted as he pushed off the thick carpet to charge toward me.

I squeaked, stumbling back. My broken arm bounced against my body, dragging a sharp cry of pain.

My eyes flew to the door; my legs prepared to bolt.

But I'd made a vow not to run.

Besides, Cut was too fast.

His arms wrapped around me, clamping in a hellish hug. "She also told me that while your generation would be the last, you wouldn't find a happy ever after. You share the same fate as her."

I stopped breathing as Cut grabbed my cheeks. "Her fate has always been your fate, Nila. No matter what you did, who you corrupted, or how many conspiracies you planned, your fate was unavoidable."

Kissing the tip of my nose, turning something so sweet into something so sinister, he murmured, "You've taken from me and I've taken from you. Now, it's time to end this so I can repair the damage you've caused."

Slipping his fingers from my cheeks to my hand, he

snatched away the scissors and carted me from Bonnie's quarters. He left his mother decomposing; surrounded by bushels of her favourite blooms, already in a tomb with flowers.

Without my cast or sling, my broken arm twinged with pain. The wooze and wash of imbalance toyed with my vision as Cut carted me down the stairs.

"I'd planned on giving you a final night of pleasure, Nila. You deserved a shower, a good meal, a good fuck before your final breath. You've robbed me, not only of being generous for your good performance smuggling my diamonds but also of my opportunity to claim the Third Debt."

The Third Debt.

I'd been granted my wish, after all.

Hadn't I whispered I would rather pay with death than rape if I had a choice?

I didn't have a choice, but the preferable ending had been selected.

My skin broke out with clammy nervousness as Cut stalked me down the main artery of the house, past rooms I'd relaxed in, nooks I'd taken refuge in, libraries I'd napped in. Turning left, we bumped into a Black Diamond brother.

His leather jacket creaked as he slammed to a halt. "Cut."

Cut yanked me closer. "Are the final touches complete?"

The brother nodded, his shaved head and mix-matched tattoos absorbing the darkness of his attire. "Yes. All ready to go, as per your instructions."

Cut sniffed, his fingers tightening around mine. "Good. I have another task for you. My mother is dead. Take her body to the crypt below the Hall. I'll deal with her remains once my afternoon is finished."

The brother nodded obediently, unable to hide his sudden shock and curiosity hearing about Bonnie. "Okay…"

Cut stomped onward, then stopped. "One other thing. Get Jasmine. I want her there. And the rest of the brotherhood."

The man frowned but nodded again. "Right you are."

He took off the way we'd come, jogging with purpose.

I squirmed in Cut's hold, wishing he hadn't thrown his gun away upstairs. If the weapon were still lodged in his waistband, I could've commandeered it and shot him point blank. There was no need to be secretive any longer. No need to hide my true intentions.

He's my last victim.

"Where are you taking me?" I skip-trotted to keep up, gritting my teeth against my pain.

Cut smiled, his golden eyes blank and cruel. "The ballroom."

Chills darted down my spine.

Ballroom.

Instead of conjuring images of finery, sweeping drapes, and sparkling dancers, I pictured a mausoleum, a morgue…the last area I would ever see.

Jethro had said a debt would be repaid in the ballroom.

Despite my courage in Bonnie's quarters, fear engulfed me now.

Debt.

The last debt…

My heels dug into floor runners, creasing ancient rugs. Cut merely dragged harder, never slowing his pace.

Hawksridge seemed to exhale around us, the portraits and tapestries darkening as Cut dragged me down yet more ancient corridors. Moving toward large double doors in the same wing as the dining room, he stopped briefly before another Black Diamond brother opened the impressive entrance.

My eyes drank in the inscriptions and carvings on the doors, of hawks and mottos and the family crest of the man who was about to kill me in cold blood.

I'd walked past the doors countless times and never stopped to jiggle the handle—almost as if it'd kept itself secret until this moment—camouflaging itself to remain unseen until the Final Debt.

Cut clenched his jaw as the large entry groaned open, heavy on their hinges and weary with what they contained.

Once open, Cut threw me inside. Letting go of my hand, he grabbed a fistful of short hair, marching me to the centre of the room.

The chasmal space was exquisite. Crystals and candlesticks and chandeliers. Needlepoint and brocade and craftsmanship. Money echoed in every corner, shoving away dust motes and proving that glittering gold was immune to tarnish and age.

The gorgeous dance floor competed with the tapestry-covered walls and hand-stitched curtains, yet it wasn't overshadowed. The glossy wood created the motif of the Hawk crest inlaid with oak, cherry, and ash.

The black velvet curtains gleamed with diamonds sewn into the fabric, and everywhere I looked, the emblem of my capturers gilded wall panels and ceiling architraves.

There was no denying who this room belonged to, nor the wealth it had taken to acquire it.

"Like what you see, Weaver?" Cut never stopped as we stormed toward something large and covered by black sheeting in the middle of the empty expanse.

There were no chairs or banquet tables. Only acres of flooring with no one to dance. Loneliness and echoing eeriness swirled like invisible threads, tainting what would happen with its chequered history.

There'd been good times and bad in this place. Wine spilled with laughter and blood shed with tears.

Goosebumps darted over my flesh, almost as if I stepped through the time-veil. Able to see previous generations dancing, hear their lilting voices on the air.

And then I saw them.

Cut grunted as I slammed to a stop, zeroing in on the portraits he'd told me about in Africa.

The Hawk women.

Unlike the dining room with its over-crowded walls of men in white wigs, chalky faces, and gruffly stern expressions, the Hawk women bestowed the ballroom with class.

Their faces held colour of pink cheeks and red lips. Their hair artfully coiled and curled. And their dresses tumbled through the artist's brush-strokes, almost as if they were real.

Cut let me look. "Beautiful, aren't they?"

I didn't reply. I couldn't. I was overwhelmed with antiquity and yesteryear.

He let me survey his family's history while I searched for the portrait that'd caught my eye. I needed to look upon the woman who started it all.

I can't find her.

Bonnie.

She found me first.

Her painting hung vibrantly, royally. She'd posed with a white poodle and an armful of lilies. Her face unlined and youthful vitality hinting at a woman of early forties rather than the ancient ninety-one-year old who'd just perished.

Up and up the family tree my gaze soared, over Joans and Janes and Bessies.

And finally, at the very top, overseeing her realm and all that she helped create and conquer was Mabel Hawk.

The shadowy sketch wasn't as intricate in detail as the rest. Her grandson, William, could only remember so much, commissioning the painting off memory. But the intensity of her gaze popped full of soul even if her features weren't drawn with precision. She looked like any other woman from the bygone era. Any other mother and grandmother. Her gown of simple brown velvet held a single diamond at her bosom while her cheekbones swept into her hairline.

She reminded me of Jethro in a way. The same potency of sovereignty and power.

"Drink it in, my dear." Cut let go of my hair, running his fingers along my collar. "This room will be the last thing you ever see."

I still didn't respond. I'd taken so much from him, and I refused to give it back in the form of begging and tears.

Time ticked onward, but Cut didn't hurry me. I let the portraits on the wall tell their story, filling me with timeworn relics, ensuring when the time came to bow on my knees and succumb to the guillotine's blade, I would be more than just a girl, more than a Weaver, more than a victim of the Debt Inheritance.

I would be *history*.

I would be part of something so much bigger than myself and would take mementoes from this life to the next.

The room slowly filled with witnesses. Black Diamond brothers trickled in, lining the walls with their black leather. Out the corner of my eye, I noticed a few with bloody knuckles and shadow-bruised jaws. Why had they fought within their ranks? What had caused their violent disruption?

The oppressive summoning from the hidden apparatus in the ballroom pressed deeper and deeper the longer I ignored it. The portraits had been studied, the room scrutinized—I had nothing left to capture my attention away from the monolithic mysterious thing.

Cut turned me to face it. "Would you like to see below the cloak?" He smiled tightly. "I'm sure your imagination has created a version of what exists before you."

I straightened my spine. "Whatever you do to me, it won't bring them back."

He stiffened.

The gentle squeak of a wheel broke the brackish silence. I looked over my shoulder as Jasmine suddenly propelled herself into the room, slipping quickly over polished wood with a horrified expression. "What the hell do you think you're doing?"

Cut turned around, dropping his touch to land on my lower back. He didn't hold me in place, but I wasn't idiotic to think I wasn't trapped and unable to move.

"I'm doing what needs to be done."

Jasmine wheeled herself right up to Cut's knees. Her beautiful face pinched with disbelief. "No! That isn't your task.

It's Jet—I mean, Daniel's."

Cut narrowed his eyes, looking between the two of us. "Fuck." He ducked down, grabbing his daughter roughly by the chin. "You knew, too. You knew all the fuck along Jethro and Kestrel were alive." He shook her. "What sort of daughter are you? What sort of loyalty do you have toward your own flesh and blood?"

Jasmine chopped her hands on Cut's wrists, breaking his hold on her cheeks. "My loyalty is to the right thing. And this is not right! Stop it. Right now."

Cut chuckled. "There is so much you don't know, Jaz, and so much you'll never learn. You're a failure and no longer a fucking Hawk. The moment I've dealt with Nila, I'll deal with you. What's good about family if it's the same family that does everything possible to destroy itself?"

Snapping his fingers, he growled at the brother who'd just arrived.

The man skidded through the doors, breathing hard as if he'd been at war rather than on whatever errands the club did.

My eyes met his. Dark floppy hair and kindness hid beneath ruthless.

Flaw.

My heart leapt, hope unspooling.

I had many enemies in this room but two people I cared about and trusted might be all I needed against Cut and his blade.

"Flaw, take my daughter to the back of the room. She's to watch from a safe distance and not to leave, understood?"

Flaw glanced at me. Secrets collided in his gaze before looking resolutely away. Nothing in his posture apologised or promised he would try to prevent the future. He merely nodded and clasped his hands around the handles of Jasmine's wheelchair. "Yes, sir."

Flaw...?

What had I done to warrant his sudden coolness?

Backing away, he dragged Jasmine with him.

She screeched and jammed on her brakes, leaving large grooves and tyre marks on the elegant floor. "No!"

"Don't argue, Ms. Hawk." Flaw dragged her faster toward the border of the room.

I couldn't believe he'd abandoned me. Wouldn't he at least try to argue for my life?

Jasmine made eye contact with me, fighting Flaw's yanking, shaking her head in despair. "Nila…where is he? Why isn't he stopping this?"

Jethro.

She means Jethro.

I wanted to tell her everything, but there was too much to that question and I had no strength to answer it. She didn't need to know what happened in Africa. She had her own issues to face once I'd departed this world at the hands of her father.

I shook my head, a sad smile on my lips. "I'm sorry, Jaz. I tried. We both did."

Tears welled, catching on her eyelashes. "No. This can't be happening. I won't let it." She reached behind her, trying to slap Flaw and scratch his hands from dragging her farther. "Let me go!"

With jerky movements, he bent angrily and hissed something unintelligible in her ear.

She froze.

Flaw used her sudden motionlessness to yank her the rest of the way.

What had he said?

How could he betray us?

My heart stopped. *Has he betrayed us or did he make another oath to Kes and Jethro I'm not aware of?*

Vexatious questions came faster, battering me with final worry. Was Kestrel awake? Was he alive in the hospital waiting for his brother to visit?

I wish I could say goodbye to him.

My tummy clenched even as I tried to remain strong.

I wish I could kiss Jethro one last time.

Cut spun around, forcing me to do the same. Flaw and Jasmine's eyes seared brands into the back of my spine. Two brothers dashed forward, gripping the ends of the black sheet hiding the apparatus, looking at Cut for commands.

He snapped his fingers with regality. "Remove it!"

Their hands gathered swaths of material and tugged. The fabric slid like ebony silk, kissing angles and gliding over surfaces, slowly revealing what I'd known existed all along.

The method of my death.

The equipment I'd hoped never to see.

There was no Jethro to stop it.

No Kestrel to fix it.

No Jasmine to ruin it.

Only me, Cut, and the awful gleaming guillotine.

The lights from the chandeliers bounced off the glossy wood of the frame, suspending a single blade ensconced in two pillars of wood. A latch at the top held it in place while the rope dangled down the side, ready to pull aside the barrier and let the blade plummet to its task.

And there...below the chopping block where my head would lay was the basket that would be my final resting place.

Cut kissed my cheek, wrapping an arm around my shoulders and guiding me toward the machine. "Say goodbye, Nila. It's time to pay the Final Debt."

Jethro

I'D BEEN AWAKE for centuries.

I'd travelled thousands of miles. I'd fought hundreds of battles. I'd lived a million lives in a matter of days.

My brain gasped for rest. My eyes screamed for sleep. But my heart pushed relentlessly toward the end.

"Stop here."

The taxi driver did as I asked, pulling to a halt beside a grass verge a few metres away from the entrance to Hawksridge. As soon as we'd landed, I'd paid the crew for their fast service and hopped into a taxi.

The flight had gone as planned. Once I'd made phone calls for Tex to gather his enforcements, Flaw to sort out the brothers, and Kill to hide on the grounds and watch from a distance, I'd focused on ensuring my body would continue to obey me and the strength I'd need for the future tasks wouldn't fail.

I'd eaten and tended to my wounds in the airplane bathroom. I'd patched up my gunshot wound as best I could and added a Band-Aid to the cut on my forehead. I asked the flight crew to give me the first-aid kit and took what pills I could to lower my incessant fever and subdue the aches and pains I didn't have time to deal with.

When we finally traded air for earth, I wasn't recharged or

ready for carnage, but I was better than I'd been a few hours ago.

I had enough energy to finish this…and then…then I would sleep for a fucking eternity and let others worry about the world for a change.

Nila, I'm coming.

Once she was in my arms, I was never letting her go again.

Looking through the taxi windshield, my eyes widened at the countless cars and SUVs decorating the entrance to the Hall. All of them black and threatening—waiting for commands.

I hope to fuck that's Tex and his men.

"That's ten pounds twenty." The driver twisted in his seat, pointing at the metre.

I threw him twenty quid from the bankroll the captain had given me in exchange for another diamond and climbed out. "Keep the change."

The driver nodded, shifting into gear and pulling away from the verge. As he drove off, I prowled toward the convoy, peering at men I didn't recognise.

No, that wasn't true.

I did recognise them. I recognised the ferocity in their gaze. The merciless stare of a hired killer. I felt their quiet thoughts and slipstream of emotional commitment to a job they'd been hired to do.

I wanted to grab them all in a fucking hug and thank them profusely for being on my side after a lifetime of war.

Vaughn spotted me first.

Nila's brother careened around a 4WD, pointing his finger in my face. "*You*. What the *fuck* is going on?" Gel plastered black hair away from his face; his eyes ready to slaughter me.

Not giving me time to reply, he grabbed his right forearm, shoving it beneath my nose. "What did you do to her? Why do I have an ache in my arm?" Grabbing me by the neck, he growled, "Tell me what the *fuck* you did to my sister!"

His internal thoughts flew haywire, screeching in fear and

fluster.

I held up my hands, submitting to his hold. "Your fight is not with me." I held my ground as he clenched his fists, tightening his grip. "I didn't touch her. I *love* her. I'm on your side, Weaver."

"Let him go, V." Tex appeared from around another vehicle, dressed all in black like his son. They truly looked alike, whereas Nila looked very much like Emma. A true family. The only thing my family had in common was insanity and golden eyes.

Damn genetics.

Damn contracts and debts and greed.

Vaughn bared his teeth, ignoring his father. "I asked you a question, Hawk. I *said* what the *fuck* is going on? I didn't ask if you're on our side. That's debatable, and we'll make up our own minds without you telling us thank you very fucking much."

I dropped my hands, my fingers itching for one of the guns holstered to the men slowly surrounding us. Each man held an arsenal on his body, fully equipped for battle and not afraid of firepower or injury.

My back ached from bowing with my neck in a headlock, but I wouldn't fight. I refused to fight with the Weavers anymore. "Let me go."

"No. Not until you talk."

"We're going to end this." My voice sounded tired to my ears, but truth rang loud. "That's what's going on."

V shook with anger. "Where's my sister?"

"At the Hall."

"Is she safe?" Tex asked, his aging face strained but resolute. In a different world, I would've liked Nila's father. His inner thoughts were gentle and quiet—almost like Kes with the ability to switch off overwhelming hate or happiness, living a mediocre life of monitored emotions. Unlike Kes, who'd learned to hide in order to live a better existence, I doubted Textile did it for fun.

My suspicions were he kept his true feelings locked away, padlocked and buried, so he didn't have to deal with a daily drowning of sorrow and regret of losing the women of his family.

Surprisingly, there was no guilt. He'd allowed me to take Nila with no fight or fury. He should feel some patina of shame for handing over his daughter, even if he'd been trained to do exactly that. There was more to his defeat than he let on. Something lurked on the outskirts of his thoughts…wrapped up in flickering pride and solemn dignity at something he'd done where Nila was concerned.

What did he do?

Vaughn suddenly released me, pushing me away from him and rubbing his forearm. "She's hurt. I feel her—always did."

My eyes shot to his, appreciating the twin-link he and Nila shared more than he knew. He might feel her physically, but I felt her emotionally. And he was right, she *was* hurt.

Tex sucked in a heavy breath, his large shoulders rolling beneath stress. I made a note to ask him what he'd done when this was all over. I wanted to know his secrets. I had a feeling he held the answers to a lot of loose ends.

But now is not the time.

Nila.

We'd stalled enough.

Is she safe? Are you safe, Nila? Please, be fucking safe.

I shook my head. "We need to go. You're right, she's hurt. My father broke her arm, and I have no doubt he means to do more than that. That's why we have to move fast."

"*What!?*" V's eyes narrowed to slits. "You'll pay, Hawk. I'll make you pay for every injury Threads has endured because of your fucking family."

My heart pattered irregularly—my rhythm always struggled when faced with such overwhelming emotion. "I'll pay whatever you want, Weaver. But for now, we have to work together." Eyeing up the cars, I counted eight in total. At least two men to a car, so sixteen men.

Sixteen men to kill Cut and whatever brothers remained patriotic to him. I didn't relish the thought of killing club members who'd served beneath me for years, but maybe I wouldn't have to if Flaw managed to separate the loyal from the traitors.

I cocked my chin at the silent mercenaries. "They work for you?"

Tex nodded. "I told you I'd hired help. I found them before you came to take Nila."

My nostrils flared. "*Before?*"

If he had them before, why not use them to protect Nila from ever falling into my hands?

Tex swallowed, looking away. "I meant *after* you took Nila. I gathered an army. I won't let you take another of my loved ones, Hawk. I won't."

His slip-up and sudden lie to switch timelines didn't make sense. There was no one else to take. Nila was the firstborn girl. We never went after Weaver sons.

So what is he hiding?

Pushing aside my curiosity, I nodded. "I know. And you won't have to." Searching for the ringleader, discarding ex-Army and Marines by the way they held their shoulders and weapons, I ordered, "Who's in charge here?"

Vaughn stomped closer, poking his annoying finger in my chest. "We are, motherfucker."

I gritted my teeth. "Fine, if that's how you want to play it. How about you give them orders on how best to infiltrate. If you know where Cut will have Nila and how to get inside the estate undetected, be my fucking guest."

Tex growled under his breath. "Watch it. We're tolerating you right now. Doesn't mean we've agreed to be your taskforce when you've already taken so much. We're here for Nila and that's it. You hear me?"

I swiped a hand over my face. "If you're here for Nila, prove it. She's in trouble. The longer we stand here comparing dick sizes, the worse she'll need help." Spreading my arms, I snarled, "You decide. You want my insider knowledge so this goes well or would you rather do things your way and risk Nila dying and yourself in the crossfire?"

Tension smouldered between us, itching for a naked flame to incinerate.

Tex looked at Vaughn. They shared a silent conversation until finally Tex exhaled heavily. "Fine. We agree to cooperate."

"Good." I crossed my arms. "I'm in control from here on out. I'm the only one who knows where to go, how to get in, and what we need to do."

"Like fuck you are. I've stayed in your house of horrors. I know enough to guess——"

Tex placed his hand on his son's shoulder. "Enough, V. Let him. I just want my daughter back, and if he says he can do that, then…let him get her back." Twisting to face an elderly man with a black beanie on his head, Tex motioned him to come forward. "Change of plans, Dec. Follow Hawk's orders. Let's move out."

The silent journey through the estate twisted me with fear.

The driveway went on for a fucking eternity, revealing our black line of cars clearly. I just hoped Cut was busy elsewhere and didn't look out the south-facing windows onto the sweeping vista as we crept over Hawksridge.

Rolling hills and soft dirt hindered but didn't slow; we chewed up distance, bringing me closer to Nila and my dreaded birthright.

I rode with the ringleader, Declan. He'd given me his resume in a few short bullet points.

Retired military.

Awarded service.

Highly trained and skilled with the best men loyalty and money could buy.

Sitting with him, I suffered flashbacks of hunting animals for food and sport. For someone like me——someone who felt not just human emotions but even the emotions of the basest of creatures—I struggled to hunt like a normal, unfeeling being.

Cut knew that.

He'd forced me to hunt until I could switch off the panic of the prey and focus on the joy of the predator.

It'd been one of his most valuable lessons.

Focus on the hawk stalking the rabbit, not the rabbit running for its life.

Focus on the dog's infectious joy bounding after a deer, not the deer galloping from death.

Those two parallels had been so fucking hard to choose between, but I'd done it. I'd even been so successful, the predator's joy infected me enough for hunting to become almost…fun.

And now I was on another hunt. About to hurt others, about to feel their pain.

But I could do it because I was the beast, not the quarry. And I was surrounded by men who focused on the same sweet victory.

That was all I needed to know. I trusted Declan and his men. I just hoped they'd be enough if the Black Diamonds decided to fight against us.

I hope Flaw came through.

I didn't want bloodshed. The Hall had seen enough fucking death. I wanted to end terror without more of it. But I was prepared for either scenario.

Hawksridge appeared above us, watching us with its impressive turrets and spires. The ancient building had been my home all my life. The grounds had been my salvation. The animals, my lifeblood.

I'd grown up running away from this place, but now, I wanted to turn my legacy around. I would rule a different dynasty from the one Cut envisioned, and I would do it on my own terms with Nila by my side.

Pointing at a service track—an un-tarmacked path with weeds growing through pebbles, I said, "Follow that road. It'll cut across the chase and head in behind the main entrance. We might prevent being seen a little longer."

Hawksridge sat perched on a hill. The design was deliberate for times of war and protection from enemies who might try to topple the estate. No ambush could happen. No entrapment. We would be seen—it was a matter of time. I just didn't want to show my hand before we were close enough to launch an attack.

Where are you, Nila?

Was she with Bonnie on the third floor?

Was she with Cut on the fourth?

Or was she already in the ballroom on the ground floor, on her knees and about to become the latest stain in a horrendous basket?

"Step on the gas." My order lurched us forward, tyres grinding gravel, skidding around bends and hurling us closer to the awaiting battleground.

I'd deliberately chosen to travel with two mercenaries and not Nila's brother or father. I needed to keep my head clear and I couldn't do that with Vaughn's emotions bouncing kamikaze in his skull or Textile's secrets gnawing a hole in my patience.

No one talked as we pulled to a stop by the stables. A wash of homesickness crippled me. Not for the Hall but for Wings. Being around so many people set my nerves on edge. My condition flickered with intensity and numbness. One moment, I was blank from sensory overload, and the next, I'd succumb to frivolous things of what the men would do afterward, what they planned to do during.

People saw fellow humans as respectful and civilized. Only, I knew the truth.

They were as animalistic as they'd been hundreds of years ago. Inner thoughts and unspoken quips painted them as vindictive, selfish, and focused on things that should never be revealed aloud.

It almost made me happy to know I wasn't as terrible as

I'd feared. I was normal. I was human. I had faults and flaws and fears, but despite all of those, I tried to be better, bolder, and braver than I truly was.

And that was what made right triumph over wrong.

Isn't it?

At least, I hoped so.

The convoy rolled to a stop, and Dec gave the order to leave the cars behind. Boots landed on gravel, and car doors quietly closed. Concentration levels of the men added to the cauldron of emotions, and I wiped away a combination of fever and sweat from trying not to listen.

Once Nila was safe and Hawksridge secured, I would need to be alone. I knew the symptoms of system failure. I knew when I'd reached my limit. A wash of nausea climbed up my gullet, and my hands shook as I wrapped fingers around the gun Dec handed me.

I was borderline.

Overtiredness and over-empathy would end up killing me if I didn't kill Cut soon.

"Come on." I waved for the men to line up behind me, a black line patrolling from the stables toward the Hall.

Leaving the cars behind, I guided the men up the hill toward the house. We stuck to the trees as much as possible, moving in short waves. Weapons were drawn as we crested the hill and made our final descent.

I didn't say a word, too focused on seeking weakness and attack points of my family's home. I searched the shadows for Kill and his men, trying to see where they hid, but spotted no one.

The closer we got to the Hall, the more my heart pounded.

V and Tex shadowed my every move and luck kept us shrouded long enough to sidle up to the ancient architecture and fan out around the buttresses of Hawksridge.

Left or right?

I couldn't decide.

Dining room wing or staircase leading to boudoirs and

parlours?

The wind howled over the orchard, sounding like someone screamed.

I froze; my head tilted toward the dining room wing...the ballroom wing.

The noise came again.

Haunting.

Lamenting.

Dragging chills over my flesh.

It came again, shrill and cut short.

It wasn't the wind.

Fuck surprise.

Fuck the regimented ambush.

Fuck everything.

Nila!

I held my gun aloft and charged.

"READY TO DIE, Nila?"

Cut's voice physically hurt me as he forced me up the crudely made steps and onto the wooden foundation. My heart tore through my ribcage.

Jasmine screamed from across the room. Her cry split the ballroom apart, tears staining her pretty cheeks. "Please."

Tears of my own threatened to wash me away, but I wanted to remain dry-eyed. I wanted to remember my last few moments in perfect clarity and not swimming with liquid.

Cut wrenched my arms behind my back; I groaned with agony from my break. The twine wrapped around my wrists, bending my forearm unnaturally.

"Please. Don't—"

Cut spun me around with his large hands on my shoulders. His golden eyes glowed with apology, and at the same time, resolution. "Hush, Nila." His lips touched mine, sweet and soft, before he marched me to the kneeling podium and pressed hard. "Kneel."

"No!"

"*Kneel.*" His foot kicked out, nudging the back of my knee, shattering my stability and sending me cracking into place. I cried out as the pain in my kneecaps matched the pain in my arm. Like a snapped needle, I lost my sharpness, my fight.

The ballroom splendour mocked me as I bowed unwillingly at the foot of my executioner.

Velvet and hand-stitched crewel on the walls glittered like the diamonds the Hawks smuggled—a direct contrast to the roughly sawn wood and crude craftsmanship of the guillotine dais.

"Don't do this. Cut…think about what you've become. You can *stop* this." My voice mimicked a beg, but I'd vowed *not* to beg. I'd seen things, understood things, and suffered things I never thought I would be able to endure. I'd been their plaything for months, their adversary for years, their nemesis for centuries. I refused to cry or grovel. I wouldn't give him that satisfaction.

I know the history of the Hawks. I know I'm stronger than they are.

"I want to live. Please, let me live."

He cleared his throat, masking any thoughts of hesitation. "In five minutes, this will all be over." Cut bent to the side and collected a wicker basket.

The wicker basket.

I didn't want to think about what its contents would be.

He placed it on the other side of the wooden block.

My heart jack-hammered, thudding faster and faster until lightheadedness made me sick.

My lungs demanded more oxygen. My brain demanded more time. And my heart…it demanded more hope, more life, more love.

I'm not ready.

Not like this.

"Cut—"

"No. No more talking. Not after everything you've done. My son. My mother. You think you've stolen everything I care about, but I'm going to steal so much more from you. From Jethro. And when I find out where Kestrel is, I'll steal from him, too." Ripping a black hood from his pocket, he didn't hesitate. No fanfare. No pauses.

"No!" I cried out as the scratchy blackness engulfed my

face, tightening by a cord around my throat.

The Weaver Wailer chilled me. The diamond collar that'd seen what I'd seen and whispered with phantoms of my slain family prepared to revoke its claim and detach from around my neck.

This was it.

The Final Debt.

Cut pushed my shoulders forward.

I struggled, willing my wrists to unlock, to find a weakness in the rope to get free.

A heavy yoke settled over the top of my spine.

No. This can't be it. This can't be!

"Goodbye, Nila."

The breeze of Cut moving to the side sent goosebumps over my nape. My breath clouded the hood. My eyelashes jewelled with unshed tears.

I hunched, tensing against the painful conclusion.

I couldn't get free.

I couldn't save myself.

I hadn't won.

Cut's boots crunched on the platform, the gentle clink of rope and pulley signalling he'd reached for the release of the blade.

I waited for his last history lesson.

Surely, I should have a history lesson.

All the debts did. He couldn't have forgotten the theatrics of the debt. His story would extend my life just a little longer.

But no words fell.

Only my breathing…

My heart beating…

My tears falling…

My body living its final seconds…

I'm dead.

I curled inside, waiting to perish.

A loud bang rang in my ears.

For a moment, I thought I'd died.

In my mind, I saw the jerk of the rope. I felt the slice of sharpness. I suffered the untethering severance.

I waited for some mystical deliverance where my soul flew free, growing wings to hover over my decapitated body.

I hung in limbo waiting for pain or freedom.

But neither came.

What was death?

How would it feel?

What should I expect?

Would the blade slice through and turn me from alive to dead? Would I know once it had happened? Would I witness the end and feel the agony as my soul snipped free?

Or would it be over so fast I wouldn't even know he'd stripped my life away?

I tensed.

Nothingness...

Am I dead?

Nothing happened.

Then every sense rushed into liveliness. The hood still covered my head. The yoke still crushed my shoulders. And the burning break in my arm still throbbed.

All my discomforts returned along with noise.

So, so much noise.

Deafening noise.

Gunfire slaughtered the air as footsteps pounded the hardwood floor of the ballroom. Men hollered. Things banged and clanged and a cacophony replaced the empty silence.

Curses. Words. Promises. They were all cut short as fighting broke out all around me.

I couldn't see, but I could *feel.*

The whoosh of wind as bodies flew past. The flinch of bullets flying too close to my skin. And Cut's hand on my head as he bellowed for it all to stop. "Black Diamonds! Attack!"

More boots. More curses. More bullets.

Thank you, thank you, thank you.

My final hopes had been answered, my prayers delivered.

Help had arrived at the last second.

Who was out there?

Who fought on my behalf?

My eyes begged to see. My body twisted to know. But Cut's fingers dug into the hood, pressing my throat against the wood and the yoke tight over my shoulders.

Instead of dying, I'd entered a warzone where my vision couldn't tell me a story.

I huddled at Cut's feet, my spine curled and knees bruised beneath a guillotine just waiting for the sharp edge to plummet.

My heart lodged in my throat, terrified a rogue bullet would slice the rope and drop the blade to butcher my tender flesh.

I was alive, but for how much longer?

How reckless was the fighting?

How could they prevent an unforeseen event from killing me all while they tried to save me?

"Fuck." Cut never stopped touching me, his fingers digging into my scalp as anarchy rained. "Over there, get him!" His orders fell on the raucous, delivered to an unseen fighter.

I had no way to judge time, but the war only increased in ferocity. More gunfire, more thuds as bodies fell and fists connected with flesh.

My ears rang with gunshots. My thoughts suffocated with violence and mayhem.

Grunts and curses bounced off portraits and velvet, changing the destiny of the ballroom from dancing frivolity to carnage brutality.

Stop.

Don't stop.

Save me.

Don't kill me.

Slowly, curses switched to moans and stampeding footsteps gave way to limping.

The fight could've lasted hours or seconds. The only thing I knew with certainty was I clung to this life—the one I didn't want to leave—and the break in my arm cemented me firmly into being.

Finally, a stranger's voice crescendoed over everything else. "You've lost, Hawk. Step away from the rope if you wish to remain alive and not meet your maker."

That voice…I didn't recognise it.

Shivers stole my muscles.

Cut could still kill me.

The battle was over, but my life could be, too.

I couldn't breathe.

One second.

Two.

Three.

Disbelief and uprising perfumed the air. Boots stomped forward, the click of a bullet entering a trigger chamber the only noise in the suddenly silent ballroom.

"Let her go, Cut."

That voice I did recognise. I would know it anywhere.

Him.

I trembled in love.

I wept in gratitude.

He'd come for me.

He'd saved me.

Jethro.

"Never. Lower your weapon, or I pull. I'll do it, Jet. You know I will."

Another voice I adored joined that of my lover. "You do and I'll shoot you until you're so full of holes even the worms won't want you."

My father.

"And if he shoots you, I'll shoot you three. You'll be fucking shredded."

My twin.

Their voices pulsed with barbarity I'd never heard before.

Three men I never thought would be in the same room together, let alone fighting on the same side. How things had changed since that night in Milan.

I wanted so much to stay alive. To launch into Jethro's arms and kiss my father and touch my twin. But no one moved as I remained trapped by the guillotine.

Hope warred with defeat.

Cut could still kill me so easily and no one would be able to stop him. If they shot him and he held the rope in his hand, the guillotine would fall. If he decided to commit suicide and die right alongside me, no one could stop him from releasing the blade.

Only the final shred of decency left in Cut could stop him from doing the unthinkable and stripping me of a future I so desperately wanted.

Do something.

I didn't know what. My mind was blank.

Play him...

Cut had welcomed me into his home, he'd had moments of civility, of *normalness*—he was human beneath his devilish ways. Perhaps...perhaps there was some way to cajole him into listening.

I whispered through the hood, "I forgive you."

It sounded condescending and forced.

Try harder.

"I forgive you for everything you've done. What you did to Emma, me, your children. I forgive you. Let me live and break the indebted history."

Jethro sucked in a breath.

No one else spoke.

Everything hinged on the bond between Cut and me.

I huddled beneath the blade...waiting for his decision. Over the past few months, we'd come to understand one another. I knew he loved his children in his twisted way. And he knew I wouldn't give up without a fight.

There was hatred between us but respect, too.

If only that respect saved my life.

The whole room paused, watching history unfold.

Feet scuffled and weapons spewed rich-smelling smoke from used gunpowder, but no one moved.

My spine tickled with tears, fearing the worst.

I'd offered my forgiveness, going against everything I'd wanted to say. I'd traded my own morals for the right to keep my life. But what if it wasn't enough? What if my only value to Cut was in pieces?

"Cut..." I breathed. "Don't let her win."

The pulley clanked as Cut flinched. I didn't need to look into his eyes to know I'd hit home. Watching Bonnie die of her body's own volition had taught me something. She had been the root of all psychotic and immoral behaviour in her family. She was the one who drove her children to the point of lunacy. She was the seed sprouting such demonic petals.

And now, she was dead.

"You don't need to obey her anymore." My voice came out half-prayer, half-beg. "Free me. End this."

Once again, silence settled like a smothering pillow.

No one moved.

Cut's body heat branded my thigh, standing, just standing. *Deliberating.*

Then...finally...the clinking of rope and mechanism sounded again, only this time I didn't fear it. Cut's leg nudged me as he secured the rope, staying the blade and my death.

I didn't breathe as he squatted beside me.

I didn't flinch as his hands landed on my shoulders, undoing the yoke and helping me to my feet.

I didn't make a noise as his fingers untied the rope around my wrists and his touch grabbed a handful of hair as he tore off the hood in one swipe.

I didn't do anything to make him regret his courageous decision.

He'd saved me knowing he was doomed himself.

Was that redemption? Was it enough to be free of everything he'd done?

I trembled as the black material freed my vision, blinking

as my eyes accommodated to light.

Cut didn't smile or grimace, he just stared.

I wanted some time to take stock of how close I'd been to dying. To look my potential murderer in the face and thank him for sparing me even while hexing him to hell.

But the moment our gazes met, Jethro stormed up the podium and yanked Cut's hands behind his back.

Bryan didn't say a word, submitting to his son.

I remained locked in the moment, reading so much into Cut's eyes but not understanding any of it. Rubbing my throat and the phantom slice through my neck, I nodded. "Thank you."

Cut shrugged in answer to all the questions I wanted to ask, before allowing his eldest to jerk him down the steps and throw him into my father's control.

The minute Cut looked away, my attention switched to the space around me.

I gasped.

The pristine ballroom had turned into a warzone. Blood spilled and broken men decorated the pretty floor. Men dressed in black and Black Diamond brothers both moaned and held their multiple wounds.

What the hell happened?

Who were these men?

Flaw came forward with Jasmine at his side. He gave me a tight smile as Jethro gripped my upper arms. "Are you okay?"

I flinched, drinking him in.

Was I in shock? A dream?

I couldn't make sense of how calmly I accepted that I was about to die and now…wasn't. I'd been granted a second life…and all I could do was nod in a daze and blink in a stupor.

"Fuck, Nila." Jethro crushed me to him. My broken arm wailed, but I didn't care at all. All I cared about was him.

I hugged him back, squeezing as hard as I could. "You're here."

"I'm here."

"You saved me."

"You saved me first."

"I love you."

"I love you more."

"It's over." He pulled back, kissing my lips with the softest flutter.

"Is it truly?"

Jethro smiled with the wattage of a thousand moons. "It's done."

My heart unfurled, and for the first time, I believed that.

The Final Debt would never be paid.

The Hawks had lost.

The Weavers were free.

The Debt Inheritance would never claim another victim.

Jethro

"NO, FOR THE final time, you're not coming." I pushed Nila aside. "You're not going to be there when I do what needs to be done."

Her mouth opened to argue, her uninjured arm hugging her broken one. "But—"

"No buts. You're not coming. No matter what you say. You. Are. Not. Coming." A sliver of the old me—the arsehole who'd collected her that first night—came back. That shell had long since broken, but it rapidly reformed.

And I let it.

I let it because what I was about to do would test every inch of my condition. It would kill me as much as it would kill Cut because I would feel everything my father would go through. I wouldn't be able to shut off his emotional screams nor freeze myself from ignoring his thoughts.

I would be with him for every lash.

Nila tried to grab my arm. "Jet—"

Dodging her hold, I pointed a finger in her face. "No, Nila. You're to stay. *Obey* for once. Don't make me ask again."

"You're not asking, you're telling."

"Goddammit." I swallowed hard, running a hand through my hair. I hadn't slept in days, my body hurt all over, and my mind barely functioned from dealing with so much death and agony in the ballroom. Seeing her on her knees with the hood on her face and guillotine above her head—it'd fucking crippled me.

I'd hurt so many people for her. I wore their souls like badges of worthless honour. And yet, she *still* argued.

I can't do this.

You have to.

I couldn't falter now. Not when the end was so close.

All I wanted to do was drag Nila to her quarters, tend to her arm, and fall asleep. I wanted today to be over so tomorrow could banish the past.

But I couldn't.

I had things to do, and I would not—no matter how much she fucking argued—let Nila be a part of them.

I looked at my sister as she wheeled closer. My eyes shot two messages: *Help and don't argue.* My voice sounded like I'd been smoking for decades. "Take Nila to her quarters."

Jasmine nodded slightly, understanding better than anyone what I was about to do and why I had to do it. Her fingers slinked around Nila's unbroken wrist.

Nila jerked, trying to free herself. "What? No way." Managing to shake Jasmine off, she planted one hand on her hip; the other she let hover by her waist, protected by her body.

Her gaze darted between Cut and me. "He's not worth it. Can't you see that? He isn't worth what you're about to—"

I grabbed her cheeks, rubbing my thumbs over her face. "Nila...shush. I need you to let me do this."

Tears sprang to her eyes. The diamond collar he'd almost extracted glittered in the false light of the chandeliers.

I forced myself to hide my nerves, soothing her with whispered confidence. "Don't ask me to stop. It's what I need to do to fix my family and yours—our very history."

Tears trickled over my thumbs as she fought my decision. "But—"

"There are no buts, Needle." Looking at Cut, I hardened

my heart toward him. He'd done the right thing in the end. He'd let her go. Nothing had stopped him from killing Nila in front of me. Only his decency and lingering affection for Emma.

When Nila had forgiven him, I thought for sure he would pull the lever. He'd never been good at accepting charity.

But for once, he went against the actions of the man who'd raised me and became a hero. He deserved a fragment of respect for that gallant move.

But he also deserved to pay a very painful toll for every other sin he'd committed.

That was his fate.

And it was my fate to deliver it.

Nila pressed her cheek into my palm, her skin warm beneath my touch. "Kite...I—"

I understood her knotted thoughts and scrambled conclusions. "I know." My voice was a breath as I kissed her. "I understand your fear, but you have to trust me."

How many times had I asked her to trust me, only to shatter the trust she bestowed?

I won't shatter it this time.

I knew what I was doing.

Don't I?

Nila's onyx eyes glowed with rebellion, and I steeled myself against yet another argument. I sensed she only wanted to support me. For me to lean on her while I did something so heinous. But I didn't *want* to lean on her. I had to do this for me, my siblings, my past and present.

I couldn't have her there because I didn't know if I'd be able to carry out the punishment he deserved. I didn't know if I'd break and crumble and submit to his power like I'd done all my life.

It would be my biggest trial. But I'd try my fucking hardest to make Cut pay.

Dropping my hands from Nila's cheeks, I stepped back. "Just trust me, okay?"

Kill morphed from the men checking on the wounded, coming toward our tight-knit gathering.

Flaw had fetched his medical equipment and put his healing knowledge to work on those needing immediate attention. I trusted him to arrange help and take those who required more than he was capable of to the hospital without alerting a massacre had just taken place.

Killian had come through for me. He'd waited outside the ballroom where Tex, V, and our team of mercenaries poured in. He had his gun pinpointed on Cut and would've pulled the trigger if we hadn't arrived at that exact moment.

He would've saved Nila without a bloodbath, but by doing so, he would've stripped me of the right to make my father pay. It'd been risky, barging in and giving Cut the opportunity to murder Nila right before my eyes, but Cut didn't know everything that I did.

He slipped.

In Africa, I'd felt a slight thawing in him. And today, as we barged in and brought death on our heels, he looked almost…relieved. As if he expected me to show up and was grateful it was over.

I couldn't understand it. But he couldn't keep it hidden any longer. He'd finally shown the truth of how tired he was. How tired we all were.

All my life, he'd been a controlling bastard with unattainable ideals and strict rules. I'd maintained my belief that he never liked us, let alone loved us. But there was something more to him. Something I never let myself focus on as it only confused my conclusion of my father.

But I sensed it now. A deeper facet poured from Cut as Kill jerked him from Textile's arms and pinched his shoulders. My father held a lot of hate and delivered many ruthless requests, but he also held compassion and guilt.

And that guilt had steadily grown more and more dominant the longer Nila lived with us.

That was another reason why I wanted to be alone with

him. I wanted to look him in the eye, drop my defences, and truly strip my father of his secrets so I could understand him for the first time in my life.

And that was why I didn't know if I'd be able to go ahead with what he deserved. because what if I found his secrets redeemed him? What if I felt something that changed twenty-nine years of believing a lie?

"Jethro…" Nila's voice dragged me back from thoughts and tiredness. My vision wavered, dancing with figments of hallucinations from lack of sleep and stress overload. The hallucinations weren't anything major, just the odd flutter of a curtain looking like a blackbird or a ripple of sunshine resembling a bumblebee or butterfly.

Innocuous things but non-existent things nevertheless.

Sleep.

I could sleep soon.

Pinching the bridge of my nose, I inhaled deeply. *Keep it together. A few more hours and I'll be free.* We'd all be fucking free, and I could rest safely for the first time since I could remember.

The minute this was over, I would visit my brother. I would tell him things were taken care of and it was safe to come home.

I missed him so fucking much.

Time to return, baby brother.

Time for me to show him I had his back like he'd had mine all my life.

"Kite…I do trust you. But you need to rest." Nila's fingers landed on my hand. "Please, whatever you're thinking of doing, it's already eating you alive." Pointing at Cut imprisoned in Kill's arms, she murmured, "You've won. The Debt Inheritance is over. Let the authorities deal with him."

I chuckled darkly. "Authorities? Nila, we *own* the authorities. No one would dare testify or incarcerate him. If you want justice, this is the only way." Cupping her chin, I smeared a strand of cotton from the hood away from her skin.

"Trust me when I say this is what needs to happen. Don't try to stop me again."

Nila dropped her gaze. Her heart raced, her emotions bubbling like the hot springs beneath the Hall, but she obeyed me. She stepped back, giving me the freedom to leave.

I sighed, thanking her silently.

Cut didn't say a word—not that he could. The minute he'd submitted to my custody, I'd returned the favour of a reeking rancid gag and duct-taped his mouth closed. His nostrils flared, white hair cascading over his forehead in a tumbled mess.

Daniel was dead. Bonnie would be soon. Cut would be the next to expire.

Nila stepped back as Jasmine wheeled closer to me and grabbed my hand. "I won't try to stop you, but don't feel like you have to—"

"Don't you start, Jaz."

"I'm only worried about what—"

I laughed coldly. "What it will do to me? Jaz, you know yourself what will happen if I *don't* do this. I'll never forgive myself. He's delivered enough agony to those we love. Don't you think it's time he felt his own medicine?"

Kill didn't say a word, gripping my father tighter in his arms.

Nila bit her lip, looking down at Jasmine, waiting for her reply.

Jaz sat stiffly in her chair. I let my condition fan stronger, singling her out in the crowd. She felt the same fear Nila did. Fear that I'd never be the same if I did this. Fear that it would forever haunt me.

That might be the case, but I owed this debt. To the miners who'd helped free me. To Kill who'd had my back. To Textile for the death of his wife. To everyone involved in the Debt Inheritance.

I wasn't doing this for me. I was doing this for *them*. And it was a sacrifice I was willing to make.

Jaz smiled softly as my eyes met hers. Her emotions

quieted, fading into one singular calling: closure.

I nodded, letting her know I understood her conclusion. "Thank you."

She smoothed the blanket over her useless legs. Legs that'd been payment for me. Disability given by our father who would now answer for his crimes.

Tonight was the night everything ended.

Cut's life was the full stop on his terrible reign.

Jaz nodded, too. Wordlessly giving me permission and strength. Her eyes narrowed on Cut. "I tried to be the daughter you wanted, but I was never good enough. I hope that thought alone haunts you for eternity."

Cut's chest rose with an influx of breath, repentance bright in his gaze.

She didn't give him forgiveness like Nila had. She'd suffered too much at his hand to be so selfless.

Her switch of fear for me and need for retribution drenched her. She wanted me to do this. She *urged* me to do this.

Good enough for me.

Cut swallowed, his face glowing, filling with things addressed to his daughter. The scramble of emotions from him smothered me and I deliberated removing his gag to say farewell to Jasmine.

However, my sister decided for me. Her fists wrapped around her wheels, shoving backward and granting space for Killian to move forward.

"Take him." Her voice hissed. "I don't want to see him anymore." Grabbing Nila's hand, she kept her anchored as Kill stormed forward, carting Cut toward the exit.

Nila's gaze met mine. I sent a silent message. *You understand why?*

Her lips twisted, but she nodded. *Yes.*

"I'll come find you when it's done." Turning my back on Nila's family and a room full of carnage, I stalked past Kill and snapped my fingers for him to follow.

I didn't stop to give directions. I trusted the biker president of Pure Corruption would obey. Whatever hierarchy existed, we were on equal footing. Kill knew the terms when he came to help me. I would pay him back for his help. I would honour the agreement we'd made.

Besides, his task was almost over.

While mine is just beginning.

Leaving the room of men, I sucked in a breath. The oxygen helped cleanse my system of thoughts and pain. I did my best to shut out Cut, but I couldn't completely ignore him.

We were bound together until the end. Blood to blood. Pain to pain. There would be no separating my mind from his until he was dead.

"Jethro—" Nila gave chase, following us out the exit, leaving the guillotine behind.

I spun around just in time for her to launch into my arms. Her black hair glistened like a raven wing. The afternoon sunshine mocked us after the darkness that'd happened in the ballroom.

Kill continued onward, dragging Cut away and granting a small oasis of silence. My arms wrapped around her tightly even though I wanted to push her away.

Her chest rose and fell, her embrace one-armed with her other dangling painfully by her side. "Please, Kite…just stop for a moment and—"

"Nila, you promised."

"I know, but—" Her eyes met mine, glossing with angry tears. "I'm not going to stop you. I understand. I really do. I just. I needed to—I need…"

My heart overflowed, and I grabbed her. My forehead nudged hers as I bowed over her. "I know what you need."

My mouth claimed hers and she sighed, melted, positively submitted to my kiss. Her tongue instantly met mine in a tangle of hot desire, invoking pleasure and pain and undeniable passion.

This kiss deleted the last one we'd shared in the mine as

she was dragged away. That kiss had been a goodbye. This kiss was a hello. An acknowledgment we soon wouldn't have to fear tomorrow. That the future was no longer our enemy but our friend. We could be together. Our promise to get married could come true. Our heartbeats unnumbered now we'd won.

Pulling away, I kissed the tip of her nose, her eyelids, her hair. "I'll be back soon."

She arched in my hold, peppering my rough cheeks with affection. "I'll be waiting for you."

"I know."

Slipping from my embrace, her gaze travelled past me to Cut. "Do you mind?"

I stiffened but didn't stop her. "By all means."

If it granted her closure, who was I to stop her saying goodbye? Cut was no threat. Even if he wasn't bound and gagged and held by Kill, he wouldn't run. I knew he'd accepted his fate and would stand regal and defiant until the end.

His almost royal bearing made me proud for a moment. Proud that I came from such strong stock, even if madness ran in his veins. If my condition had prevented me from inheriting his drive for perfection, regardless of what sins he committed, then I was glad.

I wasn't like my family.

I was unique.

I was me.

And I'd never been more fucking grateful.

Nila padded over to Cut, her bare feet disappearing into the long grass. Kill didn't speak as she stopped in front of my father. The wind whipped her hair around her jaw, slicing and slicking, looking like oil in the breeze.

"I said before that I forgive you."

Cut shifted, rolling his shoulders in Kill's grip.

"I'm not here to take that forgiveness back. I don't even know *why* I'm here." She rubbed her face, trying to re-centre herself. "I guess I wanted to say...be thankful. Your crimes have caught up with you...and I'm there to see it." Her voice lowered as she looked back up. "I'm here to see you one last time. To know you're just human. That you were doing what you thought was right, but now you have to pay. We all have to pay, Cut. Nothing is free in this world, and you've taken enough from my family that from now on, we've paid our dues and deserve happiness. I won't celebrate your death. I won't think of you with hate or cruelty. But I *will* be free of you, and I'll be happy you're no longer there to terrorize my lineage."

Shuffling away, she smiled softly. "May God have mercy on your soul, Bryan Hawk, and for you to find redemption in whatever awaits you."

Looking at me one last time, she moved back toward the Hall.

V and Tex hugged her, kissed her, then let her go.

Flaw appeared from the exit, jogging over to Nila and slinging an arm over her shoulders, joining her family. His possession didn't spark jealousy; if anything, it granted peace knowing she would be cared for and protected while I was gone.

"Thank you, Flaw." My voice travelled on the gentle wind to the Black Diamond brother. I didn't know how much war had gone on before our arrival, but he'd managed to enlist over three-quarters of the brothers to fight on our side. I would have to debrief and investigate each member and have them swear new allegiance to me, but for now, Flaw was in charge.

He saluted me casually. "No problem."

V guarded her while Tex looked dotingly at his children.

Switching his grip on Nila, Flaw relinquished her shoulders in favour of her hand. "I'll take her to her quarters and make sure she's fed and rested. Don't worry about her."

I smiled in gratitude.

Nila didn't say a word as Flaw guided her around Hawksridge, leading her toward another entrance and avoiding the nastiness of the ballroom. Tex and V followed, smearing bloody hands on their black trousers.

I would never know if Flaw's loyalty was because he

trusted me or because of his steadfast friendship with Kes. Either way, he was a good man. And his actions today had prevented yet more deaths and helped those injured with his medical help.

Turning my back on the Hall, I moved alongside Kill as he shoved Cut forward, leading us away from prying eyes and looming buildings.

We didn't talk as we traversed the lawn, circumnavigated the maintenance shed where Cut had given me the salt shaker and told me it was time for the Second Debt, and entered the woods.

Our shoes snapped twigs as we moved deeper into forest darkness.

"You sure you want to do this, Hawk?" Kill's voice grabbed my attention. He fisted Cut around the back of his neck, shoving him forward. Two of Kill's men flanked us, morphing from the trees where they'd been watching the Hall.

I appreciated the back-up, but I didn't want an audience. The minute we arrived at our destination, I would send them away.

I needed to be alone in this.

Looking at the Florida-born president, I nodded. "I know what I'll have to pay in order to get retribution. But yes, I'm sure."

Kill grinned. "When the day comes for me to claim vengeance on my own father, I'm taking it. I don't care how hard it will be to kill flesh and blood or how fucked-up I am afterward. I need closure. I understand you completely."

I didn't reply. I had no reason to. He lived the same predicament, and his approval helped fortify my resolve.

In shared brotherhood, we made our way down animal tracks and through clearings, moving ever deeper into the treeline.

The outbuilding I'd decided on existed the furthest from the Hall. This one was hidden—alone with its horrible secrets. A place I'd never been able to enter after what happened to

Jasmine, no matter what Cut did to me as a child. No matter the threats and corrections. No matter the curses and pain. I'd never stepped foot into the torture chamber again, boycotting its hateful memories.

Our clothing dappled with leaf stencils, trading sunshine for shadows as we traipsed deeper and deeper. The outbuilding nestled in the woods—swallowed whole by trees doing their best to delete the terrible atrocities.

We kept moving.

Cut didn't struggle, his breathing loud and uneven around the gag.

More flickering hallucinations played havoc with my vision. Leaves danced, turning briefly into wolves. Bracken crunched, morphing into badgers.

Goddammit, I need to rest.

My hand went to my side. The fever I'd had ever since heading to Africa hadn't broken or grown worse. If anything, it granted a heightened sense of everything, muddying outside influences, letting me focus entirely on what I wanted. What I needed. But it came with a price. A price of withering energy and health.

Soon.

Soon, I can rest.

Breaking through a final thicket, we stepped into a small glen.

The building loomed tall and ancient. Two stories high with oaks and pine surrounding it in their morbid cage. The double barn doors remained locked with a large padlock.

The key was hidden.

"Wait here." Leaving the men, I ducked into the woods and searched for the tree I needed. Cut had taken me the night he'd told me of my birthday present and inheritance of Nila. He'd marched me through the darkness, filling my head with tales of what would happen and how proud he was that soon I would show him how worthy I was and finally take the place I was born for.

My eyes searched the green gloom.

Where is it?

It took longer than I wanted, but finally, my strained eyes caught sight of the symbol of a diamond and an outline of hawk wings signalling I'd found the right one.

Climbing a few feet up the coarse bark using gnarly roots and limbs, I found the knot left behind after a branch fell away and reached inside for the packet. Jumping down, I undid the fastening and tossed out the key into my palm.

A few others jangled free, landing with a hint of rusty metal. The extras operated parts of the machinery inside. Machinery I had no intention of using or ever switching on again.

Fisting them, I turned on my heel and stomped out of the brush past Cut, Kill, and his men and toward the brittle barn doors.

My breathing turned harsh as I inserted the key into the tarnished padlock.

The mechanism turned as smoothly as the day the lock was bought, the doors creaking on their frame as I shoved open one partition. The stench of dead rodents and rotting foliage mixed with time-stale dust hit my nose.

Barring the entry with my body, I turned to face Kill.

The biker came forward, delivering my father.

I held out my arm. "Give him to me."

"You sure?"

"Very sure. I want to be alone for the next part."

Kill passed over my father without another word. He didn't try to talk me out of this. He didn't have any obligation to remind me that this was murder, not revenge. That I would become as bad as those I hated if I went through with this.

Kill was not my brother or my conscience. He'd done all he needed to. His obligations were complete.

Cut didn't struggle as I latched my fingers around his bound wrists. However, his eyes glowed with golden rage. His emotions poured forth, swamping with hatred and killable fury.

"Are we done?" Kill asked, crossing his arms over his leather jacket. "Will you be okay with your own men or do you want back-up?"

Shoving Cut into the barn, I ran a hand through my hair. "No. That's it. Your task is finished. You're free to return home, and I'll make sure to repay the favour whenever you need." Holding out my hand, Kill shook it.

"We'll wait until you're done. I'll station my men at the forest edge, just in case. Once they know you've finished, they'll leave." He cocked his head, eyeing the building. "How long will you need?"

His question weighted with hidden curiosities he wouldn't get answers to. *What will you do? What's in there? How badly will he die?*

I swallowed, dreading what my night would entail. "Until dark. I need until dark."

Kill grinned. "Six hours, it is." Moving away, his large boots created indents in the soft woodland. "Pleasure knowing you, Hawk. I doubt we'll see each other face-to-face again, but we'll stay in touch."

We'd come together for mutual advancement, and now, we would go our separate ways. It was for the best.

I waited for Kill and his men to disappear from the clearing before turning my back and entering the barn.

The moment I traded trees for tomb, I shed all resemblance of who I was.

I left behind my humanity.

I tore Nila from my heart.

I embraced the motherfucking ice my father had taught me.

This would kill me.

But it had to be done.

I stepped into the darkness and prepared to murder.

Nila

"HE WON'T BE able to live with himself."

Jasmine shook her head, wheeling toward me. "Yes, he will."

I sucked in a breath, looking toward the window. The same window where the bird of prey had delivered Jethro's note to meet me in the stable.

God, was that only a few days ago?

It felt like an entire lifetime.

I begged for a feathered messenger now to tell me everything was done, finished; that Jethro would return to me and nothing else could keep us apart.

Jasmine's wheels whispered over the thick carpet of my quarters. The soft bubble of the fish tank and gentle tick of the clock all screeched over my nerves.

Springing from my mattress, I paced the large room. On every surface scattered half-sewn garments, scribbled drawings, and hastily cut fabric. My Rainbow Diamond collection existed in all stages of creation, but I would burn every scrap if it would bring Jethro closure and erase everything that'd happened.

"Nila, stop. You're worn out." Jasmine stopped by the chaise, narrowing her eyes at my frantic pacing. "Sit down, for God's sake."

I glared, disobeying.

Flaw had done what he'd told Jethro. V and Tex had gone with the maids to spare guest rooms and Flaw had taken me quietly back to my quarters. He'd fetched a banquet of fruits, snacks, and vitamin rich food, and summoned a servant to help tend to my bruises in the shower.

I wanted to refuse the food, knowing Jethro was just as weak as I was. I wanted to decline the shower because why should I be comforted while Jethro had such a trial to endure?

But Flaw hadn't let me argue.

He'd crossed his arms and stood in my room while I showered away African dirt and dried sweat from the pain of my broken arm. Struggling to wash, I was grudgingly grateful for the sweet-smiling maid who helped me dry off with a fluffy towel and dress me in the black shift I'd worn when the weeping scabs on my back from the First Debt healed.

The steam and warmth from the shower helped ease my aches and injuries, conjuring sleepiness and lethargic healing.

By the time I re-entered my quarters, Flaw had a spread of plaster strips, gauze, and warm water—just like Cut used in Africa. He shuffled me over to the bench, shoved aside my needles and lace, and ordered me to eat while he gently felt my break, ensured my arm was in the correct position, and re-cast it with confident precision.

I'd wanted to ask him questions about his life. Find out how he became a smuggler when it was obvious his true calling was to heal. But once the first mouthful of delicious food hit my tongue, I couldn't stop eating.

And that was why I wouldn't stop pacing even though my arm still hurt, my knees still wobbled, and my eyes still burned with unshed tears. I couldn't sit still. I'd been on the brink of death, and now, I was alive with a full belly and the welcome numbing of painkillers.

What did Jethro have?

Nothing.

No one.

Out there, on his own, about to do the unthinkable.

Whirling around, I glowered at Jasmine. "He's an Empath, Jaz. How the hell does he think he'll make Cut pay without feeling everything he does to him? Whatever pain he bestows, it will boomerang back and hurt him in equal measure." Gripping my damp hair, I missed the length. I wanted to tug on the ends and find some relief from the rapidly building pressure of despair.

Jasmine sighed softly. "I learned early on that Jethro is stubborn—especially when he believes he's doing the right thing."

"But he *isn't* doing the right thing! He's going to kill—"

Her lips thinned. "And that's not the right thing? Tell me, Nila. How much disgrace, death, and debts does my family have to do to yours to make it the *right* thing?" She pointed at the closed door. "I bet if I found Tex and Vaughn and asked them what they thought of Cut's justice, they would dance for bloody joy."

I stormed toward her. The sling Flaw gave me kept my broken arm snug against my body, leaving me free to gesture with the other.

"I won't lie and say I don't want Cut to pay. That isn't what I'm worried about. I'm worried about what it will do to Jethro. What if this changes him? What if he can't wipe away—"

Jaz bent forward, capturing my hand. "Nila, shut up." Squeezing my fingers, her temper glittered in her gaze. "It isn't up to you. If Kite needs to do this—if he believes he has the strength to do this, then that's his call. He's waited almost thirty years to reap what his father has sowed. It isn't up to you, me, or anyone else to interfere."

I hated that she made sense.

My eyes once again returned to the window. My indignation and worry spilled out of me, dampening my desire to run after Jethro and stop him. My love for him flew out the window, winging to wherever he was.

"I just…" My head hung as I struggled to articulate what I truly fretted over. "I love him, Jaz. I love him so damn much. It terrifies me to think I've only just earned him and he might leave me. How can I help him if he returns broken? How can I piece together a future I want so desperately if he can only remember death and agony?"

Jasmine pulled me closer, forcing me to sit on the chaise. "Don't torture yourself with what-ifs, Nila." Her voice softened. "He *will* be able to live with himself, and I'll tell you why. You don't know what it was like living here since birth. You don't know the mind games we endured and the unsaid threats we were raised with."

Pointing at her useless legs, she smiled sadly. "I have a daily reminder of what our childhood was like. And Jethro…every time he looks at me, he remembers, too. I try to hide my inner thoughts when he's around because I don't want him to know how much I miss walking. How much I miss running and riding and even the luxury of leaving the estate and going to a shop to browse things on shelves that are eye height instead of unreachable from a chair."

My heart broke for her.

I grabbed her hand with my good one, granting back the support she'd just given me.

For all Jasmine's assurances that Jethro could withstand what he was about to do, I didn't believe her. His empathy would mean everything he did for himself, for his sister, for me, would ricochet with persecution.

I couldn't stomach the thought of how much strength that would take. How much courage to do something, knowing you would feel every inch in kind.

"I know he has to do this, Jaz. I just wish—I wish I could be there with him. To give him another emotion to focus on. To feel love even while drowning in pain."

Jaz tucked her hair behind her ear. "My brother knows what he's doing. He'll remember how to block it out. He'll remember how it felt when Cut taught him all those lessons."

My heart froze.

What if he doesn't remember how to block it out?

What's the worse fate? Remembering or not?

My fingers clutched Jasmine's harder. "Please, tell me he'll come back."

Jaz sat higher in her chair, pecking my cheek with a kiss. "He'll come back. And when he does, it will be over.

"For all of us."

Jethro

"YOU HONESTLY EXPECT me to believe you're going to be able to do this?" Cut spat at my feet the moment I removed his gag. His tongue worked, dispelling the taste of being silenced. "Come on, Jethro. We both know you don't have it in you."

I didn't answer.

Leaving him tied up, I moved toward the main attraction in the room.

Just like the guillotine had rested in the ballroom pride of place, the torturous device sat in this one. Dirty grey sheets covered the apparatus, looking part phantom, part ancient relic.

Cut shifted on the spot, his jeans rustling. "Jet, I'm still your father. Still your superior. Stop this fucking nonsense and untie me."

Once again, I didn't answer.

The longer I concentrated on what had to be done, the more I remembered my childhood lessons.

Silence is more terrifying than shouts.

Smoothness is more horrifying than sharp motions.

The key to being feared was to remain calm, collected, and most of all, with a finely balanced decorum where the prey believed they had a chance of redemption, only to take their final breath with hope still glowing in their heart.

He'd taught me that.

My father.

It was thanks to him I'd built a shell around myself and portrayed to the outside world I was strong and unflappable. While internally, I combusted with chaos and calamity.

Fisting the material, I yanked it off. The billow of moth-eaten fabric floated like wings as it settled elegantly on the floor. Dust shot into my lungs, dried leaves flurried in a vortex, and grit stung my eyes. But I didn't cough or blink.

I couldn't take my eyes off the implement of my childhood.

The rack.

My fingers shook as I stroked the well-worn wood. The leather buckles stained with my blood. The grooves of my heels as I kicked and kicked and *kicked.*

"No!"

"Stop your fucking bitching, Jethro."

"Dad, stop. I didn't do anything wrong."

Cut didn't listen. "You did do something wrong." His fingers bruised my ankles as he tightened the buckles. I kicked, doing my best to prevent the thick leather imprisoning me, but it was no use. Just like it'd been no use trying to stop him tying my hands above my head.

This wasn't the first time I'd been here, nor would it be the last.

But I wished so much I could finally be better so he didn't have to hurt me.

My ten-year-old heart punched against my ribcage. "I didn't. I can't help it. You know I can't help it."

Notching the leather one more loop, he patted my knee and walked toward my face. "I know, but that is no excuse."

I lay horizontally, looking up at my father. His dark hair turned whiter with each year. His leather jacket reeked of long rides and hard excursions.

"Haven't I been lenient the past few months? I tried to help you with kinder means. But that doesn't work with you." His face contorted with affection and disbelief. "Jet, you jumped in front of my gun. What the fuck

were you thinking?"

"You were going to shoot it!"

"Yes, it's food."

"No, it's a deer, and it felt fear." I squirmed, wishing I could make him understand the agony of hunting, of watching an animal notice the gun, feeling it understand my father's intentions and the wrecking ball of knowledge it was about to die. Animals were intelligent, beyond wise. They knew. They felt—same as us. "Can't you feel them, Dad? Can't you see how scary it is for them?"

"How many times do I need to tell you this, son?" His fingers grabbed my cheeks. "Animals are there for us to eat. We are all disposable and huntable if we don't fight back. Screw their fear. Screw their panic." His anger drenched his voice. "You. Are. My. Son. You will block it out. You will not embarrass me."

Moving toward my head, the distinct thump of his hand hitting the lever sent blood whizzing through my veins. "Okay, I'll stop. I didn't mean it. I won't do it again. I don't want to be a vegetarian. I'll hunt. I'll kill. Just don't—"

"Too late, Jet. Time for your lesson."

The lever cranked, the leather tightened, and pain began in earnest.

The memory ended, slamming me into the present. My heart raced as fast as it had back then, making me breathless with panic.

Only a memory.

Why did I come back here? Why didn't I choose an easier place?

Because this is where it all began. It needs to end here.

Fever drenched my brow as I glared at the rack. I'd lost count how many times I'd been subjected to its binds and stretching agony. Cut would leave me for hours to think about what I'd done, all while my joints popped and cracked.

Until the day he brought Jasmine along to share my lesson, of course.

We'd just been children. Trusting, gullible children.

Motherfucker.

Spinning, I marched toward my father and grabbed him by

the arm. "Even now you look at me as if I'm a disappointment. I feel you, Father. You truly don't think I'll have the strength to do this." Pressing my face close to his, I snarled, "Well, you're wrong. I'll do this because of what you did to me. Nila might've forgiven you, but I won't. I *can't*. Not until you've paid."

Cut stood taller, rolling his shoulders in my hold. His bound hands couldn't hurt me, but it didn't stop him from trying with his voice. "You always were a pussy, Kite. But if you let me go, I'll honour the inheritance. On your birthday, I'll give you what you want. I'll give you everything."

I clenched my jaw, shoving my father against the wooden rack. "I don't want your money."

He stumbled. "It's not my money. It's yours. I was just the safe keeper until you were of age."

"Bullshit." I sliced the rope around his wrists—the same rope that'd been wrapped around Nila's—and shoved him backward.

He grunted as his back slammed into the rack, his clothing smearing the dusty wood. He tried to shove off, but I pushed back. He lost his footing, sprawling over the contraption.

Without thinking, I looped the rope I'd just removed from his wrists around his neck and prowled to the other side of the single-bed sized platform. The twine hooked under his chin, forcing him to arch back, keeping him pinned and choking.

His fingers fought at the imprisonment, angry curses percolating in his chest.

I didn't give him leeway to talk. I pulled harder.

The harder I pulled, the more his emotions grew stronger. I could ignore them...for now.

"Nothing you say can save you, old man. I've learned a lot from you over the years. Let's see how much I remember."

"Wait—" Cut gurgled as I tied the rope to a hook below the rim, keeping his neck throttled. He lay awkwardly, his legs dangling off the side. Moving around to his front, I grabbed behind his knees and scooted his bulk onto the table.

He couldn't stop me, too focused on fighting the rope to

breathe.

Once his body was in position, I grabbed his flailing arms. Fisting his right, I pinned it to the unforgiving wood above his head, wrapping the leather around his wrist and fastening it tightly.

"No, wait!" His voice wheezed, his fingers clawing at his throat.

He continued to pant while I remained silent, moving down the table to capture his right leg. The leather had turned stiff with age and blood, but I managed to wrap it around his ankle, shoving his jeans out of the way and fastening tight.

"Jethro—stop."

I didn't obey.

Meticulously, I drifted to the left side of the table. His left leg tried to kick as I crushed his knee against the table. I wrestled with him to buckle the strap. I panted with exertion but won.

I was weak. Tired. Sick from traipsing around the world and dealing with complications he'd caused.

Yet, I had enough strength to subdue him.

Our gaze met as I skirted the table, reaching for his left arm.

"Don't." His eyes widened as I forcefully removed his fingers from around his neck, slamming it unceremoniously against the wood above his head. Bending over him, his chest rose and fell as I threaded the leather around his wrist and finished the final binding.

All four points secured. There would be no running, no fighting back—completely at my mercy.

"Still think I don't have it in me?" I looked down at him, pitying him a little. When I was younger, I'd always hoped he'd be lenient and let me go. I held blind belief he was my father and wouldn't hurt me too much.

But Cut knew otherwise. He remembered what he'd done to me. He recalled every scream and beg. It was his turn now.

I patted his cheek.

His lips tinged purple as he sucked in a lungful of air. "Jethro...fucking obey me and—"

"I'll never obey you again." Wanting him to remain lucid for future events, I unwrapped the rope from the hook at the base of the table and removed it from his throat.

He gasped, sucking in air while an angry red line marred his bristle-covered neck.

Leaving him to breathe, I moved toward the table beneath the grime-smeared window. No reflection or view from the outside world was noticeable. The pane had turned cloudy with age, deleting everything but us and what was about to happen.

Cut's emotions built until they threatened to eclipse my own. He wasn't terrified—not yet. He still believed I wouldn't be able to do this.

I'll prove you wrong.

Grabbing the corner of yet another dusty sheet, I whipped it off to reveal a long table of nasty implements.

My heart clenched as my eyes fell on every tool. Most had been used on me. But a few had been used on Jasmine.

I shuddered, closing my eyes against the influx of memories.

"No, leave her alone!"

Cut didn't obey. He finished tying Jasmine's hands before twisting to look at me. The leather bit into my wrists and ankles, binding me to the table. But the fulcrum had been activated, switching the table from horizontal to vertical. I hung as if crucified.

I would see everything. I would feel everything. I wouldn't be able to stop anything.

Jasmine's bronze eyes met mine, her twelve-year-old face glowing with grief.

"Don't. Please, don't." My voice battled with tears.

Cut marched toward the table to grab a tiny blade. "Seeing as hurting you doesn't teach you how to switch off your condition, I've come up with a better idea."

His boots clomped on the barn floor as he strode back to his daughter.

I fought. Fuck, I fought. The rack groaned as I threw my weight against the buckles. "Don't touch her." Jaz. My baby sister.

Pulling Jasmine to her feet, Cut wrapped an arm around her shoulders. Her dainty black shoes were no longer shiny patent but dusty and scuffed. I remember the day she got those shoes. Mum had given them to her just for being the sweetest little girl.

"You have the power to stop this, Jethro." Cut angled the blade against Jasmine's shoulder, slicing through her pretty blue dress, revealing a sliver of skin. "All you have to do is focus on my thoughts, rather than hers." He dragged the blade over her flesh, not hard enough to break the surface, but hard enough to make her flinch.

She bit her lip. Jasmine was quiet. When we played, she'd laugh and joke, but when she was afraid or in trouble, she turned mute. Nothing could get her to talk. Not the threat of the knife; not my pleas for her freedom. She stood there in her father's grasp and didn't say a word.

But fuck, her thoughts said so much. They screamed for me to help her. They hated me because I couldn't. She battled with love for Cut and loathing his actions. She crumpled me like a piece of rubbish, giving me no hope of focusing on anything else.

Cut dragged the knife again, only this time a little deeper.

Jasmine's flinch turned into a jerk, squirming in his arms.

"Stop. Don't do it again. I get it. I'm not listening to her anymore. I only feel what you are." Lies. All lies. But truth got me into this mess maybe falsehood could get me out of it.

Cut cocked his head. "What am I thinking then, boy?"

My hands balled as my joints stretched beyond normal capacity. Jasmine's thoughts overpowered me. I couldn't hear him. I didn't want to hear him.

So, I bullshitted. "You like the power over her. You like knowing you created her but can take her life just as easily as you gave it." I sounded older than fourteen. Would he believe me?

For a moment, I thought he would.

Then reality dispelled that hope.

"Wrong, Jet." Cut used the knife again. This time…he broke the skin. Tears erupted from Jasmine's eyes, but still she didn't cry out. "I hate this. I hate doing this to my children. And I hate you for making me do

it."

My fingers grazed the blade he'd used, tarnished and abandoned on the table. I could cut him. I could make him feel what Jasmine felt. But I had a better idea.

Breathing hard, I bypassed the cat o' nine tails and grabbed the large club. Resembling a billy stick the police used to carry, this one was thicker, heavier, ready to break limbs and turn bone into pulp.

I turned back to face my father. He lay prone on the rack, his eyes wide, white hair a shock of snow in the gloomy barn. "Remember this?"

He swallowed. "I remember what a fucking pussy you were when I used it."

Memories tried to take me hostage of him beating me, bruising me—teaching me lesson after lesson.

"Only fair you get to see why I screamed, don't you think?"

Cut gulped. "You knew all along I didn't enjoy what I did. I did it to try and save you from yourself. You were my children. Didn't I have a right as your father to use my flesh and blood to help my firstborn?"

I shook my head. "Using and abusing are two entirely different words."

He sneered. "And yet, only two letters separate them."

My chest hurt from breathing; my side burned from fever. I wanted this over. I'd made a commitment to make him pay, but I wasn't there to drag this out.

I wanted to finish it.

I wanted Nila.

I want to forget.

"That doesn't matter. You were still wrong to do what you did." Striding toward him, I held the club over his face. "Look at this and tell me what you feel. Don't make me work for your answers, Cut. For once in your godforsaken life, tell me the truth."

His goatee jerked as he tucked his chin into his neck,

repelling from the weapon. "You know me, Jethro. You know I love you."

"Bullshit. Try again."

He bared his teeth. "That isn't bullshit. I *do* love you. When Nila returned to London and you took your medication, I was so fucking proud of you. Never been so proud. I had the son I always knew you were. Capable, courageous, a worthy heir to everything I'd built."

"I was always those things, Father. Even as a boy, I did my best to make you see that."

The wood creaked as he shifted in the buckles. "But it was overshadowed by your condition. It made you weak. It made you susceptible. I needed someone strong, not just to look after my legacy but to protect your future family. Was it so wrong of me to want to give you the life skills needed in order to fight what you are?"

"What *I* am?" I choked on a cynical laugh. "What I am is nothing compared to what you are. You talk about life skills and transforming me into a man. I call that disabling your daughter, emotionally crippling your son, and ripping apart the only people who would've loved you unconditionally."

Cut opened his mouth to respond, but nothing came out.

He stared at me, and the one thing I'd hoped wouldn't happen came true.

His emotional rage petered out, mixing with nervousness that I was right. That he'd done the wrong thing. That somehow…he'd been bad.

Gritting my jaw, my arm flew back with ferocity. "No, you don't get to think those thoughts. Not after what you've done."

The club whistled through the air, striking his thigh with sickening power. The heavy pummel and resounding aftershock made my fever crest to unbearable heights and nausea to clutch around my throat.

Cut bellowed, his body jerking in the buckles as he writhed.

Being on the opposite end of a scene I was so familiar

337

with twisted my gut.

His agony swamped me. The unravelling sanity. The nastiness inside him giving way to fear. I wanted to vomit. I wanted to cut myself so I could focus on *my* pain and not his. I wanted to run.

But I couldn't.

If I tried hard enough, I could turn off my condition. I could return to what he'd taught me. But not today. I owed him this. I owed *myself* this. Together, we would purge everything I'd been. Everyone we'd hurt.

"Hurts, doesn't it?" I struck again, this time on his other thigh. The denim of his jeans protected him a little, but his cry boomeranged around the space.

A sour taste filled my mouth as self-hatred settled around my heart. I hated that feeling his pain meant I couldn't enjoy it. I couldn't appreciate the power as I delivered a dose of his own medicine, finally demonstrating what an awful disciplinarian he'd been.

His breathing stuttered as pain flashed through his system. I hadn't struck hard enough to break bones, but he would have a hell of a bruise.

Striding around the table, I stroked the black club. The heavy rubber was dense and threatening. There would be no escape. "What did you tell me once? That I could cry and scream as loud as I wanted and no one would hear us…?"

His eyes glowed, meeting mine. Sweat shone on his forehead. His arms fought the buckles as his knees trembled from adrenaline.

"Answer me." I struck his chest. The side of the club delivered with perfect precision against his lower belly.

"Ah, fuck!" Cut's spine bowed, his entire psyche wanting to curl up around his injuries and hide. Any sign of regret or shame at doing the wrong thing drowned beneath his sudden need for relief.

That I could deal with. Feeling another's pain had been a by-product of my condition all my life. I'd never grown used to it. However, if I stood in a room with someone dying or mortally wounded, I would eventually become numb then catatonic from their agony.

The same would happen if I continued with my father.

I had to finish what I'd started before I slipped into insanity.

He hadn't paid enough yet. He hadn't learned what he needed.

I've withstood worse.

I could stomach delivering more punishment.

Tucking the club into my waistband, I stalked around the table.

Cut gasped, his eyes watering but doing their best to follow me. "What do you want me to say, Jet? That I'm sorry? That I regret what I did and beg for your forgiveness?"

He stiffened as my hands drifted toward the lever he'd used so often. Words tumbled from his mouth. "Look, I'm sorry, okay? I'm sorry for asking so much of you when I knew you struggled. I'm sorry for hurting Jasmine. I'm sorry for what I did to Nila. Fuck, Jet, I'm sorry."

"Not good enough." Curling my fingers around the sweat-polished wood of the lever, I murmured, "I think we can do better than that."

My muscles bunched as I pushed on the mechanism. The first crank sounded like the gates of hell opening up, groaning and howling as ancient wood slipped into motion after so long.

"Wait!" Cut wriggled as the leather slowly tightened around his wrists and ankles. "Listen to my thoughts. Pay attention. I'm telling the truth."

The sad thing was he *did* speak the truth. He honestly was sorry. He burned with apologies and willingly took possession of everything he'd done.

But it wasn't enough to be sorry. He had to wish he'd never done it in the first place.

Taking a ragged breath, fighting through my weakness and fever, I cranked the lever again. The cogs and prongs slipped into place, welcoming each twist. Ducking over Cut, I pressed a little harder, pulled a little tighter. "Ready to grow a few inches?"

Cut squeezed his eyes. "Please…"

"You don't get to beg." I jerked the lever, pushing a full rotation.

The rack obeyed, separating beneath him, pulling Cut's extremities into agonising tightness. The skin on his hands and feet stretched like an accordion played to maximum, turning his flesh red as it yanked him in two directions.

Cut screamed.

I pushed again.

The table fought Cut's body, snarling against the unwilling tension, causing him to stretch beyond natural comfort.

He screamed louder.

My ears rang and my condition spluttered as too many thoughts collided in Cut's head. I felt sick for becoming this monster—a beast willingly taking my father's pain. But at the same time, I felt redeemed—as if I'd finally become the man Cut wanted me to be and only now deserved his praise.

"Tight enough for you?" My question was hidden in Cut's groans as I pressed the lever once more.

The shifting parts of the rack obeyed, slipping further apart, tearing a few ligaments, cutting into my father's flesh with its leather cuffs.

Cut didn't scream again, but a feral cry fell from his lips. His face scrunched up as his skin shocked white with agony. His back arched, his shoulders pulled tight and toes pointing. His hands remained fisted, his fingernails digging into his palms as his body fought to stay together.

I knew what he felt—not because I sensed him, but because I'd been in the exact position he had. I'd been tighter. I'd been younger. His shoulders would be the first to give out. They would pop from position in order for his joints to fight a little longer against the strain. Once the shoulders went, other joints would follow. Depending on how tight the rack stretched, knees would dislocate, tendons would snap, muscles would shred, and bones would break.

This form of torture had been one of the worst used in medieval times—and not just for the victim in the rack's embrace but for the victims watching it. The sickening rip of body parts giving up the fight. The horrifying pops of joints coming apart.

Confessions were willingly given just waiting for their turn. Would I go that far?

Would I tear Cut slowly into pieces, tightening his noose until his limbs quit fighting and just disintegrated?

Could I be that cold-hearted and merciless?

Let's find out.

My palms drenched with sickening sweat as I pushed one last time on the lever. The table cracked, the leather squeaked, and Cut convulsed with cries. "Fuck, stop. God, what d—do you want? Stop—"

"I want nothing from you." Locking the table from loosening, I removed my hands from the rack. His sockets were at breaking point. For now.

It was amazing how nimble the human body was. An hour in that position and cartilage would slowly snap, tendons stretch, and bones bellow for relief. But once freed, the body would knit back together. It would take time to realign the spinal column and soothe the blistering tears inside, but the long-term effects would be nil.

I knew.

I was walking proof.

Cupping my fingers around the club again, I prowled around the table. Cut's question resonated in my mind. *"What do you want?"* In all honesty, there was nothing I wanted. I had Nila—she was all I needed. But I wasn't doing this solely for her. Jasmine mattered, Kestrel, even Daniel.

I did this for them.

Wrenching to a halt, I looked at my father. "You know what? There *is* something I want from you." I moved from his head to his feet.

Cut tried to look down his body, but the pressure on his shoulders and arms wouldn't let his head rise.

"What...anything. Name it and it's yours. You're a good son, Jethro. We can forget this and move on."

"You're right in some respects, Father. I will forget and move on. But you lost that luxury when you stole Emma from her family and let Bonnie manipulate you for so long."

Once this was over, I would deal with my grandmother. I would make her regret playing puppet master to her own family.

"Bonnie's dead." Cut sucked in a breath, his neck straining against the pressure in his joints. "She died of a heart attack just before you arrived."

I froze.

Her death had been stolen from me. But perhaps, it was for the best. I already shook with rapidly fading courage. I already whittled beneath Cut's emotions. I wouldn't have the energy or bodily strength to take another life.

"I'm sorry." For all my hatred toward my grandmother and her strict ways, Cut did love his mother and feared her in equal measure. I let myself feel what he felt. He hurt. A lot. He was penitent and self-condemnatory but not enough to warrant salvation. Beneath his pain, he still thought he was justified.

He was wrong.

Holding up the club, I moved so the weapon was in his line of vision. "Remember who else you used this on?" I shuddered, fighting back memories of that horrible, fateful day. The day I realised he would never understand me, and I had to be strong—not for myself, but for my sister.

He'd taught me the final lesson in this place. The lesson that'd helped me remain true until Nila made me thaw.

Cut gulped. "Kite...wait."

"No, you don't get to give me orders anymore." Smashing the club into my palm, I welcomed the sting. "I've waited long enough."

Another thing about the rack—while tightening joints and stretching bones, it placed the human body into the perfect position of extra sensitivity. The natural cushioning of cartilage and fat suddenly wasn't enough to protect such an elongated pose.

Before, the strikes I delivered would've hurt him but not murdered him. The pain would've been sharp but survivable. But this…if I hit him now, the pain would be a hundred times worse. A *thousand* times worse.

Barricade yourself. Prepare.

The simplest touch could shatter a kneecap. The gentlest nudge could snap an elbow. He was the most vulnerable he'd ever been physically. It was my job to make him as defenceless emotionally.

My heart chugged. I didn't want to do this. But I would.

"I need you to know I'll be with you every step. I won't be able to turn off what you're undergoing, but I'm going to do it anyway because this isn't for me." Spreading my legs, I prepared to swing. "I'm doing this for Jasmine. You'll finally understand how your daughter felt that afternoon."

"Jet, no, don't, don't—"

Cut understood what I did: I wouldn't hold back anymore. I wouldn't be gentle or forgiving.

Before had been the warm-up.

This…this was his true punishment.

"I'm sorry."

Swallowing hard, I let loose and smashed my father's ankle with the club. The blow did what I knew it would. It pulverized his complex skeleton, shattering the talus and lateral malleolus. Biology came back; names of body parts I didn't really care about popped into my head before giving way beneath my strike.

The room seemed to explode outward as Cut sucked in the largest breath then screamed his fucking soul out.

His screams flew to the roof and bounced down.

His screams rattled the window in its ancient frame.

His screams sent me hurtling back to the day I wished I could forget.

"Stop it!" I didn't care the rack kept me immobile. I didn't care blood seeped down my wrists from fighting the leather. All I cared about was a silently sobbing Jasmine at Cut's feet. "Leave her alone!"

Cut breathed hard, swiping away damp hair from his forehead. This lesson had been the worst of them. He'd done everything he could to get me to no longer care he hurt Jasmine. He forced me to stay stoic and calm, hooking my heart rate up to a monitor so he could track my progress.

After the first few lessons, he couldn't tolerate my lying. He struggled to know if he'd made progress or not.

He hadn't.

No matter what he did to me, I couldn't stop what was so natural. I felt what others did. I couldn't switch it off. How could I when I didn't know how to control it?

So he'd upped his efforts, forcing me to hunt with him and shoot hapless rabbits and deer. He threatened to hurt Kestrel. He brought Jasmine in to watch. For a time, he didn't touch her. Just having her there made me work doubly hard.

In every lesson, she never said a word—merely watched me with sad eyes and hugged herself while Cut tried everything for me to mimic his inner calmness. To accept his ruthlessness. To become him in every way possible.

For a while, I willed it to work. I got better at lying, and Cut began to believe he'd 'cured' me. But then he hooked me up to the lie detector and heart monitor. And I couldn't bullshit any longer.

Jasmine didn't look up as she huddled at my father's feet. He'd slapped her repeatedly; he'd used his hands rather than blades, forcing me to focus on his mind rather than hers.

Become the predator, not prey.

Embrace ruthlessness, not suffering.

Become the monster, not the victim.

The pinging of the heart machine wouldn't stop shredding my hope and showing Cut just how hopeless I was. I couldn't be fixed. It was impossible.

"Please, let her go."

Cut swiped a handkerchief over his face, looking disgustedly at me.

"I'll let her go when you can learn to control it."

"I can't!"

"You can!"

"I'm telling you—I can't!"

As we roared at each other, Jasmine scuttled away. The dust from the barn layered her pink dress, staining her black tights. It was winter and frost decorated the glass, billowing our breath with little plumes of smoke.

Keep him yelling.

The longer I kept him occupied, the more chance Jaz had to escape.

I glared at Jasmine, willing her to get to her feet and run. Run out the door and never come back. She nodded quickly, understanding my silent command.

Cut stormed toward me, grabbing my cheeks and shoving my face toward the out-of-control monitor. I'd always had an irregular heartbeat whenever there was too much emotion to contain. My heart felt others; it was only natural it tried to skip into their beat, to mimic their pulses.

"What the fuck am I going to do with you, Jet? Are you ever going to get better?"

My cheeks couldn't move beneath his pinching hold; I did my best to speak without spitting. "Yes, I—I promise."

"I've heard you promise before and it never comes true."

Over his shoulder, I silently cheered as Jasmine shot to her dainty legs and tiptoed toward the double-born doors. So close…keep going.

"What else can I do to make you focus inward and not be so fucking weak all the time?" Cut prodded my chest where my teenage heart thundered. "Tell me, Jethro, so we can end this charade."

Jasmine's hands looped around the handle, yanking on the heavy exit.

Yes, run. Go.

The wood grunted like a beast hunting in the woods.

No!

Cut spun around. His eyes bugged as he dropped his hold. I couldn't move, hanging on the rack as he balled his hands and strode to the table where things of nightmares rested. "Where do you think you're going, Jazzy?"

She plastered herself against the door, shaking her head.

"Run, Jaz. Run!" I struggled. "Don't look back. Just go!"

She didn't.

She froze as Cut picked up a black club and advanced on her.

"No!" I squirmed harder, drawing more blood, more fear.

"I'm going to teach you to control it, Jet, if it's the last fucking thing I do." Cut swatted the club into his hand, making goosebumps scatter over my body.

Jasmine trembled as Cut towered over her. "You love your sister. Let's see if you can protect her by focusing for once." His hand rose, shadowing her face with his arm.

"Run, Jaz!" I screamed, tearing through her terror and kick starting her flight. Her fear kept her mute, but a sudden resolution filled her gaze.

She ran.

Pushing off from the door, she charged around my father and darted across the barn.

Cut spun, holding the club, watching his daughter bolt from him. Only, he didn't let her go. He gave chase.

"No!" I couldn't do a thing as he stormed after his child and wrenched his arm back to strike.

"Jasmine!"

And then it was all over.

The club struck her back.

The force sent her tumbling head over heels.

Her little shoes clattered against the floor as her skirts flew over her face. She came to a stop facing me, her little eyes glassing with tears, locked on mine above her.

For a second, she just lay there, blinking in shock, cataloguing her hurt. Then, the thickest, hardest, all-consuming wave I'd ever felt washed over me. Her pain drenched me. Her agony infected me. Everything she felt—her childish whims, her hopeful wishes—they all rammed down my throat and made me sick.

I vomited as Jasmine burst into tears.

Her screams echoed around us, slipping out the door, licking around the trees and rising to the crescent moon above.

I cried with her. Because I knew what'd happened as surely as she did.

Winter had watched this atrocity. Frost hadn't prevented it. Ice had let it happen. And a blizzard began deep in my soul.

I couldn't do it anymore.

I couldn't handle my sister's agony, my father's despair, my own brokenness.

I can't do this.

And neither could Jasmine.

Her tears stopped as suddenly as they began, but her eyes never tore away from mine. Her cheek pressed on the floor as her breath puffed cold smoke from bluing lips.

And she uttered the words I would never forget.

The words ensuring I stepped into an icicle prison and gave her the key. The sentence forever turning me into snow so I never, never, never *had to feel what I'd felt that day.*

"Kite…I can't feel my legs."

I howled in remembered agony, hating him all over again. He'd disabled my sister. He'd broken her back, crippled her spinal column. He'd irrevocably destroyed her life all because of me.

Me.

Fuck!

Blocking out his screams, I stormed toward the head of the rack and traded the club for the lever. While Cut trembled and shook in his restraints, I punched the mechanism, cocking it another rotation.

His broken ankle and limbs stretched further, eliciting more screams, more begs. The barn filled with sounds of popping and cracking. The gristle and ligaments finally gave up, breaking in increments.

I wanted to be sick. I wanted to wade through his pain, and for once, stop wallowing in others' misfortune. But unlike the instant with Jasmine teaching me in one violent swoop to stop, I couldn't.

"Jethro—stop. Please…" Cut's voice interspersed with deep-seated groans. I wanted so much to give in and obey. But he'd committed too much. Done too much wrong.

He hadn't paid enough. Not yet.

Shoving the club down my waistband again, I sat on my haunches and grabbed the small wheel below the rack. I knew this machine so well. Too well. It'd become a regular enemy, and I'd learned how to use it from too young an age.

Cut had felt what it was like to lay horizontal while receiving pain. It was entirely a new experience to be vertical.

Spinning the wheel, I shut my ears off to Cut's string of curses and pleas as the table slowly tilted upright, transforming from bed to wall. With every inch, Cut's body shifted as the weight transformed from his back to his wrists. His spine remained stretched, his body distended, but now the new angle meant he could see me moving around. He was the messiah this time about to die for his sins, not others.

Feeling his eyes on me, I didn't look up as I made my way toward the table of horrors. Gently, I placed the club back into its dusty spot and grabbed the cat o' nine tails.

"Have you hung there long enough, Jet?"

My father's voice roused me. My head soared up even though my neck throbbed. He'd left the clock on the stool in front of me, letting me count the time. Today, I'd been on the rack for two hours and thirteen minutes. Jasmine was still at the hospital. The doctors did all they could to fix the blunt force trauma to her spine. But they weren't hopeful.

Nothing Cut did to me now would ever be as bad as watching my sister run for the very last time.

I'd made a promise never to come here again, but that was before Cut scooped me from my bed at daybreak and gave me no choice.

"Let me down." I coughed, lubricating my throat. "You don't need to do this anymore."

He came to stand in front of me, his hands jammed in his pockets. "Are you sure about that?"

I nodded, tired and strung out and for once, blank from feeling anything. "I'm empty inside. I promise."

He gnawed on his lower lip, hope lighting his gaze. "I really hope this time you're telling the truth, son." His head turned toward the table. The dreaded, hated, despised *table.*

A thought clouded his face as he strolled over and picked up a whip with multiple strands with cruel knots tied in the cords. He'd threatened me with the whip before but never actually used it.

I tensed in the cuffs. My limbs had stopped screaming, but my joints were beyond moving. Cut knew how far I could be stretched these days without causing me too much agony.

After all, it was about keeping me immobile and sensitive, rather than ripping me into pieces.

"Let's see if your lessons have been learned, shall we?" He dragged the whip through his fingers. "Call this your final exam, son. Pass this and you'll never have to come in here again."

He didn't give me time to argue.

His arm cocked backward.

The whip and its knotted tails shot forward.

The first lick shredded my t-shirt, biting sharply into my chest.

A scream balled in my throat, but I'd finally learned. I'd learned not to focus on myself or my sister or prey or hope or happiness or normalcy. I'd learned to focus on him—my father, my ruler, my life-giver.

So I did.

Every strike, I took with pride because Cut felt proud of me.

Every cut, I accepted with gratefulness because Cut finally believed he'd earned a worthy son.

I listened to him and only him.

And it saved me from myself.

I gripped the table as a feverish weakness throttled me. I couldn't do this much longer. Every part of me was heavy with sickness and toil. I'd proven my point. I'd made him suffer. I had to end this before I drove myself into a grave beside him.

Pushing off from the wood, I stalked to face Cut on the rack.

His eyes widened, locking onto the whip.

"Let's see if you've learned your lesson, Father. Let's see if you can accept what you gave me as quietly as I accepted it."

My arm shook as the whip sailed over my shoulder. I paused as the cords slapped against my back, ready to shoot forward and strike its quarry.

Cut bit his lip. "Kite…"

I didn't wait for more. "No."

Grunting, I threw every remaining energy into my arm and hurled the whip forward. The knots found his shirt; they sliced through it like tiny teeth, blood spurting from his flesh.

And finally, his emotions switched from sadistic hatred, misplaced actions, and a lifetime of incorrect choices to begging and shaming and accepting everything in full measure.

His head bowed as I struck again, tears streaming from his eyes. Not from pain. But the knowledge he'd done this to people he'd loved. He'd willingly done this to his *children*. And there was no worse crime than that.

I'd finally broken him. Finally shown him the error of his past. Finally taught him what it was like for us. He paid homage to Emma Weaver. He said sorry to Jasmine. He repented toward Nila. And finally, *finally*, he submitted to me and my power.

His apologies layered my mind.

His regret boomed in his thoughts.

He accepted what had to happen.

We were no longer father and son, teacher and disciple.

We were two men cleaning up the mess we'd caused.

Two men alone in a world we'd created.

And we would both suffer a lot more before it was over.

Nila

HE DIDN'T COME back.
Minute after minute.
Hour after hour.
Still he didn't return.
I stared out the window, imploring him to appear.
I stroked my phone, willing a message to arrive.
I glanced at my door, begging him to enter.
But nothing.
Jethro was gone.
He'd committed to what had to be done.
And I feared I might never get him back.

Jethro

DARKNESS.

It fell over the estate like the gown from death itself, trickling like oil into nooks and crannies, stealing light.

Every thickening shadow devoured a little of what'd happened—blotting out the day, the past, everything that'd led to this moment.

Time had passed, changing me as a person, as a man, as a son. Cut and I had visited purgatory together, and a small part of us hadn't come back. I'd proven my point and won. And the saddest part was that the connection between us was the strongest it had ever been.

My heart wept for what I'd done. My muscles growled with tiredness. My entire body wanted to shut down.

Almost.

It's almost time to rest.

Needing some fresh air, I left the barn and stumbled outside. Every sensory output was on fire. I'd never been so exposed or naked, drenched in the feelings of others.

The moment night chill caressed my face, I raised my eyes to the moon, gulping in purging breaths.

The atmosphere in the barn was too thick, too putrid. I couldn't breathe properly after what I'd done.

Burying my face in my hands, I forced myself not to relive

the whipping or clubbing or Cut's tears and begs. I'd broken more than just his ankle. I'd broken his heart, his soul, his entire belief. I'd done everything I could to show Cut how blind he'd been toward his children and empire.

"Fuck." The cuss fluttered to my feet like the autumn leaves, crunching beneath my boot. How could I have done what I did? How did I hurt my father over and over again? How did I draw his blood and break his bones?

I didn't know the answer to that. But I was still standing, and my father finally understood.

It was over.

Rubbing my aching eyes, I swatted away my thoughts and took a deep breath. The moonlight cast my bloody hands in silver-chrome, turning the red black. Shoving the evidence of my crimes into my pockets, I strode through the forest, searching for the two men Kill had left to guard the woods.

It didn't take me long. I followed the reek of cigarette smoke, encountering them on the border of the glen.

They turned to face me as I approached. Their hands curled by their sides and jackets bulky in the gloom.

I didn't bother with niceties. I didn't have the strength. "It's done. You can go."

The man with a mohawk nodded. "Right-o. See you around."

I doubt it.

I left them to guide themselves out. I wouldn't play host tonight. I still had too much to do to be a gentleman.

Leaving, I faded through the forest. Once I could no longer sense them, I sat on a rock and grabbed a final breath.

This was the last decision.

Cut had been taught his lesson. I'd hurt him enough that he bordered this life and the next. He was half dead, but did I have the right to take his life completely?

He took so many others. Emma. Almost Nila. Jasmine's livelihood. My mother's soul.

My hands curled again, sticky with everything that'd

happened.

I'd contemplated all manner of things. I'd thought of, and discounted, the idea of hanging my father, drawing out his entrails and quartering him just like convicts were done in the past. I'd pondered the concept of letting him live and banishing him from Hawksridge.

I had enough of my father's blood on my hands. I'd hurt myself and him.

But I knew he wouldn't let me have the happy ending I desired if I left him alive.

Eventually, he would want vengeance. Eventually, he would forget the lesson I'd taught and come back for me—come back for Nila.

I can't let that happen.

I had to end it.

It's the only way.

Climbing off the rock was a million times harder than it was to sit down. My body seized; I tripped forward as my head swam. How much longer could I stay awake without needing serious medical attention?

Not very.

Forcing my legs to work, I left my place of solitude and returned to the barn. My fingers shook as I turned and locked the door.

Cut didn't make a sound. He'd passed out just before I'd left. Tearing my eyes from the almost unrecognisable shape of my father, I headed toward the table and selected a small knife.

No matter that history tarnished the blade, the sharpness still remained.

Moving toward Cut, his chin lolled on his chest, his arms splayed high while his legs spread wide. His arms and legs were abnormally long while his body couldn't stretch any more without skin tearing as well as bones.

Blood seeped down his torso in a crisscross lattice from the whip. Beneath his wounds, the faint lines of the Tally Mark tattoos from Emma decorated his ribcage. Emma had been the one to choose the position, just like Nila chose fingertips for ours. I hadn't seen his tally in so long; I'd almost forgotten they were there.

He had more than me and he'd carried out the Final Debt. That was the main difference between us.

Dedication versus empathy.

Sighing, I did my best to gather my shredded power. The blade turned warm in my hand. Tearing my eyes from him, I moved to the rack and groaned as I bent in half to twist the small wheel.

Slowly, the rack reclined from perpendicular to parallel.

Cut still didn't move.

Placing the knife by his unconscious head, I unbuckled his wrists then his ankles. The ankle I'd shattered hung at an unnatural angle, mottled and black with bruising.

My heart clenched that I could ever be so cruel, battling with childhood memories and adulthood obligations. Along with his ankle, I'd also broken his arm for Nila's in Africa. I'd smashed his kneecap and rearranged an elbow.

I'd done such nasty shit to the man who made me.

Don't think about it.

Snatching back my knife, I tapped his grey-covered cheek. "Wake up."

Nothing.

I tapped harder. "Cut, open your eyes."

His lips twitched, but his mind remained asleep.

"Goddammit, don't make me get the water."

I hit him, harder this time. His face slipped sideways against the table, slowly cracking the cocoon his mind had built. Whatever chrysalis he'd formed against his agony wouldn't stop him from living through the next.

It took a few swats, but finally, his eyes opened.

For a while, confusion battered him. His gaze darted to the ceiling, coming to focus on me. I didn't move as he took note of his over-stretched joints, broken parts, and lurched with blundering pain.

I was the nail being hammered by his thoughts, deeper and deeper, harder and harder into my soul. After tonight, I needed solitude and aloneness. I needed to gallop away and never live through something like this ever again.

"Get up." Slinging his useless arm over my shoulder, I plucked him from the rack.

He screamed as I slipped him off the table. Regardless of his agony, he tried to move, but his limbs were no longer operational. His legs didn't support his weight, and he fell to the dusty floor with a cry.

I went with him.

We fell in a mass of body parts, sitting side by side, our backs resting against the rack.

He gasped but didn't try to untangle himself. Shock quickly deleted much of his overwhelming injuries, letting him rest for a moment without suffering.

The fact he found peace for a second let me find it as well.

I shared in his silence, letting the air wrap around us in a dusty hug.

For a while, I didn't speak. What could I say? Over the past few hours, I'd proven I was as much a monster as he was. I hadn't found reconciliation or closure. I'd only found sadness and cruelty.

But words weren't needed.

My father, the man who'd raised me, hurt me, and ultimately cared for me in his own twisted way, slowly laid his head on my shoulder and gave me the first righteous thing of his life.

"I'm sorry, Jethro. For everything."

My heart clamoured as tears sprang to my eyes.

I couldn't speak.

Cut didn't wait for a reply. He knew he was dying. His body was broken beyond repair. There would be no healing or walking away from this. His time on earth had come to an end, and now was the time to relinquish his sorrows and regrets.

His voice was a croaky thread, but my eyes pricked with

his every word.

"I know how badly I treated my children. I know I was never entitled to what I took. I let power and bloodlust cloud me. I can't amend what I did, and I can't bring back the lives I stole, but I can ask for your forgiveness."

His head turned heavier on my shoulder, dampness soaking into my sweat-clogged shirt from his tears.

"I need to know you forgive me, Kite. I need to know you accept my apology."

Matching liquid sadness ran silently down my cheeks as I stared at the locked doors. "Why? Why should I forgive you?"

"Because you know I mean it. You sense I'm telling the truth. It wasn't just the pain you showed me or the memories I relived tonight—the same memories I have no doubt you relived as well. It was hindsight, and I've finally allowed myself to acknowledge what I never did before."

My gut knotted with everything I wanted to say. "And what was that?"

Cut sighed, taking his time to reply. "I listened to my mother for too long. Time twisted her mind. It made what we did acceptable, *expected* even. I didn't stop to think it wasn't right." He broke into a sob. It wasn't fake or forced. His emotional undoing fed directly into me and I trembled with his honesty.

Forcing himself to keep going, Cut laid his conscience at the altar of wrongness. "I'm not blaming Bonnie. I'm not blaming my past or the morals I'd been fed. I'm blaming myself for being so fucking weak to stop it. Two of my children are dead. One is disabled for life. But you came back from the grave to teach me the lesson I needed to learn."

Kestrel isn't dead.

He'll come back to me because I made it safe for him to do so.

My eyes stung thinking of what my brother would say if he saw what I'd done. Would he hate me or understand? Would he fear me or celebrate? "What lesson?"

Silence fell as Cut worked out how best to deliver his

epiphany.

He forgot I could taste his confession as clearly as a drop of expensive cognac on my tongue.

"That I'm no better than a Weaver. That being a Hawk doesn't grant immunity or power over another's life. That I'm not the monster I tried to be."

Silence reigned once again.

I had no reply. He didn't need one.

I played with the knife, running the blade through my fingers. His head never left my shoulder, his arms useless by his sides.

He couldn't move even if he wanted to, but I felt he didn't want to. This rare precious moment would never come again, and we needed to touch, to say sorry deeper than words.

Ten minutes could've past or ten hours—I lost track of time. My thoughts were with ghosts of people I'd lost. Of tragedies that'd come to an end but would never be forgotten.

Finally, my father forced his head off my shoulder and smiled sadly. "You're a good son, Jethro. I'm proud of the man you turned out to be, even after I screwed you up. I wish I could say sorry to Nila for taking the Debt Inheritance too far. I had the power all along to stop it, just as my father did, and I chose not to. I also wish I could apologise to my brother for what I did and to Rose for how terribly I treated her. So many things to apologise for." He sucked in a breath, his arms and legs like discarded puppet strings. He couldn't sit up. He could barely breathe. "So many things I've done."

I'd done that to him. I'd shown him what he'd become, and he'd finally accepted his actions were bad, but his soul...it wasn't as decayed as he feared.

Shifting, I kissed his temple. "I believe you."

His sigh expelled more than just worry but his entire scorecard of wrongdoings. He exhaled his past, living the final moments in the present. "I'm ready to go, Kite. I *want* to go. Let me die and find peace. Let me fix the wrongs our family have caused."

My heart charged faster. As awful as it'd been breaking my father, forcing him to be honest and true, I didn't think I could kill him.

Not now.

Not now we'd connected like we always should've—man to man. Father to son.

Another tear rolled down my cheek. "I accept your apology, and I grant you my forgiveness." I passed him the knife. "I don't have the power to grant redemption for what you did to Jaz or Kes or Emma or Rose or the other people you hurt, but I do promise they will know you regretted it before you passed. If they can, they will forgive you in time."

Cut clenched his jaw as I moved away.

I accidentally knocked his painful limbs to squat in front of him. "I can't kill you, Dad."

Dad.

I hadn't used that word since Jasmine's disability.

Not since the last time he'd deserved such an adoring title.

Cut smiled, his golden eyes matching mine in the darkness. "I've always loved you. You know that, don't you?"

I wanted to say I didn't. That when he shot me in the parlour. That when he hurt my sister in the barn. That every day I strived for his respect and love, I didn't know what was beneath his sadism.

But I refused to lie to a dying man.

I'd known. And that was why I trusted that eventually, one day, the goodness inside him would win. That he wouldn't remain as awful as he had.

A childish hope and finally, it had come true.

Only for him to die.

"Kite…before I go…I want to do something to right my mistakes." His voice ached with sorrow. "Something to protect you all from the instructions I set beyond the grave."

If I didn't sense his sincerity, I wouldn't have believed he could feel so much regret. But he did—mountains of it. Chasms of it. He truly hated what he'd done. To everyone, not just to Jasmine and me but also to Nila and Kes and Daniel. And Rose. Most of all Rose.

I stared at him. He wanted something...something to...

"A piece of paper? Is that what you need?"

Cut smiled crookedly. "You always were a mind reader."

"Even when you tried to beat it out of me."

The truth in our words was just that. *Truth*. Not judgement or accusation. Just a statement of what was.

Cut nodded. "I'm sorry."

"I know." Climbing wearily to my feet, I moved toward the large table with implements of destruction and opened a rickety draw. Inside, I found a mouse-chewed notepad and a gnawed-on pencil.

Taking both back to my father, I sat back down and passed them to him.

He tried to take them, but his arms wouldn't work. The tendons failing to transmit instructions.

He sighed. "You'll have to do it."

He didn't lay blame. Just spoke the facts. He accepted his punishment and didn't hate me—if anything, he was grateful to have paid for his trespasses.

"What do you want me to write?"

He took a deep breath, thinking.

Finally, he recited, "I, Bryan 'Vulture' Hawk, do solemnly pledge my death is justified and accepted. I renounce all former decree that if my death is judged as murder that my firstborn heir, Jethro 'Kite' Hawk, is cut from my will. I revoke the agreements in place to send him to Sunny Brook Mental Institute and rescind all further instruction dealing with my daughter and other inheritors."

His voice hitched, but he forced through his body's shortcomings to relay his final message. "On this day, I draw forth a new Will and Testament with Jethro Hawk as my witness and true heir that all lands, estates, titles, and fortune pass to him upon my demise. This is binding and unchangeable."

A ball lodged in my throat as Cut shifted awkwardly. "Hold the paper and help me grab the pencil."

Swallowing hard, I wrapped his fingers around the pencil and hovered it in place on the newly written Will. I didn't know if it would stand up in a court of law, but we had paid lawyers on our side. Marshall, Backham, and Cole would ensure the paperwork would be lodged and executed. And then I would destroy their practice so they would never serve law to monsters such as my family again.

Cut grunted in agony as he signed his name; his signature almost illegible. Remembering what else lived in this barn, I hauled myself to my feet for the second time. "Wait there."

I returned with a handheld video recorder and new battery that'd been stored in the safe away from vermin. I didn't let myself remember why there was a recording device in here.

Ripping open the battery casing, I inserted it into the device, and turned it on.

The first thing that came up was the last filmed event. *Me.*

Stored in this tiny recorder was what happened once Jasmine's back had been broken. I remembered the day in crystal clarity. It was never Cut's intention to hurt his daughter so much.

The video unspooled, crackling with sound.

Jasmine looked at me. "Kite…I can't feel my legs."

Instantly, Cut shed his pompous strictness of emperor of our estate and become a terrified parent instead.

He rushed to release my binds, not caring I crunched into the dirt once he'd loosened the leather. Once, I was free, he scooped up Jasmine and darted toward the exit.

"We'll go to the hospital, Jazzy. Fuck, I'm so sorry."

All he cared about was fixing what he'd done.

But I didn't let him get far.

I snapped.

I became like him. I craved his pain after what he'd done to my baby sister.

361

I wasn't proud of what I'd done. My hands trembled as the video-tape showed a devil-child leap onto his father's back and beat him over and over and over again with the club he'd used on Jasmine.

I stared transfixed as the tape continued, transforming me from abused to abuser as Cut fell on the floor, covering his face and hands.

I could've killed him that day and I would've if Jasmine hadn't screamed for me to stop.

Hearing her terror wrenched me from the blood cloud I'd swam in, putting her first rather than making my father pay.

I'd scooped her in my arms and charged to the Hall. I'd been the one to get Jasmine to the hospital all while Cut lay unconscious in the barn.

"Turn it off." Cut closed his eyes, cringing against the scratchy noises of the recording.

I couldn't breathe properly as I fumbled with the machine and switched it from memory card to fresh start.

Neither of us mentioned what we'd just seen or the past feelings of the incident. We knew who'd won that night and as a kid I'd expected harsh retribution. But Cut hadn't punished me. He'd pretended nothing had happened even while bruises marked his skin. He'd continued with my lessons but didn't hurt me any more than normal.

It was as if he wanted to be hurt for what he'd done to Jaz.

Clearing my throat, I held up the lens and pointed it at Cut.

The screen bounced in my hold, but it would have to do.

This was my insurance policy.

Cut understood immediately and dropped his head to the notepad I'd tossed in his lap. He fortified himself from our strained relationship and read my scrawled writing—for Jasmine and Kes and future heirs of Hawksridge Hall.

Occasionally, he looked up, reciting his pledge while staring into the camera. More often than not, his eyes remained downcast, reading his Last Will and Testament quickly.

My hands only shook harder the closer he got to finishing. My fever fogged my eyesight, and his voice threatened to put me in a trance.

I needed to rest and fast.

Finally, he finished.

Once his declaration was verbalized, I turned off the camera and placed it beside me for safe-keeping.

I looked at the same speck he stared at, unable to move forward but knowing I had no choice. "Thank you. Not for me, but for Jaz and the workers we employ. You've kept them in their homes and jobs."

A thought pricked me.

I'd planned on dismantling the diamond smuggling ring once Cut was dead, but his unselfish act of preserving the company and giving back my birthright reminded me it wasn't a matter of shutting down something just because I wanted to. We had people relying on us. I had to do right by them. I couldn't steal their livelihoods.

"Take care of those you love, Jethro." Cut coughed. "Don't ever let corruption turn you into me."

His words said one thing, but his heart another. He'd done what he'd been taught. But now, he wanted to go. He wanted the pain to stop, and I wouldn't deny him that.

He'd done what any human would do on their death bed. Apologised for past transgressions and accepted forgiveness for those he violated.

His soul was no longer burdened.

Picking up the knife once again, I placed my hand over his, squeezing his useless fingers around the hilt. His tendons and ligaments were no longer attached to signals from his brain. Completely disabled for the rest of his short life.

His eyes met mine. "You'll do it, after all?"

I shook my head, guiding his hand to hover over his heart. "No."

"Then what?"

"I can't kill you, but I can't allow you to live in such pain any more." My own bones howled in sympathy. My spine ached and brain overwhelmed with agony.

"You'll help me?"

I nodded.

"You're a good son, Kite." His head fell forward, using up the last of his energy. His lips landed on my forehead and kissed me.

I sucked in a breath, fighting against everything that'd passed between us. I accepted his kiss. His blessing. We held an entire world in a silent conversation.

I wished there was another way. I wished I didn't have to do this.

But Cut nodded, signalling he was ready.

Who was I to deny his final wish when I'd taken so much from him?

Without breaking eye contact, I leaned on his fist, puncturing his heart with the sharp blade.

So much pain to make him see.

And now, a quick death to make him free.

His forehead furrowed as the knife sank into his chest. He groaned as I twisted the hilt, tearing through the muscle and killing him as fast as possible.

He'd already suffered enough. I wanted him to leave without pain.

His forehead touched mine as I bowed over his dying form. His pulse thundered in his neck. His soul clung tight to his perishing body. And as the final gasp left his broken chest, I closed my eyes and kissed his cheek.

"Goodbye, Dad."

I did what I could never stomach and tethered myself to his last flickering thought. I held tight as he slipped into the afterlife. I lived his final farewell.

His eyes shot their message as well as his heart. *"Take care of those you love, Kite. Don't ever doubt I was proud of you. So, so proud."*

And then...he was gone.

It didn't take long to source enough kindling and set up a small pyre inside the barn.

All I wanted to do was rest. To sleep. To forget. But I wouldn't leave my father's corpse undealt with. That would be sacrilege. His immortal soul was free. His mortal remains had to be, too.

It took the last of my energy to move his dead body into the middle of the barn and rest it on top of the kindling. Once his hands were linked on his chest, and his broken limbs placed straight and true, I worked on building a last goodbye.

Moving as quickly as I could, I wedged more tinder around his lifeless corpse. Trudging from forest to barn, I built up enough fuel to create a fire that would last all night, a fitting send-off for my cruel father.

Once I'd buried Cut in branches, I hauled the rack closer, scooped every torture device off the table, and scattered them around him. After the fire, I wanted no remains or reminders of what went on in this place.

Stepping back, I checked my handiwork before moving toward the utility cupboard storing bleach and gasoline. The bleach had been for blood and the gasoline for the bonfires we'd occasionally had out here to cull a few trees.

Fighting the dregs of energy in my system, I poured the sharp smelling petrol over my father's corpse, the rack, the floor, the very walls of the despicable barn.

Only once every item and inch of the place had been drenched did I strike the match.

Taking the camera and Cut's last confession to a tree a safe distance away, I returned to stand by the doors and fling the sulphur rich flame onto the slick trail of gasoline.

Nothing happened.

The flames didn't catch. They went out.

Fuck.

My hands shook hard as I struck another match—letting the fire chew some of the stick before tossing it to the glistening floor.

This one worked.

The sudden whoosh of heat and orange exploded into being, rippling along the liquid path I'd set, eagerly consuming the tinder I'd given.

The cold night warmed as I stood in the entry and let the fire take firmer root. I didn't move as the crackle and singe of my father's skin caught fire. The smell of human remains burning and the whiff of smoke didn't chase me away.

I stayed vigil until the woods glowed red with heat and the air became thick with soot.

And still I stood there.

Smoke curled higher in the sky, blotting out the moon and stars.

I stood sentry like the oaks and pines, watching the fire slowly eat its way along the floor and walls, devouring everything in its fiery path, deleting the barn and its history.

Watching my father char to ash, I couldn't fight the memories of what I'd done. Of the stretching and breaking and pain I'd delivered. I buckled over, vomiting on the threshold. The intensity of what I'd lived through suddenly crushed me. I had no reserves left to ignore it.

I'm sorry.

I'm not sorry.

He deserved it.

No one deserved that.

Stumbling away from the burning barn, I tripped and jogged through the forest to the lake where Nila had been strapped to the ducking stool. There, I fell to my knees, willing the past to fade.

My body purged itself. Daniel's death. Cut's death. My mother's death. Kes's coma. Jasmine's disability. And Nila's torture.

It's all too much.

Even from my sanctuary by the water, I could still smell smoke. The aftertaste of my father burning coated my throat, and my eyes smarted with ash.

Throwing my head back, I glowered at the moon.

I'd never have another birthday where I feared the cake was laced with cyanide.

I'd never be sent back to the mental institute and kept prisoner in a straitjacket.

I'd never have to worry about Jasmine being tossed from the Hall and left to fend alone.

I'd never again bow to the wishes of a deranged family lineage.

I'm free.

Cut's free.

Those I love and fought for are free.

Feeling more animal than human, I had no control as I crawled on all fours to the water's edge. My hands squelched through the mud, moving like a beast. I gasped as I traded land for icy water. Waist deep then chest. I kept going until the mud switched to silt, welcoming rather than preventing.

I kept going.

Leaving ground and gravity, I slipped into weightless swimming.

I didn't try to stay on the surface. The moment I couldn't feel the bottom beneath my shoes, I let go. I sank below, dunking into the cold darkness.

I ran from everything, hiding in the pond.

Holding my breath, the freezing temperature stole my pain and hunger, soaking through my blood-saturated jeans and cinder-coated jumper.

With water above and all around me, I opened my mouth and screamed.

I screamed and screamed.

I screamed so fucking loud.

I screamed for my father, my mother, my sister and brothers.

I screamed for myself.

Bubbles flew from my mouth.

Salty tears mingled with fresh water and frogs sped away from my emotional unravelling.

I screamed and yelled and cursed and shouted and only the depth could hear me.

I poured forth my despair, my guilt, my condition, my fever, my battle-worn body.

I sank deeper and deeper, permitting my liquid-logged clothes to take me to the murky bottom. Plant fronds tickled my ankles, bubbles erupted from my shirt, and my hands hovered in front of my face, white as death and just as cold.

Hovering, I focused on my heartbeat—the only noise in the cavernous body of water. As seconds ticked on, it slowed...it steadied; it finally found its own rhythm away from tonight's atrocities.

Down there, I found something I'd been missing.

Forgiveness.

Only once my lungs burst for air did I kick off my shoes and push off the bottom. The rush of water over my skin washed me clean—not just from tonight but from everything. I hadn't done it out of fun. I'd done it out of loyalty to those who needed to be fought for.

I wasn't vindictive or spiteful.

I was *justified.*

I was baptised anew.

Breaking the surface, I gulped in greedy breaths, feeling a sense of rebirth. My tiredness faded, my wounds numbed, and I swam to look back the way I'd come.

There, on the horizon, the angry reds, yellows, and ochres of a raging fire danced in the dark night sky. Smoke stole the Milky Way and fire cleansed Hawksridge.

I hung in the snowy embrace of the water, just watching, always watching.

I shivered. My teeth chattered. And I craved warmth and bed and Nila.

I'd done what I needed to even though it almost broke me.

I had nothing left to fear.

Looking at Hawksridge Hall, my eyes found Nila's bedroom. The light burned in her window, a lighthouse for my drowning sorrows, a beacon leading me back to her.

I kicked toward the shore.

I need you, Needle.

I need you so fucking much.

She would put me back together.

She would understand what I'd done and accept me with no questions or ultimatums or tests.

She would love me unconditionally.

My heart calmed.

My mind quieted.

And finally, finally, *finally*, I found peace.

♡Kestrel

THERE WAS A saying that humans were capable of knowing only one thing.

One thing of ultimate, undeniable conviction where everything else—our thoughts, opinions, careers, likes, dislikes—even our entire lifespan of choices, were open to interpretation and amendments.

Only one thing was irrefutable. That one thing was: *we exist.*

We knew as a species—as an intelligent race of culture and history—that we lived and breathed and *existed.*

Nothing else outside of that was fundamental, only the knowledge we were alive. It evolved us from animals because with our existence came awareness for what a gift life was.

Some of us squandered it.

Others muddied it to the point of no redemption, but most of us appreciated the small present we'd been given and were grateful for it—no matter how lowly or high, rich or poor, easy or hard.

We existed, and that was a wondrous thing.

I'd never truly understood just how grateful I was.

But I did now.

As I lay in an in-between world where pain, death, or even time couldn't reach me, I had endless space to evaluate and understand. I'd existed as more than just a man, more than a brother, or friend, or son.

I'd existed because I made a difference to those I loved.

I cherished my sister.

I helped my brother.

And I did my best to remain true to the soul inside me rather than outside influences trying to change me.

I existed truthfully and that was all that mattered.

I wouldn't lie and say I didn't miss him. I missed the relationships with those I cared about. I missed my home, my possessions, my future. I missed worldly items because I knew I'd never see them again.

Jethro hadn't been easy to love. He'd been the cause of my sister's pain, my hard childhood. He'd been…difficult. But he'd also been the most loyal, loving, coolest brother I could've ever asked for.

He'd earned forgiveness for his issues. And I liked to think I'd played my part in helping him become a better person—a person who could live an easier life with his condition.

My time was over; my existence almost done.

And although I was sad to go, I wasn't afraid.

Because I *existed*.

And because I existed, I could never un-exist.

I would move on. I would transcend. I would grow and change and magnify to the point of whatever new experience awaited me. I would see those I loved again but not for a while.

And that was okay, too.

So I waited in my in-between world, listening to silence, hovering in nothingness, just waiting for the right time. I didn't know how I would know. I didn't know why I waited. But something kept me tethered to a world I no longer belonged to.

Until one day, I felt it.

The snip.

The silence turned to sublime music, the nothingness turned to warmth, and contentment blanketed with permission to leave. I knew he would be okay. I knew she would be okay. The family who persevered would be okay.

My father was dead.

Bonnie was dead.

Daniel was dead.

Evil had finally perished in my house.

And Jethro no longer needed me.

It took no effort, not even a sigh or conscious thought.

I just...let...go.

He had her.

He had her.

He had his very existence.

Nila would be there for him now.

He no longer needed my help.

I smiled, sending love to both of them, goodbye to everyone, and so long to a world that'd been briefly mine.

Jethro has found his reason for breathing.

It was time for me to find mine.

Goodbye...

Nila

JETHRO CAME FOR me at daybreak.

His icy touch woke me, trailing over my cheek to my lips.

I'd waited for as long as I could. I'd remained vigil by the window, imploring him to return. I'd paced thick grooves into the carpet, forcing myself to stay awake.

But I'd failed.

Jasmine left around midnight, and my body shut down soon after. Even opening the window and enduring the chilly gale couldn't fight sleep from claiming me.

After the fourth stumble and micro nap almost plummeting me to the floor, I reluctantly climbed into bed and slipped instantly into dreams. Good dreams. Bad dreams. Dreams of death and destruction then love and liveliness.

"Nila…"

His voice slinked around my soul, yanking me from slumber and delivering me directly into his control. My eyes shot wide, drinking him in. The dawn light barely illuminated my room, shyly warming the carpet and windowsill with promise of a new day.

I sat up on my elbows, cursing the sudden swirl and lack of sleep fogging my reflexes. For a moment, I couldn't see him, then his form solidified beside me.

Physically, he was in one piece. Tall and strong. Vibrant and majestic.

He stood silently, gazing intently. His eyes became fireworks in the gloom, sparking over my skin.

My gaze fell from his strained face over his chiselled chest to his half-hard cock. He stood naked. Not in a sexual manner but stripped back, bared, undressed and nude. Laying his horror, harrowing evening, and every haggard emotion at my feet.

His skin gleamed a white alabaster—looking as if he'd become a nocturnal being, an immortal monster.

Tears leapt to my eyes, understanding the brink of where he stood. He'd done things he wasn't proud of. He'd done things he *was* proud of. And ultimately, he'd come to me with nothing, leaving the past behind, asking me to forgive, forget, and help grant absolution he so desperately needed.

Sitting higher in bed, I nodded at his silent requests.

Why is he wet?

His discarded, sodden clothes stained the emerald carpet; his chest rising and falling as if he'd run a marathon. His eyes were wild. His hair wet and tangled. And his smell spoke of everything he'd done and done alone.

Copper for blood.

Soot for fire.

Metal for weapons.

And salt for sadness.

We didn't speak.

He was on the precipice of breaking.

I was the strong one in this dawn-lit moment. I was the one who had to save him.

I've got you.

Soaring upward, I scrambled out of the covers and kneeled before him. Silently, I wrapped my arms around his quaking shoulders. I'd removed the sling before falling asleep and my cast rasped against his soft skin.

I hadn't taken my shift off and the iciness of his body

thawed into mine, delivering snow storms and blizzards the longer I held him.

He's so cold.

I hugged him harder, begging him to respond.

But he just stood there, trembling, shivering, his breath scattering hot and cold into my hair as I nuzzled against his chest. "It's okay. It's okay. I'm here."

Pressing warm lips against his frigid shoulder, I crawled on my knees closer to his marble-like form.

A gasp escaped him as I smoothed back his hair, kissing my way up his neck to his ear. "You're with me now. Feel how much I love you. Concentrate on how happy I am that you're back."

I never stopped kissing him, stroking him, willing him to come back to life. "Jethro, focus. Forget everything. Let me in."

Suddenly, his back bent, and he sagged in my hold. His arms flew around me, crippling me against his hard muscles. I didn't speak, but his soul screamed for help.

I let him hold me. I let him shake and shudder.

Time held no meaning as we existed in each other's embrace and fed each other with love and togetherness. I would hold him for the rest of my life and ensure he never felt anything but acceptance, adoration, and unconditional love.

"It's okay." My voice hung around us, glittering like fireflies, warming up his ice-ridden body. "I love you. I'm here for you. Feel what I feel. Live in how much you mean to me."

With a loud groan, Jethro scooped me from the bed. His arms bunched around me, cradling me gently as he carried me toward the bathroom.

My broken arm rested in my lap as I permitted him to do whatever he needed. I wouldn't fear him. I wouldn't question him or give him any reason to sense hesitation or unwillingness.

He wasn't well. His strength had reached depletion, but something drove him onward. Something he needed to abolish to find peace.

I was his. He was mine.

I would be his everything until he'd gathered his scattered psyche and returned to me.

Silently, Jethro traded the room for the shower. The same shower where he'd caught me with the water jet between my legs. The same bathroom where I finally knew I was falling for him, despite everything.

Silently, he turned on the hot spray and walked directly under it.

My dress became instantly sodden, but I didn't care. All I cared about was reanimating my lover, protector, husband-to-be by any means necessary. Cupping his nape, I pulled his face toward mine.

He didn't fight me as our lips met.

He sucked in a tattered breath as I licked his bottom lip, worshipping him sweetly. His eyes closed, his arms gathered me closer, and the world became just us, water, and steam.

Opening his mouth, his tongue met mine hesitantly, apologetically.

I hated that he'd forgotten our promises and commitment. That he didn't trust my vow to marry him. That he wasn't sure I could love him after tonight.

Holding his neck tighter, I pressed our lips together harder.

He groaned as I tasted his sadness, licking away his worry, replacing it with welcoming passion.

Slowly, he responded. The ache inside him unfurled, the pressure and stress siphoning down the drain as more droplets cascaded over us. Our heartbeats communicated in-tune with worded confessions.

"I killed him."

"I know."

"I hated him."

"I know."

"But I loved him, too."

"I understand."

His tongue teased my bottom lip. His heart cracked open

and poured everything he'd done.

"I hurt him."

"He deserved it."

"I liked it."

"That's okay."

"I loathed it."

"That's okay, too."

"Did he deserve it?"

"Yes, he deserved to pay."

"He asked for forgiveness."

"Did you give it?"

"Yes.

"Oh, Kite…" I kissed him harder, our lips turning from dancing to fighting.

"He apologised."

"He should."

"He regretted his actions."

"Good."

"In the end, he was the father I always knew he could be."

"It's over now."

Jethro dropped me to my feet, crushing me against the tiles. My cast was drenched, but I had no concerns apart from Jethro. My dress clung to me, highlighting straining nipples, and the fact I had no underwear on beneath the shift.

Jethro tore his lips away from mine, staring at me. In my hold, he slowly came alive, shedding the holocaust and returning to me. He fell forward, trapping me between the tile and his nakedness.

The moment our tongues met again, our hearts shouted louder and louder. The more our souls conversed, the more violent and awake he became.

"I miss him."

"You can miss the man but not the monster."

"I shouldn't have hurt him."

"He hurt you."

"I should've been stronger to save you."

"You did save me."

He groaned as my hands shot into his hair, jerking hard. I didn't want him spiralling into self-hatred. Cut wasn't worth that. I'd set aside my hatred; I'd granted forgiveness. But I wouldn't let Cut's shadow ruin Jethro's hard-earned future.

I touched him. "You saved my life. More than once."

"I was almost too late."

"But you weren't. You made it."

"I should've saved you the first time I saw you."

"You *did* save me."

"How?"

"You fell in love with me."

His hands coasted up my sides, tearing at my drenched clothes. My hair plastered to my cheeks as his fingers tore at the neckline of my dress, ripping it down the centre.

Dropping to his knees, he yanked the material down my wet body until we stood naked under the steaming stream.

We hadn't turned on any lights and the window barricaded the watery attempt at dawn. Our bodies were Braille as our fingers tracked and touched.

His skin glowed white in the grey morning. His eyes such a vibrant bright.

Standing, Jethro grabbed my hips and guided us under the spray. His mouth claimed mine—desperate, hungry.

We drank water and each other, kissing, always kissing. Touching, forever touching.

There was no soap, but his hands covered every inch of me, washing away the past, the murder, the last few hours.

I repaid the favour, massaging his tense shoulders, his rigid spine, the knots in his lower back. I sluiced water over his bruises and cuts, willing the warmth to knit him back to whole.

My broken arm nullified any pressure I might've granted with my fingers, but I refused to let it hang uselessly by my side.

I forced every inch of me—parts unhurt and parts in pain—to heal him, love him, bring him back into the light.

Tugging his hair, I pulled his lips from mine.

His eyes narrowed but he didn't speak.

Tracing his mouth with my fingertip, I smiled as he nipped me gently.

Dropping my touch from his face, down his throat and chest, I didn't stop as my fingers traced muscles, dipping between his legs.

The moment my hand latched around his cock, a guttural growl tumbled from his lips. He reached for my cheeks, to kiss me, devour me, but I shook my head and dropped to my knees before him.

My broken arm rested on my thigh while my strong hand stroked him, encouraging his cock to swell and harden.

His stomach tensed, every muscle shadowed with need. His mouth fell open as his head fell back and he gripped the tiled wall for balance.

My attention fell to his stiffening erection. The fact his thoughts swam with desire pleased me so much. He gave me power over him. He let me take the memories and replace them with us.

Not only would we wash away whatever he'd committed tonight, but also the blood of the past, the unjust repayments of debts, and the dusty plains of Africa.

His cock fully swelled as his thoughts switched from self-preservation to sex.

I smiled, taking his long, thick length into my mouth.

His hand fell heavily on my head, fingers threading through my hair as I swallowed more of his cock, welcoming his musky heat onto my tongue.

I worshipped him, giving him everything that I was. My tongue swirled, teasing and adoring. His balls tightened, gathering closer to his body as I gave him what he needed.

He needed to know I was okay. That we both were. That he would find no judgement here. That he was loved just as deeply as before.

His hips pulsed in time with my bobbing head. My hand

twisted and stroked, smearing saliva and shower water over his shaft. His hand gripped my hair harder then relaxed as if remembering to be gentle.

I didn't want him to remember anything. I wanted him so far gone, so in lust and consumed by desire he let go completely.

I wanted to *rule* him.

My pace increased, my tongue danced, spearing the sensitive crown and swallowing the saltiness of pre-cum.

Slowly, his breathing changed from ragged and sad to tortured and turned on.

His fingers jerked my hair, granting pleasurable pain as his other hand slapped loudly against the wall behind me, slipping and sliding, holding himself up while his hips worked faster into my mouth.

My heart burst, knowing he'd finally found some relief from his thoughts.

I closed my eyes and let him use me. I let his groans slip into my heart. I let his tugs and thrusts fill my soul.

I didn't know how long we stayed that way. Me at his feet and water raining all around but the tearful rage Jethro suffered finally faded, complex and unsolvable but faded nevertheless.

My jaw ached; my tongue throbbed.

However, I didn't try to bring him to an orgasm. I only tried to keep him centred on me. Consumed by bliss and able to find happiness after a nightmare.

His hand suddenly left the wall, slinking with the one already in my hair. Looping fingers under my chin, he broke my mouth's suction, pulling me away from his cock.

His gaze obliterated me with such love and affection, I couldn't breathe.

"Nila..." His hands tucked under my arms, tugging me to my feet. "I need you." His cock bounced against my lower belly as he hoisted me into his arms. He stumbled a little but kept me protected. His mouth captured mine, and for a blistering moment, he kissed me so damn hard, so damn feral, my core twisted with the beginnings of a release.

His tongue was magic, granting me the same gift I'd tried to grant him, ensuring all I thought about, all I needed was *him*.

Breathing hard, he tore his lips from mine and swayed weakly from the shower.

I didn't say anything.

There were no appropriate words as he reached back to turn off the spray and grabbed a towel from the rail. Placing the fluffy towel over my body, he hoisted me higher and marched back into the bedroom.

A trail of dampness turned the green carpet almost black as he plopped me on my feet beside the bed and reverently placed the towel over my shoulders.

The dawn gave way to weak sunshine. In the ever-brightening light, the scars of our trials became more apparent. My skin looked like a mismatched carousel: the bruises of Daniel's kick and punches. The scratches from glass and car carnage. The shower-drenched cast of my arm.

And Jethro.

His body held shadows and secrets of what he'd survived to get to me. His hair covered the injury on his temple. His skin, now it wasn't cold from trauma, radiated heat with the fever he needed to break. The gruesome red wound in his side was no longer hidden. The puckered skin where stitches had come undone wept, needing a doctor and healing.

We each had our craters and defects from war.

But we would wear them with pride because we'd won.

And the moment our bodies had reconnected, I would find Flaw to help stop Jethro's fever. I would call a doctor to sew up his side. And I would hire the best team to ensure he had no long-term damages from the car accident in Africa.

Jethro's lips twitched. "I love feeling your thoughts. I love knowing you want to heal me even while your body demands I take you first."

I shivered as his husky voice layered the air.

Ever so gently, with his eyes full of love, he dried me off

from the top of my head to my toes. Once I was dry, I took the towel and repaid him. It took me a little longer and more awkward not having full use of two arms, but by the time I tugged his cock in the towel, he didn't care about a few remaining droplets on his shoulders.

Guiding me by the wrist, he stalked to the head of the bed and ripped back the sheets. Swooping me off my feet, he placed me gently on the mattress and tucked me tight. Moving to the other side of the bed, he climbed in and immediately grabbed me, spooning my back against his warm chest.

A huge sigh escaped him. For a moment, we just were. Just lived and relaxed and hovered in the anticipation of sex while soothed by the happiness of connection.

His cock remained hard, wedged against my lower back. His feet stroked mine, twitching like the tail of a predator.

"I don't know who I am anymore."

"I do. You're mine. You're Kite."

"I'll never be able to tell you what happened tonight."

"I know. I don't expect you to."

His arm squeezed my middle, and I arched into his erection.

Breathing faster, he turned me to face him, pressing his nose against mine.

His eyes delved past my soul into the epicentre of who I was. He sought answers to his fearful questions. He hunted for any lie that I didn't love him as much as I said I did. That I regretted any inch of what'd happened.

I wasn't afraid.

He would find no such farce or hidden secret.

Only once he'd searched every facet did he relax a little. Only once he fully accepted I loved him with no lie tainting the truth did he touch me. Truly *believe* me.

"I've done so much to you. I've hurt you so terribly." His hand cupped my cheek. "I don't deserve you or your forgiveness, but I give you my vow, Nila. I will *never* hurt you again. I will never put you in harmful circumstances. I will never ask more of you than you can give. I need you to be strong for me. Like I told you the night after the Third Debt, loving a creature like me is hard work. I'll drain you of every reserve. I'll feed off your love. I'll crave everything you can because you save me from life itself. But I vow that whatever I take from you, I'll give back a hundred-fold. I entrust my heart, my wealth, my very fucking soul to you forever."

His voice dwindled, fading to an almost-whisper. "I will never be able to discuss what I did, and I will never do anything like it again. I can't promise I won't have bad days. I can't assure you I won't need space or time if emotions get too strong to bear. But I *will* promise I will never love anyone as much as I love you."

His gaze entrapped me. "Can you live with that? Can you be so fucking selfless to take me at my worst, my best, my messed-up self and stand by me even when I break?"

I swallowed tears, pressing my cheek deeper into his hold. "I can."

He didn't speak, letting me gather my thoughts because I had more to say...I just didn't have the words in which to say it. "You'll never be on your own, Jethro. You never have to fear I won't understand or I'll push you away. You'll never have to run because I suddenly stopped loving you. I accept your promises and give you my own.

"I promise that no matter what happens in the future, we will work it out. I vow that no matter how life goes, I'll be by your side. I'll always love you because I've seen the worst of you and I've seen the best, and I know just how lucky I am to have met my perfect match."

The room seemed to solidify and melt as he surrendered. "I fucking adore you. I'd lay down my life—"

My good hand shot up, my fingers pressing against his lips. "No more talk of dying. Not now." My eyes drifted to his mouth; my fingertips warming as the pinkness of his tongue licked me gently.

The air between us changed.

Rapturous ecstasy replaced my blood as Jethro gathered me closer. My hand fell from his lips as his head tilted toward mine. His body heated, scalding me, drugging me with unspoken words and fleeting fondles.

I needed him.

He needed me.

We needed each other to wipe away a lifetime of conditioning and destinies. *This* was our new destiny. Right here. And no one—not debts, family, or contracts—could take that away from us.

His eyes flashed gold-bronze with brutal intention as his head bowed the final distance. His lips caressed mine before his tongue fluttered over my bottom lip. "Nila..."

My muscles turned limp, reacting to the desire in his voice.

I kissed him back.

Our lips danced, turning primal, taking, giving, wet, *consuming*. He sucked on my tongue, gruff sounds of lust and possession vibrating in his chest.

He tugged my hair, forcing my head back. With my neck exposed, he kissed his way down my chin and throat, over my collar, to my breasts. He never let go of my hair as his mouth settled over my nipple.

I cried out as he pulled hard and deep, tugging on the invisible cord between breast and core. My womb clenched, wetness wept, and I opened my legs with blatant invitation.

Rolling me onto my back, he slipped his hard body over mine. His hips fit perfectly between my open thighs, and he sighed heavily as his cock nudged erotically against my delicate flesh.

Securing my head with fistfuls of my hair, he kissed me deeply, his flavour making me drunk. Satisfaction, relief, desperation—they all had a flavour. Musky, smoky, sweet. He gave me everything. His fear. His happiness. His regret. His hope.

The kiss was a kaleidoscope of tastes, weaving us closer together.

"Thank you," he murmured, kissing my cheekbones and eyelashes. "Thank you so much."

I struggled to understand as his hands trailed down my belly. "For what?"

His mouth never left my skin. "For trusting me, even when I gave you no reason to do so. For giving me everything, even while I took more than I deserved."

My eyes remained closed, my body hovering in his masterful spell. My voice was the softest melody. "You can feel that?"

He nodded, his hair tickling my ribcage. "I feel everything when I'm with you, Nila."

I gasped as he captured my nipple again. His teeth threatened, slicing deliciously around the sensitive skin.

I turned rigid in his arms. *More. Bite me. Mark me.*

My fingertip tattoos burned with his initials. I wanted more. I'd paid the debts and survived the final one. I wanted the marks to prove it was him who saved me. He who decimated the contracts and war.

"I'm so fucking grateful for you." His slow smile was pure truth. "So awed you've fallen for me." He worshipped me, submitting to me in the most endearing male way. "You kill me every day because I can't believe how lucky I am."

"Stop. You don't need to—"

He kissed me again. "But I do. I need to make you see it isn't empty words or shallow promises. It's the honest to God truth."

My heart skipped. He'd given me so much, and he didn't even know.

The mattress cushioned me as his bulk pressed me deeper into the covers. His sculpted arms trembled as he stroked me. His fever still glowed in his skin, and injury slowed his movements, but he never stopped. Never gave any reason not to take me.

For once, I'd like to make love without fear or regret. I wanted to surround ourselves in happiness and pleasure and shut out the world.

I ran my hands over his chest.

He quivered, his muscles hot and tight beneath my touch.

"I need you, Kite." I pressed my lips into the hollow of his throat. "I need you so much."

"And you have me. Now and forever." His voice slipped from gruff to husky. He slid higher over me, dropping his head, his teeth biting my shoulder. Gathering me closer, he aligned our hips, pressing his full length against me.

Being in his arms was divine. A timeless world within a broken one. Untangling my arms from around his, I swept back salt and pepper hair, staring into his eyes. "You're beautiful."

He sucked in a breath.

"Beautiful inside and out."

"You don't know how long I've wanted to feel worthy of that. To like myself. To be able to live with what I am."

"You don't have to live with yourself anymore. You live with me. Let me love you enough for both of us."

His arms flexed, squeezing me so damn hard. "Fuck, Nila." Rolling me onto his front with a fluid show of masculine power, he hugged me as if he wanted to shatter every bone in my body. Then, as if the glued contact of our skin and overwhelming tenderness of the moment was too much, he rolled me again, pressing my shoulders onto the mattress.

He hovered over me, eyes heavy with lust, his jaw shadowed with sexy stubble. The attraction between us throbbed to unbearable levels.

We'd lived through more than anyone would in their lifetime. And despite all the wrongs we'd endured, the delicious provocative taste of danger still lurked around us.

Jethro was dangerous. He would always be dangerous—not because of his lineage or wealth but because of what he was. However, he was also the gentlest person I'd ever met, building walls and mechanisms in order to live in a world of overstimulation and noise.

He was also the strongest person I'd ever known. If I dealt

with physical imbalances upsetting me daily, I couldn't image the strength it took to stay true to yourself even when there were so many avenues in which to disappear.

His hands gripped my hips. His mouth parted, pressing against mine. Tilting his head, he deepened the kiss, sending me spiralling in his arms. His lips were soft but demanding. His tongue silky but possessing. There was no escape from such control.

I sensed him everywhere, all around me, inside me. His flaws. His triumphs. But most of all his selfless love. He loved me enough to do what he did to his father. Enough to follow me around the world. And enough to put an end to the six-hundred-year-old feud between Weavers and Hawks.

I skated my hands over his taut spine, tracing his hips to grab his cock. The heat of him was still damp from our shower.

"Ask me again. Now that it's all over."

Jethro frowned, his pulse thundering. "Ask you—"

Then understanding filled his gaze. He kissed me sultry and sweet. "Nila 'Threads' Weaver...will you marry me?"

The intensity in his voice burst my heart.

I nodded. "Yes. A thousand times yes."

"Everything you feel for me, Nila. It's so intense. *Too* intense. I need you to never take that away from me. I don't think I'd survive if you did."

"I promise."

A lazy smile—the first I'd seen in weeks—stole his lips. "I'm going to make you keep that promise."

The melancholy disappeared as the dawn switched brighter into daylight. "Oh? How so?"

His hand slipped down my body, moving between my legs. "By claiming you every day for the rest of our lives." His gaze hooded as he stroked my clit with sensuous fingers. Everything about him was wicked and wild and so shamelessly real. "Help me, Nila. Help me show you how much I love you."

I didn't need instructions.

Opening my legs, I let his touch drop downward, stroking my entrance, slowly inserting a finger.

My hand stroked him in return, rippling over the velvety stone of his erection.

My back bowed as his thumb pleasured my clit, effortlessly playing me into a ballad of pleasure.

I cried out as his one finger turned to two. The pressure became indescribably decadent.

With his free hand, he caught my hips, holding me as I rocked on his hand. "God, you're beautiful." His voice was desperate, his fingers fucking me almost leisurely but completely possessively.

Uncurling my fingers from around his cock, he pressed his erection against my thigh. "Feel me. Feel how much I want you—not just now, but for the rest of our lives."

My hands flew downward again, recapturing him, working him faster, harder.

He groaned, driving his fingers inside me, matching my vicious beat.

A ripple of bliss caught me; I moaned as his thumb continued strumming. "Jethro…"

He stopped. "Don't come. I don't want you to come. Not yet." His teeth caught my ear as his harsh breath sent delightful goosebumps over my skin. "Not until I'm inside you and claiming your body as well as your heart." His voice held a warning, growling with bite.

"Jethro…take me, please."

His lips fell into a stunning smile. His fingers withdrew, and he smeared my wetness around my throat where the diamond collar rested. A slight shadow clouded his eyes. "You'll wear this for the rest of your life."

"I know."

"I'll try to find a way to take it off."

I shook my head. "No, I like it." Holding up my hands, I showed him my tattooed fingertips. "Just like I like these. Our beginning didn't start the way a romance should, but I wouldn't part with any memento. Including the Weaver Wailer."

His forehead furrowed. "Let's not call it that. It needs a new name." His hips rocked, joining his puzzle piece with mine. His face darkened as the tip of his cock found my entrance. Without looking away, he sank inside me, impaling me slowly. His jaw clenched as my body welcomed him.

The slowness and friction of his penetration drove me mad.

I gasped as he pushed past the barrier of comfort, sinking his entire length inside me. Only once he sheathed completely and could speak through echoing pleasure did he whisper, "How about Hawk Redeemer?"

My core clenched around him. "I like it."

"Me too." The rasp of his voice drugged me as he rocked once, twice.

"Oh..." My eyes shot closed; all I focused on was where we joined. I'd never grow tired of sleeping with this man. Never cease loving him.

"Fuck, I love when you think those thoughts." His eyes gleamed with awe. "They're so strong and pure—it feels as though I'm reading your mind and not just your emotions."

"I have nothing to hide from you." My head fell back as he thrust into me again, driving deeper, changing the angle of his direction. My body accepted him in one smooth glide.

We fit together so well. We always would.

"Shit, Nila." His head fell forward. "You're so tight, so amazing, so fucking precious."

Words abandoned me as I accepted his every thrust. His cock throbbed inside, so hard and thick.

Jethro kissed me. Hard and fast. His lips trailing to my ear. "I want you forever and always. Like this. No lies. No falsehoods. Nothing between us but honesty."

"Nothing." I wriggled beneath him, craving more. "I promise."

The delirium he caused in my blood sent my thoughts scattering. I needed to come. I needed to shatter and be reborn from everything that'd happened.

"I don't think I can wait," Jethro growled, rocking his cock so the base of him rubbed against my clit. I gasped as yet more blood incinerated.

"Then don't." Holding onto his nape with my good hand, I begged. "Please...give me what you want. I need it, too."

Heat misted across my skin as he thrust harder, fucking me, adoring me, driving me up the cliff of ecstasy. Heat flushed until it was an inferno, turning me sick with sex-fever, demanding medicine in the form of an orgasm.

"God, yes. More. Please."

Jethro slammed his fists into my pillow, using the bed as an anchor as he rode me. His cock drove in and out.

I accepted every punishment, cresting higher and higher, wrapping my legs around his hips, begging, loving, soaring faster and faster toward a release.

His forehead met mine, warmth enveloped us and his pace turned frantic.

I couldn't...I couldn't handle it any longer.

Ecstasy turned to euphoria. Tingles shot from my toes, crackling through my legs, detonating in my core.

Explosion and bands of bliss.

I came. "Yes. Yes. God, *yes.*"

My pussy fisted him, clutching desperately with waves of pleasure.

Jethro cursed, but he didn't come. He hovered above me, giving me a gift, all the while watching me come apart. It made my release so singular and special—turning our moment into something so intimately vulnerable.

Only once I'd wrung myself dry did he fist the pillow and wedge his face into my throat. His guttural groan as he came undone sent another flash of intoxication through my system.

"Fuck, I love you." His growl dripped pure sexuality and unrestrained reverence.

His orgasm quaked his body, wringing him dry as he spurted inside me. I hugged him, letting him splash with his release.

We stayed clinging together long after his hips stopped twitching. Our heartbeats thundering to the same beat.

Slowly, he raised himself on his elbows and cupped my head in his hands. The intimacy between us caused sudden tears to spring to my eyes.

"You're everything I've ever needed, Nila." His voice was hoarse and deep. "Through every day, every text message, every awful debt, I gave you my heart." He nudged my nose with his. "And now, you own all of it."

My nipples tingled against his chest as my uninjured arm wrapped around his muscular waist. There was no space between us. His heart pattered against mine and I never wanted him to leave. My pussy quivered with aftershocks of our orgasm—milking Jethro's erection still inside me.

He chuckled, causing his cock to jerk. "Eager for another round, Ms. Weaver?"

I gasped, shivering with a mixture of happiness and distress at my last name. "Always."

Tilting his head, he breathed, "Kiss me, Needle."

My heart leapt into my mouth as I kissed him with everything I had left. Our lips met hot and wet, the crackling lust of sex mixing with the erotic promise of more.

My fingers disappeared into his hair, holding him like he held me. Our hearts once again spoke silently as his kiss turned demanding and infinite. His cock thickened inside me as his tongue drove in and out, fucking my mouth just like he'd fucked my body.

I couldn't love him anymore than I did. I couldn't ask for any more than I'd been given.

Whatever he'd done tonight still tainted the air around us. The undercurrent of death and destruction hadn't dissolved, but the allure of a bright and untwisted future grew stronger every minute.

It would take time for us to move on. But we *would* move on.

All of us.
Because we deserved it.
With him inside me, we were inseparable.
Now and forever.
He'd proposed.
I'd said yes.
We were each other's.
For eternity.

Jethro

MY HEART COULDN'T handle any more stimuli.

Not after yesterday's rush of terrible highs and morbidly low lows. And yet, I had no choice but to endure more.

In my right hand, I held my sister's. In my left, I held my fiancée's, unknowingly passing emotional messages as natural as breathing.

Last night, we'd become more than two people beneath the spray. We'd become one.

Things had changed between us.

There was a new layer to our connection. A deeper, unbreakable bond—an indescribable friendship.

And as much as I wanted to deny it, I needed Nila's friendship and support more than anything today.

Today.

I swallowed hard, hating the word.

I would forever remember this day. I would forever *despise* this day.

The morning had been blissful. After fucking Nila, I'd tumbled into a sleep so deep, I entered a black hole of tiredness. I didn't wake until late lunch and only because the gnawing pain of hunger drove me to service my other needs now my brain wasn't shredded with lethargy.

Once Nila and I had raided the kitchen for roast chicken sandwiches and crisps, Flaw found us and demanded we follow him to his newly created triage in the east wing.

There, he'd redone Nila's soggy cast, and stitched up the tear in my side. He'd also checked my vitals, and given me antibiotics for my fever. Afterward, he'd given me strict instructions to head for a proper check-up with my doctor at the hospital and assured me he'd taken care of the injured from the ballroom and had the aftermath well in hand.

I normally didn't give employees such trust. But Flaw was more than that now. He'd proved himself capable and loyal. If he said he had things under control, I would believe him while I focused on more important things.

Things such as healing and shedding the memories of what had happened between Cut and me. Every time I thought of my father, my heart ached with torment. Was I right to do such things? Was I wrong to regret them after everything he'd done?

I sighed, squeezing my sister's and Nila's hands. I couldn't think about that.

Not here.

Not now.

Not when the very building I stood in stripped every reserve I had, poisoning me with sadness, grief, and insurmountable helplessness.

Kestrel.

Goddamn you, brother.

My eyes burned as I focused on my best friend.

Flaw had gotten his wish. I'd returned to the hospital. However, I stood in the basement of a facility dedicated to healing and keeping the injured alive, breathing in the stench of death. Above, the living still clung to hope. But down here...down here, we stood in a morgue.

A crypt where soulless bodies froze on ice, waiting for their loved ones to determine their fate. A terrible, terrible place where the lingering emotions of destroyed relatives and broken-hearted lovers said goodbye for the final time.

I don't want to say goodbye.

Nila squeezed my hand as I swallowed back a growl, snarl, curse…sob. I didn't know how to react. I couldn't unscramble my thoughts from Jasmine's or Nila's.

In the car over here, I'd had to screech to a stop, scramble out, and sucker punch an innocent tree on the side of the road.

Jasmine.

She hadn't told me.

After Flaw patched me up, I'd searched for Nila. I'd dealt with my hunger and sickness, all I wanted to do was return to bed and spend days hiding from others, wrapped up in the love Nila had for me.

But that was before the phone rang.

That was before Jasmine called and told me to join her at the hospital.

The motherfucking hospital.

The same place I'd almost died and my brother…

My head bowed as I tugged my hand from Jasmine's, squeezing the bridge of my nose.

Jasmine had received the call earlier. The one conversation no one wanted to have. She'd enlisted Vaughn's help to take her to the hospital.

She'd gone without me.

She'd deliberately left me in the dark that my goddamn brother had fucking died.

Jasmine's hand landed on my elbow, her sniffs quiet but distinct as she cried. "I'm sorry, Jet. So sorry. I came to get you. Truly. I entered Nila's quarters and watched as you slept in her arms."

Her touch fell away; her eyes on Kes, her words directed half at him, half at me. "You looked so happy, so peaceful. After everything you've been through, I couldn't. I couldn't wake you up."

Nila let me go, moving to Jasmine's side and wedging herself where Vaughn kept a subtle touch on my sister's

395

shoulder. Nila smiled at her twin, wrapping her arm around Jasmine. "We understand. Jethro isn't well. He needed to rest. You did the right thing—"

I turned on both of them. "The right thing? How *dare* you decide what's the right thing when my fucking brother is dead! I should've been here for him. I should've held his hand and said goodbye. I should've had the freedom to tell him just how much I loved him. How much he helped me. How much I appreciated his friendship even when I pushed him away."

The pain at his passing crumpled my heart like a dirty piece of paper, screwing it into a tear-stained ball. "I should've been there."

Jasmine's skin waxed white with grief. "He was already dead, Kite. He passed when you were with Cut." Her eyes popped wide. "Forget that. I wasn't going to tell you. Forget—"

"*What?*" My spine rolled. I punched myself in the chest, seeking relief from the slowly fermenting agony. "You're telling me while I hurt our father—while I did what I thought was right—my brother *died!* Is this life's cruel joke? I stole a life. Therefore, they stole his in return!?"

I faced my brother, grabbing his ice-cold hand with mine. "Is this my fault?"

Jasmine's wheels creaked as she rolled closer. Nila came with her, moving to my side, wrapping me in her sadness and despair.

"He was my brother too, Jet. Don't you think I wanted to say goodbye? I would've given anything to be there. But we weren't." Her voice turned fierce. "And it isn't your fault."

Vaughn didn't say a word, backing away a little, never taking his eyes off Kestrel.

"Kes knew how we felt about him. He knew he was loved and wanted. He didn't die without knowing how much we'd miss him." Jasmine couldn't continue; her tears turned to sobs, and my heart cracked with her pain.

I curled my fists, pressing nails against my palm, wanting

to draw blood. I needed to hurt myself so I could focus on a singular discomfort rather than a room full of tragedy. I needed my blade. I needed to cut open my soles and activate age-old salvations so I could get through this.

But I had nothing with me.

And I couldn't leave Kestrel.

Nila curled into me, wrapping her unbroken arm around my waist, pressing her head against my shoulder. She didn't say a word, but she didn't have to.

Somehow, she pushed aside her grief at Kes's death and focused on her love for me. Standing in a room full of crippling unhappiness, she gave me a cocoon of togetherness.

Unknowingly, my body relaxed a little. I leaned into her, kissing the top of her head. "Thank you."

She didn't look up, but she nodded.

Having a moment of peace, I sucked in a heavy breath and turned to hug my sister. My back bent, gathering her crying form from her wheelchair, murmuring in her ear. "I'm sorry, Jaz. I had no right to yell at you."

She clung to me, crying harder. "I shouldn't have made the decision to let you sleep. I should've woken you. I'll never forgive myself. But I haven't moved from his side, Kite. I stayed with him until you arrived. I kept our brother company."

Pulling away, I brushed aside her tears. "Thank you."

The moment I let Jaz go to touch Nila, Vaughn placed his palm back on my sister's shoulder.

My eyes narrowed.

He glared.

I didn't want to feel what he did, but he gave me no choice.

He liked her.

He wanted her.

He hated she was hurting and would be there for her whether I liked it or not.

The complication of Vaughn developing feelings for my sister pissed me off but there was too much to focus on. And there was another person much more important to fret over.

Ignoring him, I faced Kestrel once again.

He lay stiffly on the metal table. His skin looked fake, his hair dull, his form unwanted. His arms remained dead straight beside him, the inked kestrel on his flesh glowing morbidly under the lights, while a white sheet covered his nakedness.

He still looked like my brother, but at the same time, completely different. His skin was no longer warm and pink but lifeless and cold. The pure heart inside him and huge capacity to forgive, heal, and protect had moved onto a different form, leaving us but not forgetting us.

He'd been so strong. So brave. I'd taken him for granted, expecting him to be there beside me as we grew old and grey.

Yet, now he'd forever remain young. Frozen in time, immortal to the end.

I wanted to collapse to my knees and confess everything to him. I wanted to tell him what I'd done to Cut. I wanted to purge my sins and have him carry them for me.

But I couldn't.

I would never speak to him again.

And I couldn't grieve.

Not yet.

Not after the destruction of yesterday.

And in some strange way, I felt as if Kes already knew what'd happened in the barn. As if he hadn't died because I'd taken a life and another Hawk must forfeit. But because he sensed he no longer had to fight against our father.

He was free to go.

Free to be happy.

You'll always have my gratitude and friendship, Kes. No matter where you are.

A ball lodged in my throat, but I didn't break down. It took all of my remaining strength to stare dry-eyed at my brother and whisper farewell.

"He died without pain," Jasmine murmured. "The doctor told us his heart gave out from his injuries. He was still in a coma...he wouldn't have felt it." Jaz looped her fingers with Kes's lifeless ones. "He's at peace now."

My back locked as Kes remained unmoving. His bird tattoo didn't jerk, no feathers quivered over his muscles. I kept expecting his eyelids to flutter, his lips to twitch. His laugh to explode and an elaborate hoax to be unveiled.

But unlike his prankster illusions from his childhood, this wasn't a deception.

This was real.

He was dead.

He's truly gone.

I hugged Nila closer. "He didn't die alone. You're never truly alone when you know you're loved by another."

Jaz's tears wouldn't stop, and I wouldn't force her to dry her eyes until she was ready. I'd purged and sewn myself back together in the lake after coming apart with my father's death. Today, I would help my sister do the same thing.

Nila cried quietly beside me. Her heart sorting through so many memories, so many complexities even though she'd known Kes only a short while. They'd bonded. They'd loved each other. They would forever be linked by their own relationships as well as the family tie Nila would form by marrying me.

I'm sorry, brother.

I looked at his face, his cold body and vacant shell, and said a private eulogy.

I'm sorry I wasn't there to say goodbye, but this isn't goodbye; it's just a postponement. I'll miss you, but I won't mourn you because you were too good a friend and brother to remember with sadness.

Time lost meaning as we all stood beside Kes one last time.

The moment we left, we'd never see him again. The only way we would look upon his face was to stare at pictures from happier times or watch videos trapping his soul forever.

None of us wanted to leave.

So we stayed.

The room quieted from emotional strain until we all hovered in the same thoughts. We relived our special times with Kestrel. We rifled through memories; we smiled at antics and shared childhoods.

"What are you doing here?" I looked up as the locked door to the prison cell swooped open. I'd been at the mental institute for two nights and couldn't stand another fucking minute.

Kes slinked through the darkness. "Busting you out." Holding out his hand, he grinned. "Time to leave, big brother. Time to make a run for it."

He'd tried to help me escape that night, just like he'd helped me escape so many times in our childhood.

"Now, what are you doing?"

"Focusing." Kes sat cross-legged on the floor of his bedroom, his hands on his thighs in a yoga pose.

Throwing myself beside him, I rolled my eyes. "It's not working. Your thoughts are just as horny." At seventeen and fourteen, our hormones had kicked in, and Kes was a terrible flirt.

His laugh barrelled through the room. "Least I can talk to girls."

"Yes, but I can feel them."

"Not in an interesting way, though." He winked. "You feel their silly concerns while I—" He flexed his fingers "—I feel their tits."

I punched him in the arm, so damn grateful he was my brother.

God, I would miss him.

He was gone.

It was time for us to go, too.

Moving for the first time in hours, I placed my fingertips on Kes's icy forehead. His skin seeped my warmth, stealing it the longer I touched him.

Pulling away, I had the incredible urge to touch life after touching death. To hold onto something real. Gathering Nila closer, I hugged my sister and nodded at Vaughn. Flaw would come to pay his respects tomorrow. He was close to Kes; his death would be hard on all of us.

Somehow, two Hawks and two Weavers had come together in shared grief, mourning a man who died far too young.

But that was life.

It was cruel. Unjust. Brutal. And dangerous.

Good people died. Bad people lived. And the rest of us had to continue surviving.

A week passed.

In that week, things changed a lot and none at all.

My fever finally broke, my wound healed, and my strength slowly returned. My body was still exhausted but every day, I pieced myself back together.

Nila had a lot to do with that.

The day after seeing Kestrel's body, I returned to the hospital on my own. I sought out the nurse who'd brought me the cell phone while I healed and paid her a thousand pounds for her trouble. She'd gone out of her way to give me the means to contact Nila. The least I could do was compensate her.

While there, I submitted to a full examination and the doctor's instructions to take it easy. I was cleared of any concussion or long-term maladies. I also singlehandedly arranged the transfer of Kes's body to the crematorium. As part of Cut's meticulous upbringing, all his children had Last Wills and Testaments.

Kes was no different.

I'd found his file amongst the others in Cut's study. The bones of his dog, Wrathbone, lay in the coffee table as I scattered paperwork and skimmed through Kestrel's final wishes.

I already knew he wanted to be cremated and scattered on Hawksridge grounds. We'd shared many a late night conversations as young boys about how unappealing the thought of being buried and eaten by weevils and worms sounded. We were both slightly claustrophobic, and I

401

understood his wish to be sprinkled as dust, prisoner to the breeze, and weightless as the sky.

I wanted the same ending.

However, what I wasn't expecting was a note addressed to me—penned almost five years ago. The strangeness of holding a letter from the grave clutched my stomach.

There was also one for Jasmine and Daniel.

My heart suffered thinking of Daniel's remains. He wouldn't be buried or cremated, but perhaps, he would be happier away from Hawksridge and on his own with no delinquent comments of unwanted belonging.

Respecting Kestrel's privacy, I burned Daniel's letter. Never to be read. The words remaining between two dead brothers forever.

I delivered Jasmine's to her room, leaving her to read on her own. And I took my envelope onto my Juliette balcony off my office where I'd spied on Kes and Nila as they'd galloped across the meadow.

Squinting in the winter sunshine, I slipped out the rich vellum and read my brother's parting words.

Hello, Jet.

I'm guessing if you're reading this, bad things happened.

I must admit, I didn't see myself dying before you. After all, you're the old bugger, not me. But if I died to protect you or help in some small way, then I'm glad. If I died from sickness or doing something stupid, then so be it. At least I'm free from whatever pain I was in.

I do need to ask something of you. And I need you to do it, Jet. Not just nod and pretend you will. I truly need you to do it.

Don't mourn me.

Don't think of me gone, but imagine I'm still with you because I am. We're brothers and I have no intention of leaving you. I've been your support for too long to leave you in the lurch.

So even though I'm physically gone, I swear to you I won't leave spiritually. Scatter my remains on the estate and whenever the wind blows, I'm there telling you a joke. Whenever it snows, I'm there covering you in frost. Whenever the sun shines, I'm there warming your chaotic soul.

And when you finally meet a girl worthy of your love, I'll exist within her. I'll teach her how to help you. I'll guide her how to protect you like you'll protect her. Because you're the best goddamn friend a brother could ever ask for and whoever the girl is who steals your heart, I know she's worth it.

I love her already. Just like I love you.

Never forget that friendships are forever.

I'll see you again, Kite.

I'll always be around.

I didn't cry, even though my soul raged at the unjust and loss. My hands shook as I folded the letter and placed it carefully into its envelope. Kes had written the note before we claimed Nila. He'd sat alone one night and penned a letter to be delivered after his death.

How had he managed to pour so much into a few short paragraphs? How had he known exactly what to say?

If only he'd written it after he met Nila.

He would know what he predicted came true.

Nila was my everything.

She'd replaced Kes as my crutch, and I would never take her for granted like I did him.

Never.

The breeze blew gently, smelling sweetly of hay from the stables.

I closed my eyes and just rested in the moment. No thoughts. No concerns. I let life exist around me and stole a few short seconds to connect with my dead brother.

You're still here, Kestrel.

I feel you.

Another few days passed and life found a new rhythm.

The Black Diamond brothers sorted out their own hierarchy. I put Flaw in charge as temporary president and he

403

culled the members who didn't want to walk on the right side of the law. Those we paid handsomely, made them sign non-disclosure agreement guaranteeing hefty punishments if they spoke out of turn, and let them leave the club.

As our membership was always about diamonds and business, no one had to be unpatched or excommunicated from the brotherhood. They were just employees searching for new work.

One night, once we'd all eaten—Weavers and Hawks sharing a table in the red dining room where so much pain had occurred—I took Nila by the hand to our quarters. Once upon a time, my rooms had been called the bachelor wing, but now, they were our matrimonial suite. A honeymoon before I made her my wife.

We entered the wing. However, instead of taking her to bed, I gave her a key.

Standing at the base of a small staircase leading to a storage floor above, her black eyes met mine with confusion. "What's this?"

I smiled softly, wrapping her fingers around the key. "The past week I've managed to put some of my past behind me. It's time for you to do the same." Gathering her in a hug, I murmured, "Time to let the past go so we can all move on and heal."

I didn't want to think about what she'd find up there. She had to face it. Just like I'd faced Cut.

She let me hug her, her desire for me building the longer we touched. I couldn't put this off anymore. I'd already put it off too long.

Pulling away, I let her go, dragging a hand through my hair.

She frowned, twirling the key in her fingers. "What does it open?"

Something you won't want to see.

Climbing the first few rungs of the steps, I held out my hand for her to follow. "I'll show you."

She silently chased me up the twisting stone staircase, nervousness layering her thoughts the higher we strode.

We didn't bump into anyone. There was no fear of being caught by snooping cameras or hiding from madmen with death threats. Just an ordinary house and an ordinary night. About to do a very unordinary thing.

Nila slowed the higher we climbed. "Where are we going?"

I didn't look back. If I did, I'd second-guess the intelligence of what I was doing. It wasn't my choice to decide if this was wrong. It was Nila's. "Almost there."

When we arrived on Cut's third floor, she faltered. "Tell me."

Grabbing her hand, I tugged her down the plush carpeted corridor. Up here no artwork or embroidery decorated the space. These rooms were the unseen part of the Hall. The place where secrets were stored and debts were hidden for eternity.

"You'll see." I led Nila further down the corridor, stopping outside a room she hadn't been permitted to enter. This wasn't just a room but a tomb of memories. There were still so many unexplored parts of the Hall. She'd only visited a fraction of my home and most rooms were welcoming and just like any other.

But not this one.

This one housed nightmares.

The storage mecca of every debt extracted.

The carved door depicted roses and tulips, similar to the awful flower arrangements Bonnie had enjoyed. The moment the contents were cleared, I would destroy the door, too.

Taking the key from Nila's suddenly shaking fingers; I inserted it into the lock and opened the door. The soft *snick* of the mechanism made me swallow hard. I felt as if I trespassed on things I shouldn't, entering a realm not meant for me. "After you."

My heart thudded at the seriousness on her face. "What— what's in there?"

I looked briefly at the carpet, forcing myself not to drown

in her sudden fear. "An ending of sorts, or a beginning, depending on how you look at it. Either way, you need to see and decide for yourself."

Straightening her shoulders, holding onto non-existent bravery, she brushed past me.

Her eyes widened as I switched on the light, drenching the wall-to-wall cabinets of files. In the centre were a large table, a TV, VCR, and DVD player.

Everything she'd need to read and witness decades of hardship.

Nila covered her mouth as realisation came swift. "It's all here. Isn't it?"

I nodded, steeling myself against her sudden outwash of rage. "It is."

"I can't—I don't…." She backed away. "Why did you bring me here?"

Stalking forward, I opened the one cabinet where I'd seen Cut deposit all things relating to Emma.

Nila stepped again, her bare feet tripping with a sudden wash of vertigo. I rushed to her side, but she pushed me away, balancing herself with practiced ease. "Jethro…I don't. I don't think I can look."

"I'm not saying you have to. I'm giving you the option if you wish, that's all." I moved back to the filing cabinet and grabbed the largest file. Carefully, I carried it to the table. "It's your call, Nila." Heading to the door, I murmured, "I love you. Remember that. Come find me when you're ready."

"Where are you going?"

I smiled sadly, hating leaving her but knowing she had to do this on her own. She needed to say goodbye, consolidate the horror of what my father did, and work through her hate to come back to me. "Tomorrow is Kes's funeral. Tonight, we should have one for your ancestors. Send the dead away all at once, eradicate the estate of the ghosts living in its walls."

For the longest moment, she stared. She didn't say a word. She looked as if she'd bolt or fly out the window. Then, finally, an accepting tear rolled down her cheek. "Okay."

I nodded. "Okay."

It was the hardest thing I'd ever done, but I turned and closed the door behind me.

Heading down the stairs and away from the Hall, I disappeared into the woodland and gathered branches, kindling, and twigs for the largest bonfire Hawksridge had ever seen— minus the barn that'd wiped Cut from existence.

I enlisted the help of Black Diamond brothers and carted every torture equipment and vile method of pain onto the lawn, ready to be burned.

The Iron Chair, Scold's Bridle, Heretic's Fork, Ducking Stool, whips, thumb screws—every mortal thing.

I didn't want such heinous items living beside us any longer.

Hawksridge Hall would evolve with us; it would embrace happiness and learn to accept sunshine rather than darkness.

Nila might be in a room full of ghosts.

But I intended to purge them free with fire.

Nila

"*DO YOU ACCEPT the payment for this debt?*"

Cut's voice echoed in the room, sending chills down my spine.

Silent tears oozed down my cheeks as the old video played footage of my mother and him. She stood in a pentacle of salt beside the pond. The ducking stool hovered in the background and the white shift she wore fluttered around her legs.

The memories of the day I'd paid the Second Debt merged with the horrifying scene before me.

She held herself like I had that day: hands balled, chin defiantly high.

"No, I don't accept." Her voice was lower than mine, huskier and more determined. She'd said in one of her diary entries that I was a stronger woman than her.

I didn't agree.

My mother was royalty. She might not wear a crown and blue blood might not flow through her veins, but to me, she was so queenly she put Bonnie to shame.

Bonnie was younger, her hair not quite white and her back not as bent. She clasped her hands in front of her, watching the altercation between Emma and Cut. The way Cut stared at my mother belied the lust he felt for her. His fingers grew white as he fisted, regret shadowing his gaze.

Regret?

Cut turned out to have so many avenues and trapdoors. I'd always believed he was mad. A barking, raving lunatic to do what he did. But what if he became who he was because of circumstance? What if he fell for my mother just like Jethro fell for me? What forced him to take Emma's life if he loved her?

"Get on with it," Bonnie snapped when Cut didn't move.

He flinched, but it was Emma who forced Cut to obey.

She scrunched up her face and spat on his shoes. "Yes, listen to the wicked witch, Bryan. Do as you're told."

Acres of unsaid tension existed between them. They had a connection—strained and confusing—but linking them regardless.

Cut cocked his head. "You know your orders don't work on me."

My mother balled her hands. Her perfect cheekbones and flowing black hair defied the whistling wind, hissing into the camera like a thousand wails. "Do your worst, Bryan. I've told you a hundred times. I'm not afraid of you, of your family, of whatever debts you make me pay. I'm not afraid because death will come for all of us and I know where I'll be."

She stood proudly in the pentagon. "Where will you be when you succumb to death's embrace?"

Cut paused, the grainy image of his face highlighting a sudden flash of nerves, of hesitation. He looked younger but not adolescent. I doubted he'd ever been completely carefree or permitted to be a child.

Bonnie ruled him like she'd ruled her grandchildren—with no reprieve, rest and a thousand repercussions.

"I'll tell you where I'll be." Cut stormed forward. His feet didn't enter the salt, but he grabbed my mother around the nape. The diamond collar—

My fingers flew to the matching diamonds around my throat.

The weight of the stones hummed, almost as if they remembered their previous wearer.

—the diamond collar sparkled in the sunlight, granting prisms of light to blind the camera lens, blurring both her and Cut.

In that moment, something happened. Did Cut soften? Did he profess his true feelings? Did my mother whisper something she shouldn't? Either way, he let her go. His shoulders slouched as he looked at Bonnie.

Then the sudden weakness faded and he stiffened with menace. "Accept the debt, Emma. And then we can begin."

My hand fumbled for the remote control, my cast clunking on the table-top.

I can't do this.

Once Jethro had delivered me into the room, I hadn't been able to move. My feet stuck to the floor, my legs encased in emotional quicksand. I couldn't go forward, and I couldn't go back.

I was locked in a room full of scrolls and videos.

For a second, I'd hated Jethro for showing me this place. I knew a room such as this must exist. After all, Cut told me he kept countless records and their family lawyers had copies of every Debt Inheritance amendment.

But I hadn't expected such meticulous documents.

Stupidly, I thought I would be strong enough to watch. To hold my mother's hand all these years later and exist beside her while she went through something so terrible.

In reality, I wasn't.

These atrocities didn't happen to strangers. These debts happened to flesh and blood. A never-ending link to women I was born to, shared their hopes and fears, ancestors who donated slivers of their souls to create mine.

But I had to stay because I couldn't keep them shut in the dark anymore. If I didn't release their recorded forms, they'd be forever locked in filing cabinets.

Pointing the controller at the TV, I stopped the tape as Cut ducked Emma for the second time. I'd been with her while Cut delivered the history lesson. I'd hugged her phantom body as she awaited her punishment. But I couldn't watch any more of her agony. I couldn't sit there and pretend it didn't shatter me. That while my mother was almost drowned, I'd been alive hating her for leaving my father.

Forgive me.

Forgive me for ever cursing you. I didn't know.

Leaning over the table, I ejected the cassette and inserted the tape back into its sleeve.

I'd gone through her file. I'd watched the beginning of the First Debt and fast-forwarded over the whipping. I'd spied on security footage of Emma strolling through the Hall like any welcome guest. I held my breath as she sewed and sketched in the same quarters where Jethro had broken, made love to me, and told me what he was.

I couldn't watch anymore.

Whatever went on in her time at Hawksridge was hers to keep. It wasn't right to voyeur on her triumphs over Cut or despair over her moments of weakness. It wasn't for me to console or judge.

My mother's presence filled my heart, and in a way, I felt her with me. My shoulder warmed where I imagined she touched me. My back shivered where her ethereal form brushed past.

I'd summoned her from the grave and held her spirit, ready to release her from the shackles of the catalogue room.

I have to free them all.

Shooting out of my chair, I rubbed my sticky cheeks from unnoticed tears and rushed to the other filing cabinets. Each one was dedicated to an ancestor.

I couldn't catch a proper breath as I yanked open metal drawers and grabbed armfuls of folders. Working one-handed slowed me down. I dropped some; I threw some, scattering them on the table.

Cursing my cast, I lovingly touched every page, skimmed every word, and whispered every sadness.

Time flowed onward, somehow threading history with

present.

Jethro was right to leave.

As a Hawk, he wouldn't be welcome.

The longer I stood in that cell, the more I battled with hate.

Folder after folder.

Document after document.

I made a nest, surrounded by boxes, papers, photographs, and memorabilia from women I'd never met but knew so well.

Kneeling, I sighed heavily as their presence and phantom touches grew stronger the more I read. Their blood flowed in my veins. Their mannerisms shaped mine, their hopes and dreams echoed everything I wanted.

No matter that decades and centuries separated us, we were all Weavers taken and exploited.

My jeans turned grey with dust, my nose itchy from time-dirtied belongings.

Lifting images from the closest file, I stared into the eyes of an ancestor I didn't recognise. She was the least like me from all the relatives I had. She had large breasts, curvy hips, and round face. Her hair was the signature black all Weaver women had and looked the most Spanish out of all of us.

So much pain existed in her eyes. Trials upon trials where the very air solidified with injustice and the common hatred for the Hawks.

I didn't want to sit there anymore. I didn't want to coat myself in feelings from the past and slowly bury my limbs in an avalanche of memories, but I owed it to them. I'd told my ancestors I would set them free, and I would.

Tracing fingertips over grainy images, I worshipped the dead and apologised for their loss. I spoke silently, telling them justice had been claimed, karma righted, and it was time for them to move on and find peace.

My fingertips smudged from pencil and parchment, caked in weathered filth. The video recordings ceased the earlier the years went on. Photographs lost pigment and clarity, becoming grainy and sepia.

I hated the Hawks.

I hated the debts.

I even hated the original Weavers for condemning us to this fate.

So many words.

So many tears.

Reading, reading, reading...

Freeing, freeing, freeing...

There wasn't a single file I didn't touch.

The eerie sense of not being alone only grew stronger the more I opened. The filing cabinets went from full to empty. The files scattered like time-tarnished snowflakes on the floor.

I lost track of minutes and had no clock to remind me to return to my generation. I remained in limbo, locked with specters, unwilling to leave them alone after so long.

Eventually, my gaze grew blurry. The words no longer made sense. And the repetition of each woman paying the same debts merged into a watercolour, artfully smearing so many pasts into one.

By the time I reached the final box, photographs had become oily portraits. The last image was cracked and barely recognisable, but I knew I held the final piece.

The woman who'd started it all.

The original Weaver who'd sent an innocent girl to death by ducking stool and turned a blind eye to everything else.

She didn't deserve the same compassion as the rest of my ancestors—she'd condemned us all. But at the same time, enough pain had been shed; it was time to let it go.

They all deserved peace.

The small space teemed with wraiths of my family, all weaving together like a swirling hurricane. The air gnawed on me with ghoulish gales from the other side.

Taking a deep breath, I re-entered the land of the living. I moaned in discomfort as I stood. My knees creaked while my spine realigned from kneeling on the floor like a pew at worship, slowly working my way through a temple of boxes.

I didn't believe in ghosts walking amongst us but I couldn't deny the truth.

They were there.

Crying for me. Rejoicing for me. Celebrating the end even though they'd paid the greatest price.

They loved me. They thanked me.

And it layered me with shame and ultimately pride.

Pride for breaking tradition.

Pride for keeping my oath.

They'd died.

I hadn't.

I *lived.*

I found Jethro outside.

The sun had long ago set and winter chill howled over the manicured gardens, lamenting around the turrets and edges of Hawksridge Hall.

I'd had the foresight to grab warmer clothes before embarking on finding fresh air and huddled deeper into my jacket, letting the sling take the weight of my cast. Tugging the faux fur of my hood around my ears, I wished I'd brought gloves for my rapidly frost-bitten fingers.

Jethro looked up as my sheepskin-lined boots crunched across the gravel and skirted the boxed hedgerow. Wings and Moth stood in the distance, blotting the horizon, cloaked in blankets.

As I'd made my way through the Hall, I'd seen silhouettes of people outside. I'd recognised Jethro's form. I wanted to join them—be around real people after dusty apparitions.

And now, I'd not only found Jethro but everyone I loved and cared for.

On the large expanse of lawn stood my new family. Jasmine, Vaughn, Jethro, and Tex. They all stood around a mountainous pile of branches, interspersed with the Ducking

Stool and Iron Chair and other items I never wanted to see again.

Ducking my head into the breeze, I patrolled over the grass. My hood whipped back, and I caught the eye of Jasmine.

She gave me a smile, holding out her hand.

I took it.

Her fingers were popsicles, but she squeezed mine as I bent over and kissed her cheek. We didn't need to talk. We understood. She'd lost her brothers and father. I'd lost my mother. Together, we would stand and not buckle beneath the tears.

In the distance, the south gardens glittered with rapidly forming dew-frost, glittering like nature's diamonds on leaves and blades of grass.

Jethro skirted the large tinderbox of firewood, pausing beside his sister with a large log in his hands. His eyes glowed in the darkness, his lips hiding white teeth. "I won't ask what happened. And I won't pry unless you want to share. But I built this for them. For you. For what lives in that room."

He dropped his gaze, awkwardly stroking the log. "I don't know if you'll want to say goodbye this way, but I just thought—" He shrugged. "I thought I'd make a fire, just in case."

I didn't say a word.

I let go of Jasmine, flew around her chair, and slammed into his arms.

He dropped the wood and embraced me tightly. I didn't care my brother and father watched. All I cared about was thanking this man. This Hawk. Because now he'd let himself be the person I always knew he could be, I couldn't stop falling more and more in love with him.

His lips warmed my frozen ear, kissing me sweetly. "Are you okay?"

I nodded, nuzzling closer, inhaling the pine sap and earthy tones from collecting firewood. "I'm better." I gathered my thoughts before whispering, "When you left me in there, I couldn't move. I truly didn't like you very much. But you were right. Thank you for giving me that time. For knowing what I needed, even when I didn't."

He hugged me harder. "Anything for you, you know that."

I shivered as another howl swept over the treetops. The night would be bitterly cold, but soon there would be something to warm us.

Pulling away, I smiled at my twin standing with his arms crossed and a bitter look on his face. Eventually, I would have to talk to him and tell him Jethro would be his brother-in-law. He would have to accept him. Tex, too.

I asked far more than they could offer——to love the son of the man who'd stolen Tex's wife and our mother——but that was life.

The heart had the incredible capacity to heal wrongs. And I wouldn't apologise for betraying my family name with Jethro. I'd chosen him. And if they couldn't accept that...well, I didn't want to think about it. Not tonight.

Jethro tucked flying hair behind my ears and pulled up my hood. "Are you ready?"

I rested my face in his palm, reaching on tiptoes to kiss his wind-bitten lips. "I'm ready."

Taking my hand, he kissed my knuckles. "In that case, let's put the past behind us."

It took us an hour and a half to lug the boxes from upstairs to the bonfire outside.

We formed an assembly line, a never-ending factory of willing hands to transport.

Jethro joined me in the room, respectfully gathering files and packing them into boxes. I'd left the space in a mess, but together, we created neat piles so Vaughn and Tex could carry them downstairs.

Jasmine stayed on the lawn, willingly accepting the items on her lap and wheeling them across the grass to the unlit bonfire.

The last box to go down was full of my mother's time at the Hall. I blinked back tears as I handed it awkwardly to my father.

He knew with one look what the paperwork entailed. His face echoed with heartbreak as he cradled the heavy package and took it downstairs himself. He didn't transfer it to Vaughn. He didn't let go. Hugging his wife's spirit one last time.

Once he'd gone, and the room stood empty, Jethro popped into the corridor and spoke to V.

"Can you give us a minute?"

Vaughn looked past him, his black eyes meeting mine. "You okay, Threads?"

I came forward, my heart beating faster. "I'm okay. I'll see you down there." I gave him a half-smile. "Don't start without us."

He scowled. "You know I wouldn't."

I sighed. We had a long way to go to be able to joke with one another again without a filament of mistrust and pain cloaking everything. "I know, V. Stupid joke." Brushing past Jethro, I gathered my twin in my arms.

He buckled, his spine rolling and strong arms wrapping around me. He shuddered as we stood there and squeezed. The past ten days had been good for us. We'd spent time together, skirting true issues, but I had a feeling after tonight, we'd have nothing keeping us apart and could finally talk through the events and find our closeness once again.

Letting me go, he smiled. He'd let a slight beard creep over his chin, dark and rich, making him seem exotic and untameable. "Love you, Threads."

"Love you more." I patted his chest. "I'll see you in a bit."

Vaughn nodded and disappeared down the staircase. Once he'd gone, I entered the room and waited while Jethro silently closed the door.

My heart went from fast paced to flurrying. "What are you doing?"

Jethro grimaced, striding to a filing cabinet and shoving it to the side. "There's one more box you haven't seen. One I hid."

I ghosted forward. "You hid it? Why?"

Dropping to his knees, he ran his fingernails around a wooden panel in the wainscoting. Popping open a hidden compartment, he shuffled back to pull out a dust-smeared box. This one didn't match the other drab brown ones. This one was white and narrow with the initials E.W. on top.

My heart flew into my throat.

Jethro stood up, supporting the box and swatting at dust motes on his jeans. "I hid it because I was asked to by someone I cared about."

Moving toward the table, he placed the offering in the centre. "She asked me to give this to you. She knew I'd come for you once she was gone, but she also knew I was different."

I couldn't move. I couldn't take my eyes off the carton. "Different?"

"She caught me one day. She caught me before I had the chance to have another lesson. She didn't fully understand what I was, but she guessed enough that it made her trust me. I wanted to tell her not to be so stupid. I was still my father's son. But she didn't give me a choice.

"She told me I would fall in love with you. She told me you would win. She also told me that if I let you help me, everything could be different."

A tear glassed my vision then spilled over. Talking about my mother, learning new memories I didn't share was wondrous as well as bittersweet.

I didn't notice I'd moved forward until my fingers traced her initials. "She told you all of that?"

Jethro chuckled quietly. "She told me a lot of things. She also told Kes. I think she preferred him over me—he was the one everyone fell in love with—but she trusted us with different tasks."

I finally met his eyes, tearing mine from the box. "What

did she make you do?"

Jethro nodded at the table. "She wanted me to keep this safe for you. She said one day, I would find the right time to give this to you. And when I did, she hoped it meant things hadn't gone the way they had for her. That you'd won.

"At the time, I almost hated her for being so cocky and sure. I hated I'd come across weak enough that she dare predict my future. But at the same time, I loved her for seeing things in me I hadn't even permitted myself to see. I loved she thought I was worthy of your love. I loved that she wanted me to take you because, ultimately, she knew I'd lose and you'd win and together we'd fight."

I struggled to breathe as more tears joined the first. I wanted to ask so many questions. I wanted Jethro to regale me of every time he'd conversed with my mother. I wanted to hoard his memories as my own and build a picture of her strength after she'd been taken from us.

But I didn't want to rush something so precious. Another time. Another night. When people weren't waiting to say goodbye.

Sucking in a breath, I asked quietly, "And Kes? What was his task?"

Jethro's face tightened with pain. "You already know. He completed his promise within days of you being with us." His eyes narrowed, willing me to recall.

What had Kes done apart from taking me into his quarters? He'd given me sketching paper. Become my friend. Laughed with me. Entertained me and granted normalcy while I swam in bewilderment.

"He was to become my friend."

Jethro nodded. "Your mother knew no one could replace Vaughn. You'd grown up together. You loved each other so much. But she also knew not having that connection would be one of the hardest things you'd have to face. So she asked Kes to be your brother while your true one couldn't be there."

My stomach knotted as I wrapped arms around myself.

Kes's friendship had been invaluable, but now, it'd become priceless knowing every touch and joke had come out of respect for my mother.

In a way, it could've cheapened Kes's kindness to me—knowing he'd been asked to do so—but I didn't see it that way. I saw it as a selfless deed, and I was confident enough in our mutual affection that he hadn't just done it for Emma. He'd done it for himself, for whatever bond blossomed between us.

Jethro came closer, moving behind me to envelop me in a hug. My back fell into his chest, my head tilting to the side for his kisses to land on my neck. "She also asked him to give you the Weaver Journal. I knew you thought that was a tool for my family to spy on your thoughts. That we were the ones to create such a tradition. But we didn't."

His lips trailed lovingly over my collar to my ear. "That was a Weaver secret and at least one Hawk in every generation kept it hidden. Kes was tasked to give it to you. But he wasn't asked to tell you why he'd given it. It was yours to do what you wanted—write in it or not. Read it or ignore it. The choice was yours."

How could I learn so much in such a few short sentences? How could I fall in love with the dead even more than when they were alive?

Spinning in Jethro's hold, I pressed my face against his chest. "Thank you. Thank you for telling me."

His embrace tightened. "Thank you for making your mother's premonitions come true."

We stood still for so many heartbeats, thanking the dead, reliving the secrets, rejoicing in the rightful end.

Finally, Jethro let me go. "Open it. And then we'll join the others."

I looked at the box. The air around it seemed to throb with welcome, begging me to look inside.

Jethro shuffled, moving toward the door.

I held out my hand. "Wait. Don't go."

He halted. "You don't want to be on your own?"

"No." Shaking my head, I smiled. "I want you beside me. She would want you to be here."

Biting his lip, he returned to my side.

Wordlessly, I pulled the box closer and slid off the lid.

A puff of lint flurried with the opening pressure, scattering onto the table-top. My heart stopped beating as I reached into the tiny coffin of memories and pulled out the letter sitting on top.

"It's addressed to me."

Jethro looped an arm around my waist, trembling with everything I felt.

The confusion.

The hope.

The sadness.

The happiness at hearing from her one last time.

"Open it."

The glue on the envelope had weathered and unstuck, gaping open as I turned it over and fumbled with my sling to pull forth the note.

Dear my sweetest daughter,

I've promised myself I would write this letter so many times, and every time I begin, I stop.

There is so much to say. My mind runs wild with guidelines and tips for all things you are yet to enjoy. First love, first heartbreak, first baby. I'll never get to see those things. Never see you grow into a woman or enjoy motherhood.

And that upsets me, but I know I'll be proud of the woman you became because you're part of me, and through you, I shall remain alive, no matter what happens to my mortal body.

There might also be a chance you won't achieve what I hope you will. That you'll fall to the guillotine like me. That we'll meet far too young in heaven.

But I'm not thinking those thoughts.

If you live at Hawksridge while Cut is still in power, remember two things. That man is violent, unpredictable, and cruel. But beneath it, he can be manipulated. A man who has everything has nothing if he doesn't have love. And he's never had love. I pretended to give him that. I hoped my false affection could prevent my end, but I didn't have it in me to love him true. I love your father. I can never love Cut while I have Arch in my heart.

And that was my downfall.

Anyway…

Before I prattle on about nothing, I have to tell you two things. I've hoarded these confessions for far too long.

First, I need to tell you about your grandmother.

I know by now you will have seen the graves on the Hawk's moor. You'll have seen her name on a tombstone. But what you won't know is…that grave is empty.

Like you, I believed she died at the hand of Bonnie's husband.

But that was before Cut told me the truth.

He viewed his father as weak because that was what Bonnie fed him. However, I see Alfred Hawk as one of the bravest men. He succumbed to tradition and claimed my mother. He completed the first two debts, but his affection for her—the love he could never give Bonnie—meant he couldn't attach the collar or kill her.

So he did the only thing he could.

He pretended to end the Debt Inheritance. He buried a fake corpse and set her free. He gave her a second chance but with the strictest of conditions: never contact her Weaver family again—for her sake and his.

She kept that promise for many years. I grew up believing she'd died. However, one night, I received a phone call from Italy. She was alive, Nila. She'd watched me from afar, celebrated when I had my children, and lamented when I was claimed. She would've fought for me—I know that. But she died before she could.

Now…Nila…this is the hardest part to write. The second secret I've kept my entire life, and I honestly don't know how to tell you. There are no easy words, so I'll just have to swallow my tears, beg you to understand, and hope you can forgive me.

My children.

I loved you. All of you. So, so much.

I let my fear get the better of me just before they took me. I begged *your father to hide you. But we both knew this was our only chance. Arch didn't want to go ahead with my plan. Don't hate him, Nila. It was me. All me. I take full blame, and even though I'm dead and you can't berate me, know I died with regret and hope.*

I regret you living in my path, but I'm full of hope you'll achieve what I couldn't.

I always thought a letter like this would be long and full of tears, but I know now (after so many failed attempts) that I can't over think this. I can't write everything I want to say because everything important you already know.

You know I love you.

You know I'll always watch over you.

And I know when Jet comes to collect you, you'll win. You'll win, darling daughter, because you're so much more than I ever was. You're the strongest, bravest, most brilliant daughter I could ever ask for, and that's why I sacrificed you.

Does that confuse you?

Does that make you hate me?

If it does, then I won't ask for your forgiveness. But know I believed with all my heart you had the potential to do what I couldn't. I chose you over her—over Jacqueline.

I made that decision. Right or wrong. I'll never know.

After watching you grow up, I just know you have the power to end this. And it was a risk I was willing to pay. You were the one I pinned all my hopes on. You were the one to save us all.

I love you, Nila, Threads, my precious, precious daughter.

Forgive me or not, I'll never stop caring for you, never stop watching.

Please, try to understand.

I gambled both our lives to save so many more.

Thank you for being so brave.

Love,

Your mother.

Jethro

JACQUELINE?

Who the motherfucking hell is Jacqueline?

Nila dropped the letter. "What does she mean? She *sacrificed* me?" Her emotions swelled in one huge wave of question marks. "What does that *mean?!*"

Jacqueline.

Jacqueline.

Who the fuck is Jacqueline?

Snapping out of my trance, I pulled Nila away from the table, the box, the condemning note. "Nila, it's okay. Don't——"

Her black eyes met mine, wide and horror-filled. "It's *okay?* How can you say that? All this time, I hated my father for letting you take me, but I just found out my mother was the one who orchestrated it? He wanted to hide me, Jethro! And she stopped him! She was supposed to protect me. Tell me how any of this is *okay?* I don't understand! First, I find out my grandmother was never killed, and now, I find out I have another...what? *Sister?*"

My fingers pinched into her elbows, but she tore out of my hold. "No! Don't touch me." Her cast blurred through the air as she shoved off her sling and grabbed her hair. "What does this mean? Jacqueline? Am I supposed to know who she is? What. Does. This. *Mean?*"

She whirled on me. "Who is Jacqueline, Jethro? Tell me!"

I stood there, buffeted by her emotional turbulence, wishing I had the answers.

But I didn't.

I didn't have a fucking clue who Jacqueline was.

I spread my hands in defeat. "I wish I knew, Needle. I'm sorry. My family had yours under surveillance for decades and not once has anyone called Jacqueline come up."

Nila breathed hard, her tears drying as anger filled her instead. Her eyes flew to the window where the barely-there outlines of our combined family stood around the wooden pyramid.

Her hands balled, pain flashing over her face from her break. "I know who will have answers."

My heart stopped.

I took a step toward her, trying to grab her before she did anything reckless. "Nila, listen to me. Calm down. You can't go out there like this. You can't—"

"I can't, can I?" She stomped forward, avoided my grasp, and scooped the box off the table. The letter crumpled inside as she slammed on the lid. "My mother just cleansed her soul by dumping decade's worth of secrets. It's not fair. How could she do that to me?" She sniffed, ice filling her black eyes. "I won't let her get away with this. I want answers and I want them now."

"Nila...don't. Wait until later. Stop—"

She bared her teeth. "Don't tell me what to do, Kite. She was my mother, and this is my fucked-up history. I deserve to know what she meant."

I stumbled to grab her. "You shouldn't, not tonight—"

Crushing the box, she glowered. "Watch me."

Turning on her heel, she bolted from the room, leaving me standing all alone wondering what secrets we shouldn't have uncovered.

Damn Emma.

Perhaps the tales of the dead should remain dead.

Did I do the right thing?

Had I just kept a promise to a ghost and stupidly destroyed our carefully perfect world?

I won't let that happen.

"Nila!" I charged after her, careening down the staircase and erupting onto the grass.

Her treadmill running days gave her a good sprint, and I didn't reach her in time.

I couldn't stop her slamming to a halt in front of her father.

I couldn't prevent her throwing the box in his face.

And I couldn't halt the torrent of questions spilling from her soul.

Nila

"WHO THE HELL is Jacqueline?"

I stood trembling in front of my father, fighting a vertigo wave.

Tex was almost comical as he froze, gaped, and swiped a shaking hand over his face. "How——how did you hear that name?"

Ducking, I ripped out the letter from the box at his feet and shoved it into his chest. V drifted closer, drawn by the air of animosity and questions. "Mum just told me."

Tex gulped. "What? *How?*"

Jethro came jogging over the lawn, sternness on his face. "Nila...perhaps now is not the best time."

I whirled on him. "If not now, when?" Pointing at the ready-to-blaze bonfire, I snapped, "I think now is the perfect time. Closure, Jethro. That's what this is and that's what my father owes me."

Ripping my eyes from Jethro's, I glared at Tex. "So, tell me. Who the hell is Jacqueline?"

"Threads...what's going on?" Vaughn nudged my shoulder with his. "What's gotten you so upset?"

My father didn't look up as he read the same letter I'd just devoured, his pallor shifting to a sickly yellow.

My voice throbbed as I looked between my twin and father. "Mum left a note." I pointed at it, rippling in the breeze in Tex's fingers. "That one. She not only told me our grandmother was never claimed by the Debt Inheritance, but I was *sacrificed* over a girl named Jacqueline. So my question is...*who is she?*"

"Holy shit. What the fuck?" Rubbing his jaw, V glanced at Tex. "Well? I think we deserve to know."

Taking a huge breath, Tex finished reading. His eyes darted to Jethro before locking on me and V. "She's your sister."

I'd already guessed as much, but it still hurt. "Older sister?"

The eldest who should've paid the debt. The sister who should've protected us by being the chosen one, not the saved.

Jethro came closer, barricading me against the wind. "I think you better spit it out, Tex."

Tex nodded, fighting ghosts and things I never knew. How could he keep such a secret? How could my own father be a complete stranger?

Picking up the box, I hugged it, waiting for knowledge.

His body tensed, thoughts filing into collected streams, ready to tell me the truth. "There isn't much to say. Your mother and I met young. We never planned on getting pregnant—she was averse to the idea of children right from the start. But the pill failed. When we found out, we agonised for days what to do. We couldn't abort as my parents were very religious and had recently died, making me loathe to destroy new life. But we also couldn't keep it.

"We were too young to make the choice, so we decided to let life do that for us. We got married because we loved each other, not because Emma was pregnant, and we set up life while she grew with you. However, instead of it being a happy time, it was fraught with secrets and tension. I didn't care about any of it—the strangeness of taking her name. The oddness of her family empire and unspoken obligations.

"By that point, I was happy to start our family young. Emma…she wasn't. She came from Weaver money. I'd been inducted into the business and we were financially secure. We could start building our own family—regardless if we hadn't planned it so quickly.

"Early on in the pregnancy, we found out she was carrying not one, not two, but *three* babies. The shock quickly faded into happiness, and I was glad she came from a bloodline that tended to give birth to multiples. I transformed my home office into a large nursery with three cots, three bouncing tables, three singing mobiles. Three of everything.

"But no matter what I said or how excited I became, Emma shut me out. The closer to delivery, the more she'd cry, need space, and push me away. I was told by our local doctor to leave her be—that some women required time to come to terms with their body changing and the uncertain future.

"So, I gave her time. I was there for her, I left her notes telling her how amazing our life would be, how perfect our children would be, and how happy I was to grow old with her—"

Tex stopped, wiping his eyes with the back of his hand. He stared at the awaiting bonfire and rushed onward. "She disappeared. I remember it so clearly. We'd just come back from our latest check-up and I'd left her in the lounge to make her a cup of tea. When I came back…she was gone. The front door was open, her shoes by the welcome mat. Just gone.

"She was seven months pregnant and padding barefoot around London. Winter was close, and the air was freezing. Terrified, I hopped in the car and patrolled the streets for her. It took me hours before I found her sitting in the cathedral where we were married.

"There she told me the most awful thing, the curse on her family, the debt she must pay. She tried to divorce me, telling me she'd made a terrible mistake. She tried to convince me to give up the children for adoption the moment they were born and let her run far away.

"Of course, I didn't believe her. I thought she was tired and stressed from the pregnancy. I murmured and soothed and took her home to bed. She didn't mention it again, and I stupidly thought it was over. Only, then the birth came around, and I rushed her to the hospital.

"Jacqueline was born first, then you, Vaughn, followed by tiny Nila." His eyes glistened with paternal love. "I held you all in my arms. Three small bundles with tiny red fingers and squished up faces. I fell madly in love with you within seconds.

"I kissed Emma and handed over my newborn triplets for the nurses to weigh and measure. I trusted everything was right in my world."

Tears welled in his eyes as he cleared his throat. "However, after forty minutes, when the nurses didn't come back, I began to worry. I tracked them down only to find my three children had become two."

My heart lurched, imagining such a tragic revelation.

"I rushed back with you and V, demanding an explanation from Emma. She merely shook her head and said she'd told me what happened to the firstborn girls of her family, and she wouldn't let that happen to Jacqueline.

"Behind my back, she'd arranged a private adoption; she'd bribed the nurse and doctor to wipe all record of ever having triplets and listed her delivery as twins. She did it all. She stole one of my daughters to protect her, and for a time, she believed you would be safe, Nila. She said you wouldn't be claimed as technically Vaughn was firstborn and not you.

"However, that plan showed its flaws when Cut came to collect her. She was my wife, but she had so many secrets from me. She'd told me you would be safe, but she knew better. She sacrificed you. She let them take you. And I did nothing to stop it."

Silent tears tracked down his face. "I'm so sorry, Nila."

I couldn't move.

My mother had always been a perfect memory. I'd hated her for a time for leaving my father with no explanation, but then she became a saint when I found out the Hawks murdered her. She'd been a hard woman to love. And Tex had been there for her. He'd loved her so much even when she left. He lied for her. He did everything she asked. And he'd honoured her wishes and let them take me.

I had so many questions, but I couldn't formulate them clearly. My brain remained fuzzy, slow to grasp the magnitude. All I could think about was—

"We have an older sister…" Vaughn murmured, stealing my thought. I leaned my head on his shoulder, slipping back into my body after living the past with Tex. Having my twin back and sharing the same thoughts was like wearing a favourite pair of slippers. I'd taken our ease for granted, and having him by my side while we learned something so monumental was a blessing.

My hand slipped into Jethro's. He hadn't moved. He stood on my left while my twin stood on my right.

I was the only female in an all-male gathering—apart from Jaz.

I'd been the only female for most of my life.

To find out there'd been another girl? A *sister*? A potential best-friend who had been robbed from me…it hurt. But excited, too.

I have a sister.

I could find her.

Swallowing, I asked, "Where is she now?"

Tex sniffed, reaching for the box in my hands, willing me to give it to him. I did, handing over the pieces of jewellery Emma had been wearing and whatever other knickknacks she'd treasured.

They belonged to Tex more than me. It would've been Emma's wish for her husband to possess her last trinkets. "I don't know. I've never known."

"You never tried to look her up?" Jethro asked.

Tex shook his head. "I wanted to. But Emma made me swear I wouldn't."

"But you said you hired the mercenaries *before* I came to take Nila. What did you mean by that?" Jethro was deceptively calm, as if he'd been planning to ask that question for a while.

Tex swallowed. "You caught that, huh?" Sighing, he added, "You're right. I'd enlisted the help of a P.I and protective team to track her down. I kept it a secret from everyone—even the men working for me. They didn't know why they were searching for a girl with my strict criteria. They just hunted.

"Emma said if I ever tracked Jacqueline down and the Hawks found out, they'd take both my daughters. So I kept it secret—half of me wanting them to find her so I could love her from afar, and half of me hoping she remained lost so she stayed safe." His eyes narrowed. "Is it true you would've taken both? If I'd found her?"

Jethro pinched the bridge of his nose. "In all honesty, if Bonnie was still in charge, probably. But now, you have nothing to fear. If you want to track her down, I think you should."

Tex looked at me. "Nila…what do you think? Do you want to?"

The question was too large to answer so quickly. I bit my lip. "Yes…no…I—I don't know."

"I vote yes," Vaughn piped up.

How would a girl who'd been given up for adoption, stolen from her heritage and family's legacy, ever slip into our world?

"Imagine it from her point of view," Jasmine said, wrenching our attention to her. "You two grew up together. You've been best friends all your life. She didn't have that. She might've felt like she was missing something but didn't know what."

She smiled sadly at Jethro. "I know I loved having more than one brother. It's natural to want similar people to share your life with."

Yes, but we didn't have a similar upbringing.

Vaughn chuckled, sharing my thoughts again. "You think anyone could enter our life and not want to run away? Especially once we told her what happened and why she was given up?"

Tex ran a hand through his hair. "You have a point."

"Shouldn't she be given that choice though?" Jasmine rested her hands on her lap. "I think you should find her."

We all slipped into silence, mulling over the idea. There was still so much to say but not tonight. We'd all been through so much. Jacqueline had been missing from our family for so many years. Another few days wouldn't make a difference.

Tex straightened his shoulders, looking a hundred times lighter even after recounting something so hard. "I didn't realise how much that secret weighed me down." His eyes glittered. "Every time I look at you both, I remember Jacqueline. I wonder if she looks like you, has the same habits and fears. I hate that I was glad my parents died, so I didn't have to break their hearts by stealing a grandchild."

He sighed. "I'm not one to complain; I loved your mother. But she did leave me so alone. Stranded with secrets and missing a wife I could never have."

Unthreading my fingers from Jethro, I went to my father. I'd held a grudge against him for so long, believing it was his fault for not protecting me. But I hadn't known the full story. There was no black and white—for any of us. We'd all made choices on half-facts and uncertainty. If we couldn't forgive, then what was the point in any of it?

Wrapping my arms around Tex, I hugged him hard. His arms were imprisoning jaws, squeezing me tight. "Will you ever be able to forgive me for not saving you?"

Vaughn joined our hug. "She already has, Tex."

I nodded. "He's right."

Tex hugged us even harder. "I'm so glad I have you both. I love you so much."

As we healed each other through touch, Jethro moved to the pyramid and drenched the branches, torture equipment, and boxes full of records with gasoline.

The pungent whiff of chemicals laced the night sky, and our hug ended with much needed closure. It hurt to hear the truth, but it patched up a hole inside me I didn't know I had.

My heart knotted as Jethro diligently thought of everything, making sure tonight would be a perfect end. I hated the fact I'd just gained a sister I didn't know, while he'd lost a brother he loved. Life was never fair.

Jasmine wheeled closer, touching my hand. "I know what you're thinking, and he'll be okay."

"I know. It's just so hard to say goodbye to good people."

"He was the best."

We shared a smile as Jethro held out a box of matches. His half-grin fluttered my heart, and my lips ached to kiss him.

Taking the offered box of matches, Jethro cupped my cheek and kissed me softly. "It's all yours."

Tonight, when we were alone, I would show him how thankful I was for everything he'd done.

I moved away and stood beside the kindling. The bonfire would burn for days with the amount of fuel Jethro had gathered.

Stroking the matchbox, I closed my eyes and said a prayerful goodbye.

This is to find your perfect freedom. The Debt Inheritance is gone. It's over.

Stepping to join me, Jethro's gaze glowed with love and support. Holding out a folder, he murmured, "This isn't the original—I'll get that from the lawyers next week and burn that too—but this should be destroyed with the rest of what we've done."

Taking the folder, I opened it. Tears sprung to my eyes. Inside were the pieces of Debt Inheritance I'd been given after each round of the table along with the amendment I'd recently signed under Jasmine's duress.

"Thank you. This means a lot." Holding the folder, I struggled to open the matchbox to set it alight. It would be the first piece to burn. The catalyst to decimate everything else.

A flick of flint and glow of flame appeared in my peripheral. Jethro held out a monogrammed lighter. I'd seen it the night he'd dragged me into his office and made me sign the Sacramental Pledge.

"The wood is drenched in kerosene, so it will catch easily." Holding the lighter to the corner of the Debt Inheritance folder, he waited until the paper caught fire. Taking a step back, he smiled. "Whenever you're ready."

I looked at my brother and father. They stood like two sentries against the darkness. Hawksridge loomed behind them, leering over all of us as no longer foe but friend. A few of the windows gleamed with golden lights, spilling rectangle wedges of illumination across the grass.

Jasmine sat primly in her chair, her eyes reflecting the smoking flame in my hand. The folder rapidly dissolved into leaves of blackened char.

Evil had vanished. Only happiness remained.

With no hesitation, I threw the burning paper onto the bonfire and watched with soul-singing satisfaction as the entire thing erupted with orange heat.

The icy air was battered back as flames whipped into existence and my mind quieted from thoughts of Jacqueline, my mother, and secrets. My family stood all around me, cementing me in a brand new world where nothing could separate us.

There was nothing else to say.

The flames spoke for us.

The smoke purged the past.

And the crackling spoke of a future where no debts existed.

Jethro

SOOT TAINTED MY mouth.

Smoke laced my hair.

And my eyes still burned with sparkling orange and yellow from the bonfire. We'd stayed vigil for hours. Nila and Vaughn were the only ones who threw the documented debts onto the flames.

The rest of us paid our respects and supported them silently.

I didn't save any evidence. I didn't put aside valuable proof to incarcerate the men who'd hidden my family's secrets. Partly, because their sins were our sins and it would be hypocritical to lay the blame at their feet when we all shared the crime. And mostly, because I wouldn't use others' pain as a bargaining chip.

I had more respect than that.

If the lawyers wanted to play and proved to be a problem when sorting out the final paperwork, then I had other means in which to hurt them. More *just* means. We'd dealt outside the law for so long, a few more 'loose ends' could be managed in the same way.

Tex had stared ahead, his hands clasped and face hard. If I let myself feel what he went through, I'd suffer a clout of shellshock. He hugged Emma's last remains, twirling her engagement ring from the box as if he could invoke a spell to bring her back.

But nothing would bring her back.

Nothing could undo what Emma had announced.

And I feared what Nila would do once the wounds of tonight had been tended to and she'd had more time to think about the sudden revelation of having a sister.

I hid my derisive snort. Daniel had been right, after all. His stupid joke in the car about stealing the wrong sister—he'd meant nothing by it—a stupid ploy to unsettle Nila even more.

But somehow, he'd guessed the unthinkable.

There'd been another Weaver.

A firstborn girl hidden from us.

Jacqueline.

A few minutes older than Vaughn. A few minutes older than Nila.

The love of my life had been sacrificed to a fate that wasn't hers to bear.

Did that make me happy or sad?

Happy she'd become mine?

Sad I'd put her through so much?

Who was Jacqueline?

What did she look like? How would she have reacted?

My hands balled.

One thing I was certain of—whoever Jacqueline was, she wasn't Nila. I wouldn't have fallen in love with her. I wouldn't have broken my vow or bowed at her feet.

Jacqueline wouldn't have changed history.

Succumbing to torrenting thoughts, I remained silent, locked where I would stay for the rest of my life—beside Nila.

I didn't leave as she threw paperwork and audio and video into the raging flames. Every time Nila looked my way, I kissed her. I passed her file after file, delivering my family's crimes into her hands to dispose of.

Only once the grass was empty of history did we disperse our separate ways. The fire would continue to rage on its own while we retired to different corners to rest, revalue, and regroup.

Textile was the first to disappear, wordlessly hugging Emma's box and disappearing into the orchard grove.

Vaughn rolled Jasmine toward the Hall, her wheels sucking in the mud of her tracks from carting so many files earlier in the evening.

Nila and I—we headed back to my quarters.

Her cheeks smudged with ash and charred pieces of paper decorated her hair and lined her jacket hood. She looked as if she'd been in a battle. She looked endlessly tired.

Entering the bachelor wing and my bedroom—*our* bedroom—I shrugged out of my jacket and draped it over an ancient sideboard.

Nila drifted to the middle of the carpet, staring blankly at the bed.

My heart clenched. All I wanted to do was take away the weight of decision and grant her peace. Moving behind her, I unzipped her jacket and slid it off her arms.

The scents of fire and fresh air licked around her.

"Do you want a shower?" I asked softly, massaging her shoulders.

She jumped, startled by my voice after only the crackle of fire as conversation. Turning to lock herself in my embrace, she shook her head. "I don't need a shower." Her voice echoed with need for something else. I didn't need to ask what she needed—I already knew.

I knew far more than I should.

However, I was respectful of granting some semblance of boundaries.

Nila had a lot to sort out internally. I wouldn't make it worse knowing she couldn't pretend she was okay when I knew completely she was not.

So even though I didn't need to, I asked anyway, "What do you need…"

Her head tilted up, her black eyes flashing with ebony fire.

"You." She stood on tiptoes, pressing her lips to mine. "I need you."

My cock thickened; my heart raced.

I needed her, too. So fucking much. More now than ever as she was currently lost to me. She didn't know how to take her position within this life. She didn't know how to admit to herself that if she hadn't been chosen over Jacqueline, she would never have met me. Never have fallen for me. And I would never have fallen for her.

I groaned as the true worry of her thoughts rose.

I didn't want to pry, but I couldn't let her think such incorrect things.

"I wouldn't have loved her, Needle."

She gasped, her kiss stalling.

I parted her lips with my tongue, feeding her the truth. "Only you. I don't care she was supposed to be my inheritance. I don't care you took her place. In fact, I'm so fucking glad."

Her breath hitched as I kissed her harder, crushing her to me. "I'm so happy it was you because you cured me, fixed me. I love you, Nila. Not her. Not anyone else. *You*."

Her arms, both good and broken, slung around my neck, pulling me hard against her mouth. I let her guide me to bed. I let her control the kiss. I let her grab my shirt and pull me down upon her. And I let her control whatever she needed.

I'd give her anything she ever wanted.

I'd spend the rest of my life ensuring she never had to doubt my feelings for her.

She was it for me.

It didn't matter if lies brought us together.

Fate had decided we were matched.

And we'd fulfilled that prophecy by falling head over fucking heels.

Nila

I WOKE UP the same way I'd fallen asleep.

By Jethro making love to me.

We'd remained wrapped in each other's arms for a few vacant hours of sleep. I didn't dream. I didn't fret. I just slept and recharged after such a long emotional day.

Jethro roused me with kisses and touches, bringing me to a soft release before carrying me into the shower to wash.

After the bonfire, the sun had already risen on a new day.

The day.

The day we said goodbye to Kestrel.

I feared I'd be tired as Jethro and I dressed quickly, slipping into jeans and jackets and boots. I feared I'd be muddled with sleep deprivation as we ate a quick lunch in the kitchen and strode over the gardens to the stables.

But I didn't need to fear.

The time with Jethro had recharged me better than sleep.

During the bonfire, I couldn't think about my mother without wanting to howl at the moon and demand her explanation. I wanted to kick and punch my father for holding such a terrible secret my entire life. And I wanted to hold Vaughn because it wasn't just me this news affected.

We'd been raised as each other's everything. Twins. Best

friends. Confidants.

To find out we were actually only two-thirds of a complete sibling set—it hurt.

Jacqueline.

Tex said he would continue to track down the adoptive family. He hadn't been strong enough until now to find the truth.

Then again, maybe strength kept him away.

I was third born.

I should never have had to pay the debt.

But I had, and I'd ended it.

Jacqueline owed her life to my parents for saving her. But her future children owed me their safety.

Jethro took my gloved hand as we stepped from the sun's glare into the musky world of the stables. "Are you ready?"

Cobblestones and hay welcomed along with memories of Jethro tenderly cutting my hair, putting me back together again with the same implement that'd destroyed me. Stable hands bustled about, gathering saddles and bridles, tending to the horses.

My heart leapt as I noticed Moth.

Kes's horse.

My horse.

The bridge between us I'd always cherish.

Squeezing his fingers, I nodded.

His lips smiled, but his eyes fought tears.

Today would be hard for him. But I would be there. I would *always* be there.

He sucked in a deep breath. "Okay, then."

Together, we prepared to say goodbye to Kestrel Hawk.

"YOU SURE YOU want to do this?" I eyed Jasmine as Vaughn manhandled our gentlest horse from its box. The grooms had already combed, saddled, and prepared six mounts.

I'd planned this day for the past week.

I wanted it to be perfect.

"Stop asking me that. Yes, I'm sure." Jasmine wheeled herself awkwardly over the cobblestones, her wheels catching and stalling on the uneven surface. But she didn't complain. Not once did she curse or lament. Her disability had finally been accepted and she no longer hid away in the house, regretting the life she would never have.

Her acceptance had come from a multitude of things. Vaughn Weaver's unwavering attention had been one of those things but so had Kes's death. His passing at such a young age shook all of us. Yes, she'd lost the use of her legs but she hadn't lost her life like our brother.

"Lead her over there." I pointed V at the already erected platform I'd had the Hawksridge carpenters create.

Originally, I'd planned to put Jasmine in a carriage, safely protected by walls and wheels. But the moment I told her the plan, she argued. She used to ride a lot with Kes and me when we were younger. She wanted to share one last ride with him…before he was gone.

I'd done my best to persuade her but she was damn stubborn when her mind was set.

I didn't interfere as Vaughn did his best to guide Claret to the mounting block. However, the Roan had other ideas—hay being her main focus.

Vaughn cursed under his breath, doing his best to yank the mare forward. "Come on, you bloody animal."

Christ, at this rate we wouldn't get out of the stables until dark.

Nila laughed as I stormed forward and grabbed the reins. Taking responsibility for the horse, I pointed Vaughn to a new task. "Help my sister up the ramp. I'll move Claret into position."

Tex entered the stable. His eyes darted from the horse to Jasmine in her chair. He wisely didn't mention her safety and focused on his own discomfort instead. Rubbing the back of his nape, he said, "You sure I have to be on a nag? Can't I follow on foot?"

Nila went to her father and looped her arm through his. "Kes would've wanted us all there. Please, do it for me. We need to honour his final goodbye." Pecking his cheek, Nila smiled, completely winning over her father within moments.

Try saying no to her.

Hell, I couldn't.

Hiding my smugness, I let my condition fan out. Tex still confused me. He'd stood up for his daughter in the end. He'd helped put an end to our family's madness, but inside, he still wallowed in self-hatred and guilt. That guilt ate at him like acid. If he didn't find a way to forgive himself—he'd be dealing with his own mortality in the form of sickness.

Tearing my eyes from Nila and her father, I marched forward. Swatting the mare with the tips of the reins, she plodded onward, submitting to my direction as I led her around the newly-erected ramp.

Vaughn grabbed Jasmine's chair. Almost shyly, he tucked

her jaw-length hair behind her ear before hurtling her like a fucking rocket up the ramp.

Goddammit.

"Shit!" Jasmine grabbed the handrails, ferocity etching her face.

"Just thought I'd make sure you were awake." Vaughn chuckled.

"Yes, well, I'd like to keep awake and not dead for as long as I possibly can." Her fake anger couldn't hide her enjoyment that Vaughn didn't treat her like a china doll.

Unfortunately, her emotions couldn't lie. Her heart skipped a beat whenever that damn Weaver was around.

Nila came to stand by me, her delicate hand landing on my wrist. "Stop scowling. I know what you're thinking."

I didn't look at her. The more time she spent with me, the more she could read me. She might not be able to keep secrets from me, but I couldn't keep them from her, either. "I don't know what you're talking about."

She smiled. "Yes, you do." Her eyes shouted: *My brother likes your sister.*

I clenched my jaw, ignoring her.

Claret stomped, tossing her head as Vaughn bumped her going around to the front of Jasmine's chair. His eyes locked on Jaz's. "Remember the last time you asked me to be your legs?"

Jaz cocked her head, her gaze flickering to me. "Yes."

"Did I drop you?"

She frowned. "No."

"Good, so you trust me?"

Her tongue swept over her bottom lip. Fuck, she was flirting with him. "Perhaps."

"That's good enough, I guess." Bending, he smiled. "Put your arms around my shoulders."

My stomach knotted, wanting to tell him to be careful, but Jaz immediately looped her arms around him and allowed him to scoop her useless legs from the chair.

I'd never seen Jaz so open to trusting someone she hadn't vetted and investigated within an inch of the law before. Yet she accepted Vaughn so easily.

Holding her in his arms, he completely forgot about the rest of us and the over-packed stable.

I coughed deliberately.

Vaughn grinned not giving an arse what I thought. Murmuring in her ear, he carefully placed Jasmine on Claret. Her useless legs wouldn't straddle the horse, but Vaughn held her aloft so Jaz could grab her jodhpurs and sling herself into position.

Once Jaz sat on the horse, she nodded. "You can let me go now."

V did as she requested, looking at me for instruction.

Leaving Nila, I climbed the ramp and checked the girth was tight, Jaz's legs were anchored and buckled to the custom saddle, and her balance was correct. The pommel came up extra high and the back of the saddle cradled her back with cushioning and a seatbelt.

She'd have to be careful of sores and bruises as she wouldn't be able to feel but she was as safe as she could be on a beast.

"Ready for your first ride?"

I'd never seen Jaz's eyes so bright. The thought of doing something she'd given up granted a smidgen of magic on this melancholy day. "Never been more ready."

Fighting my brotherly protectiveness, I passed her the reins. "You sure?"

Her lips pursed as she stole the leather. "Positive."

Giving her a dressage whip, I climbed down the ramp. The whip was longer than a hunting version and meant she could encourage Claret to move without having to kick or twist.

Moving toward Wing's stall, I stopped dead as Nila came out of Moth's enclosure already sitting on the dapple grey.

So many times in the past fortnight I'd thought of Kes. Pictured him still living and joking and teasing. *Laughing.* Filling the holes of our lives with antidotes only he could.

But my brother was gone and his horse, who he so generously gave to Nila, remained.

My heart skipped a beat as Nila pulled to a stop, her eyes drowning with love. For me. *Love*...something I never thought I'd earn.

I marched to the side of the large dapple and grabbed her wrist. "Kiss me."

The one sentence that started it all. The command that broke my every resolve.

Nila smiled softly. "When you ask so nicely, how can I refuse?" Bending in her saddle, I stood on my toes to reach her delicious mouth.

It wasn't a slow kiss or even erotic. Just a quick affirmation we belonged to each other and always would.

Reluctantly, I let her go. Vaughn had managed to help Tex climb onto a large Clydesdale called Bangers and Mash, and a stable hand in turn helped V clamber on top of a newer addition to the stables called Apricot.

"Head on out, everyone. I'll catch up."

Jaz obeyed, flicking her whip and urging Claret forward. A procession disappeared out the barn. Tex followed gingerly, his hands tight on the reins while V chuckled, shaking his head at his father's nervousness.

Their lack of skills was what happened when you worked in a factory all your life.

Now Nila was mine, I intended to share.

I wanted to show her Hawksridge.

I wanted to teach her how to play polo.

I wanted her to help me run the empire of diamonds and run so many facets of my world.

I also wanted to enter hers.

I wanted to travel with her on her runway shows.

I wanted to watch her sew and spend hours just sitting beside her as she crafted exquisite designs from nothing.

I want everything.

Moth snorted as Nila prevented her from following the others into the sunshine. "Do you want me to stay?"

My insides glowed with affection. "No, I'll only be a minute."

Swatting Moth on the rump, I sent Nila out to join our family. Retrieving my important requirement, I headed to Wings and secured the saddlebag to the pommel. "Ready, boy?"

Wings snorted, his eyes black and endless.

"I'm not, either." I pressed my forehead against his silky neck, just like I had whenever my condition got too bad and needed space from life. "I don't want to say goodbye but at least this way, he's still with us."

Swinging my leg over his immense side, I kicked him and followed the others.

"This is the place." I pulled on my reins, bringing Wings to a stop.

For an hour, we'd trekked through woodland and glens over chases and riverbeds of Hawksridge Estate. The moment Kes's Will had been read, I'd known what his instructions would be.

We'd had such happy times here. Away from our father and obligation. Away from even our sister. Just us and the wilderness.

"It's stunning." Nila came up beside me. Moth's breathing caused plumes of condensation in the chilly winter air.

Jasmine encouraged Claret to move further up the ridge, looking down the valley to where a small village rested in the distance. Hawksridge Hall couldn't be seen from here. That was why Kes and I had liked it.

Sitting at night, wrapped up in sleeping bags and roasting marshmallows on a fire, we used to watch the twinkling lights of the village and conjure stories for what each person did.

We pretended we lived hundreds of years ago. Discussed and argued what sort of career we would've had. I was adamant I would've been a horse farrier or black-smith. There was something about hammering hot metal until it submitted that appealed to me. Kes, on the other hand, wanted to be a carpenter. Not because he liked to create things from trees but because he reckoned women preferred a man who knew how to use his wood.

I laughed under my breath, remembering his quips.

"You're such a moron." I fired a flaming marshmallow his way.

Kes ducked, swatting the gooey mess into the ground. His shaggy hair glistened with moonlight, while the horses munched contentedly on grass behind us. "Whatever, Jet." Holding up his hands, he smirked. "These puppies were on Selena's tits last week. She told me I had good hands."

I rolled my eyes. "She's probably never been touched by a guy before and had no one to compare you to."

Kes scoffed. "I might only be sixteen, but I know how to please a girl."

Sighing, I reclined in my sleeping bag, looking at the stars. "Well, she'd be lucky to have you."

Kes shuffled closer, the crackle of the bonfire wrapping us in safety. "Same with you. You'll meet someone who doesn't just think of shopping and teenage girl idiocy one day. You'll see."

Lightening the mood, I snorted. "Perhaps, I should become a carpenter, too, so I know how to use my wood."

We burst out laughing.

My heart filled with history as I left the past and returned to Nila. "Kes will be happy here."

Nila nodded, her eyes glassing a little.

More horse hooves thudded over the hill as Tex and Vaughn finally caught up. They'd handled the trek well, allowing their horses to follow us.

Twisting in my saddle, I opened the bag and collected the urn that held my brother's ashes.

Jasmine moved closer, her lips twisting against the urge to cry. I smiled, reminding her to be happy and not dwell on what we'd lost. "Do you want to say it?"

"No. You. I think you should be the one."

Taking a deep breath, I unscrewed the lid of the copper urn and held it aloft. "To our brother. Every wind that rustles, we'll remember you. Every leaf that falls, we'll think of you. Every sunrise, we'll recall the times we shared. And every sunset, we'll value all that we've been given. This is not goodbye; this is a 'see you soon.'"

My hands shook as my chest compressed with sadness. Nila wiped away a tear and Jasmine swallowed a sob. Their emotions swelled with mine, threatening to avalanche with despair.

Needing to say a private goodbye, I kicked Wings forward and shot into a gallop. The ridgeline spread before me as I let my horse fly.

I let him gallop as fast as he could.

I let him carry me away.

And, as the thunder of his hooves blotted out the black hole of grief, I tipped the urn and sprinkled Kes's last remains.

The grey dust clouded behind me, whirling in the breeze, spiralling in the wind.

Goodbye, brother.

The wind picked up, encouraging the grey cloud to plume and soar down the valley, becoming one with the countryside.

My family had owned this estate for almost six-hundred years. It held many souls. Had seen many events. And witnessed many evolutions. My brother would remain its watcher and warrior—guarding Nila and my new family forever.

As Wings slowed, I looked at the sun and smiled.

The urn was empty.

Kestrel was gone.

From bone to ash.

From blood to dust.

His body had vanished, but I knew he still lived.

And we would meet again.

We would laugh again.
We would be brothers again.

Nila

"WHY DID WE come here?"

Jethro grabbed my hand, leading me from the Ferrari and through the car park at Diamond Alley. "You'll see."

Four weeks had gone by.

Four weeks of adjustment and simplicity.

I'd had my cast removed and my arm had knitted together, erasing Cut's crime. My father and I had discussed the revelation of Jacqueline many times, and V and I were both keen to track down our triplet and stare into the eyes of a lost relation.

Every day brought different experiences. Kes was gone. It was hard to get used to——especially as he deserved to enjoy the changes we slowly wrought on Hawksridge Hall——but time ticked onward, dragging us forward without him.

After staying with us for a few weeks——to clear the air and spend time together as a new puzzle-fitted family——my father moved back to London to oversee a busy part of the year with fabric deliveries and demands.

Vaughn stayed most weekends, chatting quietly, slowly letting go of his animosity about a past he couldn't change. Instead, he focused on a future so much brighter.

During the week, my twin spread his time between his

penthouse and Hawksridge. He and Jaz spent a lot of time together, and Jethro and V talked more and more.

I'd caught them chatting over cognac beside a roaring fire in the gaming room. The room no longer tarnished with gambling debts and almost-rapes but a place where my lover and brother found friendship.

Tinsel hair brushing dark hair, discussing the world's problems and hopefully seeing eye-to-eye on most subjects.

I'd also seen them chuckling over something juvenile in the dining room, slowly switching from enemies to friends.

I'd stop and watch, hidden by shadows, and allow residual fear to flee. The gaming room was no longer the room where the Third Debt was almost repaid, the octagonal conservatory no longer where the First Debt was extracted, and the lake no longer where the Second Debt had been delivered. They were blank canvases ready for new memories.

Hawksridge slowly shed its antiquity of brutality and pain, relaxing into a gentle ceasefire.

And now Jethro had brought me to another place I'd already been.

Diamond Alley.

The fascinating warehouse where I'd met Kill for the first time.

Arthur 'Kill' Killian had returned to Florida after the final battle and the day I almost lost my head. We had a future because of him. We had a life to look forward to because of what those men did that day.

Knocking the same door we'd passed through last time we came here, a small pang hit my heart. Kes wasn't with us today, and he wouldn't be any other day, but his presence never left. Jethro didn't bring him up often, but I knew he thought about him.

The nine-digit password was accepted and the door opened.

Immediately, Jethro handed me a pair of sunglasses and pulled me into the large diamond building. The incredibly bright spotlights warmed my skin like a tropical sunshine while tiny rainbows danced on the black velvet sorting pads of the tables.

The diamond collar I wore hummed to be amongst its kinsmen and I willingly clung to Jethro's hand as he dragged me down the corridor toward the door I'd once thought was a janitor's closet.

He didn't say a word as he opened it and entered the code to the large safe and spun the dial. Once the armoured entrance hung open, Jethro bowed. "After you, Ms. Weaver."

I grinned. "I can imagine Cut is turning over in his grave seeing Weavers stay happily in his Hall and touch his diamonds on display."

Jethro hadn't told me what'd happened in the outbuilding, and I hadn't pried. That was his trauma and triumph to bear.

Bonnie had been buried on the estate, in the catacombs beneath the house. Her sarcophagus had already been crafted as per the custom of burial rights for rich lords and ladies.

At first, I hated to think of Bonnie beneath my feet as I roamed the Hall, but after a while, I didn't mind. I'd won. She hadn't. It was her penance, not mine, to witness life move on for the better while she rotted below.

Daniel's body had never been found. His bones gnawed on and flesh devoured by predators. The Hawks had taken so much from the African soil. Karma had seen to pay that debt with his flesh.

"I don't think he would've minded as much as we think." Jethro moved toward the safety deposit boxes. "In the end, he truly was sorry for what he'd done. Without him revoking the conditions on his last Will and Testament, all of this would've been lost. We would've spent years in legal battles trying to claim our birthright and Hawksridge would've been torn to pieces by the state."

I looped my fingers, listening quietly. Whatever passed between Jethro and Cut that day was their own affair, but I was glad Jethro got closure. Cut hadn't died with hate in his heart as

I'd expected. He'd died with an apology and sorrow. I hoped he was at peace, wherever he was.

Standing in the middle of the safe, I waited as Jethro pulled out the long gunmetal grey drawer.

My heart beat faster.

I know what's in there.

The last time he'd shown me the original black diamond, he'd hinted at what he was. He used the stone as an example of his condition—absorbing light and emotions rather than refracting and preventing them from entering. The analogy was perfect for him.

Moving closer, I placed my hand on his forearm. "I should've guessed that day. I should've known what you were and convinced you to run away with me."

He chuckled. "Running was never an option, Needle. But you're right. Those drugs really fucked me up. I'd hoped you'd guess and slap me out of it."

I smiled. "I seem to remember I did in the end. I marched into your bedroom and forced you to listen."

"You'll never know how much your strength helped. How your tenacity to make me feel broke my unhappiness." His lips touched mine as his hands pulled out the black pouch.

"This is for you." He pushed the soft material into my grip.

I jerked backward. "What? No. There is no way I can accept that!"

He grinned. "Yes, you can. By accepting me, you've accepted it already. It's yours and I want you to open it."

"Jethro…"

He placed the ribbon in my fingers. "Open it."

My hands shook as I opened the velvet. My eyes narrowed. I expected one large stone tenderly nestled in padding. However, something didn't look right. Inside rested more parcels wrapped in delicate tissue paper.

Jethro crossed his arms, smugness decorating his face. "Go on. Keep going. You haven't opened it all yet."

Placing the pouch on the table, I plucked out the first packet. My fingers trembled harder as I pushed aside crepe paper. As soon as I unwrapped it, I almost dropped it. "Oh, my God."

Jethro didn't say a word as I pulled out the most stunning bracelet I'd ever seen. "This…it's…you made this from the single black diamond?"

The one stone that'd started it all. The priceless gem that'd raised his family to riches and tainted glory so long ago.

Jethro nodded. "Yes." Taking the dangling bracelet, his fingers traced the filigree pattern where gold licked around clusters of black diamonds, steadily growing bigger to one large rock in the centre of the design. "Give me your wrist."

Speechless, I held out my arm.

Jethro very gently secured the jewellery. Of course, it was the perfect size. "You had this made for me?"

"How could I not?" He kissed me again. My heart transformed into feathers wanting to take flight. "You're the reason I'm alive and happy. I want to give you everything, Nila."

Running his fingers over the uniquely shaped diamonds, he added, "This cut is called a kite. It's rare—not many jewellers remember the art." He smirked. "I thought it was rather fitting to use in the design."

I couldn't stop staring. "More than fitting. Now I have a Kite in my heart and kites on my wrist."

"For the rest of your life, I hope."

Not letting me answer, he looked at the pouch again. "There's more. Open the next one."

I couldn't pull my eyes away from the one he'd already given me. It was too much. Far, far more than I ever expected. The blackness of the stones sucked the light, glowing like an otherworldly charm.

Unable to speak, I pulled free the next crepe paper present. Tears glossed my eyes as I revealed what rested inside. "Jethro—"

Before I could kiss him or pounce in gratefulness, he dropped to one knee before me.

Stealing the black diamond ring, he grabbed my shaking left hand and smiled tenderly. "I've asked you to marry me twice. And each time you've said yes. As far as I'm concerned, you became a Hawk the moment you answered my first text. But I couldn't steal you away for the rest of your life without doing this properly."

I gasped as his voice broke. "Nila 'Threads' Weaver. Will you do me the absolute honour of accepting this ring, this man, this future? I offer you everything that I am and will become. I promise to adore you with every heartbeat and will forever protect you like I should've done from the day we met. Will you agree to be my best-friend and partner for the rest of our lives and continue to be so selfless with your love and kindness?"

He cleared his throat, forcing himself to continue. "In return, I promise to always love you, always protect you. I'll be the anchor you need and will never do anything to hurt you again."

I dropped to my knees before him. Knee to knee. Heart to heart. "I do. I accept and I promise you the same thing. I will never lie to you, hurt you, or keep things from you. I will always be there when you need me most."

His lips crashed against mine. My fingers dove into his salt and pepper hair. Everything I'd been through was in order to deserve this. *Him.* The greatest trophy, gift, and reward I could ever have dreamed of.

With his lips on mine, Jethro slipped the engagement ring onto my finger. Snug, perfect, never to be removed just like my collar.

I'd turned from seamstress to diamond heiress with the amount I now wore. The huge stone glittered menacingly in a cushion cut with baguettes on either side.

I didn't want to guess how many carats the ring held.

Breaking the kiss, Jethro murmured, "There's something

else in there. Something that isn't for you, but I want you to see it."

My eyebrow quirked, but I reached upward and plucked the pouch from the table. With the weight of my new engagement ring, I fumbled with the crepe.

Once it was unwrapped, I couldn't stop the tears this time. I huddled over the necklace where a teardrop black diamond had been fashioned with gold scroll work and the wings of a hawk and a needle with thread in the fixings. It wasn't just a necklace; it was a joining of our two houses. A gift for someone who would be treasured above any diamond or estate. A priceless necklace for a priceless child.

"You made this for our daughter."

Jethro sucked in a breath. "How did you—"

I smiled, liquid glassing my vision and heart. "I know because I know you." Stroking the diamond, I breathed, "You want a daughter over a son?"

His arms banded around me. "Nila, I want whatever you give me. But a daughter, if she's firstborn, will be the end to everything. The debts will never take place again. She'll be part Weaver, part Hawk, and I wanted her to have something to symbolise what a new beginning she will represent."

"I love you." I grabbed his cheeks. "I love you so damn much."

His entire body melted in my hold, his adoration for me glowing in every facet. "I know. And I'll never ever deserve it."

Climbing to his feet, he helped me upright. Tugging me into an embrace, he kissed me softly. "There's one other place I'd like to take you to, if you'd let me?"

My body curved into his like a comma. "I want to go wherever you want to take me."

His gorgeous face lit with a sexy smile.

Thoughts of sealing our engagement with more than just a kiss crossed my mind.

When Jethro had bundled me into the car this morning and driven off the estate, I thought it was to complete a few errands or to stand beside me while I visited my assistants at Weaver Enterprises and give feedback on an up-and-coming design line.

Our life had become somewhat normal with work and businesses to run. I loved the normalcy but loved the magical alone times, too.

I would never have expected something as spellbinding as this to happen.

It is spellbinding.

We'd made promises in the heart of Diamond Alley to love, honour, and treasure each other for the rest of our lives. What else existed if those vows weren't classified as a spell? A forever kind of spell. A spell that would keep our souls joined even after death.

My eyes fell on the large diamond on my finger.

I couldn't stop looking at it. Flashing the black gemstone, revelling in how thoughtful and incredible my future husband was.

I ran a finger over the glossy surface. "I'll never be able to thank you for what you've given me, Jethro. More than just an anchor. You've given me a home in your heart and made me belong."

He grabbed my hand, squeezing my fingers tight. "I feel exactly the same way. Now, let's go, so I can show you the next part of my plan."

"The next part?" I laughed. "Careful, you might spoil me."

He smirked. "You don't know where I'm taking you yet. It might be an awful place."

"I highly doubt it." Tossing my hair away from my face, I smiled. "Tell me then. Where do you want to take me?"

Guiding me from the safe, he grinned. "You'll see."

"In here?" I looked over my shoulder as Jethro nodded. We'd left Diamond Alley and driven into a bustling local town where knickknacks and tourists decorated the streets.

"Yep." Jethro bit his lip to stop from smiling.

"You want me to go into a coffee shop?"

He moved past me, pushing on the door until the chime above welcomed us into the decadent smell of coffee and sweets.

"But I don't even like coffee. You know that."

He smirked. "I know."

"Then why—?"

"Stop asking questions and get in there." Grabbing my wrist, he dragged me over the threshold and beelined for a tatty couch in the coffee shop window.

The couch.

The coffee.

Oh, my God.

My heart stopped. "This…it's similar to the café in Milan where I tried to kiss you when we first met."

He nodded. "Exactly."

I frowned, even as my heart thundered with love. "Why…why did you bring me here?"

He patted the couch, sinking into the soft cushions.

I followed, our knees touching as we faced each other. The softness of the settee cradled me as Jethro stroked my ring, his face alive and pensive. "That night I told you so many lies and hid so much from myself. I wanted you so much. I wanted to run the other way, to hide you, to never return to Hawksridge. But I didn't. I let a lifetime of conditioning control me, and I made the worst mistake of my life."

Looking around the tiny café—at the grandmother feeding a teacake to her granddaughter and the barista serving a couple—he added, "I've known you for months, Nila, and I haven't once taken you out on a proper date. Never been to see a movie or eaten at a restaurant."

My entire soul overflowed with affection. "You're saying you want to do that?"

"Of course." His back straightened. "I want to explore the

world with you. I want to show you off and let people know I might've planted evidence saying you ran away with me at the start of this mess—that the media believed we'd had an affair well before we did—but now, it's true, and I value you enough not to keep you all to myself."

His golden eyes darkened to bronze. "You're no longer indebted. You're free to go wherever and whenever you wish; I want to be by your side for every experience you find. I want to be the reason you smile every day and the man you hold every night."

Quick flashes of the doctored photographs and Flaw's handwritten note to the press the night Jethro stole me entered my mind. I no longer suffered any hurt or annoyance because, in the end, that was life's plan. To give me to Jethro so I could steal him in return.

My voice stayed soft, inviting. "What are you saying?"

"I'm saying, I'll be beside you no matter what you want to do. If you want to return to sewing, I'll be there holding the fabric. If you want to travel and help me with diamonds, I'll be there carrying your bags. As long as we're together, Nila. I don't care where we are."

My heart galloped with longing and love and overflowing lust. "Kite…" Leaning closer, my eyes latched onto his mouth. "As far as I'm concerned, you come first. I might not be indebted anymore, but I have no intention of running far from you. I don't care what we do as long as we do it together."

He relaxed a little. "I'll never get tired of hearing that."

"Never get tired that I love you or that I won't run?"

His smile turned into a sinful invitation. "If you run from me, I have the means to chase you. I'd find you and make you mine again."

My legs twitched as my belly fluttered.

Inching closer to me, Jethro ran the pad of his thumb over my bottom lip. "Now, if you don't mind, I believe I need to do something that I should've done that first night."

My breathing stopped. "What should you have done?"

His breath fanned over my lips. "Kissed you. You owe me the kiss you so naively offered me moments after we met."

"Naively?" My heart pounded as my core grew wet. The tension between us swirled and sparked. "Don't you mean stupidly? I remember you calling me that a few times."

His hand cupped my cheek; his thumb skimming from my lip to my ear. "Like I said. I told a lot of lies that night." His eyes drifted to my mouth. "May I? May I take back that first wrong and make it right?"

I couldn't breathe.

I nodded.

"Fuck." His body fell forward, his mouth met mine.

I parted for him, welcoming his taste and control. Scooting closer, his arms banded around me, his knees bruised mine, and the coffee shop faded into obscurity.

I moaned into his mouth, melting into his embrace. I'd never been kissed so deeply or so selflessly. He poured the past and present down my throat, rewriting history and revoking everything that'd happened. In his arms, I only remembered how happy I was and not about the sadness still clinging to us.

My diamond ring weighed on my finger. My diamond bracelet decorated my wrist. And my diamond collar locked me forever as his. So much had happened. So much pain and debts and death.

But this.

A simple kiss in a simple coffee shop in a simple world.

This made it all worth it.

This made it all *priceless*.

His tongue danced with mine, slowly pulling away from me, leaving me needy and desperate for more.

Letting me go, Jethro reached into his jacket pocket and pulled out a folded piece of parchment. "It's fair to warn you, Needle, that after that kiss I'm fucking rock hard and need you more than I can stand. I doubt I'll have the self-control to order a coffee or watch you eat a piece of cake without needing to be inside you, so I'm going to show you this before I yank you out of this place and find a dark place so I can fuck you. Then, when the violence in my blood is sated, I'll reward you by making love to you and showing how my love can both be a punishment and a play."

My mouth fell open. His torrent lapped around me, licking my nipples with promise. "We can leave now. This very second."

He shook his head, fanning out the parchment on the low coffee table. "No, we can't. Not until I show you this."

His eyes met mine, dark and delicious, his lips glistening from our kiss. "I never told you this, but the Sacramental Pledge I made you sign the night of Cut's birthday—the one you signed after breaking in my office—I burned it before I came to get you in London."

I shivered, remembering that night and what happened afterward. He'd kissed me. He'd fucked me. He'd let me win after watching me come apart. "Why?"

His fingers stroked the inked words. "Because I didn't want the burden of owning your soul when I'd taken it so cruelly." Spreading out the parchment further, working the kinks from the centre, he dipped into his pocket again and grabbed a fountain pen.

Holding it out for me, he said, "It's not a quill, but this will have to do." Sudden nervousness covered his features. "Would you? Will you sign another, now you know everything that I am?"

My eyes fell on the paper. *That's what this is?*

A new Sacramental Pledge? A new contract trumping the Debt Inheritance and everything it stood for?

I took the pen without hesitation. "I've already agreed to marry you. I'll agree to anything that puts your heart at rest and grants me you for eternity."

He sighed, his knee rubbing mine. "You're far, far too good to me."

"And you gave me everything I ever wanted." Kissing him gently, I whispered, "I'll sign whatever you want me to sign,

Kite. But…can I read it first?"

He chuckled, tucking fallen strands behind my ear. "Of course. I want you to read it. I want you to know what I need from you."

Plucking the parchment, I held it within slightly trembling hands. The night of Cut's birthday came back. The way I broke in his office. The cuts on my back killing me from the First Debt. This was so different. Our first 'date.' Our first normal outing together as lovers rather than debtor and debtee.

My eyes landed on the gorgeous calligraphy of Jethro's writing. The words were so similar to the other pledge I'd signed but at the same time so different.

Jethro Hawk, firstborn son of Bryan Hawk, and Nila Weaver, firstborn daughter of Emma Weaver, hereby solemnly swear this is a law-binding and incontestable contract.

Nila Weaver revokes all ownership of her free will, thoughts, and body and grants them into the sole custody of Jethro Hawk. In exchange, Jethro Hawk renounces his free will, thoughts, and body and grants them entirely to Nila Weaver to do as she pleases.

The previous incontestable document named the Debt Inheritance is void now and forever. No debt nor family decree will ever befall these two houses. This new agreement brings two enemies into one family where bygones are bygones and the future is bright for all.

Both Nila Weaver and Jethro Hawk promise neither circumstance, nor change of heart will alter this vow.

In sickness and in health.

Two houses.

Two people.

One contract.

One lifetime marriage and commitment.

I looked up.

My heart showered with countless droplets of adoration.

I kissed my future husband. "How is it possible that you keep making me love you more each day?"

His face shattered into tenderness.

Before he could reply, I scrawled my name and accepted everything—the past, the present, the future. The triumphs and tragedies. The deaths of good people. The demise of bad. The pain that'd ruled us for so long. And the treachery that allowed madness to rule.

But not anymore.

This was our new chapter.

Our new story.

And we would write every sentence together.

Nila Weaver.

Jethro Hawk.

Two houses.

One future...

. . .

One family.

Indebted Epilogue

OUT NOW

www.pepperwinters.com

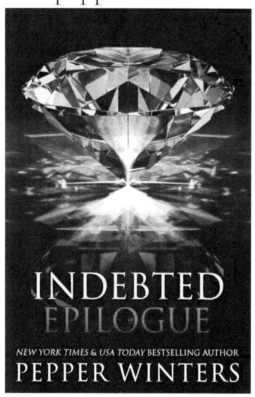

"Life after death...love after debts...is it possible after so much pain?"

**Find out in the bonus edition: INDEBTED EPILOGUE
BUY NOW**

*You don't have to read **Indebted Epilogue** if you do not wish to. It's a bonus book for Jethro and Nila to show life after the Debt Inheritance. There is also a Question and Answer session in **Indebted Epilogue**, sneak peeks into **Unseen Messages**, **Sin & Suffer**, cover reveal for **Indebted Beginnings** (yes, you heard that right), along with a couple of deleted scenes from Final Debt including a sex scene that didn't make it into the published copy.*

About the Author

Pepper Winters is a New York Times and USA Today International Bestseller. She loves dark romance, star-crossed lovers, and the forbidden taboo. She strives to write a story that makes the reader crave what they shouldn't, and delivers tales with complex plots and unforgettable characters.

After chasing her dreams to become a full-time writer, Pepper has earned recognition with awards for best Dark Romance, best BDSM Series, and best Dark Hero. She's an #1 iBooks bestseller, along with #1 in Erotic Romance, Romantic Suspense, Contemporary, and Erotica Thriller. She's also honoured to wear the IndieReader Badge for being a Top 10 Indie Bestseller, and recently signed a two book deal with Hachette. Represented by Trident Media, her books have garnered foreign and audio interest and are currently being translated into numerous languages. They will be in available in bookstores worldwide.

Her Dark Romance books include:
Tears of Tess (Monsters in the Dark #1)
Quintessentially Q (Monsters in the Dark #2)

Twisted Together (Monsters in the Dark #3)
Debt Inheritance (Indebted #1)
First Debt (Indebted Series #2)
Second Debt (Indebted Series #3)
Third Debt (Indebted Series #4)
Fourth Debt (Indebted Series #5)
Final Debt (Indebted Series #6)
Indebted Epilogue (Indebted Series #7)

Her Grey Romance books include:
Destroyed
Ruin & Rule (Pure Corruption #1)

Upcoming releases are
Sin & Suffer (Pure Corruption #2)
Je Suis a Toi (Monsters in the Dark Novella)
Unseen Messages (Contemporary Romance)
Super Secret Series
Indebted Beginnings (Indebted Series)

To be the first to know of upcoming releases, please follow her on her website
Pepper Winters

She loves mail of any kind: pepperwinters@gmail.com
All other titles and updates can be found on her
Goodreads Page.

Playlist

Avicii Hey Brother
Madonna Ghost Town
Paloma Faith Only love can hurt like this
U2 With or without you
Adele Skyfall.
Jarryd James Do you remember
Stan walker Holding You
Rhiana Dimaonds
Imagine Dragons Roots
Avicii Addicted to You
Bruno Mars I'd catch a grenade for you
Halo Starset
Chris Isaak Wicked Game
Sam Smith The Writings on the Wall.
Adele Rolling in the Deep
Avicii Wake me Up
Shawn Mendes - Stitches

Other Books by Pepper

26th January 2016
Sin & Suffer (Pure Corruption MC #2)

"Some say the past is in the past. That vengeance will hurt both innocent and guilty. I never believed those lies. Once my lust for revenge is sated, I'll say goodbye to hatred. I'll find a new beginning."

Buy Now

2016
Je Suis a Toi (Monsters in the Dark Novella)

"Life taught me an eternal love will demand the worst sacrifices. A transcendent love will split your soul, cleaving you into pieces. A love this strong doesn't grant you sweetness—it grants you pain. And in that pain is the greatest pleasure of all."

Buy Now

Early 2016
Unseen Messages (Standalone Romance)

"I should've listened, should've paid attention. The messages were there. Warning me. Trying to save me. But I didn't see and I paid the price..."

Get Release Day Alerts when this Book is Published

Early 2016
Super Secret Series Starting Soon

Please keep an eye out for the blurb and cover reveal early 2016. I'm beyond excited about this series and hope to deliver another epic tale.

*"He has millions, but without her he is bankrupt.
And he'll spend every dollar and penny to get her back."*

Get Release Day Alerts when this Book is Published

Tears of Tess (Monsters in the Dark #1)

*"My life was complete. Happy, content, everything neat and perfect.
Then it all changed.
I was sold."*
Buy Now

Quintessentially Q (Monsters in the Dark #2)

"All my life, I battled with the knowledge I was twisted… screwed up to want something so deliciously dark—wrong on so many levels. But then slave fifty-eight entered my world. Hissing, fighting, with a core of iron, she showed me an existence where two wrongs do make a right."
Buy Now

Twisted Together (Monsters in the Dark #3)

"After battling through hell, I brought my esclave back from the brink of ruin. I sacrificed everything—my heart, my mind, my very desires to bring her back to life. And for a while, I thought it broke me, that I'd never be the same. But slowly the beast is growing bolder, and it's finally time to show Tess how beautiful the dark can be."

Buy Now

Destroyed (Standalone Grey Romance)

She has a secret.
He has a secret.
One secret destroys them.
Buy Now

Ruin & Rule (Pure Corruption MC #1)

"We met in a nightmare. The in-between world where time had no power over reason. We fell in love. We fell hard. But then we woke up. And it was over . . ."
Buy Now

Thank you so much for reading.

CPSIA information can be obtained at www.ICGtesting.com
Printed in the USA
BVOW02s0224040316

439020BV00018B/30/P